SO-AZI-443

Published by Scrivenings Press LLC
15 Lucky Lane
Morrilton, Arkansas 72110
https://ScriveningsPress.com

Printed in the United States of America

Paperback ISBN 978-1-64917-197-9

eBook ISBN 978-1-64917-198-6

Library of Congress Control Number: 2022933684

Editors: Erin R. Howard and Linda Fulkerson

Cover by www.bookmarketinggraphics.com.

TRUE BLUE MYSTERIES • BOOK THREE

Persian Blue Puzzle

AWARD-WINNING AUTHOR

SUSAN PAGE DAVIS

Scrivenings
PRESS
Quench your thirst for story.
www.ScriveningsPress.com

1

"Who's Louanne Vane?" Bill McBride looked up from the envelope in his hand.

His daughter Campbell paused in setting the table for their breakfast. "Oh, we're getting mail here already?"

"Apparently not. The only item is for someone who doesn't live here. A Louanne Vane."

"Ah. Isn't she the lady who lives in the gray house? You know, beyond Ben Tatton's old house," Campbell said.

"Oh, right. You interviewed her during the Harrison case."

"I sure did. She's a very nice, very chatty woman, probably about eighty, and she has a huge Persian cat."

"Would you like to visit her this morning and take her this letter?" Bill asked.

"Sure, I'll take it over." Campbell reached for the letter and laid it to one side.

"Great. I've got a lot of errands to run, and I don't want to get sidetracked with a chatty neighbor, nice though she may be."

"The coffee's ready, but I forgot to get orange juice." They'd just moved into a large Victorian three times the size of her father's old house a few blocks away. It would take Campbell a while to recover from emptying the old refrigerator and stocking the new one.

"Add it to the grocery list. I'll stop at Kroger after my other errands."

"That's great, if I can find the grocery list."

After their breakfast of pancakes and coffee, Campbell ransacked the kitchen drawers and finally found the list pad in with the potholders. Just when she was getting used to her dad's old house, she had to relocate everything in this one. With a sigh, she sent her father on his way and had their dishes washed by the time Nick Emerson, Bill's other employee, arrived.

"So, what's up?" he asked, plopping his laptop down on his desk in the old living room they'd designated the new outer office. The largest room downstairs, it seemed the most logical place for the two junior investigators to work and interview clients, while Bill got something he'd long dreamed of—a private office.

"Dad's out running errands. I guess we work on those background checks for the university." Campbell sat down at her desk and opened her laptop just as a knock sounded on the old house's front door. She looked across the room at Nick.

He made a face and pushed back his chair. "I'll get it, but we're going to have to get us a receptionist."

"Thanks." Moving True Blue Investigations into the house from the cramped one-room office Campbell's father had maintained for years was stressful for all of them, but mostly in a good way. Still, the new space seemed almost too large for the three of them.

Nick returned to the office with a neighbor in tow. Vera Hill and her husband lived diagonally across Willow Street, and she'd shown an avid interest in their move.

"Hi, Mrs. Hill," Campbell said.

"Hello. Are you all moved in?" The older woman brushed back a strand of straight, gray hair.

"Yeah, pretty much. Last night was the first night Dad and I slept here."

"No bad dreams?"

"Not so far." Campbell was sure she was alluding to some nightmare-worthy events that happened in the house before they moved in, but the sooner they forgot all that, the better.

"Oh, well, I brought you some supper, so you won't have to cook tonight," Mrs. Hill said.

Nick was standing uncertainly, holding a covered dish with potholders. "Where do you want this, Professor?"

"Oh, in the fridge. There should be plenty of room."

Nick nodded and headed for the kitchen.

"Thank you." Campbell stood and walked closer to Mrs. Hill. "That was really sweet of you."

"Hope you like cheesy grits with sausage."

"Sounds yummy." Campbell grinned and tried not to think what that dish would do to her waistline and her dad's arteries. Maybe they could send part of it home with Nick.

"My, my, my, this looks official." Mrs. Hill looked around at the spacious room, her gaze resting on the desks, oak file cabinets, and inviting seating area near the fireplace, where they could interview clients in comfort. "So much brighter than Katherine's décor."

"Thanks. We wanted it nice and light for work and for our clients." Campbell had gladly thrown away the dark drapes and replaced the rather gloomy art prints that had graced the walls. After several attempts at persuasion, she convinced her dad to let her paint over the fifty-year-old wallpaper, and now their backdrop was a light but warm gray.

"I'm so glad we got nice new neighbors, not—" Mrs. Hill broke off, but Campbell could guess what she was thinking. Not murderers or blackmailers. The case that involved the former owner and the man who'd lived in the house next door had shocked the Hills. But Vera was resilient, and she seemed to have recovered.

As Nick returned, she glanced toward the doorway. "Is Mr. McBride around?"

"Bill's out," Nick said. "He should be back pretty soon, though. Can we help you?"

"I just wanted to ask him something. See, I'm not sure if it's the kind of thing anyone would hire a private investigator for."

Nick glanced at Campbell. "Want to run it by us?"

Campbell doubted Mrs. Hill would turn out to be a client. Middle-aged women seemed drawn to her father and loved chatting with him, and she couldn't blame them. He was extremely likable. A widow down the street had brought them cookies yesterday while they unloaded the office furniture, and another one from their church always made a point of talking to Bill after services.

But Vera's husband, Frank, was still very much a part of the neighborhood. Campbell didn't see Vera as the flirtatious kind. Maybe she had a legitimate concern.

Nick waved the older woman to the sofa near the fireplace, and Campbell joined them, taking one of the armchairs.

Mrs. Hill eyed them both soberly. "Well, see, our daughter Dorothy is divorced. Has been for four or five years. And she's got this new fella. I don't know as I'd call him a boyfriend exactly—not yet. Anyway, he's trying to interest my husband and me in investing in a fund he's keen on."

"What does Dorothy say?" Campbell asked.

"Oh, she thinks he's terrific. Says she's invested, and if she had any extra cash she'd put that in too."

"So, what do you think we could do for you?" Nick asked.

"I don't really know. Maybe find out if it's legitimate? I don't expect you to be able to tell if the investment would pay off or anything like that."

Nick chuckled. "It would take a psychic for that, Mrs. H."

"Oh, don't get me started on psychics." Mrs. Hill rolled her eyes. "I leave that to my friends. Anyway, uh, do you have an hourly fee?"

Campbell started to open her mouth about the usual retainer, but Nick jumped in.

"Tell you what, how much is your budget?"

"Oh, uh ..." She looked around the corners of the room as if embarrassed. "Maybe a hundred dollars? I'd think it would be worth that to find out if he's honest or not."

"Okay. Why don't you give us his name and any details you have on this investment plan," Nick said. "We'll give it a day and see what we can do."

Campbell sat there watching him wide-eyed, wondering if her father would sanction this huge discount for a neighbor.

The wrinkles on Mrs. Hill's forehead deepened. "What could you learn in that time?"

"For one thing, we could find out if this guy has a criminal record."

Good thought, Campbell decided, but she knew they usually charged more than a hundred dollars for a background check.

"And if you've got the name of the fund or business, or whatever it is, we can check into that too," Nick added.

"Oh, would you? It would be such a load off my mind. I'm a natural skeptic, I guess, but Frank thinks we should give the guy a chance. I mean, Dorothy seems to like him real well. He could end up our son-in-law."

"Tell you what," Campbell said, shooting Nick a don't-get-ahead-of-yourself look, "why don't you come back in an hour or so and talk to my father about this. He's got a lot of experience, and he'd have a pretty good idea how much we could find out for you."

Mrs. Hill gazed at Nick, and his eyes flickered, but he didn't contradict Campbell, for which she was thankful. Nick was a good investigator in a lot of ways, but she wasn't sure yet just how much leeway her dad gave him with clients.

"Okay, I'll do that," Mrs. Hill said. "I'll get going now and let you get back to work."

"Thanks for the casserole." Campbell walked with her into the entry, "Bring us any details you can when you come later." She closed the door behind the older woman and went back into the office.

Nick was already typing away rapidly on his keyboard. Without looking up, he said, "If we can't afford a receptionist, we should at least have a doorbell installed."

"Dad's already working on it," Campbell said. "Someone's coming in a couple of days. Meanwhile, I suggested a sign we can hang out front during businesses hours. *Walk right in*, or something like that."

Nick's dark eyebrows lowered in a frown. "I don't know. This house has a history of people walking in without being invited. If you forgot to take the sign in, you might have trespassers. Again."

Campbell chuckled, but he had a point. The hundred-year-old house had a lot of quirks she and her father would have to get used to. She couldn't easily forget being attacked in the darkness just down the hallway when a former client owned the house.

A stray thought hit her, and she clapped a hand to her mouth.

"What?" Nick said.

"A letter was delivered here by mistake, and Dad asked me to take it to the right house."

"Put it in the mailbox tomorrow," Nick said.

"No, it's just down the street, and I promised him I'd do it."

Nick shrugged and focused on his computer screen.

Campbell hurried to the dining room and retrieved the letter. The sun was blazing outside, so she didn't worry about a jacket. At quarter past nine in the morning, the temperature had already risen to nearly ninety degrees. She slowed her steps. No sense arriving at Mrs. Vane's house all sweaty.

She rang the bell at the gray frame house, and after a short wait, the elderly owner opened the door.

"Oh, Miss McBride, come on in."

Campbell smiled and stepped inside. "I can't stay long. We had a letter for you delivered at our place this morning, and I thought you'd want it, so I brought it over." She held out the envelope.

"Oh, thank you. My daughter in Arkansas."

"That's nice. Most people don't write letters anymore."

Mrs. Vane waved a dismissive hand. "Well, she's probably trying to talk some sense into me, as she'd call it."

"I wasn't aware you needed that," Campbell said with a laugh. "You seem plenty sensible to me."

The old woman's eyes sharpened. "Can you sit down for a minute? Would you like a glass of tea?"

"Oh, I shouldn't." Campbell saw the disappointment in her eyes. Her dad had been right about getting sidetracked with neighbors. She hadn't done any work yet this morning, but she wavered. "Maybe for just a minute."

"Come into the parlor." Mrs. Vane walked her into a cozy

living room full of patchwork cushions and framed family photos. Her enormous Persian blue cat sprawled on a rocking chair.

"My goodness, you're a big fellow." Campbell stepped closer. "I love cats."

"Well, he's not too friendly," Mrs. Vane said just as its paw darted toward Campbell's outstretched hand.

She pulled back, but not quickly enough to avoid a scratch on her thumb.

"Blue Boy! Naughty!" Mrs. Vane smiled apologetically. "I hope he didn't get you."

"It's not bad." A few drops of blood oozed through the claw marks, but Campbell thought she could get away without a bandage.

"Here." Mrs. Vane brought over a box of tissues, and she took one.

"Thanks. I should have known better."

"Oh, he's like that with strangers. Much better with people he knows. In fact, if you sit down, he'll probably be over in a few minutes, expecting you to scratch his belly."

Campbell wasn't sure she wanted to do that, but she managed a smile and took a seat on the sofa. "What did you want to tell me?"

Mrs. Vane settled into her favorite chair and adjusted the tail of her pullover top. "Have you ever heard of Miss Tryphenia? She's down on Second Street."

"I ... don't think so."

"Oh. Well, she's been there several years. She gives readings."

Campbell straightened and studied her hostess. "You mean, psychic readings?"

"I guess you could call them that. But she helps people."

Her mind clicking back to her earlier conversation with Mrs. Hill, Campbell tried to sort things out. Was Louanne Vane one of the friends Vera had mentioned in connection with psychics?

"Let me just get that tea."

Campbell couldn't see a graceful way out of it and decided to chalk this experience up as one she'd missed out on with family. Both her grandmothers were deceased, and she had fond memories of them. Maybe she'd find some surrogate grandparents here in Murray, where there seemed to be a disproportionate number of retired people.

Blue Boy hopped down from his chair and followed Mrs. Vane out of the room, his fluffy tail swaying with arrogance.

The hostess was soon back with two frosty glasses of tea. Campbell took a long swallow and relished the cool, sweet taste.

"Mmm. Thank you. That's really good. Now, what were you saying about your daughter and this woman who gives readings?"

"Oh, Elena. She thinks I've gone batty to visit Miss Tryphenia. But after my Leland died, my doctor recommended a grief support group. I went to it a few times, but it was so depressing."

"I guess it didn't help you to be around others who'd just had a loss too?"

"Not a bit. After the third meeting, I quit. But one of the gals there chatted with me during the refreshment time. She said she got more consolation out of a session with Miss Tryphenia. To hear her tell it, the reading was much more encouraging than the grief support group. So I thought, why not? My husband was dead, and my children all live at least three hundred miles away. Why shouldn't I find new friends in the community?"

"Why not?" Campbell smiled. "So, Miss Tryphenia is a friend."

Mrs. Vane's expression clouded. "I wouldn't say that exactly. It's a business relationship. But she does cheer me up."

"I see. So ... you go to her, and she gives you uplifting news?"

"Not always news, but encouraging thoughts, I'd say. Last week she told me something good would land on my doorstep."

"And did it?"

Mrs. Vane paused with her glass nearly to her lips and smiled. "Well, you're here."

Campbell chuckled. "I'm glad I can be considered something good."

"You did bring me Elena's letter, which the post office might have taken days to deliver."

She had a point, but Campbell figured any self-proclaimed psychic could hit the nail on the head fairly often, so long as she kept her predications vague and maintained a loose definition of terms like *good* and *bad*.

"What other kinds of things has she told you?"

"She told me where to find my lost glasses."

"Really?"

"She asked me where I'd looked already and suggested a few places. Sure enough, when I got home, I found them under a magazine on the nightstand, one of the exact places she'd mentioned."

Campbell nodded, working hard not to smile. "How long have you been consulting her?"

"About four months now. I go every couple of weeks. I'd go more often, but ..." Her eyes flickered, and she took a quick sip of tea.

"I suppose you have to pay her each time."

"Well, yes. The first few times it wasn't so much. Only twenty dollars for a reading."

"And now?"

"Now it's fifty." She frowned, but added quickly, "But we have longer sessions, and she's told me some amazing things. She said it requires more energy for her to seek them out."

"What sort of things?"

"Oh, private stuff mostly. Some has to do with my husband —things he thought and did that I had no inkling of."

"I see." Campbell was afraid she did see, indeed. The psychic was bleeding Mrs. Vane for as much as she thought she could get by making up tales about poor Leland. "I guess Elena isn't too happy about the money, is that it?"

"Sort of. And ... well, she was upset when I told her one of the things Miss Tryphenia told me about her father."

Campbell wanted to ask what that was, but she didn't want to violate the old woman's privacy. She drained her glass.

"That was delicious, Mrs. Vane. Now I should go back to the office, but maybe I can visit you again sometime."

"I'd like that. I don't get out much anymore, and it's nice to have visitors."

Campbell smiled and clasped her hand gently. "I'll try to stop in again soon." Blue Boy strolled in from the kitchen, and she scooted out the front door, careful to avoid the cantankerous cat.

2

Campbell hurried back up the sidewalk to the new house. Had she just wasted half an hour? She liked Mrs. Vane, and she couldn't just ignore people like her, who had a shaky support system at best. More than ever, she was glad she'd moved home. Her mother had been gone more than seven years, and she would hate to see her father grow old in loneliness.

Nick glanced up at her when she walked into the office.

"Dad's not back?" she asked.

"Nope."

Nick was usually more talkative, and she figured he was angry with her—shirking was probably his diagnosis. He would probably finish way ahead of her with his part of the background checks.

Murray State University had entrusted True Blue Investigations with the names of six people, three candidates for each of two job openings. She got right to work and had nearly finished her first one when her father came home.

"Hey," Bill said as he strolled into the room. "Just what I like to see—my investigators hard at work."

Campbell smiled up at him. "I'm almost ready to email you my first report so you can check it. Oh, and Mrs. Hill wants to talk to you. She'll be back in a while."

"What about?"

Nick looked up. "Some creep her daughter's dating. He wants her and Frank to invest in some fund he's pushing, and Mrs. H. isn't so sure about it."

"Okay, we can look into it."

"Nick told her a hundred dollars," Campbell said cautiously.

Nick scowled at her. "She's a neighbor."

"Well, she did help us a little on the Tatton case," Bill said.

"And she brought you a casserole," Nick said almost triumphantly.

Bill laughed. "I'll talk to her."

"We could probably do a light background on the guy," Nick said. "If he's a career criminal, it shouldn't take us long to find out."

Bill stood on the old oriental rug, one of the few pieces Campbell hadn't rejected of all those that came with the house. His gaze swept back and forth between her desk and Nick's. They had situated them at opposite ends of the large room. Each of them had plenty of space, and she was glad not to be elbow-to-elbow with Nick, the way they'd been in the old office. She and Nick didn't always get along, and a little distance seemed like a good idea.

"Okay, so if you can finish the job you're doing for Murray State by tomorrow's close of business, that would be great. Opening day is only four weeks from now."

"No problem," Nick said.

"Guess it's a rush job. They need to do their hiring fast."

Campbell was used to the way colleges worked, and she figured the administrators wished they had more time to make staffing decisions.

"True," Bill said. "How are you coming, Nick?"

"Oh, I'll be done by noon."

Campbell's shoulders slumped. He was showing off. He'd worked with her father for about three years, while she'd only been on board for a few weeks. Nick knew all the websites to check and the nuances of the reports he was reading. She hated to admit it, even to herself, but she was jealous of his ability.

"What are you working on, Dad?" she asked.

"I've still got a few picky things to handle on our change of location."

"Can I help you with that?"

"I don't think so, but thanks. I've been to the post office and the bank, and I ordered new business cards and letterheads. Now I've got to contact all our regular clients, to make sure everyone knows we've moved to Willow Street."

Campbell nodded. Her father would handle each client just right. It was better for him to touch base with them, rather than his daughter, who was new in town.

"What about all the old letterheads and business cards?"

"Scrap paper." Her father went into the hall just as someone knocked on the front door.

Nick looked over at Campbell. "Mrs. Hill."

"No doubt. She's probably been watching for him to drive in."

In the entry, Bill opened the door. Nick and Campbell listened closely.

"Well, hello, Mrs. Hill. What can I do for you?"

"It's Vera. Campbell says you're all settled in?"

"Yeah, I think so," Bill said.

"Well, I saw the new sign go up yesterday. Very classy, I must say."

Nick grinned at Campbell, and she returned his smile. Mrs. Hill had come over twice during the move to gush about how cleverly they'd figured out what happened to Katherine Tyler, who'd lived here and been her neighbor for many years.

"That's very nice of you," Bill said. "Come on in. You don't have to knock during business hours."

"Well, I wasn't sure."

"We're going to get a doorbell, but this is a business now." As Bill spoke, the two ambled into the living room-turned-office. Nick and Campbell stood.

"Hi, Mrs. Hill," Campbell said.

"Hello again, dear." She turned back to Bill and laid a hand on his wrist. "Now, Mr. McBride, as I was telling the kids earlier, we have a family matter we're concerned about. if I could have a private word with you ..."

Bill's eyebrows shot up. "Sure you can, but you know, if I'm going to call you Vera, you need to call me Bill."

"All right, but this is business. At least I think it is."

"In that case, step into my private office."

Campbell smiled at the pride in her father's tone. He was definitely glad to be out of the tiny, one-room storefront that had been his office for six years.

She looked over at Nick. "Are you really almost done with your assignment?"

"I can finish it in an hour."

She hesitated then said, "Would you mind looking at my first one and telling me if I missed anything? I want to learn to do things right for Dad. And for the clients, of course."

"Sure. Bill gave you a list of what we need to look for, right?"

"Yes, and I memorized it."

"Whatever for?"

"I've got my private investigator's exam coming up in mid-September."

Nick laughed. "That's like two months away. You're studying already."

"Of course. This is all new to me. I figured I'd better start now."

Nick shook his head. "I'll bet in school, when your teacher told you to write a term paper, you started on it the same day you got the assignment."

"Well ..." That was exactly what Campbell had done, but she was certain Nick would rag her about it if she admitted to it. "Come on, let's get at it."

Nick scanned her file quickly. "Looks good, Professor."

Campbell was determined not to scream at him for calling her that. She'd lost her job as an English professor when the small private college in Iowa downsized its faculty. But Nick could come up with lots of worse nicknames, she realized, so she thanked him and kept quiet.

All was peaceful for the next half hour as she tackled the next potential hiree. The murmur of voices drifted across the hallway, but when she heard her dad and Mrs. Hill coming out of his office, she was surprised how much time had passed. What could they possibly have been hashing over? Mrs. Hill was a talker, but her father was efficient and didn't like to fritter away his working hours.

"Well, thank you so much," Mrs. Hill said.

Campbell perked up her ears as her dad saw the new client out.

"You're welcome," he said heartily. "We'll see what we can turn up, and we'll report back to you on Thursday."

Thursday ... only two days. So her father considered this a quick job, probably more of a favor for their neighbor.

"Okay, you two," he said from the doorway. "I told Vera we'd put in a few hours on this. I'd really hate to see her and her husband get bilked."

"You think it's a scam?" Nick asked.

"I'm not sure yet. He didn't give them anything on paper, but I did a quick check on the fund name she gave me, and I didn't find anything about it. That doesn't mean it isn't real. Nick, if you're about done, I'll put you on checking the guy's background."

Nick nodded.

Turning to Campbell, Bill said, "After you finish your work for MSU, come into my office and we'll do some serious digging on the financial end."

"What about lunch?" Nick asked.

"Oh, right." Bill pulled out his wallet. "How about some sandwiches from Subway, Campbell?"

She pushed back her chair. "Or Mrs. Hill brought cheesy grits and sausage."

He winced slightly. "Let's save that for tonight."

"Actually, I'm going out with Keith tonight." She was thankful she had a legitimate reason to skip the meal.

"Of course you are." Her dad smiled indulgently. "Nick, you want anything?"

Campbell did the lunch run and brought back drinks and sandwiches. By afternoon's end, she had finished her Murray State profiles, and Nick and Bill had done a fair amount of research on Mrs. Hill's situation. They gathered around the desk in Bill's office.

"I want to do some follow-up on this tomorrow," he said. "I couldn't find anything about this fund through any of several financial services I checked. On the other hand, the Better Business Bureau has never heard of them either, so no complaints have been filed on it."

"Yet," Campbell said.

Nick pulled a skeptical face. "Maybe it's just something he made up out of thin air."

"It's possible," Bill said. "You got anything, Nick?"

"Well, this guy Dorothy Chambers is seeing—"

"Samuel Truman," Bill said.

"Right. His full name is Eliot Samuel Truman, and he's originally from Missouri. But he's going by his middle name, and he has a Missouri driver's license that lists him as Samuel, not Eliot, or E. Samuel, or E.S., or anything else."

Bill grunted. "Where does he live now?"

"Benton."

"Just up the road."

"Yeah. I checked the address. It's about eighteen miles from here. He's been there a couple of months."

"And yet, he still has a Missouri driver's license. And you're sure he's the same guy?"

"Same birth date, and I couldn't find a legal name change. However, I did find a conviction in Missouri on a misdemeanor. Petty theft."

"How long ago?" Bill asked.

"The arrest was almost ten years ago."

"Well, that shouldn't count now, should it?" Campbell asked.

Her father shrugged. "It says something about his character ten years ago."

She couldn't argue with that. "Do we know how Dorothy met him?"

"Vera says through her work," her father replied. "Dorothy is a clerk at the newspaper office."

"Has he placed any ads in the paper?" Campbell asked.

"Not that I've been able to find out. But he has subscribed to both the Murray and Paducah newspapers."

"Okay, so now what?" Nick asked.

"Find out everything you can about what he's doing here in Kentucky. He must be approaching other people about this investment too. But is that his only way of making a living? Maybe it's a sideline, and he has another job. Do it tomorrow, though. It's quitting time."

Campbell jumped up and hastily arranged her papers and shut her laptop.

"Big date tonight?" Nick asked.

She frowned but didn't answer.

"Say hi to Keith for me," he called as she left the room and headed for the stairs.

———

"This place is gorgeous." Campbell laid down her menu and looked around the inside of the log-framed restaurant. One whole wall was made of windows that overlooked Kentucky Lake.

"Yeah. A friend told me about it." Keith Fuller, her favorite police detective, smiled at her across the table. "So, how was your day?"

"Fine. First full day in the new office space. I think it's going to work well. Come by and see us."

"I will. I've got to be in court tomorrow, but maybe after that's over."

Campbell nodded. She was getting used to seeing her father and Keith head off to the courthouse to testify. She hadn't been called in yet herself, but it wouldn't be long before she had to give evidence in a case she'd bumbled into her first week in Murray.

"I had an interesting conversation with a neighbor today."

She chuckled. "Probably spent too much time at her house sipping tea."

"Oh? It's good to bond with the neighbors."

"I know, but I felt like she was looking for approval. Maybe because I'm an investigator."

"In what way?"

"She's been seeing a psychic. Miss Tryphenia."

"Over on Second Street, right?"

"Yes. Has she been there a while?"

"Years. I think she's harmless. At least, I haven't heard of any complaints against her."

"Good. It seems Mrs. Vane goes to her every couple of weeks for a reading."

"Reading of what?"

"I'm not sure exactly. I think Miss Tryphenia encourages her and pretty much tells her everything's okay. Sort of an emotional massage—a feel-good session."

"Huh."

"Mrs. Vane is widowed, and her kids all live out of state. I asked her if this woman is a friend, but she said it's all business. And she pays her plenty." Campbell frowned. "You know, Vera Hill made a remark about some friends and psychics to Nick and me earlier. I think maybe she was talking about Mrs. Vane."

"Vera Hill—she's the one across the street?"

"Right across from the Tatton house. Which, by the way, may be for sale soon. Dad said Tatton's sister was over there with a real estate agent a couple of days ago. No sign out front yet, though."

"I won't be surprised if they want to sell it quickly." Keith's brown eyes lifted as the waitress came to the table. They gave their orders, and when she'd left them, Keith reverted to the former topic. "You don't think there's anything fraudulent going on with this psychic business, do you?"

"I'm not sure. Miss Tryphenia did raise her price after the first couple sessions, and Mrs. Vane said her daughter doesn't approve of her going there."

"Well, if it's her own money she's spending, I guess she has the right to spend it where she wants."

"Why would someone like Mrs. Vane do that? Do you think it's because she's lonely?"

"That could be a big part of it. Psychics—and con artists in general—prey on people who are vulnerable. In this case, she's lost her husband, and her kids are far away. Maybe the readings make her feel less alone and more connected."

"But I know she has friends."

"They don't give her the same thing this woman gives her."

Campbell frowned. "I just don't get it. What does Miss Tryphenia give her?"

Keith reached for her hand and gave it a squeeze. "Hope."

———

When she returned home, Campbell heard voices upstairs and hurried up to the private sitting room they'd made from one of the extra bedrooms. Her father was sitting in front of the TV, watching his favorite police drama. He pushed pause as she walked in.

"Hi. How was your evening?" he asked.

"Great. How about you? How were the grits?"

He hesitated, not meeting her gaze. "Actually, I—uh—I ordered a pizza."

"Oh." That surprised her. He was usually very tactful. "What do we tell Mrs. Hill when she asks us how we liked it?" Because she would, Campbell was certain.

Her dad didn't seem to have an answer.

"Do you think we should at least taste it?" she asked.

He sighed and lumbered up out of his armchair. "Okay, one little taste, and then we hit the ice cream."

In the kitchen, she opened several cupboards before finding where they'd stashed the custard cups. Scooping small portions of the casserole into two of them, she said sternly, "I'm going to heat this a little in the microwave, Dad, and you give it a fair chance."

"Okay." He looked like an unhappy little kid.

She managed not to laugh. A minute later, they poised with their spoons over their dishes. Her dad said, "One, two, three," and they each took a bite.

"Oh. Hot." She sucked air in and out quickly to cool the food in her mouth.

Her father chewed and swallowed. His eyebrows shot up. "You know, that's not bad."

She took a drink of cold water and blew on a second bite from her dish, avoiding taking a big piece of sausage the way she had the first time. She ignored the small burn and considered the flavor. "Yeah, I've had worse. Do you want me to throw it out or not?"

"Keep it. I'll eat some for lunch tomorrow."

She nodded and put their dishes in the dishwasher while he covered the casserole and returned it to the fridge.

"Hey, you delivered that letter down the street, right?" he asked.

"Yes, I did." She related her conversation with Mrs. Vane and added, "I told Keith, and he says this psychic's been in business a long time, and they haven't had any complaints filed against her."

"It's an odd name." Her dad filled a coffee mug. "Want some?"

"No, thanks. I want to sleep tonight. I'll take some ice cream, though." While she dished it out, she said, "I did a quick search on *Tryphenia* this afternoon. It is an uncommon name. It's Greek. I think it may have been more popular in Colonial Days—not sure."

"Well, they did use a lot of weird names then."

Campbell laughed and followed him up the stairs to their private sitting room. "Tell me about it. Cotton Mather, Oceanus Hopkins."

"Yeah, I remember your mother doing a lot of genealogy research and coming up with tons of crazy names. Love Brewster was a boy, if I remember right. I think my favorite was Submit Howe." He wiggled his eyebrows. "Be thankful you weren't named Hephzibah."

"Oh, like Campbell's one of the ten most popular names. I like it, though." She curled up on the sofa with her legs under her. "Hey, I bet Tryphenia isn't her real name."

"Probably not." Bill slid into his recliner and sipped his brew. "Tomorrow let's dig deeper into Vera's situation, and when we report back to her on Thursday, maybe I'll mention Miss Tryphenia and see what she says."

"You don't want to upset her, Dad. She's got troubles enough with her daughter."

"Yeah, Dorothy's the one I'm worried about right now—or actually, her boyfriend. He's not exactly squeaky clean."

"You think he's a con artist?"

"Too soon to tell."

She took a bite of her peppermint ice cream, thinking over the evening. "Keith pretty much said psychics are con artists."

"Aren't they?"

"I don't know."

"Surely you don't believe some of them really have supernatural powers?"

"Well, no, I guess I don't. But he said they prey on vulnerable people and sell them hope."

"Keith's right. Whatever a person needs, a psychic will focus on that and promise to provide it. They bring hope that life will get better and whatever bad feelings surround the customer will go away. I saw some of that when I was on the force in Bowling Green. We tried to prosecute one guy who was conning people, and the defense was that the victim gave him all her money of her own free will, so it wasn't a crime."

"Which is basically what Keith said. But if a con artist of any stripe stole thousands of dollars from a person, couldn't you make a case that he'd deceived them?"

"It's tough, but maybe. With a good lawyer. If the customer could prove he'd promised something in return, yes. But they're crafty. They don't usually do that. There was this one guy who had a little store, and he'd sell good luck charms and worry stones. He'd tell people if something bad was in their life —negative energy or whatever—this would help get rid of it."

"What happened when it didn't work?"

"Sometimes it seemed like it did. Sometimes the situation worked itself out."

"Right." Campbell's voice was heavy with sarcasm.

Her dad set down his mug and leaned forward. "Okay, let's say a woman's upset because her son is marrying a young woman she can't stand. The con artist sells her a charm for a hundred bucks. A couple weeks later, the son and his fiancée break up."

"That's not very common."

"Maybe. But what if Mom spends more time with the girl and decides she's not so bad after all? Isn't that getting rid of the negative energy?"

"I guess."

"And, hey, it was only a hundred bucks. It was worth a shot, right?" He picked up his mug and took a deep swallow.

"What if things get worse?"

"Then the con tells Mom it's a difficult case and she needs a stronger charm. For more money."

Campbell spooned a big bite of ice cream. "It's sad that anyone would fall for that, but some folks have been known to lose their life savings to these people."

"That usually happens over a long period of time. It's the same principle, though. The con just takes longer getting to know them and gaining their trust. After a while, things feel better for the victim just because this person listens to them and takes their concerns seriously. But you're right. Usually after a while, they raise the stakes." Bill pulled his bowl closer.

"How can they do that, over and over?" Campbell asked.

"If they con the poor dupe out of a huge amount of money, they'll disappear and open a new business in another area. But this one, Miss Tryphenia, I'd say has never taken it to that level."

"Because she's been here so long?"

"Yeah. If anyone lost an enormous amount to her, she'd have to move on."

"Or be arrested?"

He shrugged. "The police would be aware of her, at the least."

"Keith said she's harmless."

"I guess time will tell."

They sat in silence for a long moment.

"Hey, Dad?"

"Yeah?"

"You mentioned Mom's genealogy research."

He nodded.

"What ever happened to all of it? She had all those big

three-ring binders full of family group sheets, and file folders of letters and records she'd copied."

"I still have it."

Campbell blinked. "Where? I didn't see it when we moved."

Her father let out a big sigh. "When I moved over here from Bowling Green, I didn't have room for all her stuff. That house was so small, and ... well, it was hard having it there to look at all the time. Not just her family tree stuff. Anyway, I got a storage unit and stashed it."

"In Bowling Green?" Campbell tried not to let her surprise show on her face.

"No, here. In case I wanted to get some things out." He looked tired.

A wave of pain washed over Campbell. She'd been in college when her mother died, and she'd come home for a week, for the service and to be with her dad for a few days. They'd sorted her mom's clothing, and she assumed he'd donated it somewhere after she went back to school. Then he'd moved to Murray.

She'd wondered on her sporadic visits where a few particular items had gone, but she didn't want to ask. If it had been too painful for her father and he'd given away or sold the Boston rocker that had once been her grandmother's, or the books her mom had loved, she supposed she could understand it. But she had felt a little hurt that he hadn't asked if she wanted any of her mother's things.

He drained his coffee mug. "I guess there's room here, if you want to have that stuff out again."

A lump formed in Campbell's throat. "Only if you want to, Dad."

He nodded, and his eyes glistened. "Yeah, let's do that sometime."

"Have you got her books?"

"Yeah. And the old dishes."

"Grandma's rocking chair?"

"That too. And Emily's old desk."

Campbell sniffed. "Thanks, Dad. I'm glad you kept Mom's stuff." She stood and rounded the table to give him a hug.

3

The next morning, Campbell packed up her laptop and rode with her father to Benton while Nick stayed at the office to do more online research on Samuel Truman.

As he pulled out of their driveway, Bill turned past the vacant house next door.

"I wonder who we'll get for new neighbors." Ben Tatton's old house was built of light-colored brick, as were many residences in Murray. She liked their white wood-frame better, but the other house would make a cozy place for someone—as long as they didn't mind living in a house where a man had been murdered.

"Are we going to Truman's apartment?" she asked a few minutes later, as they whizzed past cornfields and the South Marshall County Middle School.

"I don't think so. I don't want him to realize Vera's got someone looking at him. Let's nose around and see if we can catch any of his neighbors. He hasn't lived there very long, but we might find someone who can give us some information."

They soon learned that Truman lived in a house that had

been divided into four apartments. One of the first things Nick had ferreted out was the make and model of their target's car. They confirmed it wasn't parked at the house before they got out. A ten-year-old pickup and a Ford Fusion sat in the parking area.

"Truman's in apartment 2. Let's try number 1 first," Bill said.

Campbell walked with him to the door, taking in the neighborhood's ambiance. Older houses nearby were becoming rundown, and farther down the block sat a convenience store with gas pumps. She pulled in a deep, slow breath. Her nerves always kicked up a little when she made the first contact with a witness—or a source, as her father termed it.

The apartment door opened, and her dad smiled at a man of about thirty-five, wearing jeans, a black T-shirt, and work boots, with a couple days' worth of stubble on his face.

"Hey."

"Hi, my name's Bill McBride, and this is my daughter, Campbell. Can we ask you a couple of questions?"

"Are you selling something?"

"No, we're private investigators."

He blinked. "Fine, if you come inside. I'm packing my lunch. Gotta leave in ten minutes."

"Thanks. We won't take much of your time."

Campbell followed her father inside, amazed at the man's trust. They could be lying criminals, and he invited them in, just like that. Of course, they were neatly groomed, and her father was well-spoken. But then, so was Sam Truman, from what they'd learned.

"I'm Ted Holloway." He waved toward a couple of stools at the island in his kitchen, where he had bread, mustard, cold cuts, and cheese spread out.

Campbell sat down, and her father claimed the stool next to her.

"We're curious about your neighbor, Sam Truman," her dad said.

"Yeah? He's all right."

Bill smiled. "Could you be more specific?"

Ted shrugged and squeezed mustard onto a slice of bread. "He loaned me his car when my truck broke down."

"Anything else?"

"Oh, sure. He's brought over beer and pizza and hung out."

"What does he do for a living?"

Ted paused in arranging the sliced ham on his bread. "I think he said he's some kind of consultant."

"In what field?"

"I dunno. But he's smart."

"How do you know that?"

Ted smiled and shook his head. "You can tell just by talking to him."

Bill glanced at Campbell, and she took it as license to ask her own questions.

"Has he ever talked to you about money?" she said.

"Yeah, a little. I told him I've got a small stash, and I'm looking for an investment. I was thinking of buying shares of Caterpillar or Google, but Sam told me about this startup company he's investing in. I'm looking at it."

"Can you show us the material?" Bill asked.

Ted eyed him thoughtfully. "I don't have anything on paper yet. Sam said he'd get me a prospectus."

Campbell turned her attention to her father. Would he warn this poor, innocent guy?

Ted put the lid on his sandwich and reached for a plastic bag. "You said you're investigators. Has Sam done something I should know about?"

"We're not sure," Bill said. "He may be squeaky clean, but you might want to hold off a bit before handing over your savings."

"Really."

Ted and Bill gazed at each other for a long moment.

Bill pulled out a business card. "This is my contact information. I'm not a police officer, but I spent a lot of years on the P.D. in Bowling Green. If you want to check up on me, ask for their detective sergeant, or call the Murray P.D. and ask for Detective Fuller. They can tell you about me."

"So, is this a police case? I mean—is someone official looking into it?"

"Not yet. We're just asking a few preliminary questions for a private client who's also been befriended by Mr. Truman."

"I see."

"And we'd appreciate it if you didn't tell him we were here."

"Yeah, I can see why. Thanks." He closed his lunch box and picked it up. "Now I've got to get to work."

"Sure. Thanks for your time," Bill said. Campbell followed him outside, where house numbers for units 3 and 4 flanked the main door. Inside the entry, stairs led them to the doors of the upper apartments. Bill pushed the bell for number 3. Campbell wasn't surprised when a woman in her twenties opened the door and regarded them curiously.

"Can I help you?"

"Yes, we were wondering if you know Mr. Truman, in apartment 2," Bill said.

Her features softened. "I've met him. Why do you ask?"

Bill handed her one of his business cards. "I'm Bill McBride, from True Blue Investigations in Murray. We've had an inquiry about Mr. Truman, and we're trying to get a sense of his relationships with his neighbors, Ms., uh—?"

"Andrea Finley." Her eyebrows drew together as she peered at the card. "He's only lived in the building a couple of months, but he seems like a nice guy. Is he in some sort of trouble?"

"No, not at all." Bill smiled. "So, there's nothing about him that would make you uneasy?"

"No. My roommate and I like him a lot. He's very polite, and he'll run errands if anyone needs something."

"Is your roommate home? Maybe we could talk to her too."

Andrea shook her head. "She's teaching summer school right now. To tell you the truth, I think she's a bit smitten with Sam."

Campbell leaned in a little. "Sounds like Sam Truman's the ideal neighbor."

"Yeah, kind of. But you're making me a little nervous. Are you sure there's nothing wrong?"

"There's not," Bill said. "We would appreciate it if you didn't mention our visit to him, though. Our client is eager to know if other people are as impressed with Mr. Truman as she is."

"Oh, a job thing?"

"Something like that. He hasn't talked to you about finances, has he?"

Andrea eyed Bill blankly. "No. Why would he?"

"No reason."

"I mean, he recommends restaurants and things, and when he first moved in, he did ask us what bank we used, so he could set up his account at a place he could trust."

"I see."

Her face clouded for a moment. "He did tell us about a clairvoyant in Murray."

Campbell caught her breath.

Bill chuckled. "Now, that's interesting. Have you ever had your fortune told?"

"No, but my roommate, Sarah, went to her once. She said it was a hoot. We were thinking of hiring the woman to do readings at a party."

"Sounds like fun," Campbell said. "But you've never met her personally?"

"Not yet. I may go see her with Sarah this weekend."

Campbell glanced at her father, and he gave her an almost imperceptible nod to continue. "Do you know her name? It sounds like something I might enjoy."

"It's an odd name." Andrea frowned. "Starts with a T, I think. Did I tell you she lives in Murray? I'm sure you could find her online."

"Thanks. I'll take a look." Campbell smiled and stepped back.

"Thanks a lot for your time, Ms. Finley," Bill said.

The door closed behind them as they walked away. At the top of the stairs, Bill put a hand on Campbell's arm.

"Let's check apartment 4."

Campbell waited while he punched the doorbell on the other upstairs unit, but no one responded.

"Okay," her dad said as he rejoined her. "I'm guessing that pickup in the yard belongs to Ted Holloway. The Fusion's probably Andrea's."

As they went downstairs, Campbell glanced at him. "She seemed to think Sam Truman's the salt of the earth."

"Well, that's how these people operate, you know. They're very charming, and they make you feel as if you want them to be your best friend."

"He hasn't asked Andrea or her roommate to invest."

"Probably he learned enough from them to see they don't have much money for that kind of thing. And he probably wouldn't hit up all his closest neighbors. That might look suspicious."

"But he recommended Miss Tryphenia."

"Yeah." Bill shook his head as they stepped outside into the oppressive heat. The white pickup truck was gone. "I think we can assume that's the clairvoyant she meant. I didn't expect that."

"Me either. I almost gave away that we knew about her."

"You did fine."

"Isn't Sam Truman forty-five years old?" she asked.

"I think that's correct, according to our research."

"Well, I mean—Vera Hill's daughter must be at least forty. Don't you think Andrea Finley would be a little young for him?"

"We don't know how old her roommate is."

"True. She's a teacher." While her dad drove southward toward Murray, Campbell took a notebook from her purse and wrote down the names they'd learned and the details Ted and Andrea had given them.

"Preparing to write up your notes?"

"Yeah, my supervisor has me turn in a report every day." She grinned at him.

"You're easy to train, believe me."

She guessed Nick hadn't been so pliable. Writing reports was a breeze for her, and she loved keeping an organized file on each case, with details they could all check when needed. It made her feel like she was really helping the agency, even though she was still a newbie.

"I'm thinking it might be time for a visit to Miss Tryphenia," her father said, jerking Campbell's attention back to the case at hand.

"Really? Are you going to ask her about Sam Truman?"

"No, that's not my plan, exactly. I was kind of thinking you could go. Pose as a customer."

Campbell gulped. "Ask her to give me a reading?"

His eyebrows shot up.

"That's what Mrs. Vane called it," she said. "Not fortune telling. You get a reading."

"Reading of what? Palms? Cards? Tea leaves?"

"I don't know."

"Hmm. Maybe we should do a little more digging first." They reached Murray, and he turned off on Main Street.

"Well, Vera Hill said not to talk to her about psychics—she said she leaves that to her friends. Plural. I'm thinking maybe she knows someone else besides Mrs. Vane who goes to the psychic."

"Good thinking," Bill said. "Let's ask her tomorrow. Meanwhile, I hope Nick's got some more leads on Truman for us. So far, we haven't found any evidence that this guy has an actual job."

"Maybe he's psychic, too, and he levitates." At her dad's blank look, she said, "You know, no visible means of support."

He let out a belly laugh. "Your education was worth every penny."

"Come on, Dad. It was a stupid pun."

"I thought it was pretty good. Maybe you should consider standup comedy."

"No, thanks. I get enough laughs working with you and Nick."

They rolled past Eighth Street, their usual turn.

"Where are we going?" she asked.

"I want a visual on the psychic parlor. Can you get your phone ready and snap a picture?"

He turned at Second Street, and Campbell's pulse picked up.

"It's down there, on your side." Bill nodded ahead, and she soon located the sign. "Miss Tryphenia, Psychic Readings," he read aloud as they approached.

Campbell whipped her phone up, zeroed in on the building, and tapped. Her father slowed down, and she had time for a closeup of the sign as well.

"Got it."

"Nice work, kiddo." He accelerated gently and turned at the next corner, heading back toward Eighth and Willow Street.

———

"Nope, I didn't find anything. Not since he moved to Kentucky, anyway." Nick's dark eyebrows drew together as he scrolled through a computer file. "I checked all the accounting firms and investment brokers in the area, but I didn't find him anywhere."

"And no social media?" Bill had brought his plate of casserole and salad into the office, and he settled in one of the armchairs.

"Nope," Nick said, "unless he's got accounts under a different name."

Campbell sat at her desk eating the sandwich she'd made herself for lunch, mulling over the enigma of Sam Truman. "We need to find out what the connection is between him and Miss Tryphenia."

Her father looked over at her, and his gaze sharpened. "How much have you put online about yourself?"

"You mean Facebook and that sort of thing?"

"Yeah."

"You asked me not to talk about the business on social media, and I haven't."

"Good. Of course, your picture is on our agency's website, if anyone looks there." He frowned for a moment. "You haven't posted anything about working here?"

"No. I wanted to brag about it, but I haven't."

Nick smirked, and she hastily went on.

"When I first got here, I did post about coming to live with my father and looking for a job."

"But you never said what job you took?" Bill asked.

Campbell shook her head. "It seems most of my friends in Iowa have forgotten about me. Nobody's followed up and asked what I'm doing now."

"Not even Steve?" Nick asked with a sneer.

"Not since his run-in with the police over that medal business. I think he's been glad to stay clear of me for the past few weeks."

There. She'd wiped the smile off Nick's face. He shrugged and turned back to his screen.

"Why are you asking?" She gazed straight at her father.

"I'm thinking maybe you could sort of accidentally meet up with one of them and not tell them who you are. They might try to work their magic on you, and we'd learn something."

"Do you really want me to set up an appointment for a reading? Or are you talking about bumping into Sam Truman? He does seem to like the ladies."

"Not yet. Let's find out a little more first."

Nick looked up from his screen. "I just did a search for your name, Professor, and it found our agency website. It's third on the list."

Bill frowned. "Not good. That's the trouble with advertising when you sometimes need anonymity."

"What came up first?" Campbell asked.

"Feldman University," Nick said. "Then your Facebook page."

She groaned. So much for keeping a low profile.

"Don't worry about it." Her dad stood and went to the coffeemaker they kept on a side table. "Nick does a good job on our website. It does exactly what I wanted it to—gives the public an overview of our services and draws in new clients." He filled his mug and headed back to his seat. "Remember how Andrea said they might hire Miss Tryphenia to entertain at a party?"

"Yeah. What are you thinking?" Campbell asked.

"One of us—or somebody else we enlist—could inquire about her rates for parties and just get a general sense of her and the way she works."

Campbell lifted her chin as an idea formulated in her mind. "Maybe Reagan Brady would come over this weekend. She might do it, and she doesn't have any obvious local connections."

Her dad pursed his lips for a moment. "She's young, and she's not trained. But maybe you two could go together. If she didn't mind using her name, you could just tag along as an anonymous friend."

"The woman would see me, so she'd recognize me if I ran into her later."

"Let's think it over." Her father took his coffee mug and turned toward the door. "I'll be in my office. Campbell, work up your notes and then report to me for another assignment."

The background checks for the university had been delivered. Her father kept her busy that afternoon with updating reports and practicing skip tracing techniques while he and Nick tapped every resource they could think of for more information on Truman. Campbell spent the final hour of her workday studying for the upcoming exam.

Everyone's spirits lifted when Keith walked in the front door shortly before five o'clock.

"Hey, come in. Sit down." Bill led him to the seating area near the empty fireplace in the main office. "Can I get you something to drink?"

"No, thanks. I'm on my way to my folks' house for supper."

Keith sat and crossed his long legs as the others gathered and took comfortable seats. "So, how's it going with the psychic thing?"

Campbell's dad shot her a quick glance. "Well, we're not actually investigating the psychic. Not officially, that is. That's sort of a side thing that came up."

Keith nodded. "Campbell mentioned to me that a neighbor had some involvement with a local medium."

"There may be a connection between Miss Tryphenia and our official case." Campbell looked at her father to see if he would object to discussing it with the police detective.

"She's right, I'm afraid," Bill said. "The fellow we're looking into recommended this psychic to one of his neighbors. He hasn't been in the area all that long, and we're wondering what the link is between them."

"Who's the subject you're looking at, if you don't mind telling me," Keith said.

"Samuel Truman, or Eliot Samuel Truman," Bill said.

"Doesn't ring a bell."

Nick ran a hand through his hair. "We're pretty sure he hasn't had a run-in with the law since he moved here, but he's got an old rap sheet in Missouri."

Campbell couldn't help smiling. In her study session she'd just learned that the letters in "rap" sheet stood for "record of arrests and prosecutions."

"Why is that funny?" Nick frowned at her.

"Oh, it's not. I was thinking of something else. I haven't met this Truman character, but he sounds like a piece of work. His neighbors love him, but there's just a slimy feel about him."

"Why are you investigating him?" Keith looked to Bill for an answer.

"Because he's cozying up to our client's daughter, and she's concerned. It doesn't feel right to the client."

"How old's the daughter?"

"At least forty." Bill sighed with a sidelong glance at Campbell. "We never stop worrying about our kids, right, Soup?"

"I have no expertise in this area," she said, "but if you're an example, Dad, then yes. I agree wholeheartedly."

Keith smiled. "Your daughter's got her head on straight. What's this Truman doing that the mom doesn't like?"

"He's pushing some kind of investment scheme," Bill said. "Have you ever heard of the Billings-Phifer Fund?"

"No, but I can put out some feelers."

"I wish we could connect with him without letting on that we're investigators, but we're too easy to find online." Bill sat back in his chair and looked up at the ceiling. "Are you on social media?"

"I'm not, but a lot of officers are."

"Don't they tell you not to?" Nick asked.

"They encourage us to keep a low profile. Officers who have accounts are supposed to remember that they're representing the department and the community on there. Anyone who posts something questionable is disciplined."

"That's the way it is with Bill." Nick didn't seem happy about it.

"It's common sense." Bill didn't seem offended. "I tell them, if someone looks us up to see if they want to hire us, and they see a picture of you doing something irresponsible, they're not going to want to do business with us."

"Yeah, being active on social media can make it hard to investigate discreetly." Keith pushed to his feet. "Well, I'd better get going."

"You haven't even seen my private office yet." Bill almost pouted.

Keith chuckled. "Don't forget, I saw it when it was Katherine Tyler's private office and someone had just ransacked it."

"Oh, yeah. Well, it's a lot nicer now."

"Campbell told me you've fixed up your private quarters upstairs too. Tell you what, I'll come by again soon for the grand tour."

"Have supper with us tomorrow," Campbell said quickly.

"All right, I'd like that."

She walked with him into the entry. Keith turned to face her and reached out to brush back a strand of her hair, his hand grazing her cheek.

"I'm so glad you decided to stay in town."

"Even under Dad's eagle eye?"

"Especially. Bill's a good friend, and I know he's looking out for you. Just be careful, will you?"

"Of course."

Keith nodded and left smiling.

4

Vera Hill was prompt for her appointment Thursday morning, with homemade apple turnovers in hand.

"Oh, Vera, how wonderful." Campbell took the Ziploc bag with a cautious smile. "You know you don't have to bring us food every time you come over, right?"

She chuckled. "Cooking is one of my hobbies. Besides, your father could use a little extra poundage."

But not me, Campbell thought ruefully. Because her dad liked to eat out so much, she was trying to watch her calorie intake.

"Say, I don't think Bill's ever met my daughter Dorothy." Vera gave her a winning smile.

"Uh, no, I don't think so."

Vera leaned toward her with a conspiratorial air. "Maybe when this is over."

Campbell cleared her throat. Her dad hated to be set up by well-meaning friends. "Won't you come this way? I know Dad's expecting you."

She knocked on the door of his office and stuck her head in. "Mrs. Hill's here, Dad."

"Great. Oh, and Campbell, maybe you should sit in too."

"Okay. Just let me put these in the kitchen." She held up the bag of turnovers then stepped aside so Vera could enter.

She put the goodies in a cupboard and hurried back to join the others. Vera was seated in a comfortable chair across from Bill and telling him a story about her grandchildren, which he apparently found hilarious. Campbell smiled and drew up another chair.

Bill sobered and pulled a manilla folder toward him. "So, this man your daughter's seeing …"

Vera pulled in a breath and squared her shoulders.

"We've learned a few things about him," Bill went on, "but probably not as much as you'd like to know."

"Give me a for-instance," Vera said.

"All right. He was born in Metropolis and grew up there. Later, he lived near St. Louis for a while. He has a criminal record in Missouri, but so far, we've only found one conviction, and it was ten years ago, for a misdemeanor."

She frowned. "I suppose that sort of thing could be true for a lot of people."

"It could," Bill said. "However, I've touched base with law enforcement in Metropolis, and we did find a complaint filed against him a few years later."

"What sort of complaint?"

"Domestic. A restraining order was issued against him, but he wasn't charged with a crime at that time."

The older woman's face paled. "Do you know who filed that order?"

"His wife."

"Ex-wife?"

"I have Nick working on it, but he hasn't found a divorce record yet."

"You mean he's still married?"

"Not necessarily. It's possible we just haven't found the paperwork yet."

"Hmm." The lines on Vera's face etched deep as she ruminated on that. Campbell could almost see her protective instincts as a mother kicking in.

"The Metropolis police are familiar with Sam, but there haven't been any other formal charges there. Now, we can put in some more time on it if you want—" Bill began.

"What about that fund business? He came around yesterday wanting to know if Frank and I were ready to invest. Frank was leaning toward giving him five thousand dollars, but I said we needed to think about it some more."

"Good for you," Campbell said.

Vera glanced at her and nodded. "It may not seem like a lot of money, but at our age, we have to be careful."

"Yes, you do," Bill said.

"He did bring us this brochure." Vera opened her purse and fumbled in it for a moment then drew out a colorful pamphlet. She passed it across the desk to Bill.

"Now, this is helpful." He picked it up and opened it, scanning the contents. "This is the first evidence I've seen that there really is a Billings-Phifer Fund. We couldn't find anything online about this, and a police officer who's a friend of ours made a couple of inquiries. He came up empty too."

"You told the police?" Vera looked alarmed.

"I didn't tell him it was for you," Bill assured her. "We never reveal our clients' names without permission. I just wanted to know if this fund—or Truman—had hit their radar."

"Oh. I guess that's all right."

"We can do a little more digging into this if you want," Bill went on. "Now that we have this brochure, we might be able to find something."

"Do you think he printed it himself?" Vera asked.

"It's possible. With today's technology, it's easy to make a professional-looking sales tool like this."

Vera sighed. "I just don't know. Frank thinks we should give him the benefit of a doubt."

"There's one other—" Campbell broke off and looked at her dad.

"Go ahead," he said. "It's okay."

She turned to face Vera. "We met some of his neighbors yesterday. They mostly like Sam."

"Well, sure. As I told you, he's charming." Vera scowled. "*Too* charming in my book."

Campbell nodded. "One of them had talked to Sam about investments, and he mentioned this fund, but that man didn't have anything on paper. Another neighbor, though, said Sam recommended a psychic to her and her roommate."

Vera's eyes hardened. "Not that one on Second Street?"

"We're pretty sure that's the one," Campbell said.

"I have no use for her." Vera shook her head. "I'm pretty sure she's bilking my friend Mary out of a heap of money. Money she needs."

"Can you tell us about it?" Bill asked gently.

Vera hesitated.

"I understand if you don't want to break a friend's confidence." Bill leaned back in his chair, giving her a little more distance.

"Mary went to have one of those readings, okay? Twenty bucks the first time."

Campbell sensed that Vera might be more comfortable

focusing on her, rather than her father, so she asked, "Did she tell you about it? How did it go?"

"She thought it was great. That woman told her some things about her private life and her family that she didn't think anyone would know about. And she said there was a cloud over Mary's son, but she could help make it better."

"Make it better how?"

"She burned some incense and gave Mary a little charm. She told her to pray for her son and rub the charm while she did it."

Campbell thought about that, but she couldn't see how praying while holding a charm would be better than good old heartfelt praying.

"Is Mary one to pray ordinarily?" her father asked.

"Yes. Well, I mean, she goes to church. And then that woman told Mary to come back again the next week and tell her how it was going. But by then things had gotten worse."

"Did Mary go back?" Campbell asked.

"Yes. And that time it was forty dollars, but she got these little prayer cards and some herbal tea."

"Tea?" Bill's face scrunched up. "For herself or the son?"

"For her. It was supposed to make her calm, so that she could pray more effectively. The next time, it was lotion. That cost an extra twenty-five bucks."

"And it went on like this?" Campbell couldn't imagine continuing to give money to someone like that, but she supposed Mary was desperate to help her son.

Vera nodded. "When she told me, I asked her why she didn't go to her pastor about it. She said he couldn't do anything. Her son lives in Tennessee. But location doesn't limit Miss Tryphenia's powers. She can heal anyone from afar."

Bill's eyebrows shot up. "Heal him?"

"Heal the situation, I think. I'm not really clear on what all this was supposed to do exactly. I just know that within a couple months of that first visit, Mary had forked over more than a thousand dollars, all told."

"Wow."

"Yeah. She had to dip into her savings to pay her rent and utilities. I told her to quit going to that woman. But did she listen to me? She did not."

"She got in deeper," Campbell guessed.

"Another two thousand. That was the latest payment I know about. There could be more."

"How's the son doing?"

"Not well. He's changed jobs a couple of times, and then Mary told me he was in some kind of trouble."

"Legal trouble?" Bill asked.

"I'm not sure, but I think maybe. I don't guess he's in jail, or Mary would have told me. But maybe not, if she's too ashamed."

Campbell gazed at her father, unsure of what to say.

"And she still thinks the psychic can fix things?" he asked.

"Now she's protecting the fellow from evil. If he's been arrested—well, a lot goes on in jails, you know."

"Oh, I know." Bill fingered his coffee mug and looked around.

"Let me get you some coffee, Dad." Campbell rose. "Vera, would you like some? Or a cup of tea?"

"I'll drink some coffee with Bill. Thanks."

Campbell went to the kitchen and set up a tray with cream and sugar, mugs, spoons, and napkins. As she reached for the coffee carafe, the house phone rang. She grabbed the receiver from the wall phone.

"True Blue Investigations."

"Is that you, Miss Campbell?"

She smiled at the typical Southern use of the courtesy title with her first name.

"Yes, it is. How may I help you?"

"This is Louanne Vane. I think someone's been in my house. No, I *know* someone's been in my house."

"While you were out?" Campbell frowned but went ahead pouring the coffee.

"No. Sometime in the night."

"How do you know?"

"Things are a little messed up, like someone was looking for something. And worst of all, Blue Boy's missing."

Campbell straightened, "You're sure?"

"Yes. He's not in the house. And he never goes outside." The old woman's voice broke. "Whoever came in here while I was asleep must have let him out. Or—or taken him."

Catnapped. Campbell grimaced at the thought and didn't speak the pun aloud.

"Miss Louanne, I'll be right over. I just have to tell my dad where I'm going, okay?"

"Yes, ma'am. I'll be here."

She set aside the third mug from the tray and carried it with two servings to her father's office. Spilling Mrs. Vane's name in front of Vera Hill probably wouldn't be strictly ethical, even though the two were friends. Maybe especially because they were friends.

"Here we go." She set the laden tray on the corner of Bill's desk. "Dad, I need to run out for a few minutes. I won't be gone long, and I'll call you if I need help."

Her last phrase triggered the pucker of a frown between his eyebrows. "Okay. Got your phone?"

"I do." She smiled at Vera. "Nice to see you, Miss Vera."

She backed into the hallway and shut the door then hurried toward the front entrance.

"Hey, Campbell," Nick called as she passed the open door to their joint office space. "Got a sec?"

"Not really." But she hovered in the doorway.

"I found out why there's no divorce record for Samuel Truman and his wife."

"They reconciled?"

"Nope. She died."

Campbell stared at him for a moment. "Okay, that's very interesting. Unfortunately, I have to run an errand, but I'll be back soon. You can give me the details then."

She didn't bother to take her purse. Walking would be as fast as driving half a block. When she reached the small gray house, Mrs. Vane opened the door before she could ring the bell.

"Hello, sugar. Thanks for coming so quick."

"No problem. Can you show me where you think the intruder touched things?" Campbell had learned a few things by watching Keith examine crime scenes. She was careful not to touch anything as they went into the neat kitchen.

"Not much in here. It's just that the back door was unlocked, and I always make sure it's locked before I go to bed. As they say nowadays, I'm compulsive about checking my locks."

Campbell bent and peered at the doorknob with its button lock and the deadbolt's turn lever above it. She didn't want to open the door because she hadn't thought to bring any plastic gloves. "All right, what else told you someone had been here, aside from Blue Boy being gone? Did you hear anything?"

"No. I went to bed after the ten o'clock news last night. I got up once." Her sweet face flushed pink. "I went right back to sleep, though. And I didn't wake up again until almost eight."

"You didn't call me until nine thirty."

"It took me a while to get moving this morning. After I

dressed, I went to the kitchen to get my breakfast. Blue Boy usually comes around then, but today he didn't. So I ate, and then I started looking for him. It took me a while to convince myself he was really gone. I even checked the towel shelves in the laundry room, because once I saw him napping in there. Finally, I went to the back door just to be thorough, and that's when I noticed it wasn't locked."

"And that's when you called me?"

Mrs. Vane nodded.

"Where does Blue Boy sleep at night?"

"He has a basket." She nodded toward a cushioned wicker nest beside the refrigerator. "He doesn't always use it, though. Sometimes he'll settle on an armchair. I don't let him sleep in my room, because he wakes me up when he moves around."

Campbell followed her through to the parlor, where they'd drunk their tea on Tuesday. Sure enough, the rocking chair and one upholstered recliner had long, blue-gray cat hairs on the seat cushions, but no Blue Boy sprawled there.

"And these papers and things were shuffled." Mrs. Vane nodded toward the coffee table, where a stack of magazines and a sheaf of loose papers sat in disarray. "At first I thought maybe Blue Boy had jumped up there and knocked them crooked, but then I saw they were out of order. And I noticed my desk wasn't tidy either, and one drawer was open about a half inch."

"You wouldn't leave it that way," Campbell said.

"No. And then, when I couldn't find him …"

Campbell drew in a slow breath. "I think you should call the police."

"Really?" The older woman's anxiety was plain in her face.

"Yes. They could dust for fingerprints on the back door and these things that have been tampered with."

"Oh. Would they? A friend of mine's husband had his chainsaw stolen from his truck, and they didn't do anything."

"I know someone on the police force. Do you mind if I call him?"

"I suppose not."

Campbell pulled her cell from the pocket of her pants. "What are those papers on the coffee table? Are they important?"

"It's a document from the bank. My mortgage is almost paid off. I only have three more payments, and I was looking over the statement last night." She managed a shaky smile. "I'll be so glad when the house is all mine. When Leland died, I wondered if I'd be able to do it, but I'm nearly there."

"That's a big milestone. Congratulations." Campbell patted her shoulder. "Excuse me just a minute." She stepped out into the entry.

5

Keith glanced at the screen of his phone and smiled. Campbell never called him during work hours without a good reason, and he'd have to be engaged in something urgent not to take a call from her.

"Hi, how's it going?" he said.

Quickly, she told him she was at a neighbor's house and the reason for her visit. "Keith, I know this is probably something you'd normally send a patrol officer on, but this could be related to that case we discussed with you." Her warm voice sounded a little troubled and apologetic.

Keith paused, mentally reviewing what the McBrides had told him about the psychic and the man peddling a questionable investment opportunity.

"What's the address? I'll be right there."

Ten minutes later, he pulled up in front of Luanne Vane's house, where Campbell met him at the door.

"Thanks for coming," Campbell said.

"No problem." He followed her into the living room, where

a woman in her eighties was sitting on the edge of an armchair, breathing in quick, shallow gasps.

"Mrs. Vane, I'm Detective Fuller. I'm so sorry this happened."

"Thank you."

Keith sat down on the blue sofa near her and moved aside a patchwork throw pillow. "Can you please tell me exactly what happened this morning?"

She related how she'd noticed little things that made her more and more uneasy, ending with her frantic search for her cat and her call to Campbell, who hovered near Mrs. Vane's chair.

"Is this cat valuable, ma'am?" he asked.

"Well, he's not like some alley cat. He's a Persian blue. Leland and I paid about eight hundred dollars for him when he was a kitten, but that was ten years ago."

"So, he's a middle-aged cat."

"Yes, and he's still very handsome, but I've never shown him or anything like that."

"Could you show me some pictures of him?"

Campbell grabbed a framed five-by-seven from the top of a bookcase and put it in his hands.

"That's Blue Boy."

Keith studied the picture and nodded slowly. Very handsome, indeed. The slightly smug face sported a luxuriant blue-gray mustache. The long, thick hair fluffed all over the feline's body. His mother would go nuts over Blue Boy—but there must be a constant battle with cat hair during shedding season.

"He never goes outside," Mrs. Vane wailed.

Campbell patted her shoulder and sent Keith a silent plea with those stunning green eyes. Keith forced his attention back to the cat's owner.

"If someone opened a door, would Blue Boy try to get out?" he asked.

"Not usually. He's quite shy. Doesn't take to strangers."

"The intruder may have frightened him," Keith said. "What do you say I dust the back doorknob and these papers and things that have been moved?"

"I didn't think you'd take the trouble." Mrs. Vane's eyes were misty.

"I don't mind. I'm here to work in your best interest, and if Murray's got an active burglar, the sooner we catch him the better."

"Oh! I hadn't thought of that. But nothing's missing. Except Blue Boy." Her gaze drifted to the cat's favorite chair.

"Breaking and entering is still a crime, even if they didn't steal anything."

"I really should get back to the office," Campbell said. "I left Dad with a client. Miss Louanne, will you be all right?"

"Yes, dear. I feel much better, knowing a detective is working on this."

"You're in good hands." Campbell smiled at Keith. "I'll see you later."

It was a subtle reminder of their supper date, and he nodded with a smile.

As Campbell went out the front door, Mrs. Vane said, "So, you two are good friends, I take it?"

———

Campbell hurried along the sidewalk, her sweeping gaze taking in both sides of Willow Street in the faint hope that she might spot Blue Boy.

As she came even with Ben Tatton's old house, she stopped and scrutinized the willow tree in the front yard. A suspiciously darker patch teased from among the green foliage. She squinted at it. Squirrels wouldn't build a nest that low, would they? She took several steps onto the overgrown lawn, and the dark patch stirred.

"Oh, you naughty boy." She walked slowly toward it. "Come on, Blue Boy."

The willow leaves rustled as he climbed to a higher branch.

"No, of course you wouldn't come to me. You hate me." She still had three little scabs on her thumb to prove it. She pulled out her phone.

"Hi, Keith. It's me. I think I've found Blue Boy, but I need Mrs. Vane to coax him down out of a tree."

"Where are you?"

"Tatton's house."

"We're on the way."

Before Mrs. Vane's door opened, Vera Hill came out of the McBrides' new house and spotted her.

"Campbell! There you are." Walking toward her, Vera continued in a loud voice, "Your father is such a kind man. He's going to go on looking into—you know, that matter we were discussing."

Campbell put on a big smile and nodded but put a finger to her lips.

Vera paused. "What is it?"

In a loud whisper, Campbell replied, "Mrs. Vane's cat is in that tree. She's coming to try to get him down."

As if hearing her cue, Louanne came out her front door and down the steps, with Keith solicitously holding her elbow.

"Blue Boy's outside?" Vera's shocked tones probably reached Courthouse Square.

Campbell looked uneasily toward the willow. Sure enough, the cat was scrabbling higher yet.

"I think we should stand back and let Miss Louanne get

closer. You know Blue Boy doesn't like strangers, and I'm practically that." Campbell joined Vera on the sidewalk, and they waited together while Keith and Mrs. Vane walked toward them at the old woman's slow pace.

"Where is he?" Her quavering voice reached them.

"In that tree." Campbell pointed.

"Oh, dear."

"I didn't think he'd come down for me," Campbell said.

"No, probably not."

"What do you want to do?" Keith asked. "We could call Animal Control."

"No, no. That would only traumatize him." Mrs. Vane shook her head slowly. "Maybe one of his treats?"

"I can get it for you," Campbell said. "Where are they?"

"In the cupboard to the left of the sink. And bring a can of the seafood medley too. That's his favorite."

"Let me," Keith said.

Campbell nodded, and he jogged off toward Mrs. Vane's house.

Nick came out onto the front porch of the McBride house. "What's going on?"

"We've got a situation with Mrs. Vane's cat. It's up the willow tree, and he's an indoor cat." Campbell turned back to the two older women. "I should probably go tell my dad what's happening. I was supposed to go right back to my desk, and he'll wonder where I am."

"Of course," Mrs. Hill said.

By the time she got to the walkway, her father was on the porch with Nick.

"Hey, Soup. Nick called me out here. What's up?"

"Mrs. Vane phoned me because she thought someone had been in her house during the night. I agreed with her after looking things over, so we called Keith. The worst part is that her cat got out somehow, which is a big no-no. On my way home, I spotted him in that willow tree, so she's going to try to lure him down."

"Can we help?" Bill asked.

She shook her head. "Don't think so. Blue Boy is not a people cat. Except for Miss Louanne, of course."

"Okay. Well, Nick and I will get back to work. When things calm down, come see me, and I'll brief you on how things stand with Vera."

"Got it."

He and Nick went inside, and she stood on the porch watching as Keith returned carrying a can of fancy cat food and a bag of treats. She wanted to go closer, but Frank Hill had joined his wife and Mrs. Vane. Campbell didn't want to add to the congestion. The way she saw it, the more people staring, the longer Blue Boy would stay in the willow.

It took another twenty minutes, and Keith amiably but firmly asking the spectators, which by then included three children, their mother, and a couple from down the block, to move on. Finally, Blue Boy inched down the willow's trunk toward Mrs. Vane, who stood under the curtain of graceful, arched branches. Holding up an open can of seafood medley, she called plaintively to the cat. Only when the neighbors backed away did he make a move toward her.

He must be starving, poor thing. Campbell remembered his hostile reception when she first visited the Vane house. Had he attacked the intruder? If the burglar retaliated, Blue Boy must have been scared out of his mind. No wonder he'd streaked out the door when he had a chance.

Or maybe the burglar had tossed him out to keep him from interrupting his search and keep him from making noises that might awaken Mrs. Vane.

Unfortunately, they'd never know. As special as he was, Blue Boy couldn't tell them.

At last the cat moved to a low branch, and when the lady he deigned to live with held up the can of food, he sniffed at it. She held up both arms, and after some shifting and feinting, he jumped down onto her shoulder. She dropped the can and wrapped him in her arms.

Across the street, the lingering neighbors applauded. Blue Boy wriggled and dug his claws through her blouse in an effort to gain purchase and escape, but she held him fast.

Keith moved in cautiously and retrieved the can of seafood medley. He scooped out a blob and extended his finger over Mrs. Vane's shoulder. Blue Boy stilled for a moment, then sniffed at the fishy substance. At last he licked it and then grabbed a quick bite.

Watching from afar, Campbell sighed. She wished she'd thought to ask where Blue Boy's carrier was, but this looked like the beginning of a positive ending. Keith signaled the onlookers to be quiet. Mrs. Vane eased out from beneath the willow and walked slowly toward the sidewalk and her home, while Keith followed and offered occasional bits of food to the cat, who nestled on his owner's shoulder.

Not until the cat, Mrs. Vane, and Keith were all inside her house did Campbell quit watching. She hurried to her father's office, and he looked up from an open folder in his hand.

"Mission accomplished?"

"Yes, finally."

"So, Keith thinks there was a burglar?"

"Yes. And some bank papers Mrs. Vane had been studying last night were out of place."

"Not something the cat could have done?"

Campbell shook her head. "Oh, I suppose it's remotely possible. But how did he get outside if no one opened a door or a window? The back door wasn't locked, and Miss Louanne was certain she'd checked it last night. She lives alone, you know. Well, except for Blue Boy."

"Right. I've no doubt she's diligent about checking the locks."

Campbell sat down. "Dad, do you think someone was looking to see what her finances are like? She's about to finish paying off a thirty-year mortgage. That's something Sam Truman might be interested in. He might think Miss Luanne would start having a little extra every month to invest now."

Her father nodded. "Has he approached her?"

"Not that I know of."

"Well, I've been thinking too," Nick said from the doorway.

Campbell whirled around. "When did you come in?"

"Just now."

She considered making some remark about the rarity of his engaging in thinking, but she decided to act like a grownup instead. "So, what were you thinking?"

Nick stepped in and sat in the extra chair. "You know how the coroner checks a victim's fingernails to see if he had the attacker's skin underneath them? Well, that cat's a scratcher. You showed me your battle wound the other day. What if he scratched the burglar?"

Campbell stared at him. Was this train of thought worth considering? "I suppose a vet could scrape his claws."

Her father shook his head. "Think about it. That cat has been climbing a tree. No doubt he scratched the bark many times, and it probably cleaned out any evidence that was in his claws—unless you and Keith found some blood in the house? In that case, it might be worthwhile."

"No, I didn't see anything like that. And besides, when Blue Boy finally came out of the tree, he dug into Miss Louanne's shoulder. I saw her wincing and gritting her teeth. If anyone's DNA is under his claws right now, it's probably hers."

"Right. If they catch the burglar, they can check him for claw marks. In the meantime, let's let Keith handle the Case of the Reclaimed Cat, and we'll get back to Mrs. Hill's case. She paid us another hundred dollars—"

"Dad, you can't keep the three of us all working for a whole day for a hundred bucks," Campbell said. "You don't give whopping discounts to friends and neighbors."

"I know, but the Hills are on a fixed income, and I feel as though we're doing the community a good turn by looking into this. If someone's preying on our senior citizens, let's smoke him out."

She drew in a deep breath. "Okay. What do you want me to do?"

Bill wrote something on a memo square. "At my request, Vera discreetly jotted down Sam Truman's license plate number. You know the make and model. It's maroon. Nick, I want you to go to Benton and see if he's at his apartment. If so, sit on him for a while, and if he goes out, find out where. Oh, and before you head up to Benton, I want you to swing by Second Street."

"To see if he's over there visiting Miss Tryphenia?"

"Yeah. I don't want you to waste a trip to Benton."

"I'm on it." Nick grabbed the slip of paper and stood.

"What if he's at Dorothy Chambers's house?" Campbell asked.

Her father sucked in a breath, his eyes focused beyond her. "Doubt it. Remember, Dorothy has a job. She's probably not home this morning."

Nick strode out the door.

"Okay, what about me?" Campbell asked.

"You and I are going to see if we can find out who else Truman's been pitching this scheme to."

"You're sure it's a scheme then?"

Her dad leaned back in his chair and twiddled his Racers pen back and forth, frowning. "Not a hundred percent, but I can't find an official registration of the fund in Calloway County or anywhere else in Kentucky. If it's based out of state —which the brochure doesn't tell us—they haven't made it easy to find them."

"The address should be printed on there, right?"

"Yes, some indication of their location. Of course, it can take a while for these things to go through and show up on rosters. Weeks, maybe. But he's been pushing this thing for at least a couple of weeks now. We know that from Vera. And it would surprise me if he didn't start as soon as he arrived in the area."

Campbell picked up the glossy brochure and studied it closely. She turned it over and perused the back but couldn't find any sort of contact information, which seemed odd if the man wanted people to be able to reach him and invest.

Bill's desk phone rang, and he picked it up.

"Yeah, Nick. Okay. Keep me posted." He hung up. "Nick didn't see any sign of Truman over near the psychic's place."

"Let's hope he can pick up his trail." Campbell laid down the brochure. "You're right. There's nothing new here, and no way to ask for more information. What good is it?"

"I think it's a dummy sort of thing," her dad said. "If the fund was legitimate, there ought to be some kind of web presence. If anyone sees the name on the brochure, they should be able to find it by browsing online."

She nodded. "A website would certainly make it look more authentic."

"It would make some of them think, 'Oh, yeah, that's official.'" He shrugged.

"The I-saw-it-on-the-Internet mentality?"

"It does exist. There are people who think that if it's online, it's genuine."

"I love the Internet, but it gives crooks so many ways to scam people."

"Oh, yeah. The bad ones are going to take advantage of every new opportunity to fleece those who aren't discerning." He smiled at her. "So, are you ready to talk to some of Vera and Dorothy's friends to see if Truman has approached them?"

"Okay. And what about Andrea Finley's roommate? Do you think we could approach her without triggering an alarm for Truman?"

"Hard to say. Maybe we should talk to Andrea again and see if she discussed our visit with her roommate. Sarah, wasn't it?"

"Yes, but she was teaching. She might not be home again today."

"Well, Vera gave me the names of two of Dorothy's friends who live here in Murray. Let's start with them."

6

K eith knocked on the McBrides' front door at quarter to six. Before anyone could respond, he opened the door and called, "It's me."

"Come on back," Campbell yelled from the kitchen.

He grinned and let himself in. Campbell was pulling a pan from the oven, and a couple of saucepans steamed atop the stove.

"Smells good in here," he said.

"Thanks. Stuffed pork chops." She transferred the pan to a hot mat on the counter and pulled off her oven mitts. Her bib apron lent her a domestic air she didn't usually exhibit.

"Wow, I didn't know you could cook like that."

She gave him a sheepish look. "Rita put it in the oven before she left. We decided to have her come in one day a week to clean and start supper for us."

"Probably a wise idea."

The woman who'd lived here last had employed Rita Henry as a daily housekeeper. She was efficient and honest, and she knew the house.

Campbell shrugged and turned to switch off the oven and a burner. "Dad and I are so busy, we decided we don't have time to vacuum."

"I know what that's like."

"What do you do?" Campbell turned to face him.

"On my day off, I force myself to spend an hour cleaning up the house. And then I reward myself for all my hard work. I go fishing, or I go see my folks, something like that." *Or I come visit you.*

She smiled, and he knew she had read his mind, though he hadn't said it aloud.

"Well, Dad's upstairs. Want to give him a holler?"

"Sure."

She started transferring the chops to a platter. Keith stepped into the hallway. At the bottom of the stairs, he called, "Yo, Bill!"

"Hey, Keith. Be right there."

He went back to the kitchen, where Campbell was about to carry the serving dishes to the dining room.

"Want to grab the veggies?" she asked with the smile he could never refuse.

"Of course." He picked up bowls of mashed potatoes and collard greens and carried them in for her. The table was already set for three. Bill was more of a paper-plate guy, but tonight they were eating off fancy plates, white with blue forget-me-nots.

"Your mom's china?" he asked.

"Yeah. I washed it all after the move anyway, and I figured we might as well use it. It's too pretty to stick in the cupboard forever."

Keith knew what she meant. When his folks had moved to the lake and sold him their house in town, his mother had left him quite a few household items as a convenience to him and, he suspected, an excuse for his mother to buy new ones. He enjoyed using her old pans and linens. They reminded him of his parents' love, and that they were only a few miles away. Campbell's mom had been deceased for a long time. She must miss her horribly.

When Bill joined them, they sat down to share the meal, and the talk turned to the morning's events.

"I think Blue Boy was delighted to get back to his home," Keith said.

Campbell paused with her fork in midair. "Poor Miss Louanne."

"She'll bless your name forever," Bill said, reaching for the water pitcher.

"I'm just glad he showed up. If he hadn't, she'd have been miserable. I just happened to be the one who spotted him in that tree." Campbell took her bite and chewed, her gaze far away.

"So, was there really a burglar?" Bill asked.

"Oh, yeah." Keith picked up his steak knife to cut his chop. "Ordinarily when nothing's taken, I wouldn't dust for prints, but this was an elderly woman, and as Campbell said, she'd have been devastated if she didn't get her cat back."

"You got some prints then?" Campbell said eagerly. "Off the back doorknob?"

"No, the papers in the living room. I couldn't find any others, so I figured he was wearing gloves. But he must have had trouble leafing through the documents, so he slipped one off. I got three good right-hand prints."

"Hooray for science," Bill said. "Were you able to match them?"

"Not locally, but I'm having them run through a national database." Keith paused. "One thing this burglary has done, though—it's put the man who's looking for investments from elderly residents on the P.D.'s radar."

"You think it was Sam Truman?" Campbell's eyes almost shone.

"Let's just say I also sent the mysterious fingerprints to Missouri with an inquiry about Eliot Samuel Truman." Keith smiled. "Mrs. Vane was tickled when I asked her to let me take her prints for comparison. She said today was one of the most exciting in her life."

Bill frowned. "One thing bothers me."

"Just one, Dad?" Campbell grinned.

"Well, about this case. Mrs. Vane, so far as we know, had no connection to Truman."

"I asked her, and she'd never met him," Keith said. "However, she's a good friend of Vera Hill, whose daughter is dating Truman. She'd heard his name, in a negative context, from Mrs. Hill."

"Aha," Bill said. "And chances are Truman had learned Mrs. Vane's name from Dorothy. He probably asked her in all supposed innocence who her mother's friends were."

"Maybe," Keith said. "It's certainly a possibility. But those prints could turn out to be someone else's and no relation to the investment case."

"You mean the investment swindle."

"Now, Bill." Keith gave him the most fatherly look he could manage, which was hard since Bill was about twenty years older.

"I'm just saying." Bill waved his fork through the air, narrowly missing Campbell's ear.

"Take it easy, Dad," she said gently.

"What's your next step concerning the psychic?" Keith asked.

"Oh, so now you agree with me that the two cases are

connected?" Bill eyed him closely.

"I think Mrs. Vane could be a connection. She sees the psychic on a regular basis, and now it appears someone is looking into her finances on the sly."

"Not so sly," Campbell said.

"If that cat hadn't gone missing, she might not have noticed anything," her father said with a stubborn edge.

"But she'd already noticed plenty before she realized Blue Boy was gone. Dad, she told me she discovered the back door wasn't locked, and that her papers were messed up and a desk drawer was slightly open. Then she started tearing the house apart looking for Blue Boy."

He held up both hands in surrender. "Okay, I get it. She's more observant than I gave her credit for."

Keith nodded. "She's pretty sharp. I dusted her desk and coffee table, too, but the only prints were hers."

"How did he get in?" Bill asked.

"I think he picked a lock. But if he did, he's not a beginner. He's good at it. No scratches on the striker plate."

"Kind of sloppy of him not to lock the back door as he went out," Bill said.

"I agree. He couldn't set the deadbolt when he left, but he could have at least turned the button on the knob. That makes me think he was there early this morning."

Campbell drew in a quick breath. "You think he heard her stirring, so he got out in a hurry?"

"Could be. Either this morning or when she got up in the night to use the bathroom."

She shivered. "That's scary. Miss Louanne must be creeped out to know a man was in there while she was asleep."

"It could have been a woman," Keith said.

"Yes, it could have been Miss Tryphenia," Campbell said.

"Or someone else acting on her behalf, to find personal

information about her for the psychic to use." Bill straightened his shoulders. "By the way, I don't think I've told either of you —I learned that Miss Tryphenia's real name is Karen Potter."

Campbell stared at him. "I can see why she chose a more exotic name."

Keith chuckled. "Sorry you had to go to the trouble. We've been aware of Ms. Potter's activities for years, and I could have told you her name."

Bill shrugged. "It didn't take me long to find out. Anyhow, I couldn't do a deep search on her finances, but I found some hints that her income is sporadic."

"You mean, she has some large deposits followed by periods of low income?" Campbell asked.

"Nothing that specific, but a couple of sources who deal with her indicated that, yeah, she has her ups and downs. For instance, the landlord who owns her house said she'd been late on her rent a couple of times. But I also turned up a few large purchases she's made, ostensibly when she was a bit more flush."

"You know," Keith said, "This investment case isn't a priority for the police yet—not unless we can definitely link Truman to something solid, like Mrs. Vane's burglary. But it could blow up fast. You'll keep me in the loop?"

"Of course," Bill said. "If we find anything that shows a crime was actually committed in the investment case, we'll be in contact immediately."

"Okay. Now, as far as Ms. Potter, goes, we've watched her with a jaundiced eye for years, but—"

"But no complaints on her." Bill nodded. "That doesn't mean she's not bilking people. Just that she keeps her head down and doesn't reach too far too fast."

"Right."

"I'm thinking we need to send someone in to consult her."

Bill flicked a glance Campbell's way. "I hate to send my daughter, because her name and picture are on our company website. I'm sure Miss Tryphenia uses the Internet to find out information about her clients, and that would make her suspicious."

"Maybe my mom would help."

"Your mother? Absolutely not."

"Why?" Keith liked the idea more as he said it. "She's fascinated by the work you and Campbell do. She'd be tickled to help you out."

Bill's expression darkened. "She's a rank amateur."

"All the better. She'd act totally innocent, I assure you. I'm not on social media, and Fuller is a common name. I doubt the psychic would connect her to me quickly."

"I don't know." Bill shook his head.

Keith studied him for a moment. "Surely you don't think it's dangerous to walk into a psychic's parlor and ask for a reading? Miss Tryphenia will be all over it. Delighted to have a walk-in customer."

"Does she take walk-ins?" Campbell asked. "I'd think she'd want to make an appointment in advance, to give her time to do a little digging."

"You'd be surprised how fast they can learn stuff," Keith said. "And they can read body language better than a detective. They'll throw out a few suggestions and wait for the client to grab one."

"Such as?"

Keith smiled at her. "Well, let's see, Ms. McBride. I sense a dark cloud in your life. You've had a bad experience lately."

Campbell locked eyes with him. Deadpan, she said, "Which one?"

He laughed. "That's just it, don't you see? If she sees a tiny reaction to that, she'll fish more specifically. You've lost a loved one, or a relationship has ended badly, or you've had a financial setback."

She jerked her chin up.

"Aha," Keith said. "You recently changed jobs."

Campbell's lips tightened.

"You lost your job and had to look for another."

"But you knew all that." She looked at her father with exasperation written all over her face.

"Now, now," Bill said. "It's true Keith knew about your job loss, as well as a dangerous situation you found yourself in recently, not to mention almost losing me, or your mother's death."

"That wasn't recent." Campbell's jaw stuck out a little farther.

"No, but when he tossed around the possibilities, the financial setback was the one you reacted to. Sorry, kiddo, but I saw it myself."

"She might not zero in on the job loss so quickly," Keith said, "but she'd know something's happened, and she'd prompt you a little to tell her more about it. You'd be shocked to know how many women would say, 'Oh, that's right. My husband was laid off.' Or with a cue about family troubles, they might say, 'My daughter's husband just walked out on her and the kids.' From there, it's simple for the psychic."

Bill nodded. "They'll assure the client they can help take away that dark cloud and help give you serenity again."

"And when they sense you're buying it," Keith added, "they'll book you for another appointment next week. In the meantime, they have plenty of time to gather more facts and shock you with their insight the next time you meet. Maybe she'd find out the name of the university where you worked, but she wouldn't say so directly. She might say, 'I see an F. A name that starts with F. It has to do with your old job.' And you'd jump at it."

"No, I wouldn't. I mean, not now that I know how they work."

"You do tend to show your feelings," her dad said. "Maybe we should do some role playing, so you can practice not revealing stuff on your lovely face."

She grimaced. "I think I can do that, now that I'm aware. And I could go with Keith's mom and not give my name. I wouldn't lie, but I could give just my first name."

"Or your middle name." Bill's face was pensive, as though he was seriously considering the plan.

"Let me talk to Mom," Keith said. "Campbell could go along as a friend giving moral support. And if Mom wants to do it, I can warn her too. She can be ready not to react to real cues, but to give some vibes on a false cue."

"How would she do that?" Campbell asked.

"Well, let's say the psychic says maybe you've lost a loved one, and you tense up and say, 'Bobby.' There's no real Bobby, right?"

"Right."

"But she doesn't know that. She'll be scrambling before your next reading to find someone you were close to named Bobby."

"I don't know." Bill threw his daughter an uneasy glance. "I know you don't think she's dangerous, Keith, but I'd feel better if one of us went in."

"Most men don't seek out psychics," Keith said. "And if they do, they won't react as strongly as a woman would."

Campbell sat straighter and frowned. "That's a little demeaning, don't you think?"

Keith shrugged. "It's the truth. I'll bet ninety per cent of her clients are women."

"Maybe," Campbell mumbled. She didn't look happy.

"Well, you go ahead and ask Angela if she thinks she's up to it," Bill said. "Meanwhile, Soup, we got any dessert?"

"Yes, Rita threw a pan of brownies in the oven this afternoon."

Bill grinned. "I knew I smelled chocolate. That Rita's a treasure."

7

At ten on Friday morning, Campbell and Angela Fuller parked down the street from Miss Tryphenia's building.

"I admit I'm a little nervous," Campbell said.

"Me too." Angela pulled her car keys from the ignition. "But we're agreed, if she insists on an appointment, we'll make it as soon as she'll allow it."

"Right, so she won't have too much time to dig around and learn we both have a strong connection to a police detective." Campbell still had her doubts as to whether this was a good idea. On the other hand, she was curious about the psychic and excited to be doing something constructive with Keith's mother.

Angela smiled. "Let's do it."

They got out of the car and walked up the sidewalk. Traffic was light. Once the college semester opened at Murray State, that would change.

The sign looked amateurish, black lettering on white-painted boards, but the hand-painted font was stylish. The business seemed to occupy the front of a two-story house of yellow brick. Karen Potter probably lived here, as well as conducting her business, Campbell reflected. She looked at Angela and nodded, and her companion rang the doorbell.

When the door swung open, they were confronted by a thin woman probably in her forties. Her short, dark brown hair had spikes of blond on the tips, and her brown eyes rapidly assessed them.

"Good morning, ladies. Come for a reading?"

"Er, yes," Angela said. "That is, I hoped you'd give me one if you have a slot available."

"As it happens, I'm free right now. Won't you come in?"

She stepped back, and when they entered she led them into a dim living room. The Venetian blinds were closed, but light seeped in between the slats. A sofa and several chairs were grouped on a carpet from another decade. Beyond them, bookshelves and side tables held books and objects Campbell suspected were part of the readings, and perhaps for sale.

"The initial reading is twenty dollars."

"Oh, of course." Angela pulled a twenty from her purse and handed it over.

"Take a seat." Miss Tryphenia glided to an upholstered chair behind a small, draped table. Angela sat down in the armchair most directly facing her, and Campbell took a seat on the sofa nearby. Beyond it was an old walnut desk. A lamp and a few envelopes sat on its surface, along with a decorative, bronze-colored letter opener. Campbell forced herself to turn her attention back to the table where the other two sat.

"What are your names?"

"I'm Angela."

Campbell met Miss Tryphenia's gaze. "I'm just here as a friend. You know, moral support." If the psychic insisted she give a name, she'd decided with her father's approval to use her middle name, but she hated to do that. They'd discussed whether the woman would let them get away without giving their last names. Bill was of the opinion that she might at first, but she'd probably want more later, especially if it seemed Angela might return for a repeat performance.

The cool eyes rested on her, and for a moment Campbell feared she would ask her to leave. Instead, Miss Tryphenia turned back to Angela.

"What's on your mind today, Angela? Why did you come here?"

They'd rehearsed this type of open-ended question, and though Campbell's heartbeat increased, she remained certain that Angela could handle it.

"I have to make an important decision soon."

"Ah. Decisions are always difficult, but some people find them more stressful than others." Miss Tryphenia reached for a deck of cards. "You seem quite at peace today, except for one or two areas. Perhaps that includes the decision that looms before you."

As she spoke, she dealt out four cards, face up on the table. Campbell wished she was closer and could get a better look at them. She wasn't sure, but she suspected they were tarot cards.

"You have children." It wasn't a question, but then, most women Angela's age wearing a wedding ring had children, and many of them had grandchildren too.

"Yes, two," Angela said.

She should have made the psychic tell her how many, Campbell thought.

"I'm not seeing any large clouds over your children."

"Well, no. I mean, I wish my son would tie the knot—" Angela threw Campbell a rather panicky glance. Was it because she knew she'd just spilled personal information or because she had a particular person in mind whom she wished Keith would marry? "But no, my kids are fine."

"The cards show family, dwelling, income, and relationships. Is it one of these areas that concerns you?"

"I—well, yes. I'm worried about my friend. That's a relationship, I suppose."

"Ah." Miss Tryphenia scooped up three of the cards and laid them aside. Below the remaining one, she dealt out four more.

Angela had insisted she wouldn't lie to the psychic, which was fine with Campbell and Bill. They'd discussed several topics she could present during the reading as potential problems for which she sought advice.

One hand hovering over the cards, Miss Tryphenia said, "This friend of yours ... I sense that it's a woman."

"Yes, a longtime friend. Her husband died a few years ago, and now—" Angela broke off with a little sob.

"You think she's making a mistake."

"Yes. Well, I'm not sure. That's what I wanted to ask you about. How can I know that she'll be all right?"

"This is disturbing you. You think about it all the time."

"Yes," Angela said. "Absolutely. I've been having trouble sleeping because I worry about her."

"And the decision you must make?"

"Whether to tell her what I really think of the man she's seeing. I don't know anything terrible about him, but I don't like him. I don't like the way he treats her, and I want to tell her not to put up with it. But I don't want to lose her friendship."

"I can help you. The most important thing is for you to regain your calmness, your serenity." Miss Tryphenia smiled. "You have that in other areas of your life. Your family, your home ..."

"Yes, I've been blessed."

"And you want that peace for your friend as well."

Angela nodded. "I love her dearly, and I just don't want to

see her make a huge mistake. Her husband was a lovely man, but this—" She stopped, wide-eyed.

Inwardly, Campbell applauded her acting ability. It was true that an old friend of Angela's was widowed and had recently begun a close friendship with a new man. In reality, she'd seen no red flags and was happy for her friend. But since she didn't know all the details, she'd felt she could present the matter to the psychic as a potential problem—or even a disaster—and so far, she was doing great.

"This new man," Miss Tryphenia said softly. "Have you met him?"

"Not yet. We've discussed it, but she lives a couple of hours away, and we haven't gotten together yet. I'm just going by things she's told me." Angela's face clouded. "Of course—"

"What's troubling you?"

"Well, her husband seemed to be in fine health when he died."

After a moment's pause, Miss Tryphenia asked, "How did he pass?"

"A heart attack. So unexpected."

"And your own husband?"

"Oh, he's in good health."

"But you can't help worrying a little. It happened to your friend. It could happen to you."

Campbell made herself sit still and not show her emotion. She didn't know Angela all that well, and she wondered if she really did worry about Nathan. If so, it was the first she'd heard of it. The psychic was clever at planting that seed of doubt.

Miss Tryphenia gazed into Angela's eyes. "Do you pray a lot?"

"Yes."

"And you pray for your husband's health?"

"Of course."

Rising, Miss Tryphenia said, "One moment." She walked to a hutch and took something from it then returned to her seat. "I want you to take this and hold it. Hold it as you pray for your husband."

Angela took the small item, but Campbell couldn't see what it was. A rock, perhaps?

"I—" Angela looked across the table, lines creasing her face. "Oh, is there a fee for this?"

The psychic reached out and folded Angela's fingers around it. "That is my gift to you. To bring you peace about your husband's health. Now, about your friend ... I sense a letter J."

"J?" Angela frowned. "Her name is Carla."

Closing her eyes, Miss Tryphenia swayed a little. "And her new friend?"

"Uh—no. His name starts with a T. But ... she does have a son named Jimmy."

Campbell pressed her lips together tightly. She hoped Angela wasn't giving away too much information. Would Karen Potter be able to learn more about this family based on Angela's revelations? If so, she might arrange another session in which she revealed things that might convince a less skeptical client that she really did have supernatural powers.

"The J is strong," Miss Tryphenia said. "Is there someone closer to you with that initial?"

"Uh, well ... Oh, my sister. Of course."

"And your sister is?"

Campbell had to struggle to keep a straight face. They had discussed the likelihood that the psychic would fish for personal information, but she hadn't expected the attempt to be so blatant.

"Justine."

The woman laid out four more cards. "Ah, yes. I see it now. Your sister is very dear to you."

"Yes, we're only fifteen months apart, and we shared a room growing up."

"I have something that can keep you and your sister even closer, if you wish." She got up and took something from a drawer. "Wear this charm, and touch it when you think of your sister."

"Oh, it's lovely." Angela smiled and held it out so Campbell could see a small, silver-colored filigree heart.

"The bond is even stronger if you give her one just like it," Miss Tryphenia said smoothly. "When you think of each other, you'll sense a warmth and a peace, knowing she's safe and she's thinking of you."

Angela's eyes widened. "You don't think something's wrong, do you? That Justine isn't safe?"

"Not that, but ..." Miss Tryphenia passed an open hand over the table above the cards. "The fact that the letter J was brought to me by the cards so intensely tells me there might be something troubling her. Not a threat, or it would be clearer, but something niggling at her. Perhaps she will tell you about it."

"I see. How much are the charms?"

"Twenty dollars each."

Angela nodded slowly. "I think I can do that. It will be worth it for a closer bond with Justine."

Campbell wanted to jump up and scream, "Don't give her more money!" Instead, she remained passively in her seat while Angela took out her wallet and gave Miss Tryphenia forty dollars.

"As to your friend Carla," Miss Tryphenia said, "I will ask a blessing for her. You must have faith that all will be well."

"With her new friend, you mean?"

"Yes. You can invoke goodwill and contentment for her, even from a distance." As she spoke, Miss Tryphenia placed a small plastic packet on the tabletop. "This will help you if you crush the leaves as you think of her and burn them. Now, about your personal serenity, I'm thinking some sage incense, and perhaps some soothing lotion."

"Oh, I think I've exhausted my budget for today." Angela rose with a smile and nodded at Campbell. "Thank you so much. I'll give one of the charms to my sister soon."

"Perhaps we'll meet again," Miss Tryphenia said. "Here's my card. Call me if you want to talk again. And I hope all goes well with your relationships."

She obviously knew that Angela's largess was at its limit. She walked them to the door.

"Oh, as for you ..." She gave Campbell a smile. "I sense there is someone close to you about whose health you are concerned."

Campbell blinked. She opened her mouth to say something and then closed it.

Miss Tryphenia nodded. "I wish you both the best."

"Goodbye," Angela said.

In the car, Campbell huffed out a big breath. "You didn't have to buy those charms."

"I know, but they're pretty, even though they're just cheap gewgaws. Justine's birthday is coming up. If I give her one and tell her the story, she'll get a kick out of it. But I wasn't going to let her sell me incense and cheap lotion at high prices."

"I was proud of you. And you did a great job. She was hoping you'd tell her a lot more."

"Thanks. I was careful not to blurt out Nathan's name. I was afraid she could find us if I did, and then she might connect us to Keith." Angela stowed her purse and started the car.

"What did she give you?" Campbell asked.

"A smooth rock with 'PEACE' written on it." Pulling out onto the street, she glanced over at Campbell. "Do you think she was talking about Bill when she said you're worried about someone's health?"

"No. I think she was fishing. Hoping to lure me in as a customer too."

Angela raised her eyebrows. "Really?"

"Yes. It's the kind of general thing you could say to anyone. Do *you* have someone whose health concerns you?"

"Well, I suppose I do fuss over Nathan's cholesterol now and then, and I don't let myself think about the possibility of Keith getting hurt on the job."

"Exactly. Everyone has someone they worry about, at least a little bit."

At a red light, Angela glanced over at Campbell. "Why do you think she told me to pray? Do you think she believes in God?"

"It's possible, I suppose. More likely, she picked up on the fact that you said you'd been blessed."

"Oh, it never occurred to me that something like that would be a tip-off to her."

"She knew right away that you were a spiritual person, though not in the same way she is. Your rock says *peace*. If you'd said something else, she might have chosen one with a different word—*serenity*, or *hope* maybe."

"You're probably right. I was scared the whole time I'd say something that would tell her we were really there to find out about her, not me."

"You were wonderful. I'd nominate you for a Tony if I could."

Angela smiled. "Maybe next time I'll get a rock that says *confidence*." She drove all the way to Twelfth Street, as Bill had instructed, and Campbell watched the side-view mirror as she made a couple of turns and ended up back on Eighth.

"I'm pretty sure we're not being followed," Campbell said.

"Me too. I've been trying to pay attention." Putting on her turn signal, Angela slowed and turned in at Willow Street. Once she was saw the True Blue sign and pulled into the driveway, she let out a big sigh.

"Glad it's over?" Campbell asked.

"Well, yes. Relieved. But it was exciting, too, you know?"

"I do. I really like this new job, but it challenges me every day."

Keith joined them after Angela gave him a call, and they sat in the cozy private sitting room upstairs with coffee all around.

"Sounds like a good first contact," Bill said after Angela had detailed the reading. He'd reimbursed her the twenty dollars for the price of the reading, but she wouldn't let him repay her for the charms.

"That was my decision, and I will give one to my sister." Angela smiled. "Do you think that woman will try to get me to go again?"

"I doubt it," Keith said. "Not unless you call her. She did give you her card to make that easy for you."

"Should I do that?"

"Why don't you sit on it for a few days," Keith said. "Maybe a week. You don't want to seem too eager."

Bill nodded. "Right. We have some other pressing things to work on, and this isn't really an official case for any of us. But we may turn up something else that makes us want to go a little deeper with Miss Tryphenia." He sipped his coffee.

"If you do, you could call and say things haven't cleared up with your friend yet, and you need reassurance," Keith said. "By the way, thanks for not spilling any juicy secrets about me."

Campbell laughed. "She did a great job this morning."

"And Miss Tryphenia found out Mom's not a total skinflint." Keith looked at Angela. "Now that you know her methods of adding on a trinket here and a pack of incense there, if you call her again for an appointment, she'll figure you're ready to spend a little more money."

"That's fine by me. Well, thanks for letting me be part of the team." Angela gathered her things and rose.

"I'll walk you out." Keith stood. "I'll catch you later, McBrides."

When they'd left, Campbell let out a big sigh. "So, that's the end of it?"

"For now," Bill said. "I've got a list of Vera and Dorothy's friends that Vera made for us. I thought we'd contact them discreetly and see if Sam Truman has made any overtures to them. And we pulled a new insurance case this morning. Do you want to do surveillance for that, or split the potential investors list with me?"

"Oh, I think the investors would be much more interesting."

Her father grinned and passed her a memo sheet with three names and addresses on it. "Here you go. I'll break the news to Nick that he's on surveillance duty this afternoon." As he and Campbell walked toward the stairway, he grinned at her. "And if there's time, maybe we can dig out those juicy secrets about Keith."

Campbell approached the large house slowly, looking around at the burgeoning flower beds. The residence looked fairly new and was set in a large development among others that had much the same appearance but with different architectural details. Beautiful, she thought. "McMansions," her dad would say. "People like us couldn't afford to live here."

That was okay. The house he'd just bought wasn't as big as these and didn't have the contemporary flair, but it was perfect for the two of them and the business. One of these huge dwellings would be too much for them—and would scare away some of the folks who sought out her father for help. She renewed her determination to make the Willow Street Victorian feel cozy and welcoming.

A young woman in black pants and a white blouse opened the door. Immediately she knew this was not the friend Vera Hill had described to her.

"Hello, I'm Campbell McBride. I believe Mrs. Gilley is expecting me." She'd called Friday to make the appointment.

Though she and her dad had enjoyed a quiet weekend, she got a few butterflies whenever she thought about going out to interview Vera's friends on her own.

"She is. Come right in." The young woman didn't introduce herself, but she didn't have to. Campbell was beginning to recognize wealthy people's hired help. Mr. Gilley owned a large car dealership in town, and this elaborate home with tasteful decorations was no doubt the fruit of his labor.

The maid showed her past the open door of a formal living room and into a smaller but cozier room with large windows showcasing the expansive back yard, full of shrubbery, bird feeders, a small pond, and wrought iron patio furniture.

Her hostess rose from an armchair with a coffee mug in her hand. "You must be Campbell."

"I am."

"Trish Gilley." She extended a hand, and Campbell shook it. "Have a seat. Will you join me in coffee?"

"Oh, no thank you," Campbell said.

Mrs. Gilley nodded to the maid, and the young woman left the room.

"What can I do for you?"

Campbell quickly assessed the woman. Blond hair, surely bleached, but tastefully done. Well-cut pants and coordinated top. Huge diamond on her left hand with her wedding ring, and another ring with channel-set emeralds and diamonds on her right. She was at least fifty, but with her money, she could very well be older. A well-preserved sixty or even sixty-five.

Campbell smiled. "Thank you for seeing me. You have a lovely home."

"Thank you. You said this has to do with a private matter?"

So much for chitchat. "Yes. Vera Hill told us you'd met Sam Truman at her house, and we wanted to know your opinion of him."

"We?"

"My father, Bill McBride, and I."

She nodded shrewdly. "He's the private investigator."

"Yes, and so am I." Campbell hoped she didn't sound too green and incompetent—or too arrogant. After only a few weeks, she was still breaking in her new role. When would she feel comfortable uttering those words? Probably not until she'd passed her exam and had her license in her pocket, at the least.

"I did meet Sam at the Hills' house," Mrs. Gilley said. "I was there one afternoon, discussing plans with Vera for a fundraiser. We're collecting school supplies for low-income children. Our group does it every year." She looked around. "We'll hold our next meeting here on Monday. We're actually close to the end of the campaign for this year. The next step is distributing the backpacks and other supplies."

"That's great," Campbell said. "And Sam dropped by during your meeting?"

"The meeting was finished, and most of the others had left. I was just going over the list of items we still needed with Vera when her daughter Dorothy came in with Sam in tow."

"I see. That was the first time you'd met him?"

"Yes. I found him very likeable. Dorothy's found a good catch. If she can catch him, that is." Mrs. Gilley took a sip of her coffee.

"And did the subject of finances or investments come up that day?"

"No. Well, Dorothy did mention to me that Sam was a shareholder in an investment fund. I believe it's a group where they back promising new startup businesses."

"Was that the only time you met Sam Truman?"

"No. In fact, Dorothy phoned me the next day. I was surprised, because she and I don't generally socialize. I mean, her mother is my friend, not Dorothy. But she asked me if Paul and I would be interested in hearing more about Sam's fund. An investment opportunity."

"What did you say?"

"I agreed to have him over. It sounded like something Paul might find interesting. I expected Dorothy to come with him, but he came alone a couple of evenings later."

Campbell digested that. "And what was the result, if you don't mind my asking?"

"We invested. Not a huge amount, but enough to test out the fund and see if we got a good return."

"And did you?"

"Well, we don't know yet. It's only been about a month, but we're hearing good things from Sam. If it stays strong, we'll leave our money in the fund for at least six months, maybe a year. And if it's really good, Paul will put in some more."

"So, it sounds promising."

"It really does. Paul told a few of his friends about it, and I believe one of them invested as well." Mrs. Gilley's eyes narrowed. "May I ask why private investigators are asking about Sam?"

"We've had inquiries," Campbell said. "People who want to know if this investment fund is real, and if it's actually a good investment."

"And you think it's not?"

"I don't have an opinion on the matter. At this stage, we're just gathering facts."

"And how do the facts look so far? Is there cause to worry?"

"Not at this point."

"So ... the fund is solid?"

Campbell let out a slow breath. "So far, we haven't been able to find out a whole lot about it. Did Sam give you some information?"

"Yes. I know Paul had some brochures. And of course, we have the receipt from our investment. A sort of contract, I think. I don't know, Paul took care of it."

It all sounded rather thin to Campbell, but Mr. Gilley was a businessman, and apparently he'd seen no red flags.

Mrs. Gilley set down her mug. "Should we contact Sam?"

"No, no," Campbell said. "We haven't found anything negative. It's just that ... we haven't found anything positive either."

"Who's paying you to do this investigating?"

"I can't reveal the client's name."

"I think I'll call Sam. Or Paul will."

Campbell's heart sank. "I really wish you wouldn't do that, at least not for a few days. I assure you, if we find anything that says your investment isn't safe, True Blue Investigations will notify you."

"And if it's okay?"

"We can tell you that too. I'll make sure my father knows you want to know. But please don't tell Mr. Truman about the investigation."

Mrs. Gilley eyed her for a moment then nodded. "All right, but I will tell my husband you were here and why."

"I'd expect nothing less."

"You're making me nervous. Not that the ten grand we invested would break the bank—as I said, it was more or less a test. But if Sam Truman isn't being straight with us—"

"We'll certainly notify you." Campbell stood. "Thank you for being so frank, Mrs. Gilley. We only want to protect our client if there's a reason to do so. But certainly we wouldn't want other innocent people to be hurt either."

Mrs. Gilley got up and walked with her out to the front entry.

"We'll be in touch." Campbell gave her a nod and smile and

walked to her car. When she was inside it, she let out a deep sigh. Interviews were the part of the new job she liked least. Well, not all interviews, but the ones where people were suspicious of her motives and became upset.

She phoned her dad, and he answered immediately.

"Are you done with your assignment?" Bill asked.

"Yes. Are you?"

"Just got home. Come on back and we'll talk."

She felt better immediately. This job was entirely different from teaching college students. As an investigator, she had to ask uncomfortable questions and deal one-on-one with people who were hurting and some who'd made poor decisions. Sometimes that unsettled her as well as the person she was interviewing. She started the car and headed home. Things always seemed better when she talked to Dad.

———

After lunch, the three investigators gathered in the large office. Nick slurped from a milkshake he'd brought in with him.

"So, the insurance case is coming along?" Bill asked.

Nick nodded. "I'll probably need to stay on her this evening, to see if she goes out tonight."

"All right, call me by ten and let me know how it's going. You can come in late tomorrow," Bill said. "Meanwhile, Campbell and I interviewed four parties today who've either invested with Sam Truman or declined to invest. So far, we know of at least thirty thousand he's collected in this area in the last month, and that could be just the tip of the iceberg."

Nick whistled. "Even if that's the whole of it, that's pretty good pay for a month."

Bill shrugged. "Of course, it could be on the up-and-up, but I'm thinking it's not."

"Or it is, and he's skimming," Campbell said.

"That's another possibility. While Campbell did her last interview today, I stayed here and contacted some people in Missouri. I wanted the full story on the death of Sam Truman's wife."

"What did you find out?" Nick asked.

"There was some inconclusive evidence. Either she was accidentally overdosed on a motion sickness medicine, or—"

"Or it wasn't accidental," Campbell said.

"Right-O. The detective I spoke with liked Truman for it, but he couldn't make it stick. The coroner said she had way too much scopolamine in her system. We're talking four times the usual dose."

"Is that like Dramamine?" Campbell asked.

"No, it's a different drug altogether. Dramamine is usually a pill. This can be a pill, but it can also be injected or administered in a patch."

"A patch on your arm?" Nick asked.

"No, this goes behind the ear."

Campbell tried to fit that with the woman's death. "Was she wearing a patch when she died?"

"No, and they didn't find any injection site." Bill shook his head. "An overdose could cause hallucinations, irregular heartbeat, trouble breathing, and lots of other things."

"Did she have a heart condition?" Nick asked.

"No, but she had asthma."

Campbell stared at him. "I'm guessing this medicine isn't one asthmatics should take."

"Correct. The coroner said the medication induced a huge asthma attack. That's probably what killed her."

"And no evidence of foul play." She watched him closely to be sure she had it straight.

"Right. Truman admitted he'd used the transdermal

patches once when he went deep sea fishing, but so far as he knew, his wife had never used them. And they didn't find any packages or pill bottles for scopolamine, or any other evidence it was in the house."

Nick scowled. "So ... suicide?"

"If that's the case, where's the container for the meds?" Bill asked. "They didn't want to call it suicide, but they couldn't say for sure it was murder. She could have taken the medication somewhere else, then gone home and died there."

"It surely doesn't sound accidental," Campbell said. "Did Truman have an alibi? He must have."

"Supposedly he'd been at work all day. They were separated, but he went by her house that evening when he got off work. He found her dead in the bedroom. But he only worked twenty minutes away, and he wasn't constantly with his coworkers. In fact, he'd driven to an appointment in the next town that morning."

"And the police accepted the alibi?" Nick asked.

"There are holes in his story, but not big enough to drive a truck through." Bill got up and went to the coffeemaker. "That case was a real headache for the investigators and the district attorney."

"They never charged him?" Campbell asked.

"Not him or anyone else." He came back with a mug of steaming coffee. "On another note, this morning I talked to a woman who nearly invested with Sam Truman, but her husband put his foot down. Told her not to give Sam a penny."

"How did she react?" Campbell asked.

"She said she was disappointed at first, but after some thought she decided he was right. They don't know Sam from a hole in the ground, and they really couldn't afford to lose the money if the investment didn't work out."

"I assume you're keeping a list in the file of all the people who didn't invest, as well as those who did." Campbell arched her eyebrows at him.

"Natch. You can see it anytime."

Nick frowned. "Do you suppose if we had a list of Madam Tryphenia's clients, there'd be an overlap with Sam Truman's investors?"

Bill scowled at him. "It's *Miss* Tryphenia, not madam, but you may be right about that."

"Dad, I take it you're still open to there being a connection between those two." Campbell gazed over at him.

"There's got to be. But we have to concentrate on the Truman case first. We have a paying client for that one, and the Hills and several other people could get hurt if Vera's questions about Truman turn out to be justified."

"What do we do next?" Nick asked. "Have Mrs. Hill introduce me to Truman?"

"You're a bit young for a serious investor." Bill sat for a moment, his eyebrows drawn together. "If we could only find the connection to the psychic."

"But you just said we can't work that angle now."

Bill sighed and raked a hand through his hair. "We may have to."

Nick leaned forward and clasped his hands between his knees. "What if the whole psychic business just distracts you from Truman?"

"Good point."

"How about this," Campbell said. "Angela and I go back to Miss Tryphenia, and Angela mentions having met Sam. She could ask Miss Tryphenia if it's a good idea to invest with him. If she cautions her, wouldn't you think she really does want to serve Angela's best interests?"

"Well, maybe she'd want to keep Sam from getting his hands on all the money she might be able to get from Angela."

Campbell made a sour face at him. "I think we should do it and suggest the connection. Tomorrow."

"It's too soon," Bill said. "She only went for the first time on Friday. We need to give it more time."

"She's had all weekend to stew on what Miss Tryphenia told her Friday morning," Campbell said. "Angela could call tonight and ask for an appointment as soon as possible. And she can ask about the investment. Say she's very uneasy that someone in her family wants to do it."

His lips twitched back and forth. "Okay, but I've got to be in court by ten tomorrow morning. Let me call Angela. If she's free tomorrow, then I'll have her come here early so you and I can talk to her and go over exactly what we want out of the encounter."

"Okay," Campbell said.

Bill turned to Nick. "Meanwhile, you see if you can wind up the insurance case. Let me know if you need help on the surveillance. I could spell you later."

"Where's the woman you're watching right now?" Campbell asked.

"At work." Nick checked the time on his Fitbit. "She gets off at three. I'll have eyes on her when she leaves, to see if she does anything between there and home."

Campbell and Bill watched him walk out. When the front door closed, Campbell said, "Thanks, Dad."

"For what?"

"For following my instinct."

He smiled. "You've been on your game since you came home. I think you have *good* instincts."

Campbell couldn't help smiling. His praise gave her a

warm glow, better than any rock a psychic could give her. She got up and walked over to his chair. "You know I love you."

"I do."

She bent and kissed the top of his head.

9

"I tried to call her twice last night and again before I left home this morning, but she didn't answer," Angela told Bill on Tuesday morning in his office.

"Maybe she's gone away," Campbell said. "Should we go over there and see if she's home?"

Bill frowned. "Unfortunately, I have to be at the courthouse soon. I should be free later in the day. How about we wait until this afternoon?"

"But, Dad, we need to move this thing along. You were sure we could connect her with Sam Truman."

Bill sighed. "I don't want to get Angela mixed up in something I can't control while I'm sitting in court."

"I'm not afraid to go," Angela said.

"But still ..." Bill sat there scowling for another ten seconds, and the two women waited. "Okay," he said at last, "here's what I want you to do. Angela, don't you do anything. Go home or shopping or whatever. You can try calling her later, and if you get her, go ahead and set up another appointment.

Don't mention Campbell if you can help it, but after you schedule it, call and tell Campbell the details."

"All right," Angela said. "If you're sure."

He nodded. "Meanwhile, Campbell, you take Nick and go over there. If you find Ms. Potter, remind her that you're Angela's friend and you've decided to try a reading too."

"What's Nick's excuse?" Campbell asked. "And besides, I thought he was still working that insurance case."

"Nah, he and I both think the loss is legit. Nick's gone to see the insurance agent to close out the case. He should be back any minute. If you see the psychic, you can say he's your boyfriend."

"Oh, please." Campbell shifted uneasily. "I'm not going to lie to her, and Nick certainly is *not* my boyfriend."

"You're right. Tell her whatever you're comfortable with, except that you're P.I.s."

Campbell let out a big breath. She wasn't fond of field work with Nick. Whenever they went out together and poked into other people's secrets, they always seemed to get into something weird. But she did want to keep the case on track, and her dad was already clearing his desk and making sure he had his pen, notebook, and business cards in his pockets.

"When will you be done at the courthouse?" she asked.

"Not sure. Maybe by noon, but maybe not. You and Nick can go over to Second Street and look around. If no one's home, come back here and catch up on your reports."

"Okay." Campbell and Angela rose. While she walked with Angela to the front door, Bill hurried upstairs for last-minute preparations for his court appearance.

"There's Nick," Campbell said when she opened the door. His Jeep was just pulling into his usual spot in the driveway, leaving plenty of room for Angela to back out.

"Oh, good." Angela touched her shoulder. "I was afraid you

might go over there alone. I'm not afraid of Miss Tryphenia or anything like that, but I think it's better if you have someone with you."

"We'll be fine," Campbell said. "Say hi to Nathan for me." She was growing very fond of Keith's parents, and his dad always made her feel wanted, almost like a part of the Fuller family.

Angela greeted Nick as they passed on the walkway, and he eyed Campbell curiously as he mounted the steps.

"What's up, Professor?"

"You and I are going to the psychic's house and see if she's there. Angela hasn't been able to get her to respond to her phone calls."

"Okay. Give me five minutes and cup a coffee?"

"Sure, but get your own coffee. I want to run upstairs and change my top." Her T-shirt from Feldman University, where she'd taught English courses, might give Miss Tryphenia too many clues. Besides, she wanted a more professional look when she was out around town representing True Blue.

Her dad came out of his room as she reached the landing at the top of the stairs. He had put on a tie and jacket.

"You look spiffy," she said. "Very professional. Nick's back. I'm going to change before we leave."

"Take his Jeep," her dad said. "If Karen Potter sees you arrive in your vehicle, she might be able to trace the plate and learn more about you."

"She can do that to Nick's Jeep too."

"Yeah, but his name's not McBride, and he's not as pretty as you. Overall, I'd say Nick is better at blending in than you, and less likely to be noticed in a crowd."

"Why, thank you. She does know what I look like already. But I'll make sure we park a block or so away."

"Great. See you later."

She heard him greet Nick as she headed for her bedroom. It would take her a while to get used to living in Katherine Tyler's old room, but she was starting to like it. The famous author was now deceased, but several reminders had come with the house. Campbell especially liked the small painting of daffodils that hung above the brick fireplace in her room. The old oak bed and dresser made her feel as though she'd traveled back in time to a simpler day.

Quickly, she put on a striped blouse and brushed her hair. Nick was ready when she went down, and he drove the Jeep to Second Street and parked, at her insistence, a block from Miss Tryphenia's establishment.

"Miss Picky," he said.

Campbell wanted to crab back at him, but she forced herself to keep quiet and not start a new round of bickering. She and Nick had to get along, that was all.

"Ready?" He pulled the keys from the ignition.

She met his gaze and smiled. "Let's go."

He locked the Jeep, and they walked up the sidewalk. Nick strode past the sign and up to the entrance, where he rang the doorbell. They waited in silence for several seconds.

"Maybe you were right, and she's gone away," Nick said.

Campbell frowned. "If she went someplace for the weekend, she ought to be back."

He pushed the button again, but no one opened the door. On impulse, Campbell tried the knob, and the door swung open. She caught her breath.

"You usually yell at me if I do that," Nick said with a smirk.

"Not funny. This is a little scary."

"It's a place of business. Maybe people usually walk in."

"Do you think so?" she said. "I mean, you rang the bell. You'd think she'd respond if she was here."

"Maybe the bell doesn't work. Or maybe she's upstairs in

her private quarters, and she didn't hear it." He glanced upward. "You think she lives up there?"

"I do. Dad couldn't find any other address for Karen Potter, and it looked like she only used one or two rooms for her business." Still Campbell hesitated. "Maybe we should call him. He wouldn't be in the courtroom yet."

"We got this."

Campbell was torn between relief at the assurance that she and Nick were capable adults and the memory of too many movies where the foolhardy young woman went to see someone and found the door ajar but walked inside anyhow. On more than one occasion, she'd found herself screaming at the television, "No! Don't go in there!"

Nick sensed her reluctance to enter, and for once he gave in with a shrug. "Okay, call him."

She pulled out her phone and went to favorite contacts. "Hello, Dad?"

"Yeah?"

"Can you talk?"

"Just getting out of my car. What's up?"

"We're at the psychic's. No one answered the doorbell, but the front door's not locked. Should we walk in?"

"What happened when you went there with Angela?"

"We rang, and Miss Tryphenia came to the door."

"Hmm. Well, I'm pretty sure she lives there."

"Do you think she could be upstairs in her apartment?" Campbell asked.

"Maybe. But if she was in the shower or something like that, I'd think she would lock the front door."

"That's what I thought."

"Tell you what," her father said. "I've learned she drives a Chevy Malibu. It's about ten years old, dark blue. Look around and see if you can spot it. She may have a private parking spot behind the building or something. Take a good look and see what you see. Now, I've got to get moving. Use your common sense."

"Okay, thanks." Campbell closed the connection and relayed what he'd said to Nick. They both turned toward the street and surveyed the vehicles parked there. "I don't see it."

"Me either." Nick swung around. "There's a driveway between her building and the next one."

Campbell peered into the paved alley between the psychic's house and thrift shop next door. "Should we walk back there and take a look?"

"You can stay here if you want. I'll go."

"No, I think we should stay together."

Nick held up both hands in surrender. "Okay, let's go."

Together they walked along the side of the building on the alley. The thrift shop was only a few yards away. Campbell couldn't see any vehicles ahead, though dirty tire tracks marked the asphalt. At the back of the building, they looked around the corner, and she sucked in her breath.

"There it is."

Nick nodded, surveying the navy blue Malibu parked nose in, parallel to the house. "Looks like a back door." He walked toward it, and she followed, studying the door as they approached. "There's no doorbell, though."

Nick raised a hand and knocked firmly on the door panel. They waited, but Campbell couldn't hear anything inside. She looked at Nick, who shook his head.

"Okay, now what?" she asked.

Nick turned the knob none too gently. "It seems to be locked. Have you got her phone number?"

"Yeah."

"Read it off to me." He took out his cell phone and entered the digits.

Campbell waited while he tried to call Miss Tryphenia's phone. She thought she caught a sound.

"She's not picking up," Nick said, his ear to his cell.

"I thought I heard it ringing inside."

"Really?"

"Well, I'm not positive. Should we go in the front door and call her name?"

He frowned. "Let's try the windows first. There are a couple here at the back."

Campbell gulped and walked over to the nearest window frame, trying to picture the layout of the house in her mind. This window might be in the room where Miss Tryphenia had done Angela's reading. After noting that the window didn't have Venetian blinds, she changed her mind. This must be a different room.

She had to stand on tiptoe to get a good look. The interior was dark. She remembered how dim the psychic had kept the room while she talked to Angela. Shielding her eyes, she peered in and saw a dining table surrounded by chairs and a hutch with glass-paneled doors on the top section.

"See anything?" Nick said at her elbow.

Campbell nodded. "I'm looking into a dining room. We didn't go in there Friday, but I can see an open doorway that I think goes into the room where she did Angela's reading."

"Is there a window to that room?"

"I think it's on the front of the house. Hold on." She walked around the corner and along the alley for a few yards to another window. "I'm pretty sure this is it, but the blinds are shut."

"Let me see." Nick stepped up and pressed his face against the window, his hands between his forehead and the glass, gazing inside.

"Campbell?"

"Yeah?" She sidled close to him. "Do you see something?"

"There's a crack here, where one of the slats is crooked. Something looks funny in there."

"What do you mean?"

Nick moved aside, and she took his place.

"A table or something is tipped over," he said, "and there's some cloth on the floor."

"Well, for the reading Miss Tryphenia sat at a little table, like a card table, with a cloth over it." Campbell put her hands to her temples, leaned in, then stood still, waiting for her eyes to adjust. "I think you're right, and that's the reading parlor. That could be her little table on end, and the crumpled up tablecloth beside it. Oh, hey, there's something shiny on the floor—liquid, I think."

"Okay, we're going in," Nick said.

It was too late to call her father again. "Do you think maybe we should call Keith?"

"You can if you want, but I'd rather not until we know if there's something worth the cops looking into." He strode off toward the street. Campbell had to jog to keep up.

"You can stay out here if you want," he said over his shoulder, reaching for the doorknob.

"No way." She stepped in close behind him. They were in a short entry hall. "The room's there, on the right." She realized she was whispering as she pointed to the open door of the parlor.

Nick strode forward and stopped in the doorway.

"What is it?" Campbell hissed, impatient. He could block her, but she wasn't that short. She rose on her toes and gazed over his shoulder. She glimpsed the table lying on the dark rug and a crumpled cloth that trailed into a small pool of liquid. She gulped. "That's not blood, is it?"

"I don't think so."

Nick stepped forward, and she almost overbalanced but quickly caught herself. A little disoriented from her wobble, Campbell caught her breath. "Can I turn on a light?"

"Why not? We can shut it off again when we leave."

Wary of leaving fingerprints, Campbell nudged the wall switch up with the edge of her cell phone. Light flooded the room, and she blinked then focused on the puddle that had soaked into the carpet and seeped onto the wood flooring at the edge of the rug. "That looks like wine or cranberry juice, and there's a glass over there." She pointed to the tumbler lying on the rug near the wall.

Nick touched the wet spot and then sniffed his fingers. "I think you're right. Her chair's tipped over too." Nick reached toward it.

"Don't touch it," Campbell barked.

He flinched. "Sorry. You're right."

She looked around. Some of the fortune-telling cards were strewn on the floor. "I sat over there Friday." She pointed to the sofa. "The client's chair looks out of place, like someone shoved it aside."

"How much?"

"A foot or so."

Nick hunched over and advanced slowly into the room until he was close to the armchair. Staring down at the carpet, he said, "Yeah, I can see indentations where it used to sit."

"Should I call Keith now?" Campbell asked.

"Yeah, sure. He knew his mother was maybe coming over here today, right?"

"She told him all about it."

Nick nodded curtly and swiveled his head, taking in the books, candles, charms, and other trinkets on the shelves.

Campbell swiped the screen of her phone. Her hands shook a little, but she got to her frequent contacts.

As she waited, she noted that the desk looked almost exactly as it did during her earlier visit—lamp, letter opener. A small binder, perhaps an address book, also lay there, with a ballpoint pen beside it. She leaned closer. Not an address book, but an appointment calendar.

After three rings, Keith's voice came, deep and steady. "Hey, Campbell. What can I do for you?"

She straightened. "Nick and I are at Miss Tryphenia's house, and we need you."

"What's going on?" His tone dropped, and she sensed that he wasn't alone.

"She didn't answer her phone. Her front door was unlocked, so we came inside, since it's a business."

"Okay. What did you find?"

"It looks like somebody had a fight in here. Stuff is knocked over, and she's not here."

"Have you checked all the rooms?"

"No, just the one where she does her readings."

"Okay, I'll be there ASAP. Don't touch anything. You and Nick go outside and wait for me out front."

She pulled in a breath, but he had already disconnected. She turned to Nick. "Keith says to go outside and wait for him. And not to touch anything."

"I didn't," Nick said defensively. "Well, I don't think I did."

"I know. I'm just telling you what he said." *And reminding you that last time you touched a whole lot of things.* Even as she had the thought, her gaze wandered back to the desk. "Hold on a sec."

"What?" Nick asked.

"I just—"

She clenched her teeth. That small, hardbound notebook was practically calling to her from where it lay on the desktop. Edging closer, she studied the calendar. It was open to the previous day. Apparently Miss Tryphenia's schedule for Monday had included two readings. Campbell bent a little closer.

"No touching, remember?" Nick said sharply.

"I'm not." As much as she wanted to flip back through the pages, she turned on her heel and marched to the front door without looking back. Nick came out behind her and closed the door.

A woman was heading up the short walk toward the entry.

"Oh, excuse me," she said. "Is Miss Tryphenia in?"

"Uh, no," Nick said.

She looked from him to Campbell. "But you just came out."

"She's stepped out for a while," Campbell said. "Did you have an appointment?"

"No, but I wanted to make one. Maybe it's not in the cards." She smiled at her own pun. "I stopped by yesterday after lunch, but she was—uh—occupied."

"Giving a reading, you mean?" Campbell asked.

"No, she, uh ..." The woman swallowed hard. "There was another woman in there screaming at her."

"Oh. Did you hear what they were saying?"

"She said something like, *You leave my mother alone, or I'll sic the cops on you.* Not her exact words, but that was the gist of it."

"And that was the visitor speaking, not Miss Tryphenia?"

"I think so. She came storming out afterward. I was a little shook up by it, so I left. I mean, I wondered if I really wanted to get a reading here. But after I slept on it, I decided to come back and see if I could meet her."

"You might want to wait a day or two and then call her," Campbell said. "Her number's there on her sign, if you don't have it."

"Yeah, thanks." The visitor backed up a few steps and paused by the sign, working her phone's screen.

"Hey, do you remember what that woman looked like?" Nick walked toward her. "The visitor, I mean."

"Uh, well, let's see ... Shorter than me, dark hair about shoulder length. She was wearing a yellow top. Oh, and her face was beet red. Probably because she'd been yelling."

"How old?" Nick asked.

"Hard to say. Forty or so?"

"Thanks." He watched her as she hurried to her car and got in.

Campbell whipped out a pen and notebook and scrawled the license plate number.

"What are you doing?"

"Getting her plate number in case we need to find her again as a witness. I was hoping you'd ask her name."

"Then we would have had to explain."

Keith's SUV drew up at the curb in front of them. He and Detective Matt Jackson, with whom he frequently worked, got out.

"Hi," Keith said as he approached them. "You both know Detective Jackson."

"Yes," Campbell said. "Thanks for coming."

"You want me to show you?" Nick asked.

"We can handle it. Which room is the one with the mess?"

"On the right," Campbell said. "Oh, I turned the light on, but I didn't touch the switch with my hand. That's the only room we went into."

"Okay, we'll clear the house. You two may as well go home. If you stand out here too long, you'll draw a crowd."

"Okay," Nick said, "but right after Campbell called you, a woman came by and was going to go in."

"We told her Miss Tryphenia was out," Campbell added, and Keith nodded.

"She heard somebody screaming at the psychic yesterday." Nick gave Campbell a smug look, as though telling Keith about it first gave him cachet.

"What about?" Keith asked.

Quickly, the two of them told him what the visitor had said.

"We didn't ask her name, but this is her license plate number." Campbell copied the number she'd written down and tore out the sheet of paper for him.

"Okay, good work."

"Do we have to go?" Her voice sounded very small, and she wished she hadn't asked.

"Probably best. I'll come by after we look around."

"Thanks."

She and Nick walked to his Jeep.

"We could sit here and wait," Nick said.

"He wants us to go, so we don't draw attention to the scene."

"Right." He started the engine and pulled out into the street.

10

Back at the office, Campbell went right to her desk. Nick couldn't settle down to work, and he paced the big room a few times then paused behind her.

"What are you doing?"

Campbell didn't look up but kept tapping words into her search engine. "I got a look at Miss T's appointment book on her desk, and she had two appointments yesterday. The woman who heard the argument said she went by after lunch, and the second appointment was at one o'clock. I'm looking for the woman whose name was in the book."

Nick pursed his lips and nodded. "Pretty clever. Why didn't you tell Keith?"

"He'll find the appointment book when they go over the room."

"And you wanted to get a jump on him."

She shrugged. "Not necessarily, but I wouldn't mind." She hitched in a breath as her screen refreshed. "Aha. I couldn't turn the page in the book to see if any appointments were scheduled for today, but the last one yesterday was with a Mary Willingham."

"And you've located her?" Nick nodded toward her laptop.

"Yes, there's a Mary Willingham living in Murray. And I also recall that Vera Hill told Dad and me that a friend named Mary had paid out several thousand dollars to Miss Tryphenia."

Nick whistled softly. "Could be the same Mary, but it's a common name."

"Not so much nowadays," Campbell said. "I'm betting she's an older woman. One who might have a daughter who's angry about her wasting all that money."

Nick's dark eyebrows morphed together. "So, you think it was the daughter arguing with Miss T, not Mary?"

"According to the woman who told us about it, she said, *You leave my mother alone.*"

"Right. Now what?"

"I'm trying to find out if Mary Willingham has a daughter."

"Let me help." Nick crossed the room to his desk and went to work. Ten minutes later, he called, "Got it. I think."

"Yeah?" Campbell said.

"She actually has two daughters. One of them lives in Virginia, but the other one's in Almo. She's married. Nicole Paxton."

Campbell shoved her chair back. "How did you find all that?"

"Mary Willingham's husband's obituary."

"Of course." Campbell gave herself a mental kick for not thinking of something so simple. "Wait a sec. Vera also said her friend Mary had a son. She didn't say anything about daughters."

"Correct. The son lives in Tennessee."

"That checks with what Vera told us, except she thought he might be in jail."

"Where? Tennessee?"

"I don't know. Vera said he was in some kind of trouble, but then I had to leave. She may have told Dad more. Have you got Nicole Paxton's address? You said Almo?"

"Hold on. We should be able to get it pretty fast." Nick tapped away at his keyboard.

Campbell got up and walked over to stand behind him, watching his precise search.

"Got it." He swiveled his chair around with a grin. "Temple Hill Road."

"Let's go."

———

When they returned an hour later, Bill's car was out front. Nick veered off to his own desk, but Campbell continued on to her father's office.

"Well, hi. How'd it go this morning?" he asked.

"Up and down. Miss Tryphenia never came to the door, but we saw through a window that things looked messed up in there, so we ended up going in."

Her father eyed her sharply. "And?"

"We couldn't find her, but it looked like there'd been a struggle, so we called Keith."

"Good choice."

"Well, he sent us home." Quickly, she told him about the woman they'd met on the sidewalk and their subsequent effort to track down the one who'd ranted at the psychic.

"Did you find her?"

"Yeah. Nicole Paxton, in Almo. Her mother, Mary Willingham, was the one who was scheduled to see Miss

Tryphenia, but Nicole intervened and went herself to give Miss T a piece of her mind. Oh, and her mom's the one Vera Hill said had paid out a lot of money to the psychic."

"Got it."

"Nicole wasn't very happy that we were snooping around. I don't think she liked the fact that, A) she'd been overheard threatening to call the cops on Miss Tryphenia, and B) that the person who'd heard it passed it on to an investigator. She probably thinks she'll get in trouble. But I managed to calm her down after a bit. She's really worried about her mom."

"And her mom's worried about her brother?"

"Yeah. The brother's name is Danny. He's divorced, and he has a new girlfriend. The mom, Mary, was concerned about the relationship. And remember, Vera said he might be in jail?"

Bill nodded.

"Nicole says he's not. The police took him in for questioning on some petty charge—she wouldn't say exactly what, but she insisted he was released within twenty-four hours."

"Hmm. The police are watching him, though."

"Probably. But the mother, Mary, seems very concerned about the girlfriend. I don't know if the girlfriend is mixed up in the legal hassle or not. But when Mary went to the psychic, apparently Miss Tryphenia confirmed that her fears were justified."

"How?"

"She hinted that Danny's girlfriend wasn't good for him and that she could help."

Bill scowled. "Help how? Make the girlfriend go away? Or make her a better person?"

"I don't know, and I don't think Nicole does either. But talking to the psychic seemed to soothe her mother. Mary now feels she was right to be worried about Danny and to seek help from Miss T. She thinks the charms and prayer cards and all of that will help the situation somehow."

"So, if Danny breaks up with the girlfriend, that proves Miss Tryphenia was right?"

"I guess so," Campbell said. "Or if the girlfriend turns out to be good for him, then it will prove Miss Tryphenia was able to turn things around."

Her father gave a little grunt and shook his head. "And the psychic's there every step of the way—every paid step of the way."

"Right. That's my take. So, Dad, what now?"

He let out a big sigh. "Mary's not our client, and neither is Nicole. I don't think we should spend much time on that angle. Let the family figure it out. But I am concerned about Miss Tryphenia—Karen Potter—being missing. Let's talk about it over lunch."

Nick appeared in the doorway. "Keith's here."

"Great." Bill rose. "Come on, Soup. Let's make some sandwiches, and Keith can fill us in on his end."

She went straight to the kitchen and was soon joined by the three men.

"Hi, Keith," she called.

"Seems I'm invited to lunch," he said. "Anything I can do to help?"

Campbell had been rooting through a utensil drawer, and she looked toward a carton at the far end of the counter. "I can't find the cheese slicer. We're still unpacking, and I wonder if it's in that box."

"Let me look," her father said, heading for the carton. "Keith, help yourself to coffee or whatever you want to drink with lunch."

Nick got glasses, and Keith poured iced tea for everyone while Campbell took sandwich orders. Her father finally unearthed the cheese slicer and gave it a good washing in the sink then handed it to Campbell.

"Ham and cheese for me, please."

She accepted the slicer from him and adjusted the wire. "I don't know why we don't just buy sliced cheese."

"Next time."

Soon they were all seated with their favorite sandwiches, and Bill asked the blessing.

"Okay, Keith, give us the lowdown." Bill reached for the bag of potato chips.

"We didn't find a lot. Karen Potter is missing, but we don't have any way to know if that was by her own choice or not. I did find her appointment book on her desk. She had two appointments yesterday. The second one was at one o'clock."

Campbell raised her eyebrows. "I saw that. I'll tell you what Nick and I have done after you finish."

"Oh, okay." He eyed her curiously.

Campbell held out a jar of dill spears. "Pickle?"

"Thanks." As he helped himself, Keith said, "She did have one reading scheduled for this afternoon. I phoned the client and told her Miss Tryphenia wasn't available today, and she should call later in the week to reschedule."

"What did she say?" Nick asked.

"No problem. I didn't get any vibes from her, except maybe a little disappointment that she'd have to wait." He took a sip of tea. "Oh, and another interesting thing. Her schedule shows that she's supposed to appear at a party a week from Saturday. Parlor tricks, I guess. Read all the guests' fortunes, maybe?"

"Was the host's name Sarah?" Campbell asked.

Keith stared at her. "How did you know that? I thought you didn't touch anything."

"I didn't."

Bill picked up half his sandwich. "A woman named Sarah

lives in Sam Truman's apartment building in Benton. Her roommate told us she was thinking of hiring Miss Tryphenia to entertain at a party."

"Oh. For what it's worth, her full name is Sarah Delisle."

"And in case you find it useful, the roommate's name is Andrea Finley," Campbell said. "She's the one who told us Sam Truman recommended a psychic to her roommate."

Keith took his small notebook from his pocket and wrote down the name. "Thanks. Sometimes I forget what it's like working with you, Bill. If you're remotely involved in a case, you're usually way ahead of me."

"Not me," Bill said. "I was in court this morning. Campbell and I did visit Truman's neighbors in Benton last week, but everything else is those two." He nodded vaguely at Nick and Campbell and took a bite.

Keith eyed them with an expression Campbell couldn't read, so she continued eating her sandwich.

"Tell him about your last interview," Bill said.

"We found the woman who had the one o'clock appointment yesterday," Nick said.

Campbell swallowed. "Actually, we found her daughter. She was the one who was heard threatening Karen Potter with a visit from the police. Her mother, Mary Willingham, had the appointment, and her daughter went instead, to give Ms. Potter a piece of her mind."

"I see," Keith said slowly. Campbell could tell he wasn't entirely pleased with their aggressive investigation.

They drifted into chitchat, but when he'd finished his sandwich, a piece of gingerbread, and a cup of coffee, Keith turned to Bill.

"Okay, this is kind of a gray area for us. I know you've been hired to look into Truman's situation, but I'm going to ask your agency to leave the psychic case alone if possible. I realize that the two could overlap. Campbell and Nick did share information with us at the scene, including the witness's license tag number. That kind of cooperation is helpful, but I also realize I can't stop you from digging where you want to."

"Keith, we don't want to cause you any problems," Bill said.

"I appreciate that. Our top priority right now is to find Karen Potter and make sure she's all right. I mean, she might have had a fit of anger, knocked over a few things, and then driven to Paducah on a shopping spree. Nobody's reported her missing."

"Nick and I did," Campbell said.

"Well, yes, but nobody close to her seems to be worried about her."

"Is there anyone close to her?" Nick asked.

"That's another thing we need to figure out. She seems to be living alone at that house. I'll delve into her history and see if I can find any family or friends. Maybe someone can tell us where she is." Keith took a last swallow of iced tea and set the glass down. "Now I'd better get back to work."

"What do you want us to do now?" Campbell asked when he'd left.

Her father held out his mug for more coffee. She got it for him, and he took a sip. "I think it's time we talked to Dorothy Chambers."

"Miss Vera's daughter?" Nick asked. "I thought you didn't want her to know we're investigating Sam."

"Vera doesn't want her to know she hired us," Bill said. "But if we can ask her a few questions without letting her know her mother's paying us, it might be worthwhile." He looked at Campbell. "Maybe you could strike up a friendship? Vera told me that Dorothy goes to the gym every Tuesday and Thursday afternoon and Saturday mornings."

"Do I have to get a membership?"

"Nah, just tell them you're interested in joining, and they'll show you all around. If you spot Dorothy, finish the tour and wait for her to come out."

"Okay," Campbell said uncertainly. "Do you have a picture of her?"

He brought one up on his computer screen. "I asked Vera for one, and she sent me this."

Campbell studied it for a moment. She could see the resemblance to Vera, but Dorothy was a well-preserved forty, and in the photo she was dressed for a formal occasion. Still, Campbell thought she could pick her out at the gym.

————

The trainer's enthusiasm was nearly enough to make Campbell sign up as a member, but she knew she wouldn't stick to regular gym sessions. She was too busy, for one thing, and she preferred exercising in private.

When they'd finished the tour, she stood by the front desk holding the packet of information the trainer had given her. She nearly despaired of sighting her quarry. A spinning class had been meeting in the room across from the weight room, and the bikers began filing out.

"Oh, excuse me, I see someone I know. Thanks a lot." Campbell smiled and turned away from the trainer. "Dorothy? Dorothy Chambers?"

Dorothy stopped walking and gave her a blank look. "Do I know you?"

"I live on Willow Street, and I've met your folks. I understand you're a friend of Sam Truman."

"So what if I am?" Dorothy eyed her warily.

"Oh, it's nothing personal. It's just that I've been looking into an investment he's recommended, and I thought maybe you could tell me more about it."

"Why don't you ask Sam?"

"Well, I've never actually met him." Campbell walked slowly with her toward the door. "Someone else told me about it, and it sounded like a good thing."

"If you don't know Sam, how do you know I know him?"

Campbell swallowed hard and pushed open the door. "Actually, I've talked to a couple of people who are into this fund he's promoting. I just want to get a sense of whether it's a good, solid investment or not."

"As far as I know, it is. I've put a little money into it myself, and Sam says it should double within a year."

"Wow." Campbell paused on the walkway. "That's remarkable. How does it do that?"

Dorothy shrugged. "I don't know the details, but Sam could explain it to you. He told me I'd see some interest within a month after my investment, and I did."

"So, you've been in it a while."

"Only about six weeks, but I got a report the other day, and my eight-thousand dollar investment is now worth eight thousand six hundred."

"That sounds really good."

"Yeah."

"And it's safe? I mean, what if you suddenly needed the money?"

"Oh, Sam says I can withdraw it at any time. I could cash it out today if I wanted, and I'd be ahead six hundred dollars or more." Dorothy set down her gym bag. "Look, I've got a couple of his business cards. Why don't I just give you one, and you can call him. He's always glad to talk to people about this."

"Okay, thanks. Do you know where Sam is today?"

"I assume he's working. He's always making new contacts —you know, networking."

She took a card from her wallet, and Campbell pocketed it. "So, he's probably here in Murray today?"

"Hard to say. His apartment is in Benton." Dorothy gave her a coy smile. "He hasn't been in the area long, but he says he might buy a house down here. A permanent home."

Oh, no, Campbell thought. She thinks he's going to marry her.

"Hey, do you know if that brick house across from my mother's is for sale?" Dorothy asked.

Campbell frowned. "You mean Ben Tatton's house?"

"Yeah, that's the one."

"Uh, no, I don't think so. I mean, it's still vacant, but there's no 'For Sale' sign." She hesitated then ventured, "You know Mr. Tatton was killed last month, right?"

"Yes, my mother told me, but I don't think that would bother Sam."

"Well, as far as I know, his family hasn't put it on the market yet." A brighter thought came to Campbell. "Hey, my dad just put his house up for sale. We moved to Willow Street a week or two ago, and he listed the old house. Sam might want to look at that." She rattled off the address.

"I'll tell him," Dorothy said.

"Okay. Well, thanks so much for talking to me."

"Anytime." Dorothy picked up her bag and strode toward a green compact car.

———

Bill listened to Campbell's account of her interview and let out a big sigh. "We're not really getting anywhere. I think it's time we talked to Truman."

"He showed her a report that says she's making money," Campbell said.

"He could have doctored the report. It's just not feasible that she could double her money in a year. He showed her some numbers that will keep her calm for a while."

"What if everyone demands their money back all at once?"

"I think that's when Truman will disappear."

She blinked. "Really, Dad? He hasn't done that before."

"I don't think he was in this deep before. Remember, he hasn't changed his car registration and driver's license to Kentucky yet. If he intends to live here, don't you think he'd have done that?"

"I suppose." Campbell could see his logic.

Her dad nodded. "And now Karen Potter's missing."

"You think he's responsible for that, don't you?"

"It's a hunch. I could be wrong."

Campbell pushed to her feet. "Are we going to go track down Sam Truman?"

"I'm ready if you are."

Bill drove his Camry, and Campbell sat in the passenger seat, going over in her mind everything they'd learned.

"What if he's not home?" she asked at last.

"Then we wait."

"He could be out with Dorothy."

"He could be anywhere," her father countered. "But you just saw her at the gym, and I don't imagine she'll see him before this evening. It's a waiting game, Soup. You have to be patient."

Patience, she knew, was not her strong suit.

Campbell's phone rang just as they parked, and she didn't recognize the number but answered it.

"Hello, Ms. McBride? This is Trish Gilley."

"Hello, Mrs. Gilley." She glanced at her father, wondering if he'd recognize the name from her daily report. He nodded.

"A man came to my house this morning, looking for Sam Truman. That wasn't someone from your agency, was it?"

"No, definitely not."

"Well, I told him that I had no idea where Sam was, but it kind of made me uneasy."

"I don't blame you," Campbell said. "I don't know what to tell you, except be alert. If he comes to your house again, I'd consider calling the police."

"Well, if Paul was home, he could handle it, but I don't like it. I guess the things you said yesterday spooked me."

"It seems a bit unusual. And it never hurts to be careful."

"Right. Well, thanks. I just wanted to tell someone."

Trish ended the call, and Campbell told her father what she'd said.

"That's odd," Bill said.

"Yeah. Somehow this guy knew she was on Truman's list."

They got out of the car and walked toward the entrance to Apartment 2. A man Campbell had never seen before stood before it, pounding on the door with his fist. As they approached, he swore and shoved off from the door, swinging around toward them.

"Are you looking for Sam?" Bill asked.

"Yeah. You know where he is?" The man glared at them with steely eyes.

"Afraid not. I was hoping to find him here myself." Bill extended his hand. "I'm Bill McBride."

"You a friend of his?"

"Not really."

The man took his hand then. "Ray Walker."

Bill jerked his head toward the parking area. "Is that your pickup?"

"Yeah."

"Missouri plates."

"That's right," Ray said.

"Did you know Sam before he came here?"

"You might say that."

Campbell watched them spar verbally, racking her brain for the name Walker. She'd seen it somewhere, and not long ago, but where?

Walker hopped down the steps and hurried to the truck.

"You got his plate?" Campbell whispered.

"Yeah. Write it down."

Campbell scrounged for her small notebook and scribbled the plate number as Walker peeled out of the parking area.

"That name, Walker, is familiar," she murmured.

Her dad nodded, watching the truck speed away. "It was Truman's wife's maiden name."

11

Campbell froze for a second, picturing the online obituary she'd copied into their case file. "You're right." She dropped the notebook and pen into the front compartment of her purse. "So now we sit around and wait for Sam?"

"I don't have a better plan."

They hunkered down in the car, and after a while Campbell brought up her notes about the case on her phone. They talked about every interview they'd done since Vera hired them.

"We've about used up the retainer she's given us." Bill shook his head. "I hate to give up on it, but I don't feel we're making the progress we should."

"What about Walker? What's he doing here?"

"Good question. Maybe I'll give Nick a call."

Campbell heard the short conversation, where Bill asked Nick to do some checking into Ray Walker, with the strong possibility that he was related to Sam Truman's late wife. When he hung up, he immediately started the engine.

"We're not waiting for Sam?" she asked.

"No, Nick says Vera came by half an hour ago, and she was

quite upset. Truman's been around to their place. He's pressuring Frank for more money."

Campbell's jaw dropped. "So, while everyone's looking for him, Sam Truman is putting the squeeze on his elderly clients."

"It appears that way."

He drove back to Murray and pulled into their driveway. Nick waved to them through the office window.

"Come on," Bill said.

Campbell followed him on foot, diagonally across the street to the Hills' brick house. Vera opened the door to them before Bill could ring the bell.

"Thanks for coming! I wasn't sure what to do. Come on in, won't you?"

They followed her inside, to the living room. Frank sat ensconced in his recliner, with a rather sheepish look on his face. When he saw them, he pushed down on the lever for the footrest.

"Don't get up," Bill said, and he and Campbell took seats on the couch opposite him.

"Tea, anyone?" Vera said.

"No, we're fine," Campbell replied.

Vera settled in another armchair which, like Frank's, faced the TV.

"I was a little put out with Sam when he showed up today," Frank said. "Well, not at first. I thought it was just a friendly visit. But then he started going on about this new information he had about an opportunity. He wanted me to put a put a bundle into it."

"Not the same fund as before?" Bill asked.

"No, he said this was something new, and we could get in on it before anyone else. He said it was practically guaranteed to give a big payoff. It was tempting."

"But you told him no?"

"*I* did," Vera cut in as Frank started to answer. "I told him we never did anything that suddenly, and we'd need to talk it over. In private."

Frank pressed his lips together.

"I—I told Frank after Sam left that your lot was taking a look at Sam, just to make sure he was on the up-and-up."

Campbell caught a pleading look in Vera's eyes. *She didn't tell Frank she's paying us to do it.*

"We heard he'd approached several people in the neighborhood," Bill said affably to Frank. "We just want to make sure he's representing these opportunities as they really are."

"You think he's cheating people?" Frank sounded surprised, but he flicked a glance Vera's way. No doubt she'd expressed her opinion to him more than once.

"I wouldn't say that exactly," Bill replied. "But it's highly unusual to find an opportunity that will pay off in a big way quickly. And if people do know about something like that, they usually keep it to themselves."

"He just wanted us to have a chance to make a few bucks," Frank said. "I mean, he's practically family."

"Oh, are he and Dorothy getting married?" Campbell asked.

Vera's face wrinkled. "I hope not."

"Oh, you just don't like him because he has a nice car," Frank said with a wry glance. He looked back to Bill. "See, she thinks he's pocketing the money people give him, but there's no way. I mean, he couldn't get away with that."

"You'd be surprised what some people get away with," Bill said. "Especially in the short term."

"He pushes too hard." Vera scowled at her husband. "You heard him. He said if we didn't do it today, we'd lose out.

That's what con artists tell people, so they won't have time to think it over and make a sensible decision."

"Or maybe not," Frank countered. "Maybe it really is a limited opportunity."

"Yeah, right," Vera said. "Frank, that's our nest egg. We're going to need that money."

"But if we can make it grow—"

"Slow and steady." Vera's jaw took on a stubborn set. "You know that's what the financial planner told us last year. At our age it's better to opt for security than take a risk."

"He said if you're comfortable with it—"

She shook her head adamantly. "I'm *not* comfortable with risks, Frank. You know that."

Frank sighed and sank back in his chair.

"It's just like that psychic," Campbell said. "She told me last week that she sensed I was worried about a loved one's health."

"You didn't tell me that," Bill said.

She shrugged. "I didn't want you to think I paid any attention to it. You're healthy. But it's the kind of thing psychics do, right? They mention health and relationships and finances to see what resonates. She wanted me to come back and pay her for a reading."

"You're right," her father said. "And what Sam Truman said to you today, Frank, was what cons do. They try to convince you their investment is a sure thing, and that you need to not think about it too long. But usually they're a little smoother about it than the way you described Sam's pitch today."

"I knew it," Vera said. "He's a con man."

Bill held up a hand. "I didn't say that. But he surely seems to check some of the boxes—and he doesn't seem to have a local office or a firm he's associated with that we can go and visit."

"I think it's all on the computer." Vera scowled.

"Well, however it is, I think you were wise not to jump too quickly. You must have some of your money in a retirement account."

"We do," Frank said. "But we have some extra. You know, mutual funds and so on."

"And I think you said you go to a financial planner for that? A licensed professional?"

"Well, yes."

Vera named a franchised financial institution, and Bill nodded.

"Their representatives have to pass rigorous tests and background checks. You're probably safe with them. And if you asked them about this fund of Sam's, they could look it up. We haven't been able to find any official registration or anything for the Billings-Phifer Fund he's been selling, but your planner probably could tell you if it's on any lists of approved investments. The same goes for this new fund."

"Do you really think Sam's trying to cheat us?" Frank asked.

"I don't know, but if I were in your shoes, I'd stick with the licensed financial planner. I mean, there's always a bad apple or two, but it's not like ..."

"Not like someone who walks in off the street with no credentials," Vera said.

Bill nodded, but Frank seemed to take umbrage.

"Sam didn't walk in off the street," he said, glaring at his wife. "Dorothy brought him to meet us. He's her boyfriend."

"How did she meet him?" Campbell asked.

"She mentioned something about work. He came into the office one day, and they struck up a conversation." Vera's eyes lost focus as she thought about it.

"No doubt it was Sam who struck up the conversation," Bill said.

Frank let out a big sigh. "Now that she's divorced, it's almost as bad as when she was a teenager. I didn't expect to have to approve her dates after I retired."

"She didn't ask us to approve him," Vera said.

They were both sounding a bit grumpy. Campbell stirred and looked at her dad.

Taking her cue, Bill stood. "Well, listen, we'd better get back to work, but we're right across the street if you need anything."

Vera got up and walked to the door with them.

"Thanks for stopping by."

"Anytime, Miss Vera." Campbell squeezed her hand.

When they got across the street to the office, Nick could hardly contain himself.

"Well? Do tell."

"I think we've convinced them not to give him any of their money right away," Bill said.

"Well, wait until you hear what I learned about that Walker guy."

Campbell and her dad got coffee and sank into cozy chairs by the empty fireplace.

"Okay, how does he fit in?" Bill asked.

"Sam Truman's wife was Libby Walker. You knew that. Raymond Walker is her brother. He lives in Sikeston, Missouri."

"That's not that far away," Campbell said.

Her father nodded. "Why is he over here, looking for Truman?"

"I don't know." Nick scrunched up his face. "But he's a known hacker, and he's got a record. Five years ago, he was arrested for hacking a medical practice's billing service. They couldn't make that stick, but a couple years later, they got him for hacking into a credit union's computer system. He tried to withdraw ten grand without going through the usual channels, but he got caught, and he spent six months in jail for it."

"Very interesting," Bill said.

Nick nodded. "I'm thinking that if Sam Truman kept his appointment book in an online schedule program, maybe Walker hacked it."

Bill's eyes widened.

"That could be how he knew who Sam's clients were, Dad." Campbell stared at Nick in amazement. "Good job!"

He smiled a bit smugly. "Why, thank you, Professor."

Bill took a big gulp of coffee and stood. "Keep working on the Walker angle. See if you can find another family member and ask them why Ray's over here in Kentucky."

"What about me?" Campbell asked.

Her father shrugged. "It's almost quitting time. Write up what happened today, and then let's have a relaxing evening."

That meant TV for her dad. Campbell started to say something but stopped. He looked tired. It wouldn't hurt him to watch a cop show or two and then go to bed early. She could read the new mystery she'd picked up at the library. As much as she wanted to work on their case, that sounded good.

She gave him a smile. "Okay, Dad."

12

The next morning at eight o'clock, Campbell rode with her father to Benton again, but once more Sam Truman had eluded them. His neighbor, Ted Holloway, was just about to pull out of the parking lot and rolled down his window.

"You looking for Sam?"

"Yeah, we are," Bill said. "Is he here?"

"I saw him leave about a half hour ago."

"Oh. Well, thanks, Ted." Bill parked and rang Sam's doorbell anyway, just to be sure.

Campbell shook her head as he climbed back into the car. "You couldn't take Ted's word for it?"

"No, I couldn't. If he'd decided to back Sam and didn't want me to know about it, he might lie to me to keep the heat off Sam."

"Ted seems like a good guy."

"Well, yeah, but you never know. And a lot of people think Sam's a good guy."

"Right." She sighed and settled back in the seat. "Now what?"

"Back to Murray. I want you to talk to all the people we know Sam has had contact with and see if they've heard from him yesterday or today. Also ask them if anyone else has shown up looking for Sam."

"You're sure Walker's the one who went to the Gilleys' house, aren't you?"

"Reasonably sure, and he's got a record having to do with financial crimes. I think I'll go over to the police station and do some hobnobbing. I want to know if the department's aware of Walker's activities and tell them he's in town."

With her coffee mug at her side, Campbell went over her notes about everything that had happened officially the previous day—Karen Potter's mysterious absence, her interviews with Nicole Paxton and Dorothy Chambers, Trish Gilley's call, and the visit with Frank and Vera Hill. They had to be missing something.

The office phone rang about ten thirty, and she picked it up.

"True Blue Investigations."

"Hi, is Bill McBride in?"

"Not at the moment. This is his daughter, Campbell. May I help you?"

"Maybe. This is Pete Marin. I'm his old next-door neighbor. I know Bill moved last week, but has he sold the old house?"

"Not yet," Campbell said. "He just put it on the market."

"Oh. Well, I saw some activity over there this morning, and I thought maybe he'd come back for some stuff, so I went over there. Nobody came to the door, but the car was still parked out front."

"That's odd. Was it Dad's blue Toyota? Because he was going over to the police station when he left here."

"No, I didn't recognize it. Maroon sedan."

"Huh. Maybe the Realtor was showing the house. I'll give them a call. Thanks for the heads-up."

She hung up and told Nick what Marin had said.

"Maybe Bill's house will sell quick," he said. "That'd be good, right?"

"Yeah." Campbell didn't like the way the neighbor had described his attempt to talk to whoever was at the house. "I'm going to call the real estate office."

Her father had hired an agency that Campbell and Nick had contacted in an earlier case, Pride & Calhoun. Their office was out on Twelfth Street, across from the Barn Owl Diner.

A familiar voice answered her call.

"Pride & Calhoun. Nell Calhoun speaking."

"Hi, Nell. This is Campbell McBride."

"Well, hi, Campbell!" Nell sounded delighted to hear from her. "How's it going in the new-old house?"

"Great. We love it. We've got our office all set up and we're doing business."

"That's terrific."

"Yeah. Listen, I wondered if you'd done a showing of Dad's old house today?"

"No, not today. I've got one scheduled for tomorrow."

"Do you know if anyone was over there this morning? I ask because a neighbor called and told me someone with a maroon sedan was at the house. I was hoping it was you."

"Nope, not me. I went over two days ago to do a little staging, but I haven't been back since. And I drive a white Prius."

"Okay, thanks."

"Do you want me to stop by there on my way home?" Nell asked.

"No, I think I'll pop over now. It's only a few blocks, and I want to see what's going on myself and maybe talk to the neighbor."

"Okay," Nell said. "Let me know if there's a problem."

Campbell put down the receiver.

"She doesn't know anything about it?" Nick asked.

"Nope."

"Could be another real estate agent?"

"Nell's office would know." Campbell snagged her purse strap and shoved back her chair. "I'm going over there. Tell Dad when he gets back, will you?"

Her father had given one key to the Realtor, but he'd kept the rest for the time being, and she retrieved one from his dresser. She passed the county hospital and reached their old street in five minutes, where she pulled into the empty driveway. The Pride & Calhoun sign on the short-cropped lawn looked crisp and official. Fishing the key from her pocket, she walked up to the front door. Nothing seemed amiss. On impulse, she rang the bell.

Thump.

Campbell flinched and listened. No more noises reached her, other than a car engine on the next street and the distant bark of a dog. She rang the bell again, but nothing happened.

Looking around the yard, she hurried to the garage door and peered through the small windows. It was empty. She went behind the house and approached the back door. Her dad had given her some lessons on picking locks. She wasn't very good at it yet, but she recognized the telltale scratches on the striker plate. Someone had been messing with the lock on the back door. She tried the door, then stuck her key in the lock and turned it.

Tiptoeing through the mud room and kitchen, she held her breath. At the living room doorway, she froze. Someone was lying on the bare oak floor. She took a step, reaching for her phone. The person's foot twitched and Campbell realized the woman's ankles were taped together. She looked around but saw nobody else inside. Heart racing, she crossed the room and knelt beside her.

"Miss Tryphenia?"

Duct tape covered the woman's mouth, but Campbell was sure it was the psychic whose frantic eyes stared up at her.

"Hold on." She grabbed a corner of the tape and jerked it off the woman's face.

Karen Potter gasped and took several deep breaths. "Thank God! Who are you?"

"I'm Campbell. I came to your house last week with Angela Fuller, when you did a reading for her."

"What are you doing here?" She frowned at Campbell, who was already picking at the tape that bound her hands together.

"This is my father's old house. It's up for sale, and a neighbor called to tell us someone was in here this morning. Who did this to you?"

"I ... I'm not sure."

Campbell darted a glanced at her impassive face. The psychic might be adept at concealing her lies, but Campbell was sure she wasn't telling the truth this time.

A rattle at the front door startled her. She sprang up and strode to the door.

"Who is it?"

"Bill McBride."

Feeling lightheaded, she threw the locks off then swung the door open.

"Dad!"

"Nick called me. What's going on?"

"See for yourself." She waved a hand toward Karen, who still lay on the floor.

Bill rushed to her side and knelt on the floor next to her. "Ms. Potter?"

"Y-yes. Do I know you?"

"I'm Bill McBride. Campbell is my daughter, and this house belongs to me. We just moved out of it last week."

She blinked and looked around. "Where—how did I get here?"

"I was hoping you could tell us that while I get this tape off you."

She shook her head helplessly, but Campbell thought it was an act. Why would she lie about something like that?

"Well, we should get you over to the hospital." Bill slit the tape with his pocketknife. "It's not far. We can call an ambulance, but if you prefer, one of us can drive you over to the emergency room."

"No, don't." She put her hands to her temples. "Did someone hit me?"

Campbell leaned toward her. "A neighbor saw a maroon car out front this morning. It's not there now. Did somebody drive you here?"

Karen Potter hesitated. "I woke up and I didn't know where I was, and I was frightened. Then someone rang the doorbell. I kicked with my feet, hoping they'd hear me."

"That was me," Campbell said. "I did hear you, and I came around to the back and let myself in."

"Think about before that," Bill said. "What were you doing this morning?"

"I don't know." Karen rubbed her wrists, frowning.

"How about yesterday?"

She shook her head and winced. "Can you take me home?"

As her father helped Karen to her feet, Campbell ran over the events of the past two days in her mind.

"Ms. Potter, I went to your house yesterday, and you

weren't there. It looked like there'd been a disturbance of some kind. We called the police, and they're looking for you now."

She groaned.

"I'll call them right now and tell them we found you," Bill said.

"Can't we leave the police out of this?" Karen asked.

"I'm afraid not." Bill took out his phone. "They're already aware that you were missing. Besides, this house is my property, although it's up for sale. Someone broke in here and used it as a place to hold you against your will. That's criminal activity. I have to make the call."

Karen swore softly then focused on Campbell. "Can you drive me home, please? I don't want to be here when the cops come."

"Sure." Campbell reached for her arm.

"You should stay and talk to an officer," Bill said. "You'll have to talk to them sooner or later."

"Later then." Karen put a hand on Campbell's shoulder and walked slowly with her out the front door.

"The white Fusion is mine," Campbell said.

She got her guest into the passenger seat, helped her find the seatbelt, and walked around to the driver's side. Would there still be officers at Karen's house? If not, she wondered if she'd be invited inside.

Silent during the drive, Karen huddled against the door, staring downward. When they got to Second Street, Campbell pulled up right in front of Miss Tryphenia's sign. The front door of the house was now closed, and no police cars or officers were in sight.

Without being invited, Campbell climbed out of the car and walked around to the passenger side.

"Are you all right?" she asked as Karen slowly got out.

Karen winced as she shut the car door. "Yeah, I'm fine. You don't have to stay."

"I want to make sure you get inside all right. I noticed you don't have your purse."

With a slightly befuddled expression, Karen looked around. "Right. Do you think the cops locked the door?"

"I don't know. Would you like me to try it?"

"I can do it." Karen squared her shoulders and marched up to the entrance.

When she turned the knob, the door opened. She walked in slowly, peering around, and Campbell followed close behind.

"Well, they left a mess." Karen paused at the doorway to the parlor then stepped inside. The table still lay on its side, and she stooped to pick up a votive holder. "Ick."

"What is it?" Campbell moved closer as Karen rubbed her fingers together, spreading the dark powder she'd encountered. "Fingerprint powder. It'll come off, but it always leaves a mess."

Karen's mouth skewed. "Why did they have to come in here?"

"Who, the police?" Campbell asked. "Karen, you were kidnapped. We were concerned about you."

She gave a heavy sigh. "I guess I should thank you for finding me before Sam came back."

"Sam? You mean Sam Truman?"

Karen turned her head slowly and pinned Campbell with her gaze. "You know him?"

"Yes. And we know that you know him. So, he's the one who kidnapped you? Why didn't you tell my dad and me?"

She shrugged. "It's none of your business."

"But he might have killed you."

"I don't think he would have."

"How can you know?" Campbell asked.

Karen didn't answer. She hoisted the light table to its feet and picked up the cloth.

Campbell stepped closer. "Why would Sam do that to you?"

Karen paused her motions and stared at the shelves full of herbs and trinkets. "Sam thinks I killed his wife."

13

Keith hung up his desk phone and typed several notes into his computer. The phone rang again, and he reached for it.

"Hey, Keith, it's Bill. Can you come over to my old house?"

"Sure, if you need me."

"Campbell found Karen Potter lying on the floor here with her hands and feet duct-taped. She wouldn't go to the hospital, and she insisted we take her home. Campbell's doing that now, but I thought you'd want to take a look here. Somebody broke in and left her here. A neighbor saw a car out front this morning."

"I'll be right there."

On his way to the small ranch house, Keith tried to piece things together, without success. Bill met him at the front door.

"Come on in, Keith. I'm positive they picked the lock on the back door, not this one. The house is empty, of course, because we put it on the market."

"Who's the Realtor?"

"Nell Calhoun."

"I know her." Keith stepped inside and looked around, taking in the discarded duct tape on the floor.

"She had tape over her mouth, too, and Campbell yanked it off." Bill nudged an eight-inch strip of gray tape with his toe.

"Might be good for fingerprints. Let me call in an assist." Keith made the call for another officer and turned back to face his friend. "I was going to tell you this later, but I may as well tell you now. We got a match on the fingerprints from Louanne Vane's financial documents."

"It took you this long?"

Keith shrugged. "It wasn't exactly high priority, since nothing was taken."

"Who was it?"

"Sam Truman."

"Figures." Bill shook his head.

"I talked to a couple of officers in Missouri. You knew about his record?"

"Yeah. And the restraining order his wife filed."

"Well, his name popped up in another investigation. He wasn't charged with anything, but he was questioned after a man he'd had dealings with shot himself."

Bill said nothing but waited expectantly.

"He'd given Sam most of his life savings, and Sam told him a few months later that the investment went south. He lost everything."

"I guess that's why we have retirement funds where you can only withdraw so much per year without a penalty."

"Yeah, well, this guy had a nest egg, but he blew it all when he gave it to Sam."

Bill frowned. "That's tragic, but ..."

"Like I said, Sam wasn't charged with anything. Once the

coroner ruled it a suicide, there wasn't anything to hold him on."

"Not fraud?"

"The investigating officer looked into it, and they closed the case."

"So, there's no question that Sam actually invested the money and the fund failed?"

Keith sighed. "He did make the investment in the man's name. The client handed over the money voluntarily. The detective told me there was no evidence Truman had withdrawn it."

"I'm sensing a 'but,'" Bill said.

"But if he was clever enough, he might have withdrawn it under a different name."

"How could that be?"

"I don't know," Keith said. "If the fund was legit, they'd have safeguards. But that fund is no longer in existence."

"So maybe it was set up just for Sam or people like Sam. A shell company."

"Could be."

"And this outfit he's pushing now could be fake too."

"That's my thought, but we have no proof. There are tight banking regulations, but it takes time to investigate these things. Truman dropped out of sight for a while after the suicide case was closed. Maybe moved out of the area for a while."

"Maybe went elsewhere to enjoy that poor fellow's money," Bill said.

"It's possible."

Bill huffed out a big breath. "Can you put a rush on the fingerprints from that duct tape and my back door? I'm thinking Sam Truman brought that woman here to keep her out of the way for a short time."

"Why here?" Keith asked.

"Search me. Because it's empty, I guess. He could have cruised around town looking for real estate signs telling him what houses are up for sale. This is a middle-class neighborhood. I didn't have a burglar alarm. The houses aren't too close together. It wasn't all that hard to get into—you know someone else broke in a few months ago."

"Right. And I can't see anyone fiddling with duct tape while they had gloves on. We ought to be able to find something. You say Campbell drove Ms. Potter home?"

"Yeah."

"I'll have to talk to them both after we're done here."

"I know. I'll tell Campbell. And I told Ms. Potter this is a crime scene. She didn't want me to call you, but I told her I had to. Keep us posted, will you, Keith?"

"I sure will. Now, can you point me to the neighbor who saw the car over here?"

———

"So why would Sam Truman think you killed his wife?"

"He's just got it in his head that I was jealous enough to do that," Karen said.

"You were jealous?" Campbell frowned.

"Look, I left Missouri ten years ago because I didn't want to be around Sam anymore. And now he's come here."

"And kidnapped you."

Karen sighed. "I didn't do anything to his wife, okay? I guess he was hoping I'd confess. And now the police are starting to sniff around him again, and he wanted me out of the way. He said he was leaving, but he didn't want me talking to the cops about him before he got out of Murray."

"Why are the police looking at him again? Do you mean it's

about his wife's death?" When Karen didn't respond, Campbell said, "Or about his recent financial activities?"

"Whatever."

It seemed Karen had shared all she intended to for now, but the whole situation seemed fishy to Campbell.

"So, he restrained you and left you in a vacant house because he didn't want you to talk to the police about him?"

"He said a real estate agent or someone would find me soon."

"I'm not sure I believe that."

"Well, why don't you go catch up to him and ask him? I have work to do." Karen shoved a chair back into place.

Campbell walked slowly out to her car and drove home. If Sam Truman was that avid about keeping Karen quiet, why hadn't he killed her? And why did he choose her father's vacant house?

Dorothy Chambers. She'd told Sam's girlfriend the house was for sale. Campbell's lungs squeezed so tightly she wasn't sure she could take one more breath. She turned onto Willow Street and then into the driveway. She parked in the garage. For a long moment she sat in the car taking slow, deep breaths. Had she inadvertently aided a criminal? At last she went into the house through the kitchen.

Nick greeted her from behind his desk.

"Your dad wants to see you right away."

Campbell turned toward her father's office.

When she reached the doorway, he looked up and said, "Hey there. Is Karen Potter okay?"

"She's home and cleaning up her place, but I don't know if she's okay."

Her father nodded. "Why don't you get some coffee and join me. I need to bring you up to speed on what Keith told me."

"Dad, it may be my fault she was left in your old house."

His brow furrowed. "Why is that?"

"Dorothy Chambers. She told me at the gym that Truman was looking for a house in Murray, and I—" She gulped. "I told her your house had just gone on the market."

"I see."

"And I need to tell you what Karen said when I took her home."

"Go get the coffee, and we'll talk."

Ten minutes later, they'd finished their briefing and sat gazing at each other in silence.

Campbell took a sip from her mug and frowned. "I still don't get it. If Sam thinks Karen killed his wife, why doesn't he tell the police and have them question her? Why kidnap her?"

"Apparently Ms. Potter was never a suspect in his wife's death."

"You think she's lying, and he doesn't really suspect her?"

Bill shook his head slowly. "I don't know."

"She did lie to us a couple of times today—I'm sure of that. She said at first she didn't know who took her to the house, but later she mentioned Sam, and when I pounced, she told me he did it."

"If Sam really did say he needed her out of the way until he skipped town, I'd better tell Keith." Bill reached for the phone. "He needs to lay off questioning our old neighbors and go arrest Sam Truman."

"For what?"

"For whatever he's running from." Bill made a wry face and paused with his hand in midair. "You're right. It's hearsay, and there's not enough evidence to arrest him for fraud. But they ought to be able to make a kidnapping charge stick."

"Even if Karen won't press charges?"

"*I'll* press charges. Breaking and entering at an empty

house may not carry as much weight, but it's something solid. And he left fingerprints at Mrs. Vane's house. Let me call Keith now, and then maybe you should pay Louanne another visit and tell her to press charges. That's two B&E's the police can chalk up to Truman. That should hold him for a while."

Her father made the call and then hung up with a serene expression. "Keith will find him."

"I hope so. There's something that stymies me, though."

He quirked his eyebrows at her.

"Dad, if Sam Truman is going to skip town, why did he tell Dorothy he wanted to buy a house here?"

"That was before things got a little too hot for him in Murray, right?"

Campbell nodded slowly. "I'm wondering if he's been stringing Dorothy along. She looked a little giddy when she asked me about Ben Tatton's house—whether it was for sale. That's when I told her about your house. I'm betting she passed that tidbit on to Sam, hoping they could go house shopping together."

"Could be. But my house probably isn't in a good enough neighborhood for Truman."

"What if Sam had no intention of proposing to Dorothy or settling down here? What if he's only been pursuing Dorothy, making her think he wants to marry her and live here, as a source of potential clients for his fund?"

"And when he gets enough to bankroll him for a while, he disappears." He leaned back in his chair, frowning. "I guess it wouldn't be the first time a con man used a woman to get information."

Campbell nodded, still miserable at her part in providing Sam with useful information. "Poor Dorothy."

———

Blue Boy approached Campbell's chair on silent feet. He sniffed at her ankle. Campbell sat still, hoping he wouldn't scratch her again.

"He's getting used to you." Louanne smiled. "Once he knows you, he'll let you pat him."

"Nice." Campbell wasn't sure she wanted to try after the way he'd reacted to her last time. "Did the police tell you they found out who broke into your house and let Blue Boy out last week?"

"They said they know the man's name. He's been in the area, trying to get people to trust him to handle their investments for them. They told me they plan to prosecute him for that, and I'll be safe."

"Well, you need to keep on being cautious," Campbell said. "They haven't caught him yet, and now they think he may have committed some other crimes. Just don't let anyone in, and lock up tight."

"I had the locks changed."

"That's very wise."

"Detective Fuller advised it after we got Blue Boy back." The cat jumped up into Louanne's lap, and she stroked his thick blue-gray fur.

"Detective Fuller is a good man," Campbell said. "I want you to call me if anyone bothers you again, okay? Dad and I can be here in sixty seconds if you need help."

"I'm sure you could, dear. Faster than the police, even."

"Yes, but the police are there to help you too."

Blue Boy began to purr as Louanne patted his back. He gazed smugly at Campbell and winked one eye.

———

That evening, Campbell couldn't concentrate on her paperwork. The officers who'd gone to arrest Sam Truman hadn't found him. They'd watch his apartment door all night, but as of Keith's last update, he hadn't shown up.

"He's left town, hasn't he?" she asked.

"Maybe," her dad said. "Look, I'm having dinner with Barry McGann."

Campbell nodded. McGann was a local attorney who often sent business her dad's way.

"It could mean a new case or two," he said.

Campbell would be bored silly if she spent the entire evening alone. Nick had gone home for the night, and Keith was tied up with his police work. "Dad, I'd like to go over to Miss Tryphenia's and see if Karen is all right. If she was hit on the head ..."

"We don't know that she was," her father pointed out.

"I wish I'd checked before I undid her hands. I didn't see any blood, though. Do you think she could have been injected with something?"

"Impossible to say. But I don't think you should go alone." Bill headed for the door.

Campbell sighed. He hadn't said she couldn't go. But who was there to go along with her?

"Karen seemed fine when I drove her home. I mean, she talked to me civilly. Until she told me to leave."

"I'm just sayin' ..."

"I know. I'll be careful."

He paused in the doorway, his car keys in his hand. "I know you're a big girl, but in this business we have to take precautions. Why don't you call Nick and ask him to meet you there? Now I've got to go."

Campbell closed her laptop and went to her room for a lightweight jacket. Was she being foolish? She'd gone to check on a cat earlier. No, to be honest, she'd gone to check on Miss Louanne. She couldn't stand the thought of another intrusion on the sweet old woman's life. But Karen Potter? She wasn't exactly an endearing person, at least not according to Campbell's limited encounters with her.

As she went down the stairs, she took out her phone and tapped on Contacts and Miss T. The ringing sound came, but no answer.

"That does it," she muttered. "I'm going over there."

Leaving lights on both inside and on the porch for her return, she went to her car and pulled out. She'd make a quick stop at the psychic's house and then come straight home.

Second Street was quiet in the twilight. She parked near the house and got out, looking around cautiously. A couple other vehicles were parked nearby, but neither had any occupants.

Lights shone inside the house. She went up the short walkway and rang the bell but wasn't surprised when no one came to the door. As she turned the knob and found it unlocked, she had a feeling of *déjà vu*. Karen Potter had been attacked and kidnapped. Why on earth was she still leaving her door unlocked, especially after business hours?

She almost went inside but remembered her dad's stern admonition and pulled out her phone and hit favorites.

"Nick?"

"Yeah?"

"You busy?"

"Kinda."

Campbell grimaced. "Well, I'm over at Miss T's house, and once again she's not answering the doorbell but has left the front door unlocked."

"Peachy."

"Dad's meeting with Mr. McGann over dinner, and I didn't want to—"

"Campbell, I'm on a date. If you find a body, call me back."

She huffed out a breath. He'd hung up on her, and not for the first time. Nick Emerson made lava erupt in her chest.

She took three deep breaths then opened the door and looked into the small entry.

"Karen?"

No one answered, and she tried again, louder.

"Karen? It's Campbell. Are you home?"

Annoyance propelled her inside. Karen was almost as infuriating as Nick. What was the point in having a doorbell if you never answered it? And if she found a body, she had no intention of calling Nick again. The police would do fine, thank you. In her mind, she gave her young colleague a flippant slap on the back of the head.

Three steps took her to the parlor doorway, and she gazed inside. And froze.

The psychic lay on her side on the floor, with a stain that looked suspiciously like blood spreading onto the carpet beneath her.

Campbell ran to the still form and knelt beside her. "Karen? Karen, can you hear me?"

She reached out and touched the woman's hand but got no response. Karen's eyes were closed, and one hand clutched her side, where blood had flowed between her fingers and onto the floor. Campbell couldn't tell whether or not the blood was still oozing. She took Karen's limp wrist in her hand and felt for a pulse.

Please, Lord, let her be alive.

She didn't feel that tiny movement of the veins. Slowly she lifted her chin. Ambulance? No, she'd call the police and let them call in the EMTs if they thought it appropriate. She was glad she had Keith in her list of frequent contacts. She should have called him first, but she'd do it now and ask for his help.

She pulled out her phone and swiped it to clear the screen.

Arms came around her neck from behind her. She jumped and writhed, but a sturdy forearm pressed tighter against her neck.

14

Slowly Campbell became aware of darkness. When she moved, fabric rubbed against her face. Her hands weren't bound, for which she was glad. She grabbed at the cloth that covered her head and yanked it off.

A cool breeze made her shiver. Stars glittered overhead, and she'd been lying in grass. The air smelled sweet. Flowers? Sitting up, she peered around her. What were those shapes?

She caught her breath. Tombstones surrounded her. Someone had left her in a cemetery.

Her shaking increased, and she pulled in another breath.

God, help me! I don't know where I am, or why I'm here.

Who would do this to her?

She remembered asking Karen Potter the same question earlier in the day. Was Sam Truman behind this? He'd kidnapped Karen. Had he repeated his crime?

Then she remembered the body on the floor in Karen's parlor and began to shake all over.

She held her arms, trying to get warm, but she couldn't still her shivering. Her hands gripping the sleeves of her windbreaker didn't seem to help a bit.

Sam had taped Karen's hands and feet when he kidnapped her. Campbell's were free. Did that mean a different person had done this?

Her throat hurt. Gingerly she raised a hand to it and winced. Definitely tender.

Rolling to her knees, she patted her pockets. Hadn't she been holding her phone when she was assaulted? She tried to remember those final moments. Arms encircling her neck. Panic as she tried to kick backward at the assailant's legs.

A low whirring sound grabbed her attention. She whipped her head toward it and saw a glow in the blackness of the grass. Her phone? Was it possible? The attacker must have tossed it down near her, but why?

She grabbed it and tapped the screen. It said 12:15 a.m. She'd been unconscious at least four hours. She gulped and tapped the phone icon. "Dad!"

"Campbell, are you all right?"

"No. Yes. Oh, Dad!" Pain lanced her throat. She couldn't help the catch in her voice, or the tears streaming down her cheeks.

"Where are you?"

"I'm in a cemetery."

"What, the big one in town?"

She looked around and said hesitantly, "I don't think so. It's ..."

A vehicle hummed by on a road a hundred yards away.

"I don't think it's that big. It's near a road, though. I just saw a car, and it was going forty or fifty miles an hour. I think." She shook her head. "I'm not a very good judge of speed, Dad."

"Okay," he said. "Take a deep breath and then tell me what happened."

"Well, I went to Karen Potter's house, and she didn't answer the doorbell, like before. The door was unlocked again. I called Nick, but he was busy, so I went in."

"Aw, Soup—"

"I know, I know. Stupid of me. But I was so mad. Nick told me to call him again if I found a body. And then—" She sobbed.

"Easy, baby girl. What happened?"

"I found a body."

"You're joking. No, you're not, are you? Was it Karen Potter?"

"Yes. Dad, I'm pretty sure she's dead. But that was like eight o'clock or eight thirty. I checked her pulse, and I was about to call Keith when someone came in behind me and choked me."

"Good grief, Campbell! Did you see his face?"

"No. It was some kind of chokehold from behind. Like a wrestler maybe would do?"

"Or a military man."

Her head ached too badly to think hard about that. "I guess maybe. I must have passed out. The next thing I knew, I woke up out here. I was cold, and something was over my head." She stooped to pick up the fabric she'd discarded and shone the light of her phone on it. "It looks like a pillowcase."

"Hang on to that."

"Okay. And, Dad, he left my phone here with me. Why would he do that?"

"He probably didn't think of it."

"No, I was holding it when they grabbed me. I'm pretty sure I dropped it. But when I woke up a few minutes ago, it was lying in the grass beside me."

"Not your typical assailant," her father said.

"That's what I thought. Dad, you've got to call Keith and tell him to go to Karen's house right away."

"I will. Meanwhile, you said you're near a road?"

"Yes, and—" She looked up as the headlights of another vehicle became visible. "Another car's passing right now."

"Can you yell to them? Get their attention without jumping out in the road?"

"No, I'm too far away for that. I'm back quite a ways from the road." The car had passed, and she squinted at the field of tombstones before her. "I can't tell how far."

"I want you to get up to the road," he said. "There may be a sign that will tell you what road it is, or which cemetery."

"Okay." Keeping her phone to her ear and carrying the pillowcase, she stepped cautiously between the grave markers, weaving between them in the direction of the roadway. After stumbling a few yards, she came across a paved path. "Oh, Dad? I found a road between the rows of headstones."

"Okay, follow that if you can."

"It doesn't go directly toward the paved road. It's kind of sideways." She looked up. "Oh, there goes another car. No, two."

"That tells me it's a well-traveled road, since it has traffic after midnight." Just walk along the path until you find one that goes toward the road. Can you do that?"

"Yeah, I—I think so."

"Kiddo, are you sure you're all right?"

She touched her Adam's apple. "My throat's a little sore, and my head aches."

"Did they hit you over the head?"

"I don't think so. Oh, wait. I think this path is heading for the road, but it's at an angle."

"Okay, Campbell, find the biggest gravestone that's near you and read the name on it."

She looked around and headed for a monument taller than she was. "Uh, Brandon."

"Great. I might be able to match that to a cemetery."

"In the middle of the night?"

"You're right. If it was daytime, I could call the county clerk's office. Let me think."

"I'm almost to the road, Dad."

"Good. Tell me if you see anything up there."

She walked on in silence, her feet thudding on asphalt. Finally she reached the edge of the two-lane road and looked both ways.

"There's a streetlight to my left, but it's quite a ways from me. There are woods across the road. I think I'm near the farther end of the cemetery. From the streetlight, that is."

"How far is it?"

"I don't know. A tenth of a mile, maybe?"

She walked toward it, along the edge of the pavement. "Oh, wait. There's a sign up there."

"Near the streetlight?"

"No, I'm nowhere near the light yet. This is at the front of the cemetery, near the road." She quickened her steps. "You there, Dad? It says Elm Grove Cemetery."

He let out a little laugh. "Good job! I know exactly where that is."

She frowned. "Where?"

"You're on Route 94—out a few miles. It's the road that Main Street morphs into."

"Okay."

"There should be a church on the other side. Look at the streetlight again."

"Oh."

"What?" he asked.

"I see the steeple. The lights are in the churchyard."

"Yes! Go over to the church, okay? I'll pick you up there in ten or fifteen minutes. Find a place to sit down that's not obvious to passersby, but where you can see me when I drive in."

"Got it." She walked along and stumbled. Catching herself quickly, she avoided turning her ankle. "Dad, I'm going to walk on the edge of the pavement so I don't fall, but don't worry. I'll be careful if cars come along."

"Just get over to the church and wait there. I'll get there as fast as I can, but I need to call Keith. I'm hanging up, but I'll call you back after I talk to him and get on my way."

She walked on slowly, using her phone as a flashlight. On her right, she passed a darkened house set back from the road. She could make out the church's sign now, and the front steps and parking lot. With a big sigh, she looked up at the illuminated steeple. *Lord, thank you for putting this here for me.* That was silly, she thought. This church had probably been here for decades, and it wasn't put here for her. *You understand, Lord. I'm grateful.*

———

Keith and Patrol Officer Jerry Stine rolled up before the psychic's house in an unmarked car.

"Bill said his daughter reported the front door was unlocked," Keith said.

Jerry nodded. "You want me to go around back?"

"Yeah. We've been here before. You know the layout."

They got out of the vehicle, and Jerry faded into the darkness as he reached the corner of the building. Keith pulled in a deep breath. The thrift shop to the right was dark, but lights shone from several of Karen Potter's windows.

He went up the walkway and tried the knob. The door swung open. At least four hours had passed since Campbell was here, but they couldn't take anything for granted. He drew his service weapon and called, "Police. Anyone home?"

The echoes of his voice floated back to him, followed by eerie silence. Keith walked quietly to the parlor's doorway and looked in at the body lying on the rug.

At the sound of footsteps, he turned toward the doorway with his gun ready. Jerry stepped into sight. "Back's unlocked, too, Detective."

Keith nodded. "Call it in and ask for a backup radio car. We'll need a couple officers."

He knelt by the inert woman. Before he even placed his fingers on the victim's throat, he knew she was dead.

He looked over his shoulder. "She's dead, Jerry. We need to clear the rest of the house."

"Right." Jerry quickly relayed the information. Gun drawn, he headed for the next room.

Keith's cell phone whirred, and he glanced at the screen. His pulse kicked up a notch when he saw Bill McBride's name.

"Yeah, Bill?"

"I've got Campbell, out at the church on 94. She's okay."

One of several heavy weights lifted from Keith's chest. "Thanks. Anything I need to know right away?"

"No. I'm taking her home. We've got the pillowcase the assailant put over her head."

"Good. It'll probably be tomorrow before I can talk to you, but we found the scene as she described it."

"Clear," came Jerry's muffled voice from the back of the house.

"Karen Potter's dead, then?" Bill asked.

"Yeah. I sorry Campbell had to see this. Are you sure she's all right?"

"She's a little shook up, but she's handling it well."

"Okay. I'll come around in the morning." Keith stuck his

phone in his pocket and headed into the hallway. This case was bad enough without the woman he cared about being in the middle of it. She was safe now, and that was a huge relief.

Jerry came to the door of the kitchen and nodded. Keith went up the stairs.

"Police. Show yourself," he cried at the doorway on the left. No answer. He raised his gun, took a breath and looked inside. Bathroom. No one in the shower. He turned across the landing to a closed door. A dim light glowed at the threshold. "Police. Come out with your hands up."

Again, there was no sound.

He stood to one side and cautiously turned the knob. The door opened at his push. He swung into the space with his gun at the ready. A lamp on the bedside table bathed the room in soft light. Blue splotches flashed on the wall as the patrol car arrived outside, casting the scene in unreality. He checked the closet and looked under the bed then turned to the doorway. "Clear."

———

"Keith found the body you saw," Bill told Campbell as she buckled and adjusted her seat belt in his car.

"I guess there was no hope I'd dreamed it." She gazed at him bleakly in the glow from the spotlights aimed above at the steeple.

"Afraid not. You were right—Karen is dead."

"Did he say how?" She couldn't get the bloody scene out of her mind. "Was she shot?"

"No, he didn't say much."

Campbell breathed out a deep breath.

"Any thoughts at all on the person who attacked you?"

"It sure seemed like a man. He was taller than me, and so strong." She shuddered and touched the sore area on her neck.

"Would you have recognized Sam Truman?"

She shrugged. "I haven't ever actually seen him."

"You've seen his picture."

"But I didn't see this guy's face."

"Right." Bill put the gearshift in Drive and swung around the parking lot in a wide arc then eased toward the road.

Campbell leaned back against the headrest and closed her eyes. Her dad tended to his driving for a moment, heading them back toward Murray. "You sure you're okay?"

"Yeah. Are you going to stop by Karen's house?"

"Keith and his team are there. They'll handle it. We'd do best to keep out of their way."

She accepted that. Keith was very efficient and skilled at his job. Because of their close connection to the case, she was sure he'd keep her and her father updated.

"So, you'd called me several times before I answered?" she asked.

"Yes. I was worried sick when I got home and you weren't there. I should have called Nick."

"It's not Nick's fault. I made the decision to go in there on my own."

"He should have been with you."

The anger in her father's voice surprised her. He sounded as if he was ready to strangle Nick. And she'd thought Nick was the golden boy in her dad's eyes. But then, people could get mad at their kids too.

"It's really not his fault. When he said he didn't want to come, I should have called you or Keith."

Her dad's lips twisted. "Well, least said soonest mended. Lesson learned, right?"

"Right. I won't make that mistake again." He flicked her a glance, and she added, "I promise."

They passed the advertisement made up of a pontoon boat floating in the air on posts.

"Dad, this doesn't seem like Sam Truman's M.O. to me. What do you think?"

"I don't know. He kidnapped Karen last night and left her in an isolated place. Didn't she tell you he just wanted her out of the way for a while?"

"Yeah, but he restrained her. Whoever took me tonight didn't duct tape me. And he left my phone, so I could call for help. I think he just wanted to slow me down. Maybe give him time to run away before I contacted anyone. And he didn't let me see him, so I can't identify him." She huffed out a breath in frustration.

"He killed someone this time, though."

"That's another point. If Sam wanted to kill Karen, why didn't he do it when he kidnapped her? Why leave her taped up in a place where she'd be found alive?"

"I don't know, kiddo. Tell me about the body. Do you think she was strangled?"

"No. There was a lot of blood. It seemed to have come from her abdomen."

"Stabbed? Shot?"

"I don't know. I didn't have time to get details. I was going to call 911, but I was sure she was dead, so I decided to call Keith instead. I was still kneeling, holding my phone, when someone grabbed me."

"You said you thought he was taller than you. How could you tell?"

She scrunched her eyes nearly shut as they bumped over the railroad tracks. "I ... I think when he pulled me backward, I managed to get to my feet."

"Honey, think. Did you see his hands? His arms? His feet, even."

Slowly she shook her head. "Afraid not." She gave him a sheepish smile. "I'm a lousy witness, aren't I?"

He smiled. "I'm surprised you didn't say 'am I not.' But you're the best kind of witness there is, sweetheart. A live witness."

Her chest ached as she inhaled. "Yeah. I'm thankful for that."

15

The next morning, Campbell opened her eyes to find sunlight flooding her new bedroom. She reached for the alarm clock, turned it toward her, and squinted. Eight forty. With a moan, she sat up.

"Dad, you let me oversleep," she said fifteen minutes later, standing in his office doorway.

"I thought you could use it. We got in pretty late last night." He sipped from his favorite mug.

"You made coffee."

"Rita did. Nick may have some in the other room too."

She closed her eyes for a few seconds. She'd all but forgotten Rita's existence. The housekeeper made herself nearly invisible on her working days, while Campbell and her dad came and went, and the house seemed to stay magically clean.

"Have you heard from Keith?" she asked.

"We talked briefly. He'd like to interview you, but I asked him to wait until ten."

"Thanks. I guess I could go to the police station."

"He's over on Second Street again this morning. He said he'd drop by later."

"Okay. So ... any news?"

"They picked up Sam Truman, finally, when he went back to his apartment early this morning. Keith interviewed him, but he plans an extended session with him today. He wasn't able to tell me anything Truman said, of course."

"Of course." Campbell found she was a bit disgruntled even though she knew Keith was just following standard procedure. Part of what she liked about him was his consistency in sticking to procedure. Doing the job right was important to Keith.

"Hey, listen," her dad said, "I was thinking it might be good for you to have a few sessions with a therapist."

"What?" She stared at him. Her father had never suggested such a thing before, and it made her feel slightly inadequate, as though he thought she was weak.

"You've seen a lot of bodies in the past few weeks, honey," he said gently.

"Dad, I'm fine."

"There's a reputable practice out of Paducah that has offices here in Murray—"

"Really, Dad. I'm okay. Talking to you about those things is as good as seeing a therapist. No, better."

"Well, thanks for your endorsement, but I'm not sure I'd be doing as well. I don't have the training, and—"

"Thanks, but no. You always tell me we can talk about anything."

"That's true. We can."

She nodded. "We had a good talk last night. If I feel like I need another dose, I'll come to you."

"Okay."

She plodded to the kitchen, still thinking about what her

father had said and trying not to resent it. He was just trying to take care of her. The washing machine chugged quietly in the adjoining laundry room, a comfortingly regular rhythm.

Rita was just removing a pan of muffins from the oven. She turned to set them on a hot mat on the counter and smiled at Campbell. "Good morning. Raisin and oat bran muffins, hot from the oven."

"Wow. Thanks, Rita. Join me?"

Rita glanced at the clock. "I might. But I'd like to dust and vacuum your room and change your bed this morning, if you don't mind."

"Mind? I feel like a princess when you clean my room." They'd never had a cleaning woman before. When her mother was alive, they couldn't afford one on Bill's salary as a police officer. Campbell wished her mom was still here with them for many reasons, but one was for the simple joy of the freedom she felt with Rita performing the mundane chores of housekeeping. And her father certainly enjoyed never having to vacuum his own office anymore.

Campbell filled two coffee mugs and took the creamer from the refrigerator while Rita tipped the hot muffins out of the pan onto a cooling rack. They sat down together at the table.

"Bill said you had a rough night." Rita chose a muffin and slid it onto a small plate.

"Yeah, you could say that. I woke up in a cemetery."

"That must have been terrifying."

"It was pretty scary all right." Campbell flipped a hot muffin onto her plate. "Rita, did you know the psychic, Miss Tryphenia?"

"I never met her. I know a couple of people who've gone to her for fun. How about you?"

"Keith's mother and I visited her a while ago. Angela had a reading." Campbell wasn't sure whether or not Rita had heard of the psychic's death, so she decided to change the subject. "Want butter?"

"No, thanks."

Campbell rose and selected a table knife from the drawer and returned with it and the butter dish, congratulating herself that she'd chosen the right drawer on the first try.

"I hope it doesn't take too long for this house to feel like home."

"The memories of Ms. Tyler will fade in time," Rita said. "I love the changes you've made."

"It helped a lot to paint and refurbish upstairs. It's a big house. Dad and I like having our sitting room upstairs in one of the rooms Kath—that woman never used."

"Right. Is the furniture up there mostly your father's old living room things?"

"Yeah. We bought new for the seating area in the big office. Figured it would give a better impression to clients. But his old set is comfortable, and I think he feels good having his own stuff around him."

Her father poked his head in from the hallway.

"I'm going to go meet with Hayden Nesmith."

Campbell frowned. "Didn't you just take a case for Dunn & McGann?"

"Yeah, but that one will wrap up within a week. And the police have got Sam Truman now, so that case for Mrs. Hill is pretty much over too. We'll meet with the Hills about it tomorrow, after things calm down a little. Maybe you can call Vera and set up an appointment?"

"Sure. What else do you want Nick and me to do today?"

"I've put Nick on looking deeper into the Walker family, but like I said, we probably won't do much more on that. You can look over the file I started on the case Barry gave us. It's marked *Fontaine*."

"Okay."

"Oh, and Nell Calhoun called to ask if it was okay to show the house this morning. I told her she might want to postpone it until we know for sure the police are done there."

"Want me to go over and see if it looks okay?" Campbell asked.

"Maybe I can swing by there after I meet with Hayden."

Campbell didn't reply, but she knew he was leery of sending her anywhere alone right now.

As he turned away, Rita rose and took her dishes to the dishwasher. "I'd better get to work."

"Thanks for making muffins, Rita. They're really good." Campbell considered eating another one and decided on a cup of yogurt instead. She carried it with a spoon and her coffee mug down the hall to the office.

"Well, hey, sleepyhead," Nick said.

"Morning."

"Bill said some ninja choked you and dropped you off in a graveyard."

Campbell set down her things and slid out her desk chair. "That about sums it up."

Nick leaned back, frowning. "Don't you think it's odd that someone got the jump on the psychic? I mean, how wacky is that?"

"Huh?" She stared blankly at him across the room.

"She should have seen it coming," Nick said.

It took a moment for that to soak in. "Oh, right. If she's psychic, she'd have known. Duh." Campbell shook her head at the tired joke. Sometimes Nick really acted like a junior high doofus. "So, what about you? Have you had any brilliant revelations this morning?"

"Well, I found out Sam Truman and Karen Potter were pretty close when they were kids."

"How close?"

Nick wiggled his eyebrows up and down. "Would you believe high school sweethearts?"

"I don't know. Should I?"

"Well, they first met when they were sent to the same foster home."

"Ouch." Campbell eyed him closely and decided he wasn't kidding. "And then?"

"They were only together in the same place for a few months. Then Karen was adopted. Later they reconnected when they went to the same high school."

"And started dating?"

Nick frowned. "It's not really clear yet. I've talked to one of Sam's teachers and two former students who knew them both. The consensus seems to be that Karen had a major crush on Sam, but he was a bit cool toward her. I'm going to try to dig up more classmates and see if I can get a better picture and then try to build a family tree for Libby Walker."

"You do that. Dad told me to take a look at the Fontaine file."

"Oh, and I checked one other thing," Nick said as she booted up her laptop. "Bill said whoever grabbed you last night used some special ops move to put you out."

Without thinking about it, Campbell touched her throat. "Well, I'm not sure. He choked me from behind. I'm just glad he let me go without finishing the job."

"Maybe he thought you were dead, hence the cemetery."

She shook her head. "If that were true, why would he cover my face with a pillowcase, and why did he leave my phone with me?"

Nick's face scrunched up. "Good point. Anyway, I checked Sam Truman for military service. Sure enough, he was in the Marines right after high school."

"Did he go to college? I'm wondering when he met Libby."

"No college. I don't know when they met. She didn't go to their high school."

Campbell opened her yogurt and pecked a few keys on the laptop, opening the electronic file on the Fontaine case. The law firm wanted True Blue to find a missing person. A wealthy landowner in the county had recently died, leaving his estate to his four children equally, but one had not been in touch with the family for more than five years. The will was written several years ago, and apparently this daughter no longer lives at the last known address the family gave Dunn & McGann.

Compared to the Truman case and the psychic's murder, it seemed pretty tame. Boring even. But she'd known a lot of P.I. work was humdrum, and this was something Dad had asked her to do. She finished her yogurt and went at it, connecting with the first of several websites her father had taught her to use when doing a trace.

She was soon immersed in the hunt. When her dad walked into the room, she was surprised to find she'd been at it for two hours.

"Hey." She threw him a big smile. "Guess what? I've found a legal name change for the woman we're trying to trace in the Fontaine case."

"Great."

"Why would someone do that and not tell their family?" Campbell asked.

"Lots of reasons. Probably the most common one is that she wants to distance herself from them. Make it harder for them to find her. She may have wanted to start a new life of her own, without being tied to them."

"Wow. That's a little depressing."

"It happens."

"So, what do we do now?"

"Confirm a new address for her under the new name."

"Then we contact her?" Campbell asked.

"No, this isn't the same as when we have a private client. We tell Dunn and McGann and let them contact her. She may not want anything to do with her family, even if it means giving up a legacy."

"I see. So, Dad, I'm practically an amateur, and I found this in two hours. Why didn't the law firm do it themselves?"

"We're fast, for one thing. We have access to sites people like her family wouldn't have. And people like Barry McGann have better things to do with a morning, so they outsource the grunt work. It's kind of like telling a secretary to take a letter, instead of typing it up yourself."

Keith Fuller appeared at the doorway and knocked on the jamb. "The sign on the front door said, 'Walk in,' so I did."

They all greeted him.

"I came to see if you're ready to give me a statement about what happened last night." He gazed directly at Campbell as he spoke.

She nodded. "Sure. Do you want me to go over to the police station?"

"No, we can do it here if you want. Unless you want a lawyer to sit in."

"I don't think I need one, but how about my dad?" She glanced at him.

Bill held up both hands. "Hey, if you want me, sure, but I have a ton of stuff to do. Lyman and Nesmith just dumped several cases on us, and I need to set up new files."

"Okay." Campbell rose. She had nothing to worry about in an interview with Keith, she was sure, although she couldn't help a few nervous flutters. She didn't like the idea of being the one questioned. In her job with her dad, they were usually the ones doing the asking.

Keith smiled. "I've asked Officer Mills to meet me here."

She felt more at ease. Denise Mills was a smart, no-nonsense Calloway County native, and she was rapidly making her mark as an excellent patrol officer.

"Sure. Let's get some coffee while we wait, and then we can go up to our sitting room. It's quiet up there." She'd vaguely registered the vacuum cleaner running overhead an hour or so ago, and she figured Rita was finished upstairs.

"Great."

Her father said, "When you're done, why don't we have a general debriefing? I'm sure Nick has a few things to tell you."

Nick looked up. "Yeah, I'm working on Sam Truman's past."

"Sounds good." Keith headed for the single-serve coffee maker, and Bill went toward his private office.

Denise brought a tape recorder for their session. She declined coffee, and Campbell took her and Keith up to the cozy room she and Bill used for a living room.

"Oh, is that your mom?" Denise homed in on a framed eight-by-ten on the bookcase.

"Yeah, that's from a camping trip we took near Pilot Knob when I was about eight." Campbell's heart squeezed as she gazed at herself, grinning with her hair in braids, and her mother encircling her with a loving arm as she smiled at the cameraman, her husband. "I told Dad we needed some pleasant memories on display when we moved here. Without a little brightening up, this house would look pretty grim."

"Well, your mother was lovely." Denise glanced around the room. "And this looks nice and homey. You did a good job of decorating."

"Thanks." Campbell had shelved several hundred of her own books here and added a few antiques from Trends and Treasures. They'd found a few more things they both liked, including a lamp and a beautiful old walnut coffee table, in the house's attic.

Their tribute to the former owner was a framed poster of one of Katherine Tyler's book covers. The author's niece had taken several others but had given this one to Campbell. It had formerly hung downstairs in what was now Bill's office. Campbell loved the artwork that graced the cover of the novel *You'll Be Sorry*. The scene of a placid Kentucky farm at sunset was gorgeous, but a sinister figure lurking near the barn always made her shiver.

"Have a seat," she said. "I'll get that pillowcase from my room."

When she returned holding the pillow slip that had blinded her the night before between her thumb and index fingers, Denise held out a large plastic evidence bag, and Campbell dropped it in. She forced a smile and planted herself on the sofa. Keith took Bill's recliner, and Denise perched beside Campbell and set up the recorder on the coffee table.

After giving the time and their names for the recording, Keith smiled at her. "Just tell me what happened last night, Campbell. Take your time."

"To start with, I was terrified. First there was the shock of finding Karen dead. Then I realized someone was behind me, and I wondered if I was next. He was choking me, and ... and I thought he'd kill me." She put her hand to her throat. "And I ... I guess I blacked out."

"Scary," Denise murmured.

Keith's eyes brimmed with sympathy. "I'm so sorry you had to go through that." He cleared his throat. "When you're ready, tell me about when you woke up—when you became aware of your surroundings."

She'd gone over and over the sequence of events in her mind countless times, and she laid it out for Keith and Denise.

When she'd finished, he asked her to give more detail on a couple of points.

"I think that does it," he said at last. "If I have any more questions, I'll call you or come by."

Campbell nodded. "Keith, how was she killed? There was a lot of blood."

"We won't know for sure until we get the autopsy report."

"I figure she was either stabbed or shot."

"You know I can't tell you much," Keith said. "The medical examiner said he didn't think she was shot."

"Stabbed then."

He said nothing, and she took that as a tacit agreement.

"Do you want to go downstairs now and talk to Nick?" she asked. "I don't want him to come up here and leave no one in the main office downstairs, in case someone walks in."

"Sure."

Campbell stood. "Keith, I asked Dad, and I'll ask you. If that was someone other than Sam Truman who kidnapped me last night, why didn't he just kill me, the way he did Karen?"

After a moment's pause, Keith shook his head. "All I can think of is that whoever attacked you had a beef with Karen, not with you."

"Do you think it's possible that the person who killed her isn't the same one who attacked me?"

"At this point, I'm open to anything. I try not to jump to conclusions that don't have evidence to back them up."

The three of them went down and joined Nick in the fireplace area. Her father ambled in and took a seat.

"So, what have you learned, Nick?" Keith asked.

Nick stretched out his long legs. "While y'all were upstairs, I was able to get hold of one of Karen Potter's classmates. She sat next to Karen in homeroom during their senior year."

"And?"

"Sam Truman was a year ahead of them, and he'd already graduated and enlisted in the Marine Corps. This gal didn't keep touch with Karen after graduation, but during that school year, Karen was definitely pining for Sam and thinking they'd get married once his hitch was up."

"Odd," Keith said. "I talked to Sam this morning, and he said he'd never made plans to marry Karen Potter. They did date a few times before he left school, but he said she was too intense. She was clingy, and she wanted to move things along faster than he did—as far as cementing their relationship, I mean."

"Going into the Marines was a good excuse to get away from her for a few years, I guess," Campbell said.

Keith let out a little sigh. "Sam insists he didn't kill Karen, but when they started dating, he says she practically begged for his class ring."

"Yeah, her classmate said she was obsessed with him." Nick nodded as if that settled everything.

Campbell frowned. "As a foster child, I'm surprised Sam could afford a class ring."

"According to him, he had after-school jobs and saved his money." Keith shrugged.

"He was probably already running his cons," Nick said. "I'll bet he stole kids' lunch money in primary school."

"Easy, Nick," Bill said. "Let's not make assumptions."

Campbell was glad her dad had stepped in, or she might have said something much harsher. She turned to Keith. "Am I allowed to know what he said about last night?"

"At first he wouldn't admit he had anything to do with it. He did admit he snatched Karen two nights ago, and that he put her in Bill's old house yesterday morning. He couldn't get around that—we found his prints on the duct tape, and his car matched the description the next-door neighbor gave us."

"So, why did he kidnap her?"

"Like Karen told you," Keith said, "he claims he just wanted her out of the way for the day, so he could tie up some loose ends before he left Murray."

"That seems extreme." Campbell pushed back a lock of hair. "Why was he leaving town? Dorothy thought they'd go house hunting together."

"Sounds like a repeat of his relationship with Karen in high school," Nick noted.

"He wouldn't say, other than he was done with his business here." Keith hesitated. "I have ideas of my own. We'd been going around talking to a lot of his investors, and so had you and Bill."

"Yeah, we have," Campbell said. "So, even though we never came face to face with him, he knew someone was digging into his little scheme."

"I'm afraid so. One of the clients probably told him."

Denise spoke up for the first time. "He's been acting the way typical con artists do—stringing people along and never delivering."

"But he did marry Libby Walker," Campbell pointed out.

"Which turned out to be a mistake." Nick nodded sagely.

Campbell wasn't convinced everything was as cut-and-dried as he supposed. "Maybe *she* made the mistake marrying him. She was the one who had to file a restraining order, remember?"

"I'm sure there's more to the story that we don't know yet," Keith said. "The Walker family was from the same general area as where Sam and Karen grew up, but not the same school district. They lived maybe forty or fifty miles apart. I'm not sure yet how Sam met Libby."

"I think he met her right after he was discharged from the

Marines," Nick said. "Or maybe even before that—when he was home on one of his leaves."

"But not before he enlisted?"

"I don't think so." Nick's lips twitched. "If Karen expected him to come home and present her with an engagement ring, she got a rude awakening."

"There's something that still bothers me," Bill said, and they all looked at him. "The police in Missouri thought Sam killed Libby, but they couldn't prove it."

"Well, the evidence was inconclusive," Keith said. "They couldn't say for sure that it was murder, and he was never charged."

"But Karen Potter said Sam thinks she killed Libby. So why didn't he go to the police with that?"

"It's been ten years," Campbell mused. "He's had plenty of time to accuse her."

"He probably didn't have proof either." Keith leaned back with a sigh. "Both Sam and Karen claimed they didn't kill Libby."

"That doesn't mean they're both telling the truth," Denise said.

"Good point." Keith gave her a little nod. "And if not one of them, then who?"

16

"We've still got people at the crime scene," Keith said. "We know Sam's been in that house, but we can't prove it was last night."

Campbell was well aware of the shortcomings of forensic science. She made a face. "On TV, they always see a unique tattoo on the assailant's arm, or they find a piece of a rare plant that only grows near his house."

Keith laughed. "I guess you know by now that it doesn't happen that way."

"I sure do. Did you find a weapon?"

"That's something I shouldn't talk about."

"Okay. But when you *can* talk about it, I'd like to know."

Keith leaned toward her and touched her hand. "We'll get to the bottom of this, Campbell."

She didn't answer.

He stood, and Denise followed his lead. Bill sprang to his feet.

"Thanks for coming, Keith. You too, Denise. I'll walk you out."

Keith gave Campbell a wistful look. "I'll call you tonight."

She nodded.

"You don't look happy, Professor," Nick said as the others left the room.

She couldn't help the thoughts swirling round and round in her brain. "What if they don't find out who did it—any of it?"

Nick sat still for a moment then met her gaze. "Remember when we were looking for your father?"

"Yeah."

"You felt that way then. Truth is, so did I. I couldn't stop thinking, *What happens if we never find Bill?* But we shouldn't be feeling that way now. We've already learned a lot. We should be saying, *What can we do right now, today, that will shed more light on all this?*"

She breathed in and then out. "Okay, what can I do right now? Do we have a suspect list?"

"Get some paper."

She went to the tray where they put used copy paper for recycling and took a sheet. As she took a pen from her desk, she heard her father go back to his office and close the door. She went to Nick's desk and sat down at one end.

"Okay, who do you think killed Libby Walker Truman?" Nick asked.

"Sam. They were separated, and she'd filed a restraining order."

"Write him down."

She scrawled *Libby Truman's murder* at the top, and *Sam* beneath it.

"Now, who else?"

"Who do you think did it?"

"Karen Potter."

She wrote it down. "They both say they didn't."

"Yeah. So, who else?" Nick's dark eyes dared her to come up with another name.

"I don't know. I don't know who she hung around with over there, or who she may have had problems with."

"Her brother's been over here, chasing Sam. Do you think it's because he thinks Sam killed her?"

"Maybe."

"There are other siblings in the Walker family."

She looked up in surprise. "How many?"

"Two sisters."

"Huh. I can't see sisters killing her. She probably had a job, though, so there'd be bosses and coworkers. We can't get a good picture of her life and the people she interacted with from this far away."

"Do you think we should go to Missouri?" Nick asked.

"Not really. Dad would probably say it's a waste of money. I'd rather concentrate on Karen Potter's murder."

"Sam," Nick said.

Campbell started a new column called *Karen Potter's murder* and put Sam's name at the top. "How about a disgruntled client?"

"Sure. How about another psychic?"

She blinked at him. "Do you know of another one in town?"

"There's someone else doing business in the county. If you look at a bigger town, like, say, Paducah, there's probably several."

"But some people we know are connected to her," Campbell said. "That's the trouble, isn't it? We don't know many of her connections."

"We know a few of her regular customers. Write them down. If we ask them all how they learned about Miss Tryphenia, they may give us the names of more. Let's try to talk to as many as we can."

Campbell wrote Louanne Vane, Mary Willingham, and Sarah Delisle's names. "We could work on it for weeks and get nowhere."

"That's true. And remember, the police are working on it too."

"Yeah. With Dad bringing in a lot of new cases, we probably can't afford to spend much unpaid time on Karen's death."

"You may be right."

She glanced at the time. "That reminds me—Dad asked me to set up an appointment with the Hills tomorrow, to wrap things up with them. I forgot earlier, so I'd better do that now. Then I'm supposed to confirm that address in the Fontaine case."

She pulled the extra chair away from Nick's desk and went back to her own with dissatisfaction eating at her. It didn't feel right to walk away from investigating Karen's death and do these mundane tasks. Didn't Karen deserve justice?

"Dad might prefer that we just work on the new stuff the lawyers gave him," she said. "We'd better clear this with him."

"Clear what with me?" Bill asked from the doorway.

"Oh, revisiting all the people we know were clients of Miss Tryph—Karen Potter, and trying to expand the list." She held out the paper in her hand and pointed to the three she'd listed.

"Hmm." He squinted at it. "You've talked to Mrs. Willingham's daughter, but have you actually met Mary?"

"You're right. We haven't talked to her personally. I guess I didn't want to upset her."

"Well, if she hasn't already heard that Karen Potter is dead, she will soon. That in itself will probably upset her. I think she'd be willing to talk to you."

"Should we pay her a visit?"

Bill nodded. "I think it's time. But I should get started on the work Hayden Nesmith gave us. You and Nick could go together." He shot Nick a glance.

"Okay by me." Nick pushed back his chair.

Bill's focus returned to his daughter. "Oh, and I called Barry with the information you got on the Fontaine case. He was very pleased with the quick turnaround."

"I'm glad." The praise boosted her flagging confidence. "Anything special we should ask Mrs. Willingham?"

"Tread softly. She probably hasn't heard about Miss Tryphenia's death yet. But see if she had any further contact with her after her daughter blasted the psychic."

"Right." Campbell reached for her purse. The desk phone rang. She glanced at her dad and reached for the receiver. "True Blue Investigations. Campbell McBride speaking."

"Oh, Campbell, sugar, it's Louanne. I just heard about Miss Tryphenia. Did you know?"

"Uh, yes." Campbell met her father's gaze. "I did know that she died, Miss Louanne," she said distinctly, for his and Nick's benefit.

"Sugar, I'm so upset. Could you come over? I need someone to talk to. Even Blue Boy is nervous. Maybe have some tea?"

"Um, hold on a second, Miss Louanne."

She pushed the mute button on the phone base. "She wants me to go have tea with her."

Bill considered for only a second. "Go. Take Nick with you, though, and don't stay too long. Calm her down, see if she knows anything. Then go to Mary Willingham's."

Campbell nodded and pushed the button. "Miss Louanne? I can come over now. Is it all right if I bring a guest?"

"That handsome detective?"

Barely able to hold back a laugh, Campbell said, "No, I meant my coworker, Nick Emerson. Have you met him?"

"I don't think so."

"Well, he's a nice-looking boy too. And he *loves* cats." She speared Nick with a meaningful gaze as she spoke.

Nick returned an expression that screamed his incredulity.

"All right," Campbell said cheerfully into the phone, "Put the kettle on. We'll be right over."

As she hung up, her father laughed, but Nick shoved his hands to his hips and scowled at her. "Since when do I love cats?"

"It seemed like a good way to get her to accept you. Do you hate cats?"

"Hate is a very strong word."

Bill said sternly. "You'd better play nice with Blue Boy."

Nick swallowed hard. "Yes, sir."

It always amazed Campbell how subservient Nick acted toward her father. She glanced back and forth between them.

"Sorry. You're not allergic to them or anything, are you?"

"Don't worry. I'd have told you if I was." Nick sighed and stuck his phone in his pocket. "Your car or mine?"

Bill strolled toward the coffeemaker. "Hey, she said you were good-looking. Don't knock it."

―――――

"I'm all aflutter." Miss Louanne's hands shook as she set down a tray with three fogged glasses. Instead of a hot teapot, as Campbell had for some reason expected, she'd presented iced tea.

The hostess handed a glass to Campbell and one to Nick, then sat down with a big whoosh of a sigh.

"I had an appointment scheduled with her for Monday afternoon." The old woman took a gulp from her glass.

"Did you see her this week?" Campbell asked.

"No, I only go every two weeks."

"That's right."

Nick sat on the other end of the couch, while Blue Boy occupied his usual chair. The cat opened one eye and observed them for a moment, then closed it again. Nick glanced at Campbell, and his lips twitched. She imagined he was glad the large cat hadn't sashayed over and jumped into his lap. She'd told him how antisocial Blue Boy could be—in fact, she was surprised he'd stayed in the room when she and Nick entered.

"How did you hear about Miss Tryphenia dying?" Campbell asked.

Tears glistened in Miss Louanne's eyes. "Vera Hill called me and said it was on the early news. She didn't have any details." The old woman gazed at her bleakly. "You said you knew ..."

"Yes." Campbell cleared her throat, trying to decide how much to tell her.

"We saw Detective Fuller this morning," Nick said.

Campbell was grateful for his atypical tact. "Yes. He was at the house earlier."

"And he told you about it?" Miss Louanne asked eagerly.

"We spoke about Miss Tryphenia, yes." Campbell felt guilty not revealing more. How much had the police told the reporters? Would it come out that she was the one who'd discovered the body?

"When was the last time you spoke to her?" Nick asked Mrs. Vane.

"At my last reading. I was so looking forward to Monday. I wanted to tell her about Blue Boy getting out and ask her if I should be afraid that burglar will come back."

"I'm pretty sure the police have him in custody now," Campbell said.

Miss Louanne caught her breath. "They arrested him for breaking in here? I'm so glad. I knew they had his fingerprints, but I didn't think they'd caught him." She looked at the lethargic cat. "You hear that, Blue Boy? That bad man is behind bars for what he did to us."

Campbell shot Nick a helpless glance.

"Do you know his name?" Miss Louanne asked. "Because a man was here yesterday, asking if I had a good retirement plan, and it made me think of that criminal who broke in here and went through my mortgage statement."

"Uh ... what did he look like?" Campbell asked.

Nick took out his cell phone, tapped it a few times, and held it out to their hostess. "Did the man who came by yesterday look like this?"

As he passed the phone, Campbell saw that he'd brought up a photo of Sam Truman's Missouri driver's license.

"Yes, that's him!" Miss Louanne squinted behind her bifocals. "Hmm, Truman. Like the former President, when I was a little girl."

"That man is the one the police think broke in here and let your cat out," Nick said.

"Oh, my. And he came back yesterday."

"They arrested him last night," Campbell said. "You don't need to worry about him coming back here."

"Did you let him in the house yesterday?" Nick asked.

"No. I didn't trust the man. I told him I was all set with my Social Security and my retirement fund. I sent him on his way." She gave a firm nod.

Campbell wondered if she'd given the con man more information than was wise. Sam had been scouting for a retiree with a fat IRA and a nest egg, she was sure. The fact that Miss Louanne's children were scattered, with none close by to look after her finances, would have been a plus.

"Miss Louanne, I think we ought to let the police know this man was here again yesterday," Campbell said carefully. "They've heard he was going around talking to some people and trying to get money from them. If you tell them about your encounter, it might help them piece things together."

"Oh, if you think it would help." Miss Louanne looked a bit flustered and pink in the face. "I'm always happy to help our local police."

"Would you mind if I called Detective Fuller now?"

"No, go ahead."

"All right. Excuse me." Campbell stepped out into the entry and called Keith's number. He answered right away. Quickly, she told him she and Nick were at Mrs. Vane's house and that Sam Truman had approached her the day before.

"That was brazen of him," Keith said.

"I thought so too. Do you want to interview her? She's very impressed with your work."

"I'm tied up right now, but I could send Officer Mills over."

Campbell felt a surge of relief. Denise Mills would get along just fine with Miss Louanne. "Great. Should we stay with her until Denise gets here?"

"If you can. I'll send her right away."

"Oh, and she knows Miss Tryphenia's dead," Campbell said. "That's why she asked me to come over. I told her I knew already, but not *how* I knew, if you get my drift."

"Right. I'll tell Denise to soft pedal the details if she starts asking about her favorite psychic."

17

C ampbell followed GPS directions to Mary Willingham's address in an upscale Murray neighborhood.

"Nice house." She pulled into the driveway and parked in front of the double garage.

"They built it before her husband retired," Nick said.

Campbell arched her eyebrows at him.

"I had a chat with Vera. She said it was the Willinghams' dream home. But then her husband died after just three or four years of retirement."

"So sad."

"Yeah." Nick looked up at the stately stone house. "They didn't have long to enjoy it together."

"How long ago did he die?"

"A couple of years. By the look of things, she has enough dough to enjoy an occasional visit to a psychic."

"You heard Nicole," Campbell said. "The money she spent at Miss Tryphenia's was a lot more than most older women spend on their leisure pastimes."

"She didn't say how much."

"Vera Hill said Mary gave the psychic three thousand or so altogether—that she knew of."

"I guess it could have been more. If her friends disapproved, she might have stopped telling them." Nick opened his car door.

"Yes, and Vera did say Mary had to dip into her savings to pay her bills."

Campbell got out and walked to the door with Nick. The silver-haired woman who opened it eyed them with interest but a hint of caution.

"May I help you?"

"Mrs. Willingham, my name is Campbell McBride, and this is Nick Emerson. We're private investigators. We were concerned about you because we know you're a client of Miss Tryphenia's—that is, Karen Potter's."

The woman was frowning now. "I'm sorry, what concern is that of yours?"

Nick seemed content to let Campbell take the lead, so she plunged on. "Miss Tryphenia died last night, and we thought you might be able to help us get a better picture of her relationship to her customers. We're contacting several of her clients."

"Well, I ..." She opened the door wider. "Of course. Please come in."

She led them to a spacious living room with floor-to-ceiling windows looking out on a large back yard bordered by trees.

"Please, sit down." She perched in a wing chair and gazed at Campbell with troubled hazel eyes. "I had no idea she was dead. Do you know how it happened?"

"She was killed," Nick said. "The police are handling it."

"Heavens."

"I'm sorry for your loss." Campbell wished she'd handled

the introduction and breaking the news more gently, but it was too late to worry about that now. "I understand you'd been a client for some time."

"Well, a year or so. My husband died, and I ..." She let it trail off and pulled in a shaky breath. "I enjoyed my visits with her, and she ... she was able to advise me on some personal matters."

"Did she give you good advice?" Campbell asked.

"I thought so."

"May I ask you what sort of problems she advised you on? If you feel comfortable sharing, that is. We're trying to understand how she helped people."

"Well, after Leon died, I felt very alone. I suppose I was depressed. The first time I went to Miss Tryphenia, it was to see if she could help me with—I don't know—some closure, I guess."

"Was she able to do that?"

"Yes. She talked to me at length and had me tell her some of my good memories of Leon. That in itself was satisfying. My children don't want to sit and listen to their mother ramble."

Campbell smiled. "I've lost my mother, and I find that it's helpful if my dad and I talk about her frequently."

"Yes, it's so true. I mean, there were some hard times, and our marriage wasn't perfect, but with Miss Tryphenia's help, I saw that the unpleasant things don't really matter. I try to look back on the happy times now, and I think about Leon's good points—how he took care of the family, how he was there for me when I had surgery, how he taught Danny to play ball, how his eyes would light up every time I made pecan pies."

"And after a while, you started sharing other things with Miss Tryphenia? Things that worried you?"

Mrs. Willingham waved a hand through the air. "Oh, well, you know. Kids. You think once they're grown your worries are over, but they're not. My girls seem to have good husbands and a fairly peaceful life, and they gave me three lovely grandchildren. But Danny!"

"He's your only son?"

"Yes." She huffed out a quick sigh. "He's divorced, and that was very sad. His ex-wife took up with a musician. That was a decade ago, though. He came home and stayed with me and Leon for a while after she left him. But then he started dating again. He moved out. Wanted his own place—and his privacy, I suppose. And his employer transferred him down to Tennessee."

"This was before Leon died?"

She nodded. "Danny didn't introduce me to most of his girlfriends, but I think there were several. And then Chrissy came along."

"Chrissy troubles you?"

"You have no idea."

Campbell glanced sidelong at Nick, but he seemed content to sit back and listen.

"She's not good for him," Mrs. Willingham continued. "I can't say for sure, but it seems like he drinks more since he started dating her. I know he lost his job with UPS. I don't know what happened—he wouldn't tell me. But he came to me asking for money. That's how I found out he was out of work." She shook her head. "He says he's working on a construction crew now, but I'm not sure what to believe. And there was some mix-up with the police."

"Police?" Campbell asked softly.

Mrs. Willingham waved a hand. "I don't know the details. He was upset I even knew he'd had trouble, but his sister told me. Anyway, apparently that's been cleared up."

After a pause, Campbell said, "Tell me more about Chrissy."

"Oh, she's a nail girl. Fingernails, you know. She does manicures at a hair salon. Some career, eh? But she's moved in with Danny. Maybe she's helping him pay the rent, I don't know, but I made it clear that I couldn't support him now. He's forty-four years old, for pity's sake."

Campbell schooled her expression. Mrs. Willingham's disdain made her feel sorry for Chrissy. "And when you told Miss Tryphenia all this, what did she do?"

"She encouraged me to think of the good things again—the good things about Danny. She showed me how to channel positive thoughts and energy toward him. She said it would help him make better choices."

"Did she give you any objects to help with that?"

"Well, I get candles from her. I tried incense, but I don't like it." She wrinkled her nose. "It gives me a headache."

"What about ... prayer cards or charms?" Campbell asked.

"Yes, she's in favor of those."

"But you pay her for them."

"Oh, yes." Mrs. Willingham smiled. "I don't mind paying her. She's helped me get past all the negative energy and focus on a bright future."

"On hope," Campbell said, recalling what her father had told her about psychics.

"Exactly. I meditate on Danny's best nature and hope for a good future."

Nick leaned forward, his lips pursed as though he wanted to say something. Campbell nodded at him.

"Where does Chrissy fit into all that? With the psychic, I mean."

Their hostess's face clouded. "I really don't like Chrissy."

"You've met her, then?" Campbell asked in surprise.

"A couple of months ago. She's the first woman Danny's introduced to me, but I gather they've been together for more than a year. Miss Tryphenia said she could sense darkness and bad energy around me when I talked about Chrissy."

"Did she recommend that you do anything about that?"

"Nothing negative to Chrissy, if that's what you mean. Just an increase in positive thinking for myself and for Danny, to build up the potential in him and my own serenity."

"How exactly do you do that?" Campbell asked.

"I pray, I meditate, I burn the candles and send positive thoughts toward Danny. And she gets a special tea for me that calms me if I'm feeling uneasy."

Nick shot Campbell a glance and said, "What's in it?"

Mrs. Willingham smiled. "Just herbs. Soothing blends. Chamomile and things like that. I looked it up online, and it's all perfectly safe. A little lemon and mint." She looked up with a sharpness of anxiety on her features. "You said she was killed. May I ask how?"

Afraid Nick would give away more than they should, Campbell said quickly, "The police say someone killed her in her house. I expect it will be on the evening news. Again, I'm very sorry."

The older woman spread her hands. "Incredible. She was such a nice person. Who would want to kill her?"

"Some people didn't like her as much as you do," Nick said.

Campbell wished they were sitting closer, so she could jab him with an elbow. The last thing she wanted was for Mrs. Willingham to think they suspected her daughter of foul play.

"That's true. Frankly, my daughter Nicole said she was a fraud. I couldn't make her understand how wrong she was. She wouldn't let me keep my last appointment with her. In fact, she said she was going to go see her and tell her to leave me alone."

The sadness in her expression made Campbell feel

sympathy for her. She reached over and pressed Mrs. Willingham's hand.

"I'm sure Nicole thought she was only looking out for you."

"Yes, I suppose so."

"She may have felt you were wasting money that you'd need later," Nick said.

Campbell wished he hadn't said it, but she appreciated the gentle tone he used.

"She did, but I felt it was money well spent. It eased my mind, much more than a tense discussion with Nicole would do. I've had to exercise some positive energy on my thoughts of her too. And I called Miss Tryphenia the next day and rescheduled. But now, I guess I won't see her again."

They sat for a moment in silence. Campbell considered asking to see the tea bags, candles, and other items purchased from the psychic, but she was sure they'd be the same as some of those she'd seen in Karen Potter's house. She really couldn't think of any more useful information she could glean here.

She took a business card from her purse. "Thank you for speaking with us. Here's my business card. It has my phone number on it, and you're welcome to call me at True Blue Investigations anytime."

Once they were back in her car, Nick said, "I don't think she regrets a penny of it."

"Neither do I." Campbell grimaced. "I was afraid you were going to push her too far and upset her."

"Sometimes you have to nudge the client a little, if you want to learn something worthwhile."

"Did we really accomplish anything here?" Campbell started the engine.

"I think so. We learned how much she hates the girlfriend."

"So? Lots of mothers dislike their sons' girlfriends. Mary

didn't do anything against Chrissy that we know of. She's into positive energy for Danny, not malevolence toward Chrissy."

"As far as we know," Nick said. "But people get emotional about that stuff. Some people get more upset about money than their loved ones' unhealthy relationships. Like the daughter. What her mom's spending with the psychic was enough to make Nicole take action. She's probably thinking her inheritance is being squandered. But Mary seems a lot more passive. Drink soothing tea, pray, think good thoughts. Nicole, on the other hand, is one to rant and yell at people."

"Are you saying you think Mary's daughter may have gone back to Karen's house and killed her?"

"No, but ... keep an open mind, okay?"

———

"Come on, Sam. You're holding back. What aren't you telling me?" Keith held Sam Truman's gaze across the table in the interview room.

"I didn't kill Karen."

"Tell me something new."

"Look, if I'd wanted to kill her, I'd have done it sooner. I wouldn't have taken her to that empty house."

"That ploy didn't work," Keith said. "I think you got tired of her not cooperating."

"I just wanted to tie up a few things before I left town. Karen's been known to interfere with my plans in the past. I was just making sure on Wednesday that she didn't put a monkey wrench in things."

"What things? Did she know something about you that you didn't want her to make known?"

Sam pressed his lips together and said nothing.

"Tell me about your plans for that day," Keith said. "You

wanted to tie up loose ends. What kind of loose ends? We know you went to visit several people and asked them to invest money with you. Some were already investors, and you asked for more. Others were potential investors you hoped to bring into the fund."

Sam looked away. "I admit, I needed some cash before I— for the business trip I was planning."

"Business trip. Look, we know you'd already collected north of forty thousand dollars from people in Calloway County over the last six weeks. How much more did you need?"

The suspect still didn't respond.

Keith shook his head. "You've been charged with breaking and entering at two houses—Louanne Vane's and Bill McBride's. That of itself will bring you several months in jail. The kidnapping charge is more serious, and now it seems you've kidnapped not one, but two women. Campbell McBride gave me her statement. Don't think you'll get away with assaulting her and transporting her to a different location."

"I didn't hurt her."

Was Truman admitting to kidnapping Campbell? Keith didn't want the suspect to clam up now.

"Okay, so you didn't hurt Ms. McBride. The bruises on her neck say otherwise."

Truman blinked a couple of times. "I'm not a killer. If she has bruises, I'm sorry."

"Oh, you're sorry. Tell that to the judge and see what it gets you, especially if your victims' doctors testify that they had concussions, or that they were in mortal danger."

"I didn't hurt Karen either."

"Really? How did you get her to let you duct-tape her hands and ankles? How did you get her to that vacant house? She's dead now, Sam. You need to own up to what you did."

"I didn't kill her," he shouted.

Keith said nothing, and Truman shrank back in his chair as far as the shackles that kept his hands fastened to the table would allow.

"I'm sorry Karen's dead, but I didn't do it." His voice was quieter now, full of fatigue.

"Who did?" Keith asked.

"If I knew, I'd tell you."

"Still think Karen killed Libby?"

Sam's head jerked up. "Yeah, I do."

"Why?"

"She was jealous."

"No, I mean why do you think that? We know Karen was your girlfriend before you went in the military, and that she thought you and she would get married. What makes you think she killed your wife?"

"Things she said back then. She threatened my wife, and she—she tried to get me to arrange something with her."

"You mean, to kill your wife?"

Sam shrugged. "Karen wanted me to get rid of Libby so we could be together."

"She said that in so many words?"

"Oh, yeah. Many times. I told her no, and no, and no. And then Libby died. It wasn't a suicide. Karen was into herbs and teas and stuff like that. She knew how to do it and get away with it."

Keith reached for his coffee mug but was suddenly repulsed by the thought of drinking anything. It was probably cold anyhow. "Okay, Truman, tell me again what happened last night."

"I've told you a dozen times already."

"Again. And don't tell me you were at home. We know you weren't."

Sam groaned. "All right, I went to Karen's. When I walked in, she was lying on the floor and another woman was bending down beside her. I wasn't sure what had happened, so I grabbed the woman. I—I thought maybe she was hurting Karen. I admit I knocked her out, okay? I didn't know who she was. I'd never seen her before. Then I checked Karen, and I saw that she was dead. I thought that other woman did it."

"Why didn't you call us?"

"I figured you'd blame me. Which you do." Sam lifted his chin and looked Keith in the eye. "Look, if I killed Karen, why wouldn't I kill this other person? But no, I didn't. I keep telling you, I'm not a killer."

"Then what?"

"I didn't think I should leave her there. When you found out Karen was dead, I didn't want you to find this other woman, too, and think I hurt both of them. So, I ... I ran up to Karen's room and grabbed a pillowcase. I put it over the second woman's head and took her out to my car."

"Where did you go?"

"You know where I went."

"I need you to tell me, Sam."

"I drove out of town. Out Main Street. After a few miles I saw a cemetery. It seemed like a good place."

"So, you bundled up the woman you didn't know and drove her five miles out of town and left her there. Come on, Sam. That doesn't make sense."

"Well, it did to me at the time. I mean, if she came to and saw me in the room, she'd think I killed Karen, just like you do. Or, if she did it, she could try to blame me. But if she woke up some other place, she wouldn't remember anything about me, and it would give me a chance to get back into town and maybe work up an alibi."

Keith found himself wanting to believe him. The whole

thing was crazy, and Campbell could have been killed in the middle of it, but still ...

"What about Dorothy, Sam?"

"What about her?"

"Did you plan to marry her? Or just take her money and her parents' savings?"

Sam gazed up at him with weary eyes. "I think I'll take that lawyer now."

"You sure? I told you we've frozen your bank accounts, but the court can appoint one for you."

"Yeah, yeah. I've told you my story. Now I think I need a lawyer. Don't you?"

"Yes, I do." Keith was amazed he'd waited so long. He got up and left the room.

18

On Friday morning, Campbell and Nick sat down with Bill in the main office with their coffee, so he could dole out specific assignments for the new cases.

"I know you're both antsy about the Truman case, and I'm meeting with Mr. and Mrs. Hill this afternoon," he told them. "I've given you the minimum amount of work we need to get done today to stay on top of these new cases. Get that information to me, and I'll let you follow up on whatever leads you have on Truman, but honestly, I don't expect you to turn up much that's new before I close the file for Mrs. Hill."

When he headed toward his own office, Nick was frowning at Campbell. "I think there's a lot more we can find out."

"We have to do the boring stuff first."

"Yeah, but that won't take long, especially if we work together."

Campbell hesitated. Nick was a pain, but he was also a good, solid worker. She could put aside her annoyance long enough to get the job done.

"Okay, and then what?"

"There are lots more people to talk to in Missouri. I've got the names of at least four people I'd like to touch base with." He took on a wistful air. "Too bad we're not across the river."

"Well, we're not. I'm sure Mrs. Hill isn't going to pay for us to go over there. Besides, Sam Truman's in jail now. That should be enough to put Dorothy off him and satisfy Vera."

"Yeah," Nick said. "Vera's probably ecstatic."

"I wouldn't be too sure. Nobody likes to see their kids sad. Dorothy really liked him. Maybe loved him. She's probably devastated."

"I guess you're right. They showed Sam's picture on the news last night and everything. Said he was arrested for assault, unlawful restraint, and breaking and entering, and that he was a person of interest in the Potter murder."

"Dad and I saw the report."

He nodded. "Well, let's get at it. I think we can be done here by ten. That will give us four hours to work on Truman's case before the Hills come over."

If we skip lunch, Campbell thought. Too bad Rita wasn't here today. She'd have gladly whipped up something.

She dove into their assignments with Nick. He wasn't far off—they uploaded their reports to her father at quarter past ten. After congratulating each other and refreshing their coffee, they split Nick's list of contacts in Missouri.

"Hey, you two, we gonna have lunch?" her father asked from the doorway.

Campbell checked the time and was surprised to see it was after twelve. She was typing up notes from her last call, but Nick was still on the phone.

"Sorry, Dad. Guess we lost track of time."

"Been pretty busy?" Bill asked.

"Yeah. I think we've found a few pertinent facts. At least I have."

"Tell you what, I'll go get some takeout from August Moon. When I get back, we should have just about enough time to eat while you and Nick update me."

Campbell grinned. The Chinese buffet was fast becoming her favorite restaurant.

When Nick ended his call a moment later, he was also enthusiastic.

"Get me some of that firecracker chicken."

"Not me," Campbell said. "Too spicy. I'll take honey lemon chicken. Oh, and don't forget the crab Rangoon."

"How could I?" Her father grinned and tossed his car keys in the air, catching them adroitly. "Every time we go there, it's the first thing you head for."

He returned with enough food for at least two meals, and they gathered in the dining room to share.

"Okay, what have you got?" he asked when they had all loaded their plates. "Campbell, you first."

"I was able to talk to one of Libby Walker's sisters as well as one of her classmates." Campbell poured herself a glass of iced tea. "Apparently everyone in that part of Missouri thinks Sam did it."

"Anything else?" Bill asked.

"The classmate and Karen were friends in school. Not best friends, but she was well aware of Karen's crush on Sam. I did tell the sister that Karen Potter is dead, and she was stunned. She said Karen had harassed Sam to no end after he started dating Libby. In fact, Karen tried to crash their wedding reception. Her father called in the hotel security to show her out and make sure she didn't come back in while the party was in swing."

Bill nodded soberly. "Nick, how about you?"

"Well, I talked to Keith about that restraining order Libby filed on Sam after they separated. Seems Sam wouldn't stay away from their house, and he tried to break in the door one time. That's when she called the cops."

"Did he hurt her?" Campbell asked.

"Nothing in the file says so," Nick replied. "But I spent most of my time trying to find Ray Walker. I called that neighbor of Sam's in Benton—Ted Holloway. He said Walker came around there yesterday, trying to find Sam."

"What time?" Bill asked.

"Right after Ted got home from work. In fact, he said Walker was sitting in the parking lot. He figured he was waiting for Sam to come home. He gave Ted a number to call if he saw Sam."

"I'm guessing you got that number from Ted," Bill said.

"Yeah, but he wouldn't talk to me. So, I got to thinking, where's this guy staying? And I started calling all the local hotels. I hit paydirt at the Holiday Inn Express."

"They told you he's staying there?" Campbell bristled. "They're not supposed to do that."

"I have a source there," Nick said.

Campbell shot a glance at her father, and he winked at her. Oh, she thought. Probably a girlfriend. She frowned. That didn't make it right.

"And what did you learn?" Bill asked smoothly.

"Walker's been staying there at least three nights. And he hasn't checked out yet. Since it's past their checkout time today, he's probably planning to stay there tonight."

"Good work," Bill said.

"Should we tell Keith?" Campbell asked.

"Let's see if we can catch up with Ray for a friendly conversation first."

"But—" She broke off, trying to reason it out. Bill was Keith's friend. He would share any leads he got with Keith, especially if he found evidence of criminal activity. So far, all they knew for sure was that Ray Walker had been looking for Sam and talking to his clients. That didn't lessen the tension in her stomach.

Her father checked his watch. "If I didn't have to meet with the Hills, I'd head over there now."

"Campbell and I can go," Nick said.

Bill hesitated then nodded. "Okay. You've both done good work on this. Just be discreet. And be careful."

"Are you going to close the Hills' account?" Campbell asked.

"I think so. The police and the district attorney are handling the case against Truman. There's no need for the Hills to stay involved, or to keep paying us."

Nick reached for the carton of egg rolls. "Tell me when you're ready, Professor."

"I'm ready now," she said.

"Oh, well then, as soon I finish my lunch."

He would probably keep eating all day if she didn't remove the takeout cartons. Campbell rose and closed up the moo goo gai pan and the fried rice.

Twenty minutes later, Nick pulled his Jeep into the parking lot at the hotel.

"See any Missouri license plates?" He drove the length of the lot slowly, and Campbell scanned the cars' tags.

"No, but what if they've backed in?"

"Missouri requires two license plates," Nick said.

"Huh." Once again, he had more knowledge than she did. She was used to the Kentucky law that only required one. She watched carefully until Nick turned around at the end of the lot. "Florida, Tennessee ..." She didn't bother to note the Kentucky plates. "Oh, there's one." She'd missed it on the way in.

"Okay, let's park as close to him as we can."

"I don't think that's his car."

"It may not be, but—"

"He was driving a pickup when Dad and I met him," she said. "And we wrote down his license plate, and that wasn't it."

"You got me." He pulled into an empty spot and took out his phone.

"What are you doing?" she asked.

"Texting my source." His thumbs flew as he tapped out the message.

Campbell sighed. She'd never be able to text that fast. *Quit comparing yourself with Nick! Just because he's a quick texter and knows about Missouri license plates doesn't make him a better P.I. than you. Besides, he has a lot more experience at this. He* should *be better.*

He lowered his phone and looked over at her. "What?"

"Nothing. Just thinking about my exam. I need to study more."

His boyish smile was quite charming. "They won't ask you about the nineteen states that only mandate one plate."

Pressing her lips together tightly so she wouldn't snap out a reply, Campbell returned his gaze. "All right, I admit you're pretty good."

"Wow. That's the best compliment I ever got in my life. From you, anyway."

His phone hummed, and he looked down at it.

"Don't know if he's in his room. Let's go in."

"Do you know his room number?"

"How would I know that? It's illegal for them to give it out."

"Right." She had a feeling Nick had his ways.

They went inside and straight to the front desk, where a young woman in her early twenties was on duty. When she looked up and grinned at Nick, Campbell was struck by her appearance. Her hair was the same color as Nick's, and she had that same mischievous gleam in her smoky blue eyes.

"Hi, Nick!" She looked furtively around as though realizing her loud greeting may have been overheard by others.

"Hi, Jenna."

"How's Uncle Justin?" Jenna asked.

"He's good. You got anything for me on—you know?"

"Well, I absolutely can't give out a room number. You know that." She lowered her voice to a whisper. "I could lose my job."

"Right. I wouldn't expect you to do that. But if someone came to see a certain guest, you might be able to ring their room, right? To tell them they have a visitor."

"I can do that." She picked up the receiver of a phone below the level of the counter.

Nick leaned his elbows on the surface and leaned toward her, way farther than was reasonable. He smiled as he kept his eyes focused downward to where she was pushing buttons.

Campbell glanced around the lobby. Two men got off the elevator and walked toward the door chatting. A housekeeper was busy washing the French doors that led out onto a terrace at the back of the building.

"Oh, Mr. Walker?" Jenna said distinctly. "This is the front desk. There are two people here to see you." Her smile faded. "No, I'm pretty sure they're not police officers. One is a Mr. Emerson. All right, I'll tell them." She hung up and nodded toward the elevator. "He'll be down in a minute."

"Thanks." Nick sauntered over to a sofa from which he had a clear view of the elevator.

Campbell went and sat down beside him. "Uncle Justin?"

"She's my cousin."

"Never would have guessed." She supposed that was better than using a girlfriend to get what he wanted, but not by much. "What if he goes out another door?"

"And why would he do that?"

"Oh, I don't know. I just thought maybe someone who thinks their visitors at a hotel must be cops ..."

Nick made a face at her. "Oh ye of little faith."

Campbell snorted, but fifteen seconds later, the elevator doors opened, and Ray Walker emerged, peering about timidly. His gaze landed on them, and she and Nick stood.

"Hi, Mr. Walker." Nick stepped forward with his hand extended. "I'm Nick Emerson, and this is my colleague, Campbell McBride."

"Colleague?" Walker took Nick's hand but eyed Campbell with suspicion.

"We're investigators, and we understand you've been looking for Sam Truman."

His face darkened. "Look, I already told the police everything I know about Sam."

"Oh." Nick's features went slack.

"We're not with the police," Campbell said quickly. "Did you know that Mr. Truman is in custody?"

"Yeah, I heard. I was going to go back to Missouri, but the cops asked me to stick around until they clear this up, so I'm still here."

"Clear what up?" she asked.

"They want to make sure I had nothing to do with that woman's death. Which I didn't. It's all on Truman."

"Like your sister's death?" Nick asked.

Campbell could have kicked him.

"What do you know about Libby?" Walker scowled at Nick.

"We know she was married to Sam, but they were separated when she died," Campbell said as calmly as she could. "According to the coroner, it was suicide."

"The coroner was wrong. They changed it to an open verdict."

Campbell glanced uneasily at Nick. Walker was built like a linebacker, and she had no desire to make him angry.

"Hey, I've seen you before." The big man eyed her closely.

"Maybe," she said. "I do live in Murray."

"No, no, it was in Benton, when I went up to Sam's apartment the first time. You were with—"

"My father," she supplied. "Bill McBride."

"Right. You were looking for Sam way back then."

"Yes, we were."

His eyes flicked back and forth between her and Nick. "What's your interest in him?"

"We're not allowed to say."

Nick said, "Client confidentiality."

"Huh. Well, I hope your client's happy, now that Sam's in jail."

"Are you?" Nick asked, and again Campbell felt he was pushing things too far.

"I'll be happy if they reopen my sister's case. Can't say I'm too happy about sticking around here. Or being harassed by amateurs."

"Well, thank you, Mr. Walker." Campbell tugged on Nick's sleeve and nodded toward the door.

Nick hesitated then gave in. "Right. Have a nice day." He waved blithely at Jenna. His cousin watched them, wide-eyed, from behind the counter as they headed for the door. She'd probably overheard the entire conversation.

Outside, Campbell followed Nick to the Jeep and climbed in on the passenger side. The whole interview dissatisfied her.

"Well, that was a bust." Nick buckled his seat belt.

"How were we to know the police had already questioned him and made him skittish?"

"We should have known. Keith's thorough."

That was true. They were probably going over ground the

detective had already covered. She should have asked Keith before they went to the hotel. He probably would have told them not to go, but he also would have told her they'd already talked to Walker.

"Well, at least we know he's still in Murray. If they had any evidence he committed a crime, he'd be in jail too."

Nick scrunched up his face. "He wouldn't kill Karen Potter. Why would he? He thinks Sam offed his sister. If he came all the way over here to murder someone, it would be Sam. And he wouldn't have made so much noise trying to locate him."

"I suppose that's true."

"You bet it's true."

Nick didn't lose his sullen expression during the drive back to Willow Street. Campbell kept quiet and thought about the encounter. She sure hoped Walker didn't complain to the police that they were harassing him. Reporting the conversation to her dad would be stressful enough.

19

When they reached home, they went in through the front hall. Nick held up a hand, and she stopped right behind him. Voices murmured from behind the closed door of her father's office.

"The Hills are still here," she whispered.

Nick nodded.

At that moment the door opened, and she came face to face with Vera and Frank.

"Hi," Campbell said with a smile and a quick glance at her dad.

"Hello, honey." Vera took her hand. "Your father was just explaining everything to us. I guess your work on this case is over."

"I hope we met your expectations."

"More than that," Vera said. "I never in my wildest dreams expected to see Sam arrested."

"But it's not for cheating people," her husband put in stubbornly.

"That's correct." Bill stepped out into the hall behind the

couple. "I'm not even sure he's been formally charged. My understanding is that he's being questioned about Ms. Potter's murder."

"Miss Potter." Vera face took on twice its normal wrinkles, and she shook her head. "Imagine that. Not Miss Tryphenia."

"That was her stage name," Frank said.

Bill shrugged. "Well, her business name, anyway."

"A lot of people will be disappointed when they learn their favorite psychic died." Frank didn't look happy.

Vera nodded. "Louanne will surely find it distressing. So tragic. But Dorothy—" She grasped Campbell's arm. "Dorothy was just shattered when she heard Sam was involved. I didn't want it to end *this* way. She's adamant that he's innocent."

"Time will tell," said her dour husband. "Come on, Vera. Let's give these people some peace."

"Thank you again," Vera called as he guided her to the door.

Nick jumped toward it and held it open for the couple. He called a last goodbye before shutting it.

"So, that's that," Campbell said.

"Unless you learned something in your interview."

"Hardly. We're lucky we got out of there without getting our heads bitten off."

Bill nodded. "The Hills are satisfied, even though the result wasn't what they expected. So now we move on."

The front door opened, and Keith walked in.

"Oh, good, you're all here," he said.

"Come on in, Keith," Bill said heartily. "What's up?"

Keith ambled into the large office with them. "I have a little news on Sam Truman."

"New evidence?" Campbell asked.

"First of all, he's confessed to assaulting you and taking you to the cemetery."

She stared at him. "I'm surprised he admitted it."

"I was too, a little. He's still trying to convince us that, while he may snatch women and break into houses, he isn't a murderer. I've also been networking to see what else we could find on him. It seems Truman's wanted in Arkansas for fraud."

"He was up to his investment tricks in Arkansas?" Nick asked.

"It seems so. He used an alias there—Eliot Trottman. But they found him pretty quickly in IAFIS."

Campbell raised her eyebrows, and her father said, "That's the Integrated Automated Fingerprint Identification System."

She nodded, disappointed that she hadn't known that after all her studying for her license exam. More to bone up on.

"I guess he tried his luck in Arkansas in between Missouri and Kentucky," Keith said. "There may be other places he plied his tricks that we don't know about yet, but Arkansas wants him when and if we're finished with him."

"Wait, you won't let him go, will you?" Campbell asked.

"He'll definitely be charged with assaulting and kidnapping you and Karen Potter, and for unlawfully restraining her and breaking and entering. I'm not sure we can prove anything else on him, but we'll try."

"And he still insists that Karen killed his wife?" Nick asked.

"Yes, more adamantly than ever. Now that we know about his escapades in Arkansas, he spilled a few things. He maintains he's not a killer, but he said Karen killed Libby hoping he'd go back to her."

"As if a guy would want to get chummy with a woman who killed his ex," Nick said, scowling.

"He says Karen messed around with a lot of herbs and drugs in her teas." Keith ran a hand through his hair. "Not recreational drugs. She was careful not to get mixed up in illegal substances."

"Oh, murder's okay, but drugs are a no-no," Nick muttered.

Keith ignored him. "According to Truman, she once hinted to him after he and Libby separated that he could get rid of her very easily with a concoction of legal drugs that wouldn't point to him. To hear him tell it, he was horrified, and he insists that when Libby died he knew she'd done it."

"Then why didn't he say so at the time?" Campbell wasn't buying that story anymore, and she didn't mind saying so.

"He thinks Karen knew about his borderline legal financial activities. He was afraid if he pushed for a deeper investigation on her for the murder, she'd rat him out for financial misconduct. Not that he'd admit to fraud. He insisted he stayed inside the law, but that Karen could do him some damage if she started testifying against him."

Nick's jaw dropped. "That woman was nuts. So, instead of killing her, Truman came over here from Missouri to harass her and kidnap her, and then somebody else killed her? I don't believe it."

"I'm not sure I do either," Campbell admitted. "If she loved him, why do something that might point to him as a suspect?"

Keith sighed. "Truman said Karen thought he and Libby might be close to reconciling. He hoped they were, but Karen went ballistic. That's when she poisoned Libby."

"They're both nuts," Nick said.

Keith stood. "We're still working on it. I'm determined to either prove Truman killed Karen Potter or find out who did. And I'd rather not have to worry about innocent citizens getting hurt while we do it."

Bill threw Campbell an apologetic glance. "You should probably know that these two had a chat with Ray Walker at the Holiday Inn this afternoon."

Keith's eyes sharpened. "Oh?" His gaze drilled into Campbell.

"I approved the interview," Bill said. "I'm sorry, Keith."

Campbell couldn't meet his gaze. "He said the police told him not to leave town."

"That's right, we did." Keith looked a bit sourly at Bill. "I thought you were done with this case."

"We are," Bill said firmly. "I've just closed it out with Mrs. Hill. We're not working for her anymore."

"Let us take it from here, okay?"

"Sure thing," Bill said. "I admit, it seemed we had a personal stake after Campbell's experience. I shouldn't have sent these two to find Walker."

"Well, now's the time to step back."

"Right." Bill walked with him to the front door.

Campbell let out a big breath. Keith hadn't even said goodbye to her. Was he really angry? She'd thought they were getting close. Had she just blown her chances of having a long-term relationship with him?

"It's my fault," Nick said. "I got all gung ho about it. I'm sorry."

She looked at him in surprise. "It wasn't just you. Like Dad said, we all felt like it was personal. If he hadn't needed to meet with the Hills, Dad would have gone to the hotel himself."

———

After supper that evening, Bill and Campbell cleaned up the kitchen together.

"I know you think the legal cases are boring," he said as he wiped down the countertop, "but they're our bread and butter."

She knew it was true. Mrs. Hill hadn't paid them enough to compensate three people for nearly two weeks' work.

"I don't mind it." She put the soap cube in the dispenser

and closed the dishwasher. "I'll admit, the personal cases are more interesting, but it was kind of nice this afternoon to have a few hours of quiet, non-dangerous work. And the lawyers pay you well, right?"

"Pay *us* well. Yes."

"Then it's worth it." She walked over to him and slipped her hand through the crook of his arm. "What are your plans for tonight?"

He eyed her keenly. "Not going out with Keith?"

"He's so busy. Besides, you heard him this afternoon. I'm not his favorite person right now."

"You underestimate yourself. He was a little upset with all of us, but I take responsibility. He'll come around."

"He's worried about the case."

Her father nodded. "I think you're right. He's afraid they'll never find out who killed the psychic."

"Since I'm their main witness for that, it makes me feel ... I don't know ... incompetent."

He drew her into a quick hug. "Honey, stop putting yourself down. You were in danger, no matter how much Sam Truman insists he doesn't kill. I shudder every time I think about him choking you."

Campbell touched her throat. "I know. What if he didn't let go soon enough?"

"Sometimes I wonder ..." He paused and looked at her bleakly. "Did I do the right thing, bringing you into the business? Your life was never threatened when you were teaching literature. What would your mother have said about all this?"

"We can't think about that, Dad. If Mom were still alive, our lives would be different now. You might even still be living in Bowling Green."

"Maybe." Bill stepped back. "Enough of this. We've got a

couple hours of daylight left. Let's go crack open that storage unit."

"Really?" The downbeat mood vanished, and Campbell felt a jolt of excitement. "Right now?"

"If you want."

"I do! Let me get a sweater." She ran up the stairs.

The storage business was a scant mile from home. Why had he never mentioned it before? Her father drove slowly between two long rows of units with garage-type doors fronting them. When he'd stopped before one situated two from the end, he sat for a moment in silence.

"When was the last time you were here?" Campbell asked.

"I don't know." He rubbed his forehead. "I'm sorry. I should have kept more of Emily's things out for you."

"No. If it was too painful ..."

His shoulders slumped.

"Dad, if you don't want to do this tonight, it's okay." She deliberately tamped down the craving inside her.

"No, let's do it." He opened his door.

Campbell fumbled to get her seat belt off and hopped out of his car. He was already unlocking the door. It rumbled upward, and he switched on a bare lightbulb overhead.

The concrete-floored room was only half full. Still, it was more than she'd expected. A few pieces of furniture she'd forgotten about stood there, including the frame for the canopy bed that she'd once slept in back in Bowling Green.

"You kept my bed?"

"Thought you might want it someday." He looked at her with worried eyes. "Do you want it now?"

"I like the bed I have, but thanks."

He stepped between a pile of cartons and a battered old desk. "We ought to take all this to Willow Street and save the monthly fee."

Campbell did a quick appraisal. "There's room there, if you want. Or we could wait a while."

He sighed.

She reached out and touched the back of the old rocking chair. "I'd kind of like to have this at home."

"Your grandma's chair."

"I suppose it's fifty years old or so."

"More than that," her father said. "Emily told me it belonged to *her* grandmother originally."

Campbell's lips curved upward. "I didn't know that. It's a real heirloom."

"Generations of your ancestors have sat in it and rocked their babies."

She liked that thought. Something else caught her eye. "Why's there a fishing pole in here?"

"That's your mother's. One of the last things we did together was a day of fishing."

"Ah."

Bill sniffed. "There's a lot of stuff in those boxes."

"We sorted out her clothes. You got rid of them, right?" Campbell was taller than her mother had been. She'd kept only a few items she could wear.

"Yeah, but there's some pocketbooks and things. Jewelry."

"You gave me most of her jewelry."

He lifted one shoulder. "I didn't know what to do with the rest, after you took what you wanted."

"I guess I could go through it again. We can donate what we don't want to Angel's Attic."

"That's a good thought."

The charity shop had become a favorite browsing place for Campbell over the last few weeks. She lifted the flap on a carton. "Books, too, I guess. Though I'd like to keep some of her books."

"Yeah." He smiled sheepishly. "A few months ago, I was looking for a book on Kentucky geology. I knew we had it, but I couldn't find it anywhere. Then I remembered—it was one your mother had picked up on a trip to the Blue Ridge. It's probably packed away here with her other books."

"You didn't come look for it?"

He shook his head.

"Okay, that settles it. Let's take all the boxes of books and anything else we can fit in the car tonight. We'll leave the furniture for another day. But anything you think we might want in the new place, let's get it now. We'll sort it and donate what we don't care about."

Bill touched a black footlocker with his toe. "I think this is full of extra blankets and bedspreads. I just didn't have room for a lot in the old house, and I was too depressed to hold a yard sale."

"Well, now we have a guest room. Hey, is my old baby quilt in there? I haven't seen it in ages."

"Probably. And somewhere there's a box with some of your baby clothes. Emily saved them, so I saved them."

She smiled and patted his shoulder. "Thanks. And you mentioned some of the old dishes?"

"Yeah. There's a lot of stuff we never used, but most of it came from either my family or hers. You know, things like bone dishes and salt cellars."

"Antiques," Campbell said with a hint of glee.

He raised his eyebrows in an if-you-say-so expression. "Hey, just because something's old doesn't mean you have to keep it forever."

"No, you're right. How about we go through and keep only the things we love. Well, really like anyway. Huh?"

He nodded cautiously.

"The rest we can sell online. That will save the hassle of a yard sale." She knew the chaos would unsettle him, watching strangers paw through her mother's things. Bill liked to go to yard sales, but she could understand why he didn't want to hold one of his own.

"I guess."

"Sure," Campbell said. "That way, we can do it a little at a time. And we never have to see the people who buy her stuff." The idea appealed to her more strongly by the minute. Selling the items at an online auction would mean less chance of running into a woman wearing her mom's old necklace.

Her dad fell into the plan and hefted a carton of books. Campbell poked around and found several boxes marked "Em's stuff" and two that held carefully padded dishes. She carried them out to the back seat while Bill filled the Camry's trunk with book boxes.

At the back of the stash, she found four boxes marked "Family Tree." One peek inside the first box told her the binders, folders, and loose papers would take days, not hours, to sort. It wasn't hard to make the decision to leave those cartons for another time.

"Trunk's full," Bill announced after a quarter hour's work. He lowered the lid. "Any room left inside?"

"Just a little. Let's see if there's anything else we want to take now."

They stood together in the doorway. A small empty cage stood on newspapers atop her mother's desk—the cage she'd kept a hamster in nearly twenty years ago.

"I think Mr. Squiggle's cage can go to the dump," she said. "What's in the desk? I didn't look."

"It's pretty much the way she left it. I took out a few bills she hadn't paid, and anything that looked like it needed my attention and left the rest."

Campbell closed her eyes for a moment. "Is her red pen-and-pencil set still in there?"

"Probably."

"And the letter opener from when she visited the Smithsonian?"

He nodded. "I didn't take it out."

Campbell smiled and slid open the flat desk drawer in the middle. "Oh, look." She lifted a small magnifying glass with a filigree handle. "I definitely want this. And, Dad, here's a packet of her stationery." She fingered pale blue sheets of paper with a delicate cutwork design at the top.

"I took her address book," Bill said defensively. "I needed it to answer all the condolence cards."

"I remember," Campbell said. Even before she'd headed back to school after the funeral, they'd been pouring in. Her father had assured her he could handle it, and she was sure he did, but it must have worn him down. Especially alone. She ought to have stayed longer to help him, but it happened in the middle of a semester, and she couldn't have kept up with her studies if she hadn't gone back.

And Bill couldn't not respond to friends' outpouring of sympathy. Both his own mother and Emily would have been disappointed if they'd known. She bet he'd sent a handwritten reply to every single card. Nowadays, people put a blanket "Thank you all so much" out on social media and called it good. But the McBrides were Old School. Not that her father felt he had to be "proper" in every single instance, but he was polite in social situations. Always.

She remembered how her feet had ached the day after the funeral. They'd stood side by side at the funeral home, and later at the cemetery and then their house, greeting people, thanking them, hearing their reminiscences of Emily. She'd been exhausted by the time everyone left, and her dad was pale and quiet. She'd insisted he turn in early, though she wasn't sure he'd sleep.

She looked up at him and touched his shoulder. "Hey, I'm going to take a few things out of this drawer. We'll leave the rest for next time, okay?"

"Whatever you want, kiddo."

"Right now, I want to go home and have a cup of hot cocoa and watch the late news with you."

He looked at his watch. "We can get home in time for *Crime Scene Mysteries*."

Her father still loved cop shows. "Terrific."

"Of course, by the time we unload everything ..."

"We can unload tomorrow."

His nod told her that was a relief. Maybe they could press Nick into service, helping them. Of course, tomorrow was Saturday. Nick would probably spend the weekend jet skiing or with his RPG friends, playing some paranormal fantasy game. Maybe Keith ...

No, she wouldn't ask him. A strong, dark feeling hovered over her, telling her Keith wouldn't come around tomorrow.

20

Saturday morning, Campbell wasn't surprised to find that her father was up before her. She drifted downstairs and found the front door wide open and a man in coveralls kneeling beside it.

She found her dad in the kitchen, measuring ground coffee into the filter.

"Morning. Is that the doorbell guy? Working on Saturday?"

He turned halfway toward her and nodded. "I called yesterday to see what the holdup was, and he said he'd come next week. I told him we'd waited long enough, and I'd give him a bonus if he did it today."

"Wow. Way to throw your weight around, Dad." She took the glass carafe from the machine and filled it with water while he put the coffee can away.

"I got thinking about it, and I don't want to take any risks with my baby girl."

She smirked but said nothing. As long as he didn't refer to her that way in front of other people, she could live with it.

"I told him we want one of those doorbell cameras."

"Oh, boy."

"I know, more technology to learn."

"I'm serious. Half serious, anyway. If Katherine Tyler had one, we'd have solved that case a lot quicker."

"My thoughts exactly. He'll help us download what we need on our phones and computer network to see the video whenever we want. And they can add an alarm to the back door as well. I'm having it put on the one that comes in here from the garage, not the outside door." He nodded toward the panel in question.

Campbell handed him his favorite mug. "Thanks. I feel loved."

"You're always loved."

She smiled and kissed his cheek. "I know, but this feels extra special. You never bothered with alarms and such for your old office or for your house when you lived alone."

He shrugged and busied himself with the toaster and a bag of bagels. Campbell reflected that he'd probably never had a burglary before she moved home. What did that say about her?

"Got plans for today?" she asked.

"Oh, after we unload the car, I thought I'd go over my fishing gear. Mart and I keep talking about getting together for a day on the lake." He glanced at her. "We should have brought your mother's rod back for you."

"No, you and Mart go ahead. A guy day would do you good."

"Well, we haven't set it up yet, but I was thinking maybe next week."

"Good morning."

At the cheerful greeting, Campbell whirled toward the hall door and realized her mouth hung wide open.

"Hi, Keith," Bill said. "Didn't expect to see you this morning."

"I see you're upping your security."

"Yeah, I figured it was time."

Campbell tried to remember how bad her hair had looked this morning. Too late to fix anything now. "We've got coffee and bagels. And juice."

"And eggs, if anyone wants to cook," Bill added.

"I'd take some coffee," Keith said. "Already had breakfast."

"Hey, I'm going to try to set up a fishing day with my friend Mart Brady next Saturday." Bill looked expectantly at Keith. "You know him. I wondered if you or your father would want to join us."

"I'm so busy, I doubt I could get a whole day, but Dad would probably love it. Give him a call."

At that moment, the workman came into the kitchen carrying his toolbox. "Ready for the other alarm. Where's the door you want it on?"

"Let's take our coffee into the dining room," Campbell said to Keith, scooping up her mug.

"Here, you can have this bagel," her father said. "I'll make myself another one." He shoved a plate with a toasted everything bagel on it into Campbell's free hand.

She and Keith went into the dining room and sat at the long table. Reaching for the butter dish, she asked, "Want half? It's not my favorite kind."

"Sure. I seem to remember you like blueberry bagels."

"Or cheese." She smiled and stood for a moment to grab a butter knife from the old-fashioned sideboard. "So, what brings you here?" She wanted to add, "Me or the case?" but she didn't. He was dressed casually, so she didn't think he was on duty.

"Can I pick your brain?"

She set her jaw as she buttered her half of the bagel. "I'll consider it."

229

"Great. I've been going through Karen Potter's appointment book backward, from her most recent sessions on back. I was a bit surprised when I saw that a man went to her for a reading about three weeks ago."

"Most of her clients were women," Campbell said.

"Right. Since this was unusual, I went to see the man. He was at his workplace, and he seemed a bit embarrassed. Seems he and his wife had been to a party the week before where Karen was the entertainment. She read tarot cards for the guests. Just quick encounters. They'd mosey over to her table and give their names, and then she'd tell them something about themselves."

"Anything specific?"

"Nothing too pointed. I'm thinking she had the guest list ahead of time and had discussed some of them with the hostess. She came out with things like, 'Stop worrying so much about your boss. Things will come around at work.' Or 'Trust your instincts. You're smarter than you think.' Innocuous stuff."

Campbell tilted her head to the side, wondering where this was going. "But?"

"This guy got a more sinister word. She basically warned him to be careful and watch his back. It upset him."

"Did he have any ideas as to what she was referring?"

"He said he didn't. His wife got a totally generic reading. 'You'll meet up with an old friend soon,' something like that."

Campbell thought about it for a minute. "I'm guessing it bothered him so much, he made an appointment with her."

"Yes. Without telling his wife. He wanted a full reading. His wife just brushed off the party predictions. She thought it was good fun, but mostly nonsense."

"She was probably right." She took a bite of the bagel. It was cold, and she wished she hadn't accepted it.

"Between you, me, and the lamppost, yeah," Keith said. "But Mark Boothby didn't think so. It creeped him out."

"Wait a second." Campbell swallowed quickly. "Mark Boothby?"

"You know him?"

"If it's the guy I think it is, he goes to Dad's church. Our church."

Keith's eyebrows lowered and he lifted his mug. "That's interesting."

"Why?"

"It's getting odder and odder. First, a man goes to the psychic. Couple that with his being a regular church attendee."

"Religious people don't usually mix with paranormal stuff, you mean?"

He shrugged. "Faithful believers. I'm not saying never, but it's not the norm."

"I'll give you that. So, he went for the reading? What happened?"

"Miss Tryphenia told him there was a dark cloud in the offing for him. An unknown source of sadness. He couldn't pin her down on what it meant—if someone was going to die, or what."

They ate for a moment in silence.

Campbell washed down her last bite with coffee. "So that's it? Is there more to the story? Did the wife meet the old friend?"

Keith stared at her. "Not that I know of, but Mark said he was actually afraid the two were connected. That the reunion with this hypothetical old friend would bring him sorrow. He admitted he was starting to feel paranoid about it and grilling his wife every evening about who she'd seen that day, where she'd been, and especially if any old friends had surfaced."

"Wow. But nothing's happened?"

"Not according to what Mark is telling me."

"Have you talked to the wife?"

"He begged me not to."

"Has he heard Miss Tryphenia is dead?" Campbell asked.

"Yeah, I think he's relieved but a bit unnerved by it. He's wondering if somehow her death is connected to the dark cloud over him."

"You don't think he was involved?"

"No way. He's got an ironclad alibi."

Her father came in carrying his mug of coffee and a plate holding a toasted bagel and a banana.

"So, what's up?" he asked cheerfully as he took a chair.

Campbell almost hated to tell him, since her dad always seemed friendly with Mark. "Dad, Mark Boothby went to Miss Tryphenia for a reading a few weeks ago."

Her father blinked twice and looked over at Keith. "Nah." He took a bite of his bagel.

Quickly, Keith repeated the story.

"Huh." Bill was working on his banana by this time. After chewing a bite pensively, he shrugged. "Oh, well. Some people are more suggestible than others. Karen probably did that party hoping to gain a few more customers. And it worked."

"Yeah, it did," Keith said. "I've found three people so far who were at that party and booked readings with her afterward."

Bill laid his banana peel on his plate. "So, Keith, please enlighten us. We know you technically aren't supposed to discuss an active case with us."

Keith stared down into his nearly empty mug.

"Can I get you some more coffee?" Campbell asked in her most innocent voice.

"Please."

She took his mug and her own and retreated to the kitchen.

When she returned and passed Keith his fresh coffee, her father was finishing his bagel.

Sitting down, she sipped her coffee and waited. Her dad spoke first.

"So, Keith was saying that he'd visited a lot of Karen Potter's clients, and he ran into a snag with Mary Willingham."

"Oh?" Campbell looked at Keith.

"She was reluctant to talk to me." He scrunched up his face. "This murder has scared a lot of people, I'm afraid. Her family's not happy that she used Ms. Potter's services, and that, combined with the murder, has made her skittish."

"What can you do?" Campbell asked.

Bill leaned toward her. "It's more what *you* can do. You've visited her before. Keith thought maybe she'd talk to you more openly than she will him."

"But ... isn't this official police business?"

"Well, yes," Keith said. "But if some acquaintances, say, you and my mom, were to go have a conversation with her ... I just want to make sure of two things. One, is Mrs. Willingham okay? Her kids don't seem to be very supportive. And two, if there's anything at all she can tell us about Karen and the way she operated, it might help us."

"You're pretty sure Sam Truman didn't kill Karen?"

"He's still high on my list of suspects. We haven't found a weapon. Truman's DNA is in the house, but so is at least fifty other people's."

"Karen had a lot of clients."

"She did," Keith said, "and some friends too. We've got her address book, as well as her appointment book."

Campbell froze with her mug halfway to her lips. "Wait a sec. You said you didn't find a weapon."

"That's right. And we'll be announcing in a press

conference that she was stabbed. But we didn't find anything in the house that seemed to match the wounds."

"When I saw her appointment book, it was lying on her desk in that room," Campbell said.

Keith waited, watching her closely.

"There was also a letter opener lying beside it. Bronze, all one piece, with an etched or stamped design that looked Middle-Eastern. Was that in her desk when you processed the scene?"

"A letter opener. I don't think so, but I'll check."

"Do you think it would match the wounds?" Bill asked.

"From what the M.E. said, it might very well."

Bill sipped his coffee. "Wasn't this supposed to be the night she was performing at a party for Sam's neighbor?"

Keith grimaced. "I've already spoken to the hostess, Sarah Delisle. She said she'd only been to see the psychic once, and Karen's appointment book bears that out. Sarah was impressed and booked the party. But of course, she's had to change her plans now."

Campbell stroked the handle of her Campbell's Soup mug with her thumb. "Did you ask her if Karen inquired about the guest list?"

"I did. She said it was going to be a very informal affair. She gave Karen a few names when she booked, and she was going to relay others to her, but she hadn't gotten around to it."

Campbell nodded. "Okay, if your mother's agreeable, I'll go see Mrs. Willingham with her. Should I call her?"

"Go ahead. I've mentioned it to her. She said she was game if you were. It may not yield anything, but I really don't want this case to go cold."

"We really don't want to see you release Sam Truman," Bill said.

Keith smiled grimly. "Don't worry about Sam. We've got enough on him that he's not going anywhere for a long time."

———

That afternoon, Campbell drove with Angela to Mary Willingham's neighborhood. She and her dad had unloaded his car, but with everything else going on, she hadn't opened a single box yet. They'd simply stacked them in the upstairs sitting room for later.

She pulled her Fusion in at the curb in front of Mary Willingham's house.

"What a lovely home," Angela said.

Campbell glanced at the car in the driveway, parked outside the garage. Tennessee license plate.

"I wonder if that's her son's car."

Angela met her gaze. "Shall we?"

They both got out and walked up the driveway. "I didn't plan on her having company," Campbell said.

Angela nodded. "If it gets awkward, we'll just make our excuses and leave."

"Okay. And if she offers tea, let's accept." Campbell glanced over at her. "I keep wondering about that calming tea she got from Miss Tryphenia."

"Surely the psychic wouldn't put anything noxious in a product she sold to a client."

"I wouldn't think so, but I'd still like to check the ingredients."

At the front door, Campbell's finger was poised to ring the doorbell when she caught voices coming from inside and paused.

"I swear, if you ever give another penny to one of these fakers, I'll—"

"You'll what?"

Campbell looked at Angela, whose eyes had widened.

Inside, the man said, "I don't know, but I'll sure do something."

"Good luck with that," the woman replied. Campbell could imagine Mary pulling back her shoulders and glaring at him. "It's my money. I can do with it what I please."

"For now."

"What's that supposed to mean?" the woman shrieked.

Campbell caught her breath. Angela opened her mouth and shook her head helplessly.

"Maybe this wasn't such a good time to visit," Campbell whispered. Her instinct was to retreat to her car and wait a few minutes. She swallowed hard, battling the impulse to flee. "She could be in danger."

Angela nodded, her eyes anxious. "We can't just walk away."

Making a quick decision, Campbell pushed the doorbell and stood a little to the side, in case a furious man yanked the door open.

Instead, Mary Willingham eased it open a few inches. She looked the two visitors up and down from behind her glasses and said, "May I help you?" Her voice trembled.

"Hi. We met the other day. I'm—"

"Oh, yes, Miss McBride."

"That's right. Campbell." She gestured toward Angela. "This is my friend Angela."

"Hello." As she spoke, Mrs. Willingham let the door move a few more inches. Campbell could see into the entry beyond her. A fortyish man, red faced and sharp eyed, stood in an arched doorway to the living room.

"Do you have a few minutes?" Campbell asked. "Angela is

also a client of Miss Tryphenia's, and when I told her about you, she was eager to meet you."

Angela smiled. "I was hoping to talk to someone else who knew her. Maybe exchange our pleasant memories of her."

"Well ..." Mary glanced over her shoulder and then faced them again. "I ... I have company."

Campbell lowered her voice. "Mary, is everything all right?"

She pressed her lips together for a moment. "It's just my son. A friend drove me to Paducah this morning, and we had lunch out. Danny was waiting when I got home. Apparently he'd been sitting quite a while and was upset."

Campbell nodded slowly. "We heard shouting."

First darting another glance toward her son, Mary said, "He—he tried to call me, but I had my phone off. I turned it on when I got back here, and he told me he'd called several times."

"I see. But I don't want to leave until I'm sure—"

"What's going on here?" Her son pushed the woman aside and glared at Campbell. "I heard you say something about that fake medium who was murdered. Are you a cop?"

"No," Campbell said quickly. We're just concerned friends. We were hoping to visit with your mother for a moment."

"About what?"

"I'll put the teakettle on," Mary said. "Now, Danny, step aside and let the ladies in. This is my friend Campbell—" She got that far smoothly but threw a panicky glance Angela's way.

"And I'm Angela," Keith's mother said with a big smile. "You must be Danny. It's so nice to meet you."

"We're not finished," Danny said, bearing down on his mother with a harsh look.

Mary laid a hand on her son's arm. "It's all right. Campbell and I know each other. You go on now."

He glared at her. "I was planning to stay here tonight. I

didn't think you should be alone after what happened to that woman."

"Nonsense. There's no need for that." Mary managed a smile, but her voice still quivered. "I've got friends to look in on me, and Nicole isn't far away."

"Fine. I'll call you tonight, Mother, to make sure you're all right." His expression remained frosty as he stomped past Campbell and Angela, out the door.

At once, Campbell turned to Mary and held out her hands. "I'm so sorry. We didn't mean to intrude."

"I'm glad you did." Mary plodded a few steps into the living room and sank down on the nearest chair. "I'm embarrassed that you saw that, but relieved you helped end it. For now, at least." She lifted her gaze to Campbell's. "I'm sure I haven't heard the last of it."

Campbell sat down on the sofa near her. "If there's anything we can do for you, we'd be happy to help out."

Mary gave a wry chuckle. "Not unless you can get back the money I paid Miss Tryphenia. I'm afraid that's the only thing that would pacify Danny. But I know that's impossible. If she were alive, I wouldn't dream of even broaching the subject with her. She gave me everything she promised."

"But not peace with your son."

Mary sighed. "I don't know if that will ever happen."

Angela cleared her throat. "Mrs. Willingham, perhaps I could make that tea you mentioned."

"Oh. I'm sorry." Mary started to rise, but Angela held up a hand.

"Please don't get up. I'm sure I can find things. Is the kitchen back there?" She leaned to one side and peered out into the entry.

"Why don't we all go to the kitchen," Mary said, her voice

stronger. "It's cozy there, and I can direct you where to find the tea."

Ten minutes later, the three women were seated on cushioned chairs around a small pine table, waiting for the tea to steep in Mary's porcelain teapot splashed with cherry blossoms.

"He's right about one thing," she said ruefully. "I didn't realize how much I'd spent. Nicole came over yesterday and had me tot up all the money I'd given to Miss Tryphenia. I was shocked. She said I could have bought a new car with it. I suspect she told her brother, and that's what prompted him to come storming up here today."

"I'm sure they're just looking after you," Angela said gently.

"They don't want to see anyone take advantage of you," Campbell added.

Mary put a hand to her forehead. "I'm not sure I'd call it that. They really despised Miss Tryphenia. But I truly enjoyed her company—more than that of my own children, if I'm being honest." She looked earnestly at Angela. "You knew her."

"Slightly. I had one session with her, but I was planning to go back."

Good way to put it, Campbell thought.

Angela held out her wrist, on which a silver chain bracelet was looped. "I purchased this charm from her, and one just like it for my sister."

Mary leaned in to examine the lacy metal heart. "Oh, that's nice. I have a charm as well—an angel. I got it at my first reading. Miss Tryphenia told me to rub it as I was praying for my family. It seemed silly at first, but—" She looked deep into Angela's eyes. "Do you think that sort of thing helps?"

"Rubbing the charm? I'm more of the opinion that it's what's in our hearts that matters when we pray."

"Mm. Well, I suppose the tea is ready now." Mary reached for the cherry blossom pot. "Sugar, ladies, or lemon?" When they'd all fixed their brew the way they liked it, she asked, "Do you have children, Angela?"

"Yes." Angela smiled. "I have a son and a daughter."

"Do they know you visited Miss Tryphenia?"

"My son knew, but my daughter didn't. She lives farther away."

"How did your son take it?"

With a glance at Campbell, Angela said, "He was all right with it. He seemed to think it was just ... a lark on my part."

"And was it?"

"Well, I didn't take it too seriously. It was interesting, but you know, more of an entertaining outing than anything else. And a reminder to stay close to my family."

"I did take it seriously." Mary sipped her tea, not looking at either of them. "Maybe too seriously. I really thought—at first, anyway—that it was helping with Danny's situation. But since he found out ..."

"Things aren't going so well?" Angela asked gently.

Mary frowned. "He and Chrissy did have a big fight this week. I thought that was a good thing—I didn't care much for her. But today ... today he seemed really torn up. I'd been hoping they'd break up, but now I wonder if he'd have been so upset about the psychic if things were going better in his personal life."

"That can happen," Campbell said. "When things go to pieces in one area, it affects how we see everything else."

"I really thought I was helping him." Mary bit her lip. "Now she's dead, and Danny's furious with me. I really wish I'd never started going to her."

As they drove back to Willow Street a half hour later,

Angela looked over at Campbell. "Do you think she's really all right alone?"

"As long as Danny Boy doesn't pay her another visit and upset her again."

"Yeah." Angela sighed. "I discreetly checked the contents on every variety of tea in her cupboard, by the way. They're all from commercial packagers. Nothing looked to be compiled by hand, I guess you'd say. And no loose tea leaves, just teabags of various sorts."

Campbell drew up at a red light. "I asked Keith about the teas Karen sold to people. He said they didn't find any evidence at her house that she was putting together her own blends. Everything they found was bought elsewhere, as you say, in sealed boxes or tins."

"But she did have herbs and things in bulk. She'd burn sage and incense for her clients."

"I know." Campbell didn't like it, but there was nothing more they could do in that regard.

"Well, I hope her son goes back to Tennessee and doesn't hang around here to bother her again," Angela said.

"He only lives in Paris." Nick had found that information online. "That's not very far away."

"Oh. That is close." Angela fell silent for a moment, then she said, "Do they really think Miss T killed Mr. Truman's wife? I mean, it's been a decade or more, right?"

Campbell nodded, watching the light. "The police in Missouri think Sam Truman killed his wife himself. Keith leans toward the theory that Karen Potter killed her. Whether or not they can prove it either way is another story."

21

Keith headed for McCracken County as soon as he was free to leave the courthouse. Sam Truman had been arraigned on four charges. The police had verified that Truman's investment fund was mythical. Keith wasn't sure the fraud charges would stick, but the kidnapping and B&E counts surely would. He wished they could have added murder to the list, but this would do for now. They'd told Ray Walker he could leave.

He wished Campbell wouldn't have to testify against the con artist, but her brief kidnapping was one of their strongest charges against Truman, and he'd confessed to it. Karen Potter wouldn't be there to relate her story, but Campbell would be lucid and believable. He knew she'd comply willingly, but still, he wished her could spare her that experience.

For a Monday morning, this was a beautiful day. No clouds, and he hoped he'd be able to solve Karen Potter's murder soon. He was nearly to Symsonia, where he had an appointment with a man who'd invested seven thousand dollars in Truman's fund, when he was called on the radio.

"Come back," the dispatcher told him. "The prisoner has escaped."

What on earth? At the arraignment, Sam had pleaded guilty to snatching Campbell and breaking into Bill's house and Mrs. Vane's. And now he'd escaped? When Keith walked out of the building, all that was left was paperwork. With a heavy heart, he looked ahead for a place where he could turn around on the highway.

His cell phone rang, and when he saw Detective Matt Jackson's name on the screen, he pulled into a turn-around and threw the transmission into park.

"What's going on, Matt? I thought the arraignment went smoothly."

"So did I. But after they finished up and were taking Truman out to transport him, he gave them the slip."

Keith gritted his teeth. "How is that possible?"

"I don't know."

"Was there someone waiting for him?"

"We don't think so. But there were a lot of people milling around. The officer escorting him got distracted. I'm wondering if he car-jacked someone, but I really don't see how he could have."

"He was handcuffed?"

"You bet."

Keith sighed and reached for the gear shift. "I'll be there as soon as I can."

———

Campbell stopped at the post office on Chestnut Street for a roll of stamps. She and her dad had spent a peaceful Sunday together. After church and dinner out at the Sirloin Stockade, they'd opened a few of the boxes they'd retrieved from the storage unit and found places in the new house for some of her mother's heirloom dishes and a few of her books. Campbell had even found time to study for her exam.

Today, True Blue was back on routine investigations. She drove the few blocks back to Willow and eased past Nick's Jeep in the driveway, to the garage. Her dad's car was there, so he was still in the office. She had a couple bags of office supplies to carry in, and she'd recruit Nick to lug in the case of copy paper.

When she turned around with her arms full, she froze. It took her only a moment to figure out that the man standing beside her dad's workbench with a chisel in one hand was Sam Truman. She'd never met him before, but she'd seen plenty of pictures—not to mention the coveralls. If they weren't enough of a giveaway, the handcuffs certainly were.

"You're Sam." She felt stupid, standing there and staring at him with a bag of printer ink in one hand and file folders in the other. Her throat was dry as the dust on her mom's old dishes. "You're the one who left me in the cemetery."

"I'm not going to hurt you," he said.

"Why are you here?" She glanced toward the kitchen door with the spanking new alarm on it. "You had court this morning, right?"

"Right. And I decided not to go back to the jail."

"Stupid of you." *Oops, did I say that? The cops are probably out beating the bushes in the park for him.* She licked her lips. "What do you want?"

"Help getting these off." He held up his chained hands. "I thought you might have bolt cutters in here. And maybe you could get me a change of clothes? A T-shirt and some sweats would do."

"Why on earth would I help you?"

"Because I didn't kill you the other night."

She stopped breathing. Everything stopped. A million things raced through her mind, but one took precedence. "You said you're not a killer."

"And I'm not."

She leaned back against the door of her car and studied him. "So, since you're not a killer, you think I owe you a favor because you didn't kill me? That doesn't even make sense."

"What are you, the logic police?"

She was about to pull out a snarky reply when the door to the kitchen was yanked inward. She shifted her gaze. Nick stood there on the threshold, gaping at them.

"Hey, Nick." She forced a smile. "We've got company."

Without uttering a word, Nick reached up to a button on the doorframe and stabbed it with one finger. The overhead garage door rumbled and began to slide closed.

Truman stared at the moving door. It was nearly halfway down when he dove forward, the chisel still in his hand, and rolled under the descending door panel.

"Go tell your father," Nick said, pulling out his cell phone.

As she ran past him into the kitchen, Campbell heard him say, "This is Nick Emerson. Samuel Truman, in handcuffs, just ran out of the garage at True Blue Investigations on Willow Street."

————

Keith pulled into the McBrides' driveway and hopped out of his SUV. One of the two garage doors was up, and he strode inside. Matt Jackson and two uniformed officers were gathered around Campbell, and Nick and Bill hovered near the open doorway to the kitchen.

As Keith entered, Campbell was saying, "He was already in here when I drove in. He must have come in through the little door." She nodded at the normal-sized door for humans set in the side of the garage, then she pointed toward the kitchen. "We got an alarm on that door over there, but not the outer one."

Keith went straight to her side. "Campbell, are you all right?"

"I'm fine. He was almost polite. And he reminded me that he's not a killer."

She sounded her usual self, if a little surprised at this turn of events.

Jackson stepped forward. "Apparently Truman got inside the garage and was looking for tools to help get his cuffs off when Ms. McBride drove in."

"Wasn't the garage locked?" Keith asked.

"It was," Bill replied. "I think he picked the lock on the man door. Or maybe I left it unlocked, but I don't think so."

"But why on earth would he come here?" Keith asked.

Campbell cleared her throat. "He said wanted me to help him. Return his favor for not killing me."

Keith shook his head in disbelief. "Well, Matt, when we arrested him, he was in Benton, getting his things out of his apartment. His car is probably still sitting there. My guess is that's where he's headed now."

"I've already alerted Marshall County," Matt said. "They'll have an unmarked car at his building before he can get there."

"It's a good twenty miles," Keith said. "He'll need wheels. Did you find out if he stole a car near the courthouse?"

"Working on it."

"Well, let's put as many officers as we can on the street, checking this neighborhood. He'll be plenty conspicuous in handcuffs and a jail-issued jumpsuit."

Matt turned away, and Campbell quickly related the rest of the story to him.

"So, you came to the door?" Keith drilled into Nick with a keen gaze.

"I saw Campbell drive in, and I heard the garage door go up, but she didn't come inside. I thought maybe she needed help carrying stuff. But when I'd disarmed the alarm and opened the door, Truman was standing there, holding a chisel. I thought he was threatening Campbell. I hit the switch to put the door down, but he was too quick."

Keith stood still for a moment then sighed. "Okay, I'll check in with you later." His impulse was to stay at Campbell's side, but that was silly. She'd be safer now than ever, with practically the entire local police force swarming her street. He walked out into the yard and scrolled through his phone contacts. Ted Holloway, Truman's closest neighbor, didn't answer. He was probably at work. Keith tried Andrea Finley. She picked up on the second ring.

"Andrea, this is Detective Keith Fuller. We met a few days ago."

"Of course, Detective. How can I help you?"

"Are you in your apartment?" Keith asked.

"Uh, yes."

"Okay, listen to me. If Sam Truman comes around, do *not* open your door to him."

"I thought he was in jail."

"He escaped after his arraignment. Lock your door now."

"It's locked."

"Good. Can you see out your window into the parking lot? I'd like to know if Truman's car is still there."

"Hold on."

He could hear her breathing as she walked into another room.

"Yes, it's in his usual spot. I can see it from my living room window."

"Thanks. Is your roommate, Sarah, at work?"

"Yes, she left a couple hours ago."

"Maybe you can get a message to her to be careful when she comes home. If we haven't caught Truman by then, he might approach one of you neighbors for help."

Andrea gulped. "Okay, I'll text her now."

Keith thanked her and relayed the information to Matt.

"I think you're right," Matt said. "He'll try to get his car and his other things back. We're on it."

Most of the officers had left, taking direction from Jackson for the search. Diagonally across the street, an older woman stood on her front porch, and Keith recognized Mrs. Hill from earlier encounters. He ambled across the pavement toward her.

"Hi, Mrs. Hill. Did one of our officers speak to you yet?"

"Yes. They wanted to know if we'd seen a man run out of the McBrides' garage."

"Did you?"

"I'm afraid not." Her face went a deeper shade of pink. "I was watching one of my programs."

"Oh. Well, he's probably left the neighborhood, but you should go inside and lock your doors until we catch him."

"Are Bill and his daughter all right?"

"Yes, everyone's fine. Apparently the man was hoping to find some tools in their garage."

"I was afraid Campbell was hurt. Another bad experience for her, poor girl."

Keith's heart echoed her sentiments, and he tried to put reassurance into his smile. "I just spoke with her, and she's doing great."

"It was that Sam Truman, wasn't it? You know, I hired them to look into that man's past. I heard on the news he was going to court this morning. I wish I'd seen him sneaking around. I'd have called 911, you can be sure of that."

"We appreciate it," Keith said.

She nodded grimly. "I won't ask you how he escaped, but if you ask me, my Dorothy is the one who escaped."

Keith swallowed hard. He didn't envy Dorothy Chambers the earful she'd get from her mother.

"Best to go inside and lock up, Mrs. Hill."

———

"How about a cup of nice, strong, hot coffee?" Bill asked as he reset the alarm on the door between the garage and the kitchen.

"I think I'd rather have iced tea. It's got to be over eighty now." Campbell walked over to the window and leaned on the sill. "I wonder how the neighbors are taking this."

"I saw Keith talking to Vera a minute ago," Bill said. "I think the police are telling everyone to be alert and stay indoors."

"Are they going to make a general announcement when it's over?" Campbell turned to look at her dad. "I hate to think Truman might try the same thing on somebody else that he did on me."

"Keith and Matt are pretty savvy. They'll have the officers check all the tool sheds and places like that in the area." As he talked, he opened the refrigerator and took out the jug of Campbell's favorite low-calorie tea.

"Still, there are several elderly people on this street." She frowned. "I wonder about Mrs. Vane, for instance. She lives alone. It must have been scary for her to see all the cops converging here."

"Give her a call," Nick said over his shoulder, heading for the big office.

"You sure you'll be okay?" Bill asked.

"I'm fine, Dad. Really. I'm sorry I gave you another scare." Since Louanne's number was in her cell contacts, Campbell pulled her phone out and used it rather than the landline. After several seconds, she tensed. "She's not answering."

"Give her time." Her father held out a full glass of tea. "Old folks move slower, remember?"

She shook her head and hit disconnect. "It rang and rang, Dad."

"She may be out shopping."

"I want to go check on her."

Her dad's face took on that stubborn, unhappy look she knew too well. "I don't want you going out right now."

"Well, someone should go over there."

He looked out the window and sighed.

"Most of the cops have moved on," Campbell observed. She laid a hand on his shoulder. "I'll take Nick with me."

"I was going to send him to pick up some lunch."

"It will only take five minutes to put my mind at ease."

"I'll go with you," He set the glass on the counter. "Come on." He pulled out his wallet as he walked down the hall. At the doorway to the main office, he said, "Nick, I'm going with Campbell to check on Mrs. Vane. Here's some cash. Go pick up some tacos or something for lunch, okay?"

"Sure." Nick came over and accepted the cash Bill held out. His gaze detoured to Campbell. "Quesadillas for you, right?"

"You got it," she said with a smile.

They all went out the front door, and her father made sure both the lock and the alarm were doing their job. Normally, Campbell would have left the front door unlocked, but today she said nothing. Operating the business out of their home had seemed like a good idea—convenient, frugal. Now she wondered if they were asking for more trouble.

Nick got in his Jeep, and she and her dad headed down the sidewalk, toward the vacant Tatton house of pale yellow brick.

"Hey, look." She pointed. "There's a For Sale sign up."

"How about that. I guess we should brace ourselves for new neighbors."

"Don't you start telling prospective buyers about the murder," Campbell said.

"Would I do that?"

"You might."

Bill chuckled. "I think the Realtor will tell them. At least she should."

They strolled up Mrs. Vane's driveway and onto the front porch of her neat little gray house.

Meow!

Campbell stared at her dad. "That's Blue Boy."

"At least he's inside this time." Bill punched the doorbell. They heard it chime, and then, *Mroow!*

"He sounds upset."

Her dad rolled his eyes. "You speak cat now?"

"Don't you?"

He laughed.

Campbell leaned against the door with her ear to the crack where it would open. On the other side, the cat wailed again, and then she heard scratching.

"Dad, he's clawing the door."

"What do you want me to do about it?"

She pushed the doorbell button again then called, "Louanne? Louanne, it's me, Campbell."

There was no response, except Blue Boy's pitiful meow. When she looked beseechingly at her father, he shrugged.

"She's out, and he doesn't like being left home alone."

Campbell looked around the yard then strode toward the garage. There must be a window she could look through to see if Mrs. Vane's car was gone.

By the time she returned panting to the front porch, her father was peering through a parlor window.

"Her car's still here." Campbell ran up the steps.

"I can't see much in there," Bill replied.

A gray-blue ball of fluff popped onto the windowsill inside. Blue Boy opened his mouth, displaying a pink tongue, razor-sharp fangs, and his displeasure.

"Let's try a different window," Bill said.

Campbell wasn't about to argue. She followed him off the porch and along the side of the house. At the third window they tried, her dad stiffened.

"I think I see her. Call 911."

"Oh, no." Campbell's hands shook as she drew her phone from her pocket.

"She's lying on the kitchen floor," her father said. "Ask for an ambulance." He tried to raise the window, but it wouldn't budge.

Campbell made the call and gave the pertinent details. While she spoke, her dad went all around the house, searching for a way in.

"Okay, thanks." Campbell turned to him. "She said there are still officers on this street. She's sending one now to help us get in, and the ambulance should be on the way."

She'd barely gotten the words out when a patrol car slid into the driveway, lights flashing. Patrol officer Mel Ferris jumped out and jogged toward them. They met him at the porch steps.

"She's in the kitchen, lying on the floor," Bill said. "There's a back door near her, but it's locked."

"Show me."

Bill looked at Campbell. "Stay out here and bring the EMTs around."

The hospital was only a few blocks away, and she could already hear the approaching siren.

By the time she had guided the responders to the back of the house, the back door was open, and her father and Officer Ferris were inside. They stepped back and gave the EMTs space to work.

Campbell drew her father aside. "Is she alive?"

"Yeah. It looks like she fell."

"How did you get the door open?" Campbell eyed it critically. No way had Mel Ferris kicked it in.

"I told Mel I could pick the lock in under a minute, and he let me."

"I thought that door had two locks. I saw it after Blue Boy got loose."

He grimaced. "The second one wasn't locked. She may have been out here in the back yard this morning and didn't throw the deadbolt when she went in. Who knows?"

"Unless someone else was in here and only engaged one lock when he left."

Bill's face tightened. "She's conscious. She told Mel that she fell and whacked her head. No intruder."

"Glad to hear it." Campbell exhaled heavily. "Can I go over to the hospital? None of her kids live close, if I remember correctly. Someone should be with her."

"Sure, go ahead. Do you have a way to contact any of her kids?"

"No, but maybe Vera Hill does. They're good friends. Or you could poke around for her address book." She waited while the EMTs loaded Mrs. Vane on a stretcher and wheeled her out to the ambulance. Her father walked with her to her car.

"I'll make sure the house is secure," he said.

"What about Blue Boy?"

"We shut him in the bathroom, but I'll let him out so he can get to his litter box."

"Make sure he's got food and water too. I'll tell Mrs. Vane we'll feed him again if she has to stay at the hospital overnight."

Across the street, Vera and Frank were both out in front of their house, gazing fixedly at the activity on Louanne's side of the street.

"Looks like I'd better go calm the neighbors too," Bill said. "I'll see if Vera's got the contact info."

An hour later, Campbell sat in a chair beside Louanne in an exam room, waiting for results from the CT scan the doctor on duty in the ER had ordered. Louanne had dozed off on the gurney after being assured that Blue Boy was in good hands. Her face was nearly as white as the cotton pillowcase beneath her head, but her breathing was steady. Campbell leafed listlessly through an old magazine until her phone whirred.

"Dad?" she said softly. "What's up?"

"I thought you'd want to know—Keith just called me. They got Sam."

"In Murray?"

"No, he stole a truck from in front of the farm store and headed for Benton. The Marshall County Sheriff had four deputies waiting for him when he went to his apartment building. He still had on the handcuffs. It's a wonder he didn't have a wreck on his way up there."

Campbell closed her eyes and sent up a silent prayer of gratitude. "Thanks, Dad. Did you tell the Hills?"

"Nick's going there now. We'll spread the word up and down the street. Did you eat?"

"No, not yet." Her stomach was by now uncomfortably empty.

"I put your share of the Mexican food in the fridge. You can have it when you get home. Oh, Vera got hold of Louanne's daughter. She'll get here this evening."

"That's good news. Thanks so much, Dad."

The doctor breezed in, and Louanne opened her eyes.

"Mrs. Vane, things look pretty good," the doctor said. "I'm going to let you go home, provided you have someone with you."

"Her daughter's on her way," Campbell said.

Louanne's eyes widened, and Campbell smiled at her then looked up at the doctor.

"I'll stay with her until her daughter gets here." She reached out and gave Louanne's hand a gentle squeeze.

22

Keith didn't like visiting prisoners at the county jail, but with Sam Truman's past escapades in mind, he didn't want to risk taking him out of the building. On Wednesday morning, he pulled into the parking lot and took out his phone. He scrolled to Campbell's number. At least he could give himself something to look forward to later.

When she answered, he couldn't help smiling. "How's your day going so far?" he asked.

"Pretty good. Dad walked me through some legal stuff that will help me with his routine cases and may also help me on my exam."

"Sounds good. I wondered if you'd like to have dinner together tonight."

"Tonight? Sure. I'd love to."

Keith went into the jail smiling. His meeting with Truman took place in the visitors' room, but outside normal visiting hours.

When the guard brought Sam in and seated him across the table, Keith gazed at him for several seconds in silence.

Unfortunately, in the two days since the prisoner's escape and recapture, the detective hadn't made much progress on the Potter murder case. But he'd had some success in other areas.

"All right, Truman," he said. "Your statement panned out. Detective Carson in Metropolis called me this morning. They got a warrant and emptied your safe deposit box. The evidence you told me about was there—along with twenty grand in cash. They'll hold on to the money in case the court finds you guilty of fraud and you need to make restitution to some victims."

Truman's face tightened. "I didn't defraud anyone. That money is mine."

"Only if the judge says so. We'll see." Keith ran a hand through his hair. "Okay, so why didn't you tell the police after Libby died that you had evidence Karen Potter did it?"

Truman sat there stony-faced.

"It would have taken the suspicion off you at the time."

"They didn't suspect me. They thought it was suicide."

He had a point there. Sloppy police work, as far as Keith was concerned. The autopsy showed Libby had a large dose of scopolamine in her bloodstream, but they hadn't found any container in her house, or a prescription from her doctor.

"Why did you remove the evidence? You were deliberately protecting Karen Potter when you took away that box of patches with her fingerprints on it."

No answer.

"Were you in it with her, Sam?"

"No!" Truman looked away. "Libby and I were starting to talk about getting back together. Why would I kill her?"

"Is that why Karen killed her?"

"Probably."

"But you wouldn't give the police proof of that. You deliberately tampered with evidence in a murder case."

"The district attorney agreed not to charge me with that yesterday, when I told you about the tea Karen made with her medicine."

"That's true. And they've located the doctor who prescribed the scopolamine the year before to Karen's mother. We think that after her mother died, Karen kept the box of patches."

Sam shrugged. "Probably so."

"Did you know about the prescription before Libby died?"

"No. Why should I? I keep telling you, Karen and I weren't close anymore. She wanted to be, especially when she heard Libby and I were separated. But I told her I wasn't interested."

Keith watched him closely. "Do you think she gave Libby the scopolamine tea for revenge, or did she think you'd change your mind once Libby was out of the way?"

"I don't know, okay?" Sam glared at him. "For the last time, I don't know, and I don't know how she got Libby to drink the stuff either. Maybe she convinced Libby she was ready to let bygones be bygones. All I know is, when I walked in the house, Libby was dead and these empty medicine packets were in the trash, with some soggy patches. I admit I fished them."

"How do we know Karen was even there?"

"You don't, I guess. But that's what happened."

"Why didn't she take the packets away with her? You removed them and washed out the tea things."

"She probably figured the police would say Libby killed herself—which they did, at first."

"But you took evidence from the trash and didn't tell the police."

"I made a mistake, okay?" Hate radiated from Sam's eyes. "You wouldn't know a thing if that McBride character hadn't stirred all this up."

"What do you mean?" Keith asked.

"You know what I mean. Dorothy's busybody mother hired the P.I. to dig into my business. If he'd kept out of it, Kentucky never would have had a problem with me. I'd be gone by now, and you'd never had heard my name."

Keith didn't like to think that was true, but it could be. "Okay. But I can think of only two explanations where Libby's death is concerned."

Sam pulled in a slow breath, but as Keith had hoped, he was too curious to stop now. "What might they be?"

"Either you and Karen were in it together—"

"We weren't."

"—or Karen had so much dirt on you that you didn't dare cross her by turning her in. We know you took money from a lot of people over there, and they never saw a return on those so-called investments. I'm thinking Karen knew too."

"I'm done. If you have more questions, I want my lawyer here." Sam slapped the table and yelled, "Guard."

———

"Miss McBride? Campbell?"

"Yes, this is she." Campbell frowned into her phone. She ought to know that voice.

"It's Mary Willingham."

"Oh, hi, Mary. How may I help you?"

"I hate to bother you, but I—I wondered if I could persuade you to drop by my house this evening. My son just called me, and he's on his way here. Frankly, I don't want to be alone when he comes."

Campbell's brain whirred. Keith was supposed to pick her up in half an hour for their date. But this was Mrs. Willingham. She'd reached out to Campbell, not to her daughter Nicole.

"I could stop by for a few minutes," she said. "I wouldn't be able to stay long."

"Oh, I'm sorry. I shouldn't have—"

"No, it's all right," Campbell said quickly. "I can be there in —" She checked the time. "Hmm. Twenty minutes, all right?"

"Yes, thank you so much."

Before Campbell could say more, Mary disconnected. She quickly pulled up Keith's number. When he answered, she said, "Hey, can we change the plan a little bit and I'll meet you at the restaurant instead of here?"

"Sure. Everything all right?"

"I'm not sure. Mary Willingham just asked me to come by her house. Danny's coming to see her again, and she wants someone there when he arrives."

"Are you sure? I could meet you there."

"I'm not sure at all," Campbell said. "I mean, arriving with a police officer might be the wrong message to send her, not to mention Danny."

"I tell you what, if you're not at the restaurant by ten past six, I'm heading straight for her house."

"Okay. I told her I couldn't stay, so I should be there on time."

She grabbed her purse and headed out of her room. Bill was in sitting room, watching the early news. He looked up when she paused in the doorway.

"Is Keith here yet?"

"No, I'm going to meet him there."

"Okay, have fun."

She skittered down the stairs. Should she have told her father about Mary's call? If he sensed she was concerned, he'd want to go with her, or even follow her over there in his car and wait outside. That's what happened when your loved one had brushes with criminals. But she wouldn't be alone. She and Mary would provide a measure of protection for each other.

She climbed into the car and locked the doors before opening the overhead garage door. Recent events had changed her too, made her more cautious. After backing out, she even sat and watched while the door went down, making sure nobody ducked inside.

Was this how it would be for the rest of her life? Always wary, always on edge? Campbell didn't like it. Her uneasiness gave her new empathy for older women, like Mary and Louanne, who lived alone. She had her father in the same house to look out for her, and if she needed them, Nick and Keith. *I'm blessed. Thank you, Lord for people who care about me.*

Watching the rearview mirror, she rolled the car carefully around so she could drive out into the street headfirst. One good thing at least had come from the series of frightening events she'd encountered since moving back to Kentucky. In the middle of confusing and dangerous happenings, she'd seen that she couldn't always control them. That realization had moved her closer to God.

She checked her mirrors often on the way to Mary's house. Was she being silly? Who would follow her? The man who'd kidnapped her was in jail. Again. She smiled and touched her turn signal then swung into Mary's street. The sun was low, but they still had at least an hour of daylight. No cars sat in the driveway, and she took that as a good sign.

After parking, Campbell got out and paused to admire the rosebushes along Mary's walkway. Stooping to smell the white blooms of one bush, she heard the front door open. Mary stood on the threshold.

"Hi," Campbell called.

"Thanks for coming." Mary walked slowly onto the porch and peered down the street. "He's not here yet."

"Do you not feel safe, Mary? Maybe it would be a good idea to call Nicole and ask her to come over too."

"No, she's as angry as Danny. When I confessed to her how much I'd actually given to Miss Tryphenia, she went into a royal rage. In fact, she's the one who told Danny about it."

"Do you know why he's coming again today?"

"I hadn't told them everything." Mary lowered her gaze. "I didn't tell Nicole or Danny about one large payment I'd given her to cleanse the air around Leon's grave. We went together last spring. She prayed and waved some branches and blew powder into the air. Nicole went over my old bank statements and noticed the withdrawal."

"Oh, dear." Campbell swallowed hard.

Mary came down the steps, reaching for her with a beseeching hand. "I didn't mean to spend so much of my savings. That was for me to live on, and for the kids to share when I go."

"I'm guessing Danny thinks you wasted his inheritance."

Mary nodded, tears seeping from her eyes. "I don't think I could bear it if he and Nicole were both hammering on me about it."

"Come here." Campbell drew her into a hug. She tried to imagine how she'd feel if her father gave all his savings to a psychic, but she couldn't. Her dad would never do something so foolish. Of course, he was only fifty. Mary's children were nearly his age. She had no guarantees that he'd have all his wits about him when he reached Mary's age.

Not that she felt Mary wasn't competent. Just a little oblivious, perhaps. She rubbed the older woman's shoulders then stepped back.

"Come on, Mary. Let's go inside and sit down."

"You said you can't stay long."

"Well, I'm supposed to be somewhere at six." She didn't

wear a watch, usually relying on her cell phone, but she knew she'd be cutting it close.

Mary had on a decorative bracelet watch, and she squinted at it. "It's ten till now. You'd better go."

"Not yet. Come inside." Keith would understand—and he'd said he'd come over if she was tardy. Campbell guided Mary up the steps and into the house, her arm around the woman. She closed the door firmly behind them and flipped the lock lever.

In the living room, Mary sank down in her favorite wing chair. "I'm sure Danny wouldn't be quite so upset if things hadn't gone haywire for him with Chrissy."

Campbell nodded and eased down on the sofa. "You told me they'd had a fight."

"Well, it's over now. She's moved out. Which is a relief to me, you understand, but Danny is furious with the world—especially me."

"He can't think it's your fault they broke up."

Mary's eyes flared. "Oh, can't he? It seems Nicole spilled the beans. I never should have told her why I consulted Miss Tryphenia."

"But you first went to her when you were mourning Leon."

"Danny doesn't care about that—except for the money. He's mad that I asked for help because of his problems, and that I talked about him to a stranger." She jumped and looked guiltily toward the front window. "I think I hear his car. Campbell, there's one other thing I didn't tell him. When you were here last Saturday, I told you I'd been to Paducah with my friend."

"I remember," Campbell said. "Danny was waiting when you got home."

Mary nodded.

The doorbell rang.

"She took me to see a new psychic," Mary said quickly. "We

went up there to consult her. But I can't tell my kids that. If they find out—"

"I understand."

Mary rose, and Campbell drew in a deep breath and stood, wishing Mary had kept that last little tidbit to herself.

In the entry, Mary opened the door. "Hello."

Campbell saw that it was indeed Danny Willingham on the front porch. She hesitated in the living room doorway, not sure if letting herself be seen would help Mary or escalate the situation.

"Mother, we need to talk."

"I'm always willing to talk to you."

Danny strode past her through the entry. He stopped when he noticed Campbell.

"Why am I not surprised?"

"Hello." Campbell tried to project confidence, while Mary dithered a moment then closed the front door.

"You need to go," Danny said sternly. "And don't come back. Leave my mother alone."

"I was invited to come." Campbell held his gaze.

"I'm sure you were."

"You mother is a competent adult. You have no right to tell her whom she may invite as a guest."

He cocked his head to one side. "Oh, la-di-dah, aren't we?"

Campbell's face heated. Before she could think of a suitable reply, Danny turned on his mother.

"It's time you quit associating with con artists and their friends."

"But—" Mary sputtered.

Campbell stepped forward and said firmly, "I am neither a con artist nor a friend of con artists. I don't know what you think you know, but you have no right to speak to your mother like that."

"Oh, don't I?" He whirled to face her. "How much has she paid you, hmm?"

"Not a cent. I have a job, thank you."

"I'm sure you do." Disdain poured from his eyes. "I can get a court order to keep you away from her."

"Danny!" Mary stepped beside him and grabbed his arm. "Stop it. Be reasonable. Campbell is a friend, nothing more."

"Sure, and she came here with another friend to talk to you about that wretched psychic. The one who bankrupted you."

"Daniel Jonathan! How dare you? Nobody has bankrupted me, and Campbell had nothing to do with Miss Tryphenia or the money I gave her. Nothing."

"So you say." Danny's eyes narrowed as he surveyed Campbell. "You're mixed up in this. I don't know how deep, but I do know Chrissy and I would still be together if you and that fake psychic hadn't gotten into the picture."

Mary tugged at his sleeve. "Please, Daniel. She had nothing to do with your romantic troubles."

"Oh, didn't she? Nicole said the psychic performed incantations to make Chrissy break up with me."

"Th-that's not true." Mary threw a panicky glance Campbell's way.

"Let's sit down and discuss this calmly," Campbell said.

"Sure, you'd like to talk, wouldn't you? It would give you a chance to find out more about me and how to wreck things for me, although I can't see how they could get worse. I'm already broke, and—How many spells did you put on me, you witch?"

He stepped menacingly toward Campbell, and she faltered backward, her heart pounding. "I am not a witch. You are out of line, and I suggest you leave now."

"Do you?" He lifted his fist and took another step toward her.

Mary grappled with his arm, holding on around his elbow. "Stop it! Stop it, Danny!"

He shook her off in a movement that wouldn't have dislodged Blue Boy, but Mary was frailer and somewhat unsteady. She fell away from him with a gasp, landing with the upper half of her body on the sofa.

"That's enough!" Campbell ran to her side. "Are you all right, Mary?"

Her hostess looked up at her. Her eyes widened, and she let out a scream. Campbell whirled to find Danny standing directly behind her with a foot-long vase in his hand. He held it by its slender neck, above Campbell's head. Her throat closed.

"Put it down," came a roar from the doorway.

Keith's voice always delighted her, but never so much as in that moment.

"Put it down now." He advanced into the room until Campbell could see him without turning her head. He'd drawn his weapon. "Police. Put that thing down. Do it *now*."

With a baffled air, Danny bent his knees and lowered the vase to the carpet.

"Hands in the air," Keith said.

Campbell was able at last to pull in a painful breath. She turned to Mary.

"Are you all right?"

"I—I think so. My ankle ..." Mary nodded toward her left foot, keeping her eyes on Keith and her son.

Campbell knelt and gently tugged up the hem of Mary's white pants. "This one?"

"Yes. I think I twisted it when I fell."

Keith was handcuffing Danny.

"I'll call for rescue," Campbell said.

"Oh, no, dear, you don't need to."

"I think we do."

Keith looked her way. "Everyone all right?"

"Mrs. Willingham needs a medical check."

Keith hit the button on his shoulder radio and asked for a patrol car and an ambulance. He gave the dispatcher a few more details while Campbell carefully untied Mary's shoe and slid it off.

Twenty minutes later, Danny Willingham was in the back of Officer Jerry Stine's patrol car and Mary, under protest, was wheeled out the front door on a stretcher. As the EMTs paused at the back of the ambulance, another car drove up and parked at the curb. Nicole Paxton leaped out and dashed up the driveway.

"Easy, ma'am. Please stop there," Officer Denise Mills said, holding up a hand and stepping between Nicole and the ambulance.

"What's going on?" Nicole cried. "This is my mother's house. A neighbor phoned and told me about the ambulance and police. Is she all right?"

"I'll have to see some identification, ma'am."

"That's asinine." Nicole pushed past Denise, who gave up and strode along beside her.

"Detective Fuller," Denise called to Keith, "a family member has arrived."

Campbell walked quickly with Keith to meet Nicole.

"What's happened to my mother?" Nicole's gaze flitted past them to Danny's car. "Is my brother here?"

"He's here," Keith said. "Your mother will be fine, I'm sure. She has a slight injury. We're sending her to the hospital to get checked out, if you'd like to go there."

The EMTs were raising the gurney on a lift into the ambulance.

"Mom?" Nicole ran to them. "Mom? Are you okay?"

"I'm fine, dear." Mary waved to her. "The officers insist I

see a doctor about my ankle."

"I'm coming with you," Nicole said.

"No, no. You can meet me at the hospital if you want. I'm sure they'll release me after a quick look. Bring your car over."

Nicole hesitated. "All right."

Campbell glanced at Keith then stepped up and touched Nicole's sleeve. "Ms. Paxton, it's a twisted ankle. Nothing too serious. But you may want to have a word with the detective."

Nicole looked at her blankly for a moment then marched up to Keith. "How was she hurt? And where is my brother?"

"Easy, Ms. Paxton," Keith said. "Let's step out of the way, and I'll answer your questions." He drew her toward the front steps. Campbell followed but stayed a few steps away.

"Well?" Nicole demanded.

"Your mother was injured when your brother Danny pushed her."

"What? That's crazy. Danny wouldn't do that."

"I saw it happen," Keith said evenly, "as did Ms. McBride."

Nicole turned on Campbell. "Why are you even here? Were you bothering my mother?"

Campbell resisted the urge to turn around and walk away. "I assure you I wasn't bothering her. She called me and asked me to come because Danny was on his way here. She was afraid of him, Nicole. Afraid of what he might do."

Nicole eyed her in silence for a moment. "Why didn't she call me?"

"I don't know, but she did call me, so I came. I was here when Danny arrived, and he was belligerent."

"How?" Nicole whipped around to face Keith. "What are you saying?"

"Let the police sort this out," Keith said. "You can probably do the most good right now if you go to the hospital and be with your mother."

The ambulance was pulling out, and Nicole gazed after it, breathing hard. "Where's Danny?"

Keith pointed to the patrol car, where Danny sat slumped in the back seat.

"No." Nicole started walking toward it.

"Ms. Paxton," Keith said firmly, and she turned around. "Ms. Paxton, I know this is hard, but I'm telling you exactly what happened. When I arrived, I saw your brother push your mother hard enough to make her fall, and then he menaced her and Ms. McBride with an object."

"What kind of object?"

"Let the police handle this," Keith said. "We'll be able to tell you more after we conduct more interviews and take statements. If your mother doesn't stay all night at the hospital, you might consider staying here with her or taking her to your home. I don't think she should be alone tonight. She needs some TLC."

Nicole swallowed hard. "Can I talk to Danny?"

"Not at this time."

Her face hardened. "All right, I'll go to the hospital." She glanced at the open door of the house. "Can I lock the house first?"

"Do you have keys?" Keith asked.

"Yes."

He nodded. "Go on to Murray-Calloway County. We'll make sure the knob lock is engaged before we leave."

She hesitated but then turned and walked toward her car. Her steps slowed as she neared the patrol car, but she didn't stop.

Keith blew out a long breath. He stepped closer to Campbell and touched her cheek gently. "Are you sure you're okay?"

"Yes. Good timing, by the way."

He nodded. "I'm sorry about dinner."

"I guess you have to go back to the station?"

"It will take them a while to process him."

"He might cool off, and you've got to eat sometime," Campbell said.

"Yeah, but not sit-down-dinner eat. How do you feel about burgers?"

"Very good right now."

He nodded and pulled out his cell and tapped it a few times then put it to his ear. "This is Keith Fuller. Thanks for holding my reservation, but I won't be needing it tonight." He smiled at Campbell. "Pick your fast food, lady."

He went to speak to Denise then went onto the porch to lock Mary's front door.

Campbell met him next to her Fusion. "I'll take my car so you don't have to bring me back over here."

"Some date." Keith let out a big sigh. "There's something I want you to know before we leave."

She paused beside her driver's door and looked up at him.

"After you called me and said Danny Willingham was coming here again, I made a quick call to the Paris, Tennessee police department, to see if they had any useful information on him. They told me a Ms. Chrissy Perlman was hospitalized this morning, after her boyfriend beat her."

Campbell gasped. "Danny?"

"Let's just say they have a suspect they were looking for down in Paris. I told them we might have a lead on him up here. I think Danny's got more than what you saw to answer for."

"Poor Mary."

"You won't tell her?"

"I'll leave that to you."

23

Campbell gazed at the nested flaps on a cardboard box but hesitated to open the carton.

"Whatcha got?"

She looked over her shoulder. Keith stood in the doorway wearing jeans and a short-sleeved polo shirt.

"Well, hi, stranger."

He walked over and leaned down to give her a quick kiss. "It's been a busy week."

"I know. For us too. Dad's been cracking the whip on Nick and me all week. This is the first chance I've had to go through a few of Mom's things that were in storage for the last ... I don't know, six years?"

"Wow. Want some privacy?"

"Actually, I'd rather have company. Dad's gone off fishing with Mart Brady and your dad today, and I'm all alone. I thought it was a good time to go down memory lane, but now I think some support would be nice."

"Your father has a hard time with the memories?"

"Sometimes. Mostly he's all right, but ... well, he went to

the scene of her accident, you know. It was pretty bad. We had a closed casket at the funeral, but he saw."

"That's rough." Keith nodded toward the box. "So, do you know what's in there?"

"I'm not sure. It's just marked 'Em's stuff.' That's why I picked this one from the twelve or so boxes we brought home. For a surprise."

"It's the first one you've opened?"

"Dad and I did a box of books and one of dishes together. This one, I haven't got a clue."

He stood patiently beside her, but she couldn't quite make herself turn back the flaps.

"You don't have to open it," he said softly.

"I want to. It's just …" Her eyes burned with tears, and she dashed one away with her wrist. "Oh, Keith. I'm hopeless."

"I wouldn't say that."

His warm arms slid around her, and she turned toward him and snuggled against his chest. She let him hold her for a long moment of comfort then pushed gently away.

"I have some news for you, if you want to hear it."

"That bad?" She gazed up into his eyes.

"It's good, actually. We've made an arrest in the Karen Potter case."

"What? Who?"

"Danny Willingham."

She stared at him.

"After the things he said about psychics the other night, and the way he attacked you, well, I applied for a warrant for his car, since it was up here anyway."

"You found something in his car? Don't tell me." She laid her outspread hands on his chest. "You found the letter opener, didn't you? Karen's letter opener."

"Not quite that conclusive. We found blood in the console

compartment in his car. I learned last night it's a match to Karen Potter."

"But Karen … She wasn't in his car." Campbell searched Keith's face.

"Matt and I had a session with him. He took the letter opener, all right, after he stabbed her with it. He figured if we didn't find the weapon, he'd be okay."

"Where is it?"

"He threw it into the lake down in Paris."

"And didn't clean his car."

"Not well enough."

Campbell let out a big sigh. "I thought it would be someone closer to her. A client at least, if not Sam or someone in Libby's family. Danny never met Miss T."

"Not until the night he killed her. He was so mad when his sister told him their mother had spent more than they thought on the psychic that he drove up here and attacked her in her house."

"Wow."

Keith eyed her closely. "Be thankful you didn't go over to Karen's a few minutes earlier. If you had walked in on Danny at the scene, I'm sure he would have killed you too."

"Or Sam," she said. "He might have stumbled on Danny at Karen's house."

"Instead, he found you and spirited you away."

"Well, I'm not sending him a thank you note."

Keith chuckled. "I don't think that's in the etiquette book." He looked over at the box. "So … your mother's things?"

"I'm ready."

"You sure?"

Campbell nodded and pulled in a big breath.

THE END

AUTHOR'S NOTE

Dear Reader,

Thank you for choosing *Persian Blue Puzzle*. Writing the True Blue Mysteries is a joy for me, but also a challenge. I don't usually set my books in a real town, but these take place in Murray, Kentucky, the seat of Calloway County, where I live.

One dilemma I found in writing the stories was where to place Bill and Campbell's new home. After much thought, I decided to put it on a fictional street. Since Murray has many streets with trees in their names, I perused a list of its streets and came up with one that hadn't been used—Willow Street. I admit I'm a little vague about its exact location, and but it's "off Eighth Street."

Another question was where to put Miss Tryphenia's house. If you go looking for Second Street, where she lives in this book, you won't find it. Murray has numbered streets running across the "trees" and other named streets, but apparently First and Second were lost sometime in the misty past. So, if you drive out to Third Street and go another block, you won't find Second. This is fiction, and so are these two streets. Enjoy your visit!

    Blessings,
    Susan Page Davis

ABOUT SUSAN PAGE DAVIS

Susan Page Davis is the author of more than one hundred books. Her books include Christian novels and novellas in the historical romance, mystery, and romantic suspense genres. Her work has won several awards, including the Carol Award, two Will Rogers Medallions, and two Faith, Hope, & Love Reader's Choice Awards. She has also been a finalist in the WILLA Literary Awards and a multi-time finalist in the Carol Awards. A Maine native, Susan has lived in Oregon and now resides in western Kentucky with her husband Jim, a retired news editor. They are the parents of six and grandparents of eleven. Visit her website at: https://susanpagedavis.com.

MORE MYSTERIES FROM SUSAN PAGE DAVIS

Skirmish Cove Mysteries

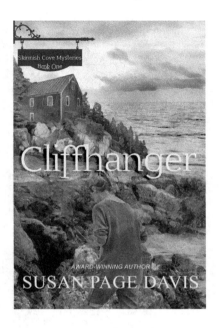

Cliffhanger

by Susan Page Davis

Skirmish Cove Mysteries - Book One

A charming themed inn, breaking waves, and a missing guest. What more could one ask?

The Novel Inn's reopening goes smoothly until a guest vanishes. The new owners prepare for their first large group—a former squad of cheerleaders meeting for a reunion. Things go awry when the head cheerleader fails to show up. Sisters Kate and Jillian, the innkeepers, enlist the help of their brother Rick, a local police officer. They're confident the missing woman will be found, but they soon learn to expect the unexpected, even during a walk on the beach.

———

True Blue Mysteries

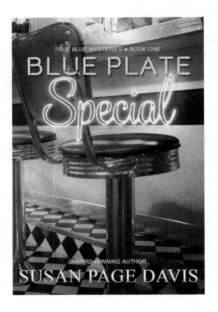

Blue Plate Special

by Susan Page Davis

Book One of the True Blue Mysteries Series

Campbell McBride drives to her father's house in Murray, Kentucky, dreading telling him she's lost her job as an English professor. Her father, private investigator Bill McBride, isn't there or at his office in town. His brash young employee, Nick Emerson, says Bill hasn't come in this morning, but he did call the night before with news that he had a new case.

When her dad doesn't show up by late afternoon, Campbell and Nick decide to follow up on a phone number he'd jotted on a memo sheet. They learn who last spoke to her father, but they also find a dead body. The next day, Campbell files a missing persons report. When Bill's car is found, locked and empty in a secluded spot, she and Nick must get past their differences and work together to find him.

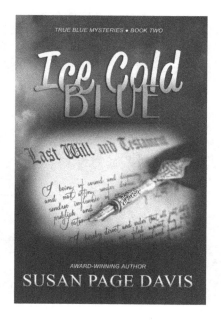

Ice Cold Blue

by Susan Page Davis

Book Two of the True Blue Mysteries Series

Campbell McBride is now working for her father Bill as a private

investigator in Murray, Kentucky. Xina Harrison wants them to find
out what is going on with her aunt, Katherine Tyler.

Katherine is a rich, reclusive author, and she has resisted letting Xina
visit her for several years. Xina arrived unannounced, and Katherine
was upset and didn't want to let her in. When Xina did gain entry,
she learned Katherine fired her longtime housekeeper. She noticed
that a few family heirlooms previously on display have disappeared.
Xina is afraid someone is stealing from her aunt or influencing her to
give them her money and valuables. True Blue accepts the case, and
the investigators follow a twisting path to the truth.

HISTORICAL FICTION FROM SUSAN PAGE DAVIS

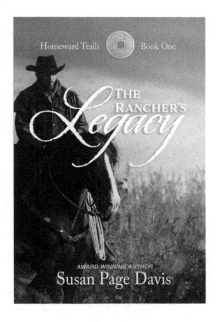

The Rancher's Legacy

Homeward Trails - Book One

Historical Romance

Matthew Anderson and his father try to help neighbor Bill Maxwell when his ranch is attacked. On the day his daughter Rachel is to return from school back East, outlaws target the Maxwell ranch. After Rachel's world is shattered, she won't even consider the plan her father and Matt's cooked up—to see their two children marry and combine the ranches.

Meanwhile in Maine, sea captain's widow Edith Rose hires a private investigator to locate her three missing grandchildren. The children were abandoned by their father nearly twenty years ago. They've been adopted into very different families, and they're scattered across the country. Can investigator Ryland Atkins find them all while the elderly woman still lives? His first attempt is to find the boy now called Matthew Anderson. Can Ryland survive his trip into the wild Colorado Territory and find Matt before the outlaws finish destroying a legacy?

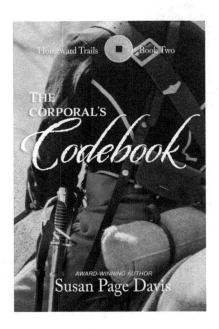

The Corporal's Codebook

Homeward Trails - Book Two

Historical Romance

Jack Miller stumbles through the Civil War, winding up a telegrapher and cryptographer for the army. In the field with General Sherman in Georgia, he is captured along with his precious cipher key.

His captor, Hamilton Buckley, thinks he should have been president of the Confederacy, not Jefferson Davis. Jack doubts Buckley's sanity and longs to escape. Buckley's kindhearted niece, Marilla, might help him—but only if Jack helps her achieve her own goal.

Meanwhile, a private investigator, stymied by the difficulty of travel and communication in wartime, is trying his best to locate Jack for the grandmother he longs to see again but can barely remember.

———

The Sister's Search

Homeward Trails - Book Three

Coming in July 2022

Historical Romance

A young woman searches for her missing brother and finds much more awaits her—if she can escape war-torn Texas.

Molly Weaver and her widowed mother embark on an arduous journey at the end of the Civil War. They hope to join Molly's brother Andrew on his ranch in Texas. When they arrive, Andrew is missing and squatters threaten the ranch. Can they trust Joe, the stranger who claims to be Andrew's friend? Joe's offer to help may be a godsend—or a snare. And who is the man claiming to be Molly's father? If he's telling the truth, Molly's past is a sham, and she must learn where she really belongs.

———

Scrivenings
PRESS
Quench your thirst for story.
www.ScriveningsPress.com

Stay up-to-date on your favorite books and authors with our free e-newsletters.

ScriveningsPress.com

T. S. Eliot's *The Cocktail Party*

Edited by Nevill Coghill

T. S. Eliot's
The Cocktail Party

edited with notes and a commentary by
NEVILL COGHILL

FABER AND FABER LTD
3 Queen Square, London

This edition first published in 1974
by Faber and Faber Limited
3 Queen Square, London W.C.1
Printed in Great Britain by
Robert MacLehose and Company Limited
The University Press, Glasgow
All rights reserved

ISBN 0 571 10592 0 (Hard bound edition)
ISBN 0 571 10472 X (Paper covers)

To Elliot and Henzie Martin Browne

Dear Martin and Henzie,
I would like you to accept the
dedication of this book as a mark of
my admiration for the work you have
both done, on the stage and in the study,
to enrich our understanding and delight
in the plays of T. S. Eliot.
                    Yours affectionately
                        Nevill Coghill

Contents

(*An asterisk in the text signals a note*)

1　*The Cocktail Party*

I WISH to acknowledge my indebtedness to two critics. To Mr. E. Martin Browne, who was responsible for the first production of this play at the Edinburgh Festival, 1949: for his criticism of the structure, from the first version to the last; for suggestions most of which have been accepted, and which, when accepted, have all been fully justified on the stage. And to Mr. John Hayward, for continuous criticism and correction of vocabulary, idiom and manners. My debt to both of these censors could be understood only by comparison of the successive drafts of this play with the final text.

T. S. E.

November 1949

IN addition to some minor corrections, certain alterations in Act III, based on the experience of the play's production, were made in the fourth impression of the text.

T. S. E.

August 1950

Persons

EDWARD CHAMBERLAYNE
JULIA (MRS. SHUTTLETHWAITE)
CELIA COPLESTONE
ALEXANDER MACCOLGIE GIBBS
PETER QUILPE
AN UNIDENTIFIED GUEST, *later identified as*
    SIR HENRY HARCOURT-REILLY
LAVINIA CHAMBERLAYNE
A NURSE-SECRETARY
TWO CATERER'S MEN

The scene is laid in London

Act One. Scene 1

The drawing-room of the Chamberlaynes' London flat.
Early evening. EDWARD CHAMBERLAYNE, JULIA
SHUTTLETHWAITE, CELIA COPLESTONE, PETER
QUILPE, ALEXANDER MACCOLGIE GIBBS, *and an*
UNIDENTIFIED GUEST.

ALEX

You've missed the point completely, Julia:
There *were* no tigers. *That* was the point.

JULIA

Then what were you doing, up in a tree:
You and the Maharaja?

ALEX

My dear Julia!
It's perfectly hopeless. You haven't been listening.

PETER

You'll have to tell us all over again, Alex.

ALEX

I never tell the same story twice.

JULIA

But I'm still waiting to know what happened.
I know it started as a story about tigers.

15

ALEX

10 I said there were no tigers.

CELIA

Oh do stop wrangling,

Both of you. It's your turn, Julia.

Do tell us that story you told the other day, about Lady Klootz and the wedding cake.

PETER

And how the butler found her in the pantry, rinsing her mouth out with champagne.

I like that story.*

CELIA

I love that story.

ALEX

I'm never tired of hearing that story.

JULIA

Well, you all seem to know it.

CELIA

Do we all know it?

But we're never tired of hearing *you* tell it.

I don't believe everyone here knows it.

[*To the* UNIDENTIFIED GUEST]

You don't know it, do you?

UNIDENTIFIED GUEST

No, I've never heard it.

16

CELIA

Here's one new listener for you, Julia;
And I don't believe that Edward knows it.   20

EDWARD

I may have heard it, but I don't remember it.

CELIA

And Julia's the only person to tell it.
She's such a good mimic. *clever at imitating*

JULIA

Am I a good mimic?

PETER

You *are* a good mimic. You never miss anything.

ALEX

She never misses anything unless she wants to.

CELIA

Especially the Lithuanian accent.

JULIA

Lithuanian? Lady Klootz?

PETER

I thought she was Belgian.

ALEX

Her father belonged to a Baltic family —
One of the *oldest* Baltic families
With a branch in Sweden and one in Denmark.   *Lady Klootz*
There were several very lovely daughters: 30
I wonder what's become of them now.

17

JULIA

Lady Klootz was very lovely, once upon a time.
What a life she led! I used to say to her: 'Greta!
You have too much vitality.' But she enjoyed herself.
[*To the* UNIDENTIFIED GUEST]
Did *you* know Lady Klootz?

UNIDENTIFIED GUEST
No, I never met her.

CELIA

Go on with the story about the wedding cake.

JULIA

Well, but it really isn't my story.
I heard it first from Delia Verinder
40 Who was there when it happened.

[*To the* UNIDENTIFIED GUEST]
Do *you* know Delia Verinder?

UNIDENTIFIED GUEST
No, I don't know her.

JULIA
Well, one can't be too careful
Before one tells a story.

ALEX
Delia Verinder?
Was she the one who had three brothers?

JULIA
How many brothers? Two, I think.

18

ALEX

No, there were three, but you wouldn't know the third one:
They kept him rather quiet.

JULIA

Oh, you mean *that* one.

ALEX

He was feeble-minded.

JULIA

Oh, not feeble-minded:

He was only harmless.

ALEX

Well then, harmless.

JULIA

He was very clever at repairing clocks;
And he had a remarkable sense of hearing —   50
The only man I ever met who could hear the cry of bats.

PETER

Hear the cry of bats?

JULIA

He could hear the cry of bats.

CELIA

But how do you know he could hear the cry of bats?

JULIA

Because he said so. And I believed him.

19

CELIA

But if he was so . . . harmless, how could you believe him?
He might have imagined it.

JULIA

My darling Celia,
You needn't be so sceptical. I stayed there once
At their castle in the North. How he suffered!
They had to find an island for him
60 Where there were no bats.

ALEX

And is he still there?
Julia is really a mine of information.

CELIA

There isn't much that Julia doesn't know.

PETER

Go on with the story about the wedding cake.

[EDWARD *leaves the room*]

JULIA

No, we'll wait until Edward comes back into the room.
Now I want to relax. Are there any more cocktails?

PETER

But do go on. Edward wasn't listening anyway.

JULIA

No, he wasn't listening, but he's such a strain —
Edward without Lavinia! He's quite impossible!
Leaving it to me to keep things going.
70 What a host! And nothing fit to eat!
The only reason for a cocktail party

For a gluttonous old woman like me
Is a really nice tit-bit. I can drink at home.

[EDWARD *returns with a tray*]
Edward, give me another of those delicious olives.
What's that? Potato crisps? No, I can't endure them.
Well, I started to tell you about Lady Klootz.
It was at the Vincewell wedding. Oh, so many years ago!

[*To the* UNIDENTIFIED GUEST]
Did *you* know the Vincewells?

UNIDENTIFIED GUEST
                No, I don't know the Vincewells.

JULIA
Oh, they're both dead now. But I wanted to know.
If they'd been friends of yours, I couldn't tell the story.   80

PETER
Were they the parents of Tony Vincewell?

JULIA
Yes. Tony was the product, but not the solution.
He only made the situation more difficult.
You know Tony Vincewell? You knew him at Oxford?

PETER
No, I never knew him at Oxford:
I came across him last year in California.

JULIA
I've always wanted to go to California.
Do tell us what you were doing in California.

CELIA

Making a film.

PETER

Trying to make a film.

JULIA

90   Oh, what film was it? I wonder if I've seen it.

PETER

No, you wouldn't have seen it. As a matter of fact
It was never produced. They did a film
But they used a different scenario. 腳本

JULIA

Not the one you wrote?

PETER

                    Not the one I wrote:
But I had a very enjoyable time.

CELIA

Go on with the story about the wedding cake.

JULIA

Edward, do sit down for a moment.
I know you're always the perfect host,
But just try to pretend you're another guest
100   At Lavinia's party. There are so many questions
I want to ask you. It's a golden opportunity
Now Lavinia's away. I've always said:
'If I could only get Edward alone
And have a really *serious* conversation!'
I said so to Lavinia. She agreed with me.

22

She said: 'I wish you'd try.' And this is the first time
I've ever seen you without Lavinia
Except for the time she got locked in the lavatory
And couldn't get out. I know what you're thinking!
I know you think I'm a silly old woman   110
But I'm really very serious. Lavinia takes me seriously.
I believe that's the reason why she went away —
So that I could make you talk. Perhaps she's in the pantry
Listening to all we say!

EDWARD
No, she's not in the pantry.

CELIA
Will she be away for some time, Edward?

EDWARD
I really don't know until I hear from her.
If her aunt is very ill, she may be gone some time.

CELIA
And how will you manage while she is away?

EDWARD
I really don't know. I may go away myself.

CELIA
Go away yourself!*   120

JULIA
Have you an aunt too?

EDWARD
No, I haven't any aunt. But I might *go* away.

CELIA

But, Edward . . . what was I going to say?
It's dreadful for old ladies alone in the country,
And almost impossible to get a nurse.

JULIA

Is that her Aunt Laura?

EDWARD
                No; another aunt
Whom you wouldn't know. Her mother's sister
And rather a recluse.

JULIA
                Her favourite aunt?

EDWARD

Her aunt's favourite niece. And she's rather difficult.
When she's ill, she insists on having Lavinia.

JULIA

130 I never heard of her being ill before.

EDWARD

No, she's always very strong. That's why when she's ill
She gets into a panic.

JULIA
                And sends for Lavinia.
I quite understand. Are there any prospects?*
                                        money

EDWARD

No, I think she put it all into an annuity.

24

JULIA

So it's very unselfish of Lavinia
Yet very like her. But really, Edward,
Lavinia may be away for weeks,
Or she may come back and be called away again.
I understand these tough old women —
I'm one myself. I feel as if I knew   140
All about that aunt in Hampshire.

EDWARD
                        Hampshire?

JULIA

Didn't you say Hampshire?

EDWARD
                        No, I didn't say Hampshire.

JULIA

Did you say Hampstead?

EDWARD
                        No, I didn't say Hampstead.

JULIA

But she must live somewhere.

EDWARD
                        She lives in Essex.

JULIA

Anywhere near Colchester? Lavinia loves oysters.

EDWARD

No. In the *depths* of Essex.

JULIA

Well, we won't probe into it.
You have the address, and the telephone number?
I might run down and see Lavinia
On my way to Cornwall. But let's be sensible:
150 Now you must let me be *your* maiden aunt —
Living on an annuity, of course.
I am going to make you dine alone with me
On Friday, and talk to me about everything.

EDWARD

Everything?

JULIA

Oh, you know what I mean.
The next election. And the secrets of your cases.

EDWARD

Most of my secrets are quite uninteresting.

JULIA

Well, you shan't escape. You dine with me on Friday.
I've already chosen the people you're to meet.

EDWARD

But you asked me to dine with you alone.

JULIA

Yes, alone!
160 Without Lavinia! You'll like the other people —
But you're to talk to me. So that's all settled.
And now I must be going.

EDWARD

Must you be going?

PETER

But won't you tell the story about Lady Klootz?

JULIA

What Lady Klootz?

CELIA

And the wedding cake.

JULIA

Wedding cake? I wasn't at her wedding.
Edward, it's been a delightful evening:
The potato crisps were really excellent.
Now let me see. Have I got everything?
It's such a nice party, I hate to leave it.
It's such a nice party, I'd like to repeat it.   170
Why don't you *all* come to dinner on Friday?
No, I'm afraid my good Mrs. Batten
Would give me notice. And now I must be going.

ALEX

I'm afraid *I* ought to be going.

PETER
                    Celia —
May I walk along with you?

CELIA
                    No, I'm sorry, Peter;
I've got to take a taxi.

JULIA
                    You come with me, Peter:
You can get *me* a taxi, and then I can drop you.

27

I expect you on Friday, Edward. And Celia —
I must see you very soon. Now don't all go
180 Just because I'm going. Good-bye, Edward.

EDWARD

Good-bye, Julia.

[*Exeunt* JULIA *and* PETER]

CELIA
Good-bye, Edward.
Shall I see you soon?

EDWARD
Perhaps. I don't know.

CELIA
Perhaps you don't know? Very well, good-bye.

EDWARD

Good-bye, Celia.

ALEX
Good-bye, Edward. I do hope
You'll have better news of Lavinia's aunt.

EDWARD
Oh . . . yes . . . thank you. Good-bye, Alex,
It was nice of you to come.

[*Exeunt* ALEX *and* CELIA]
[*To the* UNIDENTIFIED GUEST]
Don't go yet.
Don't go yet. We'll finish the cocktails.
Or would you rather have whisky?

28

UNIDENTIFIED GUEST
Gin.

EDWARD

Anything in it?   190

UNIDENTIFIED GUEST
A drop of water.

EDWARD

I want to apologise for this evening.
The fact is, I tried to put off this party :
These were only the people I couldn't put off
Because I couldn't get at them in time ;
And I didn't know that *you* were coming.
I thought that Lavinia had told me the names
Of all the people she said she'd invited.
But it's only that dreadful old woman who mattered —
I shouldn't have minded anyone else,
    [*The doorbell rings.* EDWARD *goes to the door, saying:*]
But she always turns up when she's least wanted.   200
                    [*Opens the door*]
Julia!
[*Enter* JULIA]

JULIA

Edward! How lucky that it's raining!
It made me remember my umbrella,
And there it is! Now what are you two plotting?
How very lucky it was my umbrella,
And not Alexander's — *he's* so inquisitive!
But *I* never poke into other people's business.
Well, good-bye again. I'm off at last.

                                        [*Exit*]

EDWARD
I'm sorry. I'm afraid I don't know your name.

UNIDENTIFIED GUEST
I ought to be going.

EDWARD
Don't go yet.
210   I very much want to talk to somebody;
And it's easier to talk to a person you don't know.
The fact is, that Lavinia has left me.

UNIDENTIFIED GUEST
Your wife has left you?*

EDWARD
Without warning, of course;
Just when she'd arranged a cocktail party.
She'd gone when I came in, this afternoon.
She left a note to say that she was leaving me;
But I don't know where she's gone.

UNIDENTIFIED GUEST
This is an occasion.*
May I take another drink?

EDWARD
Whisky?

UNIDENTIFIED GUEST
Gin.

EDWARD
Anything in it?

30

UNIDENTIFIED GUEST
Nothing but water.
And I recommend you the same prescription . . .   220
Let me prepare it for you, if I may . . .
Strong . . . but sip it slowly . . . and drink it sitting down.
Breathe deeply, and adopt a relaxed position.
There we are. Now for a few questions.
How long married?

EDWARD
Five years.

UNIDENTIFIED GUEST
Children?

EDWARD
No.

UNIDENTIFIED GUEST
Then look at the brighter side.
You say you don't know where she's gone?

EDWARD
No, I do not.

UNIDENTIFIED GUEST
Do you know who the man is?

EDWARD
There was no other man —
None that I know of.

UNIDENTIFIED GUEST
Or another woman
Of whom she thought she had cause to be jealous?   230

EDWARD

She had nothing to complain of in my behaviour.

UNIDENTIFIED GUEST

Then no doubt it's all for the best.
With another man, she might have made a mistake
And want to come back to you. If another woman,
She might decide to be forgiving
And gain an advantage. If there's no other woman
And no other man, then the reason may be deeper
And you've ground for hope that she won't come back at all.
If another man, then you'd want to re-marry
240   To prove to the world that somebody wanted you;
If another woman, you might have to marry her —
You might even imagine that you wanted to marry her.

EDWARD

But I want my wife back.

UNIDENTIFIED GUEST

That's the natural reaction.
It's embarrassing, and inconvenient.
It was inconvenient, having to lie about it
Because you can't tell the truth on the telephone.
It will all take time that you can't well spare;
But I put it to you . . .

EDWARD

Don't put it to me.

UNIDENTIFIED GUEST

Then I suggest . . .

EDWARD

And please don't suggest.
250   I have often used these terms in examining witnesses,

32

So I don't like them. May I put it to *you*?
I know that I invited this conversation:
But I don't know who you are. This is not what I expected.
I only wanted to relieve my mind
By telling someone what I'd been concealing.
I don't think I want to know who you are;
But, at the same time, unless you know my wife
A good deal better than I thought, or unless you know
A good deal more about us than appears —
I think your speculations rather offensive.   260

UNIDENTIFIED GUEST

I know you as well as I know your wife;
And I knew that all you wanted was the luxury
Of an intimate disclosure to a stranger.
Let me, therefore, remain the stranger.
But let me tell you, that to approach the stranger
Is to invite the unexpected, release a new force,
Or let the genie out of the bottle.
It is to start a train of events
Beyond your control. So let me continue.
I will say then, you experience some relief   270
Of which you're not aware. It will come to you slowly:
When you wake in the morning, when you go to bed at
      night,
That you are beginning to enjoy your independence;
Finding your life becoming cosier and cosier
Without the consistent critic, the patient misunderstander
Arranging life a little better than you like it,
Preferring not quite the same friends as yourself,
Or making your friends like her better than you;
And, turning the past over and over,
You'll wonder only that you endured it for so long.   280
And perhaps at times you will feel a little jealous

B   33

That she saw it first, and had the courage to break it —
Thus giving herself a permanent advantage.

EDWARD

It might turn out so, yet . . .

UNIDENTIFIED GUEST
Are you going to say, you love her?

EDWARD

Why, I thought we took each other for granted.
I never thought I should be any happier*
With another person. Why speak of love?
We were used to each other. So her going away
At a moment's notice, without explanation,
290 Only a note to say that she had gone
And was not coming back — well, I can't understand it.
Nobody likes to be left with a mystery:
It's so . . . unfinished.

UNIDENTIFIED GUEST
Yes, it's unfinished;
And nobody likes to be left with a mystery.
But there's more to it than that. There's a loss of personality;
Or rather, you've lost touch with the person
You thought you were. You no longer feel quite human.
You're suddenly reduced to the status of an object —
A living object, but no longer a person.
300 It's always happening, because one is an object
As well as a person. But we forget about it
As quickly as we can. When you've dressed for a party
And are going downstairs, with everything about you
Arranged to support you in the role you have chosen,
Then sometimes, when you come to the bottom step

There is one step more than your feet expected
And you come down with a jolt. Just for a moment
You have the experience of being an object
At the mercy of a malevolent staircase.
Or, take a surgical operation.   310
In consultation with the doctor and the surgeon,
In going to bed in the nursing home,
In talking to the matron, you are still the subject,
The centre of reality. But, stretched on the table,
You are a piece of furniture in a repair shop
For those who surround you, the masked actors;
All there is of you is your body
And the 'you' is withdrawn. May I replenish?

EDWARD

Oh, I'm sorry. What were you drinking?
Whisky?   320

UNIDENTIFIED GUEST
Gin.

EDWARD
Anything with it?

UNIDENTIFIED GUEST
Water.

EDWARD
To what does this lead?

UNIDENTIFIED GUEST
To finding out
What you really are. What you really feel.

What you really are among other people.
Most of the time we take ourselves for granted,
As we have to, and live on a little knowledge
About ourselves as we were. Who are you now?
You don't know any more than I do,
But rather less. You are nothing but a set*
Of obsolete responses. The one thing to do
330   Is to do nothing. Wait.

EDWARD
Wait!
But waiting is the one thing impossible.
Besides, don't you see that it makes me ridiculous?

UNIDENTIFIED GUEST
It will do you no harm to find yourself ridiculous.
Resign yourself to be the fool you are.
That's the best advice that *I* can give you.

EDWARD
But how can I wait, not knowing what I'm waiting for?
Shall I say to my friends, 'My wife has gone away'?
And they answer 'Where?' and I say 'I don't know';
And they say, 'But when will she be back?'
340   And I reply 'I don't know that she *is* coming back'.
And they ask 'But what are you going to do?'
And I answer 'Nothing'. They will think me mad
Or simply contemptible.

UNIDENTIFIED GUEST
All to the good.
You will find that you survive humiliation.
And that's an experience of incalculable value.

EDWARD

Stop! I agree that much of what you've said
Is true enough. But that is not all.
Since I saw her this morning when we had breakfast
I no longer remember what my wife is like.
I am not quite sure that I could describe her   350
If I had to ask the police to search for her.
I'm sure I don't know what she was wearing
When I saw her last. And yet I want her back.
And I *must* get her back, to find out what has happened
During the five years that we've been married.
I must find out who she is, to find out who I am.   — *darkness*
And what is the use of all your analysis
If I am to remain always lost in the dark?

UNIDENTIFIED GUEST

There is certainly no purpose in remaining in the dark
Except long enough to clear from the mind   360
The illusion of having ever been in the light.
The fact that you can't give a reason for wanting her
Is the best reason for believing that you want her.

EDWARD

I want to see her again — here.

UNIDENTIFIED GUEST
                    You shall see her again — here.

EDWARD

Do you mean to say that you know where she is?

UNIDENTIFIED GUEST

That question is not worth the trouble of an answer.
But if I bring her back it must be on one condition:

37

That you promise to ask her no questions
Of where she has been.

EDWARD
I will not ask them.
370   And yet — it seems to me — when we began to talk
I was not sure I wanted her; and now I want her.
Do I want her? Or is it merely your suggestion?

UNIDENTIFIED GUEST
We do not know yet. In twenty-four hours
She will come to you here. You will be here to meet her.
                              [*The doorbell rings*]

EDWARD
I must answer the door.
                    [EDWARD *goes to the door*]
                              So it's you again, Julia!
[*Enter* JULIA *and* PETER]

JULIA
Edward, I'm so glad to find you.
Do you know, I must have left my glasses here,
And I simply can't see a thing without them.
I've been dragging Peter all over town
380   Looking for them everywhere I've been.
Has anybody found them? You can tell if they're mine —
Some kind of a plastic sort of frame —
I'm afraid I don't remember the colour,
But I'd know them, because one lens is missing.*

symbol of hunter

UNIDENTIFIED GUEST [*Sings*]
     As I was drinkin' gin and water,
        And me bein' the One Eyed Riley,

Act I Scene 1   THE COCKTAIL PARTY

> *Who came in but the landlord's daughter*
> *And she took my heart entirely.*

You will keep our appointment?

EDWARD
I shall keep it.

UNIDENTIFIED GUEST [*Sings*]   390
Tooryooly toory-iley,
What's the matter with One Eyed Riley?
[*Exit*]

JULIA

Edward, who *is* that dreadful man?
I've never been so insulted in my life.
It's very lucky that I left my spectacles:
This is what I call an adventure!
Tell me about him. You've been *drinking* together!
So this is the kind of friend you have
When Lavinia is out of the way! Who is he?

EDWARD

I don't know.

JULIA
You don't know?

EDWARD
I never saw him before in my life.

JULIA

But how did he come here?   400

39

EDWARD
I don't know.

JULIA
You don't know! And what's his name?
Did I hear him say his name was Riley?

EDWARD
I don't know his name.

JULIA
You don't know his *name?*

EDWARD
I tell you I've no idea who he is
Or how he got here.

JULIA
But what did you talk about
Or were you singing songs all the time?
There's altogether too much mystery
About this place to-day.

EDWARD
I'm very sorry.

JULIA
No, I love it. But that reminds me
410 About my glasses. That's the greatest mystery.
Peter! Why aren't you looking for them?
Look on the mantelpiece. Where was I sitting?
Just turn out the bottom of that sofa —
No, this chair. Look under the cushion.

EDWARD

Are you quite sure they're not in your bag?

JULIA

Why no, of course not: that's where I keep them.
Oh, here they are! Thank you, Edward;
That really was very clever of you;
I'd never have found them but for you.
The next time I lose *anything*, Edward,   420
I'll come straight to you, instead of to St. Anthony.*
And now I must fly. I've kept the taxi waiting.
Come along, Peter.

PETER

I hope you won't mind
If I don't come with you, Julia? On the way back
I remembered something I had to say to Edward . . .

JULIA

Oh, about Lavinia?

PETER

No, not about Lavinia.
It's something I want to consult him about,
And I could do it now.

JULIA

Of course I don't mind.

PETER

Well, at least you must let me take you down in the lift.

JULIA

No, you stop and talk to Edward. I'm not helpless yet.   430
And besides, I like to manage the machine myself —

41

In a lift I can meditate. Good-bye then.
And thank you — both of you — very much.

[Exit]

PETER

I hope I'm not disturbing you, Edward.

EDWARD

I seem to have been disturbed already;
And I did rather want to be alone.
But what's it all about?

PETER

I want your help.
I was going to telephone and try to see you later;
But this seemed an opportunity.

EDWARD

And what's your trouble?

PETER

440　This evening I felt I could bear it no longer.
That awful party! I'm sorry, Edward;
Of course it was really a very nice party
For everyone but me. And that wasn't your fault.
I don't suppose you noticed the situation.

EDWARD

I did think I noticed one or two things;
But I don't pretend I was aware of everything.

PETER

Oh, I'm very glad that you didn't notice:
I must have behaved rather better than I thought.

If you didn't notice, I don't suppose the others did,
Though I'm rather afraid of Julia Shuttlethwaite.   450

EDWARD

Julia is certainly observant,
But I think she had some other matter on her mind.

PETER

It's about Celia. Myself and Celia.

EDWARD

Why, what could there be about yourself and Celia?
Have you anything in common, do you think?

PETER

It seemed to me we had a great deal in common.
We're both of us artists.

EDWARD

                I never thought of that.
What arts do you practise?

PETER

                You won't have seen my novel,
Though it had some very good reviews.
But it's more the cinema that interests both of us.   460

EDWARD

A common interest in the moving pictures
Frequently brings young people together.

PETER

Now you're only being sarcastic:
Celia was interested in the art of the film.

43

EDWARD

As a possible profession?

PETER

She might make it a profession;
Though she had her poetry.

EDWARD

Yes, I've seen her poetry —
Interesting if one is interested in Celia.
Apart, of course, from its literary merit
Which I don't pretend to judge.

PETER

Well, I can judge it,
470   And I think it's very good. But that's not the point.
The point is, I thought we had a great deal in common
And I think she thought so too.

EDWARD

How did you come to know her?

[*Enter* ALEX]

ALEX

Ah, there you are, Edward! Do you know why *I*'ve looked
in?

EDWARD

I'd like to know first how you *got* in, Alex.

ALEX

Why, I came and found that the door was open
And so I thought I'd slip in and see if anyone was with you.

44

PETER

Julia must have left it open.

EDWARD

Never mind;
So long as you both shut it when you go out.

ALEX

Ah, but you're coming with me, Edward.
I thought, Edward may be all alone this evening, 480
And I know that he hates to spend an evening alone,
So you're going to come out and have dinner with me.

EDWARD

That's very thoughtful of you, Alex, I'm sure;
But I rather *want* to be alone, this evening.

ALEX

But you've got to have some dinner. Are you going out?
Is there anyone here to get dinner for you?

EDWARD

No, I shan't want much, and I'll get it myself.

ALEX

Ah, in that case I know what I'll do.
I'm going to give you a little surprise:
You know, I'm rather a famous cook. 490
I'm going straight to your kitchen now
And I shall prepare you a nice little dinner
Which you can have alone. And then we'll leave you.
Meanwhile, you and Peter can go on talking
And I shan't disturb you.

EDWARD

My dear Alex,
There'll be nothing in the larder worthy of your cooking.
I couldn't think of it.

ALEX

Ah, but that's my special gift —
Concocting a toothsome meal out of nothing.
Any scraps you have will do. I learned that in the East.
500 With a handful of rice and a little dried fish
I can make half a dozen dishes. Don't say a word.
I shall begin at once.

[*Exit to kitchen*]

EDWARD

Well, where did you leave off?

PETER

You asked me how I came to know Celia.
I met her here, about a year ago.

EDWARD

At one of Lavinia's amateur Thursdays?

PETER

A Thursday. Why do you say amateur?

EDWARD

Lavinia's attempts at starting a salon,*
Where I entertained the minor guests
And dealt with the misfits, Lavinia's mistakes.
510 But you were one of the minor successes
For a time at least.

PETER
I wouldn't say that.
But Lavinia was awfully kind to me
And I owe her a great deal. And then I met Celia.
She was different from any girl I'd ever known
And not easy to talk to, on that occasion.

EDWARD
Did you see her often?

ALEX'S VOICE
Edward, have you a double boiler?

EDWARD
I suppose there must be a double boiler:
Isn't there one in every kitchen?

ALEX'S VOICE
I can't find it.
There goes *that* surprise. I must think of another.

PETER
Not very often.
And when I did, I got no chance to talk to her.   520

EDWARD
You and Celia were asked for different purposes.
Your role was to be one of Lavinia's discoveries;
Celia's, to provide society and fashion.
Lavinia always had the ambition
To establish herself in two worlds at once —
But she herself had to be the link between them.
That is why, I think, her Thursdays were a failure.

PETER

You speak as if everything was finished.

EDWARD

Oh no, no, everything is left unfinished.
530 But you haven't told me how you came to know Celia.

PETER

I saw her again a few days later
Alone at a concert. And I was alone.
I've always gone to concerts alone —
At first, because I knew no one to go with,
And later, I found I preferred to go alone.
But a girl like Celia, it seemed very strange,
Because I had thought of her merely as a name
In a society column, to find her there alone.
Anyway, we got into conversation
540 And I found that she went to concerts alone
And to look at pictures. So we often met
In the same way, and sometimes went together.
And to be with Celia, that was something different
From company or solitude. And we sometimes had tea
And once or twice dined together.

EDWARD

                    And after that
Did she ever introduce you to her family
Or to any of her friends?

PETER

                    No, but once or twice she spoke of them
And about their lack of intellectual interests.

EDWARD

And what happened after that?

48

PETER

                    Oh, nothing happened.
But I thought that she really cared about me.   550
And I was so happy when we were together —
So . . . contented, so . . . at peace: I can't express it;
I had never imagined such quiet happiness.
I had only experienced excitement, delirium,
Desire for possession. It was not like that at all.
It was something very strange. There was such . . .
    tranquillity . . .

EDWARD

And what interrupted this interesting affair?
[*Enter* ALEX *in shirtsleeves and an apron*]

ALEX

Edward, I can't find any curry powder.

EDWARD

There isn't any curry powder. Lavinia hates curry.

ALEX

There goes another surprise, then. I must think.   560
I didn't expect to find any mangoes,
But I *did* count upon curry powder.

                                [*Exit*]

PETER

That is exactly what I want to know.
She has simply faded — into some other picture —
Like a film effect. She doesn't want to see me;
Makes excuses, not very plausible,
And when I do see her, she seems preoccupied
With some secret excitement which I cannot share.*

EDWARD

Do you think she has simply lost interest in you?

PETER

570 You put it just wrong. I think of it differently.
It is not her interest in *me* that I miss —
But those moments in which we seemed to share some
        perception,
Some feeling, some indefinable experience
In which we were both unaware of ourselves.
In your terms, perhaps, she's lost interest in me.

EDWARD

That is all very normal. If you could only know
How lucky you are. In a little while
This might have become an ordinary affair
Like any other. As the fever cooled
580 You would have found that she was another woman
And that you were another man. I congratulate you
On a timely escape.

PETER

                    I should prefer to be spared
Your congratulations. I had to talk to someone.
And I have been telling you of something real —
My first experience of reality
And perhaps it is the last. And you don't understand.

EDWARD

My dear Peter, I have only been telling you
What would have happened to you with Celia
In another six months' time. There it is.
590 You can take it or leave it.

50

PETER
But what am I to do?

EDWARD
Nothing. Wait. Go back to California.

PETER
But I must see Celia.

EDWARD
Will it be the same Celia?
Better be content with the Celia you remember.
Remember! I say it's already a memory.

PETER
But I must see Celia at least to make her tell me
What has happened, in her terms. Until I know that
I shan't know the truth about even the memory.
Did we really share these interests? Did we really feel the
same
When we heard certain music? Or looked at certain pictures?
There was something real. But what is the reality . . .   600
    [*The telephone rings*]

EDWARD
Excuse me a moment.*
            [*Into telephone*]
            Hello! . . . I can't talk now . . .
Yes, there is . . . Well then, I'll ring you
As soon as I can.
        [*To* PETER]
    I'm sorry. You were saying?

51

PETER

I was saying, what is the reality
Of experience between two unreal people?
If I can only hold to the memory
I can bear any future. But I must find out
The truth about the past, for the sake of the memory.

EDWARD

There's no memory you can wrap in camphor 樟腦
610 But the moths will get in. So you want to see Celia.
I don't know why I should be taking all this trouble
To protect you from the fool you are.*
What do you want me to do?

PETER

See Celia for me.
You knew her in a different way from me
And you are so much older.

EDWARD

So much older?

PETER

Yes, I'm sure that she would listen to you
As someone disinterested.

EDWARD

Well, I will see Celia.

PETER

Thank you, Edward. It's very good of you.
[*Enter* ALEX, *with his jacket on*]

52

ALEX

Oh, Edward! I've prepared you such a treat!
I really think that of all my triumphs   620
This is the greatest. To make something out of nothing!
Never, even when travelling in Albania,
Have I made such a supper out of so few materials
As I found in your refrigerator. But of course
I was lucky to find half-a-dozen eggs.

EDWARD

What! You used all those eggs! Lavinia's aunt
Has just sent them from the country.

ALEX

                              Ah, so the aunt
Really exists. A substantial proof.

EDWARD

No, no . . . I mean, this is another aunt.

ALEX

I understand. The real aunt. But you'll be grateful.   630
There are very few peasants in Montenegro
Who can have the dish that you'll be eating, nowadays.

EDWARD

But what about my breakfast?

ALEX

                        Don't worry about breakfast
All you should want is a cup of black coffee
And a little dry toast. I've left it simmering.
Don't leave it longer than another ten minutes.
Now I'll be going, and I'll take Peter with me.

PETER

Edward, I've taken too much of your time,
And you want to be alone. Give my love to Lavinia
640 When she comes back . . . but, if you don't mind,
I'd rather you didn't tell *her* what I've told you.*

EDWARD

I shall not say anything about it to Lavinia.

PETER

Thank you, Edward. Good night.

EDWARD

Good night, Peter,
And good night, Alex. Oh, and if you don't mind,
Please *shut the door after you*, so that it latches.

ALEX

Remember, Edward, not more than ten minutes,
Twenty minutes, and my work will be ruined.

[*Exeunt* ALEX *and* PETER]
[EDWARD *picks up the telephone, and dials a number*.]

EDWARD

Is Miss Celia Coplestone in? . . . How long ago? . . .
No, it doesn't matter.

CURTAIN

Act One. Scene 2

The same room: a quarter of an hour later. EDWARD *is alone, playing Patience. The doorbell rings, and he goes to answer it.*

CELIA'S VOICE

Are you alone?
[EDWARD *returns with* CELIA]

EDWARD
    Celia! Why have you come back?
I said I would telephone as soon as I could:
And I tried to get you a short while ago.

CELIA

If there had happened to be anyone with you
I was going to say I'd come back for my umbrella. . . .
I must say you don't seem very pleased to see me.
Edward, I understand what has happened
But I could not understand your manner on the telephone.
It did not seem like you. So I felt I must see you.
Tell me it's all right, and then I'll go.   10

EDWARD

But how can you say you understand what has happened?
I don't know what has happened, or what is going to happen;
And to try to understand it, I want to be alone.

55

CELIA

I should have thought it was perfectly simple.
Lavinia has left you.

EDWARD

Yes, that *was* the situation.
I suppose it was pretty obvious to everyone.

CELIA

It was obvious that the aunt was a pure invention
On the spur of the moment, and not a very good one.
You should have been prepared with something better, for
    Julia;
20 But it doesn't really matter. They will know soon enough.
Doesn't that settle all our difficulties?

EDWARD

It has only brought to light the real difficulties.

CELIA

But surely, these are only temporary.
You know I accepted the situation
Because a divorce would ruin your career;
And we thought that Lavinia would never want to leave you.
Surely you don't hold to that silly convention
That the husband must always be the one to be divorced?
And if she chooses to give *you* the grounds . . .

EDWARD

30 I see. But it is not like that at all.
Lavinia is coming back.

CELIA

Lavinia coming back!
Do you mean to say that she's laid a trap for us?

56

EDWARD

No. If there is a trap, we are all in the trap,
We have set it for ourselves. But I do not know
What kind of trap it is.

CELIA
Then what has happened?
[*The telephone rings*]

EDWARD

Damn the telephone. I suppose I must answer it.
Hello . . . oh, hello! . . . No. I mean yes, Alex;
Yes, of course . . . it was marvellous.
I've never tasted anything like it . . .
Yes, that's very interesting. But I just wondered   40
Whether it mightn't be rather indigestible? . . .
Oh, no, Alex, don't bring me any cheese;
I've got some cheese . . . No, not Norwegian;
But I don't really want cheese . . . Slipper what?* . . .
Oh, from Jugoslavia . . . prunes and alcohol?
No, really, Alex, I don't want anything.
I'm very tired. Thanks awfully, Alex.
Good night.

CELIA
What on earth was that about?

EDWARD
That was Alex.

CELIA
I know it was Alex.
But what was he talking of?   50

57

EDWARD
I had quite forgotten.
He made his way in, a little while ago,
And insisted on cooking me something for supper;
And he said I must eat it within ten minutes.
I suppose it's still cooking.

CELIA
You suppose it's still cooking!
I thought I noticed a peculiar smell:
Of course it's still cooking — or doing *something*.
I must go and investigate.
[*Starts to leave the room*]

EDWARD
For heaven's sake, don't bother!
[*Exit* CELIA]
Suppose someone came and found you in the kitchen?
[EDWARD *goes over to the table and inspects his game of
Patience. He moves a card. The doorbell rings repeat-
edly. Re-enter* CELIA, *in an apron.*]

CELIA
You'd better answer the door, Edward.
60 It's the best thing to do. Don't lose your head.
You see, I really did leave my umbrella;
And I'll say I found you here starving and helpless
And had to do something. Anyway, I'm *staying*
And I'm not going to hide.
[*Returns to kitchen. The bell rings again.*
EDWARD *goes to front door, and is heard to say:*]

Julia!
What have you come back for?
[*Enter* JULIA]

58

JULIA
I've had an inspiration!

[*Enter* CELIA *with saucepan*]

CELIA

Edward, it's ruined!

EDWARD
What a good thing.

CELIA

But it's ruined the saucepan too.

EDWARD
And half a dozen eggs:
I wanted one for breakfast. A boiled egg.
It's the only thing I know how to cook.

JULIA

Celia! I see you've had the same inspiration   70
That I had. Edward must be fed.
He's under such a strain. We must keep his strength up.
Edward! Don't you realise how lucky you are
To have *two* Good Samaritans? I never heard of that before.

EDWARD

The man who fell among thieves was luckier than I:
He was left at an inn.*

JULIA
Edward, how ungrateful.
What's in that saucepan?

CELIA
Nobody knows.

59

EDWARD

It's something that Alex came and prepared for me.
He *would* do it. Three Good Samaritans.
80   I forgot all about it.

JULIA

But you mustn't touch it.

EDWARD

Of course I shan't touch it.

JULIA

My dear, I should have warned you
Anything that Alex makes is absolutely deadly.
I could tell such tales of his poisoning people.
Now, my dear, you give me that apron
And we'll see what I can do. You stay and talk to Edward.

[*Exit* JULIA]

CELIA

But what has happened, Edward? What has happened?

EDWARD

Lavinia is coming back, I think.

CELIA

You think! Don't you know?

EDWARD

No, but I believe it. That man who was here —

CELIA

90   Yes, who was that man? I was rather afraid of him;
He has some sort of power.*

60

EDWARD

I don't know who he is.
But I had some talk with him, when the rest of you had left,
And he said he would bring Lavinia back, tomorrow.

CELIA

But why should that man want to bring her back —
Unless he is the Devil! I could believe he was.*

EDWARD

Because I asked him to.

CELIA

Because you asked him to!
Then he *must* be the Devil! He must have bewitched you.
How did he persuade you to want her back?
 [*A popping noise is heard from the kitchen*]

EDWARD

What the devil's that?
[*Re-enter* JULIA, *in apron, with a tray and three glasses*]

JULIA

I've had an inspiration!
There's nothing in the place fit to eat: 100
I've looked high and low. But I found some champagne —
Only a half-bottle, to be sure,
And of course it isn't chilled. But it's so refreshing;
And I thought, we are all in need of a stimulant
After this disaster. Now I'll propose a health.
Can you guess whose health I'm going to propose?

EDWARD

No, I can't. But I won't drink to Alex's.

JULIA

Oh, it isn't Alex's. Come, I give you
Lavinia's aunt! You might have guessed it.

EDWARD *and* CELIA

110   Lavinia's aunt.

JULIA

Now, the next question
Is, what's to be done. That's very simple.
It's too late, or too early, to go to a restaurant.
You must both come home with me.

EDWARD

No, I'm sorry, Julia.
I'm too tired to go out, and I'm not at all hungry.
I shall have a few biscuits.

JULIA

But you, Celia?
You must come and have a light supper with me —
Something very light.

CELIA

Thank you, Julia.
I think I will, if I may follow you
In about ten minutes? Before I go, there's something
120   I want to say to Edward.

JULIA

About Lavinia?
Well, come on quickly. And take a taxi.
You know, you're looking absolutely famished.
Good night, Edward.

[*Exit* JULIA]

CELIA
Well, how did he persuade you?

EDWARD
How did he persuade me? Did he persuade me?
I have a very clear impression
That he tried to persuade me it was all for the best
That Lavinia had gone; that I ought to be thankful.
And yet, the effect of all his argument
Was to make me see that I wanted her back.

CELIA
That's the Devil's method! So you want Lavinia back!   130
Lavinia! So the one thing you care about
Is to avoid a break — anything unpleasant!
No, it can't be that. I won't think it's that.
I think it is just a moment of surrender
To fatigue. And panic. You can't face the trouble.

EDWARD
No, it is not that. It is not only that.

CELIA
It cannot be simply a question of vanity:
That you think the world will laugh at you
Because your wife has left you for another man?
I shall soon put that right, Edward,   140
When you are free.

EDWARD
No, it is not that.
And all these reasons were suggested to me
By the man I call Riley — though his name is not Riley;
It was just a name in a song he sang . . .

CELIA

He sang you a song about a man named Riley!
Really, Edward, I think you are mad —
I mean, you're on the edge of a nervous breakdown.
Edward, if I go away now
Will you promise me to see a very great doctor
150 Whom I have heard of — and his name *is* Reilly!*

EDWARD

It would need someone greater than the greatest doctor
To cure *this* illness.

CELIA

Edward, if I go now,
Will you assure me that everything is right,
That you do not mean to have Lavinia back
And that you do mean to gain your freedom,
And that everything is all right between us?
That's all that matters. Truly, Edward,
If that is right, everything else will be,
I promise you.

EDWARD

No, Celia.
160 It has been very wonderful, and I'm very grateful,
And I think you are a very rare person.
But it was too late. And I should have known
That it wasn't fair to you.

CELIA

It wasn't fair to *me*!
You can stand there and talk about being fair to *me*!

64

EDWARD

But for Lavinia leaving, this would never have arisen.
What future had you ever thought there could be?

CELIA

What had I thought that the future could be?
I abandoned the future before we began, ✓
And after that I lived in a present
Where time was meaningless, a private world of *ours*,   170
Where the word 'happiness' had a different meaning
Or so it seemed.

EDWARD

I have heard of that experience.*

CELIA

A dream. I was happy in it till to-day,
And then, when Julia asked about Lavinia
And it came to me that Lavinia had left you
And that you would be free — then I suddenly discovered
That the dream was not enough;* that I wanted something
        more
And I waited, and wanted to run to tell you.
Perhaps the dream was better. It seemed the real reality,
And if this is reality, it is very like a dream.   180
Perhaps it was I who betrayed my own dream*
All the while; and to find I wanted
This world as well as that . . . well, it's humiliating.

EDWARD

There is no reason why you should feel humiliated . . .

CELIA

Oh, don't think that you can humiliate me!

Humiliation — it's something I've done to myself.
I am not sure even that you seem real enough
To humiliate me. I suppose that most women
Would feel degraded to find that a man
190 With whom they thought they had shared something
        wonderful
Had taken them only as a passing diversion.
Oh, I dare say that you deceived yourself;
But that's what it was, no doubt.

EDWARD

I *didn't* take you as a passing diversion!
If you want to speak of passing diversions
How did you take Peter?

CELIA
Peter? Peter who?

EDWARD

Peter Quilpe, who was here this evening. *He* was in a dream
And now he is simply unhappy and bewildered.

CELIA

I simply don't know what you are talking about.
200 Edward, this is really too crude a subterfuge
To justify yourself. There was never anything
Between me and Peter.

EDWARD
                Wasn't there? *He* thought so.
He came back this evening to talk to me about it.

CELIA

But this is ridiculous! I never gave Peter

66

Any reason to suppose I cared for him.
I thought he had talent; I saw that he was lonely;
I thought that I could help him. I took him to concerts.
But then, as he came to make more acquaintances,
I found him less interesting, and rather conceited.
But why should we talk about Peter? All that matters   210
Is, that you think you want Lavinia.
And if that is the sort of person you are —
Well, you had better have her.

EDWARD

           It's not like that.
It is not that I am in love with Lavinia.
I don't think I was ever really in love with her.
If I have ever been in love — and I think that I have —
I have never been in love with anyone but you,
And perhaps I still am. But this can't go on.
It never could have been . . . a permanent thing:
You should have a man . . . nearer your own age.*   220

CELIA

I don't think I care for advice from you, Edward:
You are not entitled to take any interest
Now, in *my* future. I only hope you're competent
To manage your own. But if you are not in love
And never have been in love with Lavinia,
What is it that you want?

EDWARD

           I am not sure.
The one thing of which I am relatively certain
Is, that only since this morning
I have met myself as a middle-aged man
Beginning to know what it is to feel old.   230

67

That is the worst moment, when you feel that you have lost
The desire for all that was most desirable,
Before you are contented with what you can desire;
Before you know what is left to be desired;
And you go on wishing that you could desire
What desire has left behind. But you cannot understand.
How could *you* understand what it is to feel old?

CELIA

But I want to understand you.* I could understand.
And, Edward, please believe that whatever happens
240 I shall not loathe you. I shall only feel sorry for you.
It's only myself I am in danger of loathing.
But what will your life be? I cannot bear to think of it.
Oh, Edward! Can you be happy with Lavinia?

EDWARD

meaningless humdrous existence No — not happy:* or, if there is any happiness,
Only the happiness of knowing
That the misery does not feed on the ruin of loveliness,
That the tedium is not the residue of ecstasy.*
I see that my life was determined long ago
And that the struggle to escape from it
250 Is only a make-believe, a pretence
That what is, is not, or could be changed.
The self that can say 'I want this — or want that' —
The self that wills — he is a feeble creature;
He has to come to terms in the end
With the obstinate, the tougher self; who does not speak,
Who never talks, who cannot argue;
And who in some men may be the *guardian* —*
But in men like me, the dull, the implacable,
The indomitable spirit of mediocrity.
260 The willing self can contrive the disaster

68

Self knowledge
old, middle age.

Of this unwilling partnership — but can only flourish
In submission to the rule of the stronger partner.

CELIA

I am not sure, Edward, that I understand you;
And yet I understand as I never did before.
I think — I believe — you are being yourself
As you never were before, with me.
Twice you have changed since I have been looking at you.*
I looked at your face: and I thought that I knew
And loved every contour; and as I looked
It withered, as if I had unwrapped a mummy.   270
I listened to your voice, that had always thrilled me,
And it became another voice — no, not a voice:
What I heard was only the noise of an insect,
Dry, endless, meaningless, inhuman —
You might have made it by scraping your legs together —
Or however grasshoppers do it. I looked,
And listened for your heart, your blood;
And saw only a beetle the size of a man
With nothing more inside it than what comes out
When you tread on a beetle.   280

EDWARD

                    Perhaps that is what I am.
Tread on me, if you like.

CELIA

                    No, I won't tread on you.
That is not what you are. It is only what was left
Of what I had thought you were. I see another person,
I see you as a person whom I never saw before.
The man I saw before, he was only a projection —*
I see that now — of something that I wanted —

69

No, not *wanted* — something I aspired to —
Something that I desperately wanted to exist.
It must happen somewhere — but what, and where is it?
290   Edward, I see that I was simply making use of you.
And I ask you to forgive me.

CELIA
                    You . . . ask me to forgive *you*!

CELIA
Yes, for two things. First . . .
                    [*The telephone rings*]

EDWARD
                    Damn the telephone.
I suppose I had better answer it.

CELIA
                    Yes, better answer it.

EDWARD
Hello! . . . Oh, Julia : what is it now?
Your spectacles again . . . where did you leave them?
Or have we . . . have I got to hunt all over?
Have you looked in your bag? . . . Well, don't snap my head
        off . . .
You're sure, in the kitchen? Beside the champagne bottle?
You're quite sure? . . . Very well, hold on if you like;
300   We . . . I'll look for them.

CELIA
                    Yes, you look for them.
I shall never go into your kitchen again.
[*Exit* EDWARD. *He returns with the spectacles and a bottle*]

EDWARD

She was right for once.

CELIA
She is always right.
But why bring an empty champagne bottle?

EDWARD

It isn't empty. It may be a little flat —
But why did she say that it was a half-bottle?   ✳
It's one of my best: and I have no half-bottles.
Well, I hoped that you would drink a final glass with me.

CELIA

What should we drink to?

EDWARD
Whom shall we drink to?

CELIA

To the Guardians.

EDWARD
To the Guardians?

CELIA

To the Guardians. It was you who spoke of guardians.   310
                    [*They drink*]
It may be that even Julia is a guardian.   ✳
Perhaps she is *my* guardian. Give me the spectacles.
Good night, Edward.

71

EDWARD
Good night . . . Celia.

[*Exit* CELIA]
Oh!
[*He snatches up the receiver*]
Hello, Julia! are you there? . . .
Well, I'm awfully sorry to have kept you waiting;
But we . . . I had to hunt for them . . . No, I found them.
. . . Yes, she's bringing them now . . . Good night.

CURTAIN

Act One. Scene 3

The same room: late afternoon of the next day. EDWARD
alone. He goes to answer the doorbell.

EDWARD

Oh . . . good evening.
[*Enter the* UNIDENTIFIED GUEST]

UNIDENTIFIED GUEST
Good evening, Mr. Chamberlayne.

EDWARD

Well. May I offer you some gin and water?

UNIDENTIFIED GUEST

No, thank you. This is a different occasion.

EDWARD

I take it that as you have come alone
You have been unsuccessful.

UNIDENTIFIED GUEST
Not at all.

I have come to remind you — you have made a decision.

EDWARD

Are you thinking that I may have changed my mind?

73

UNIDENTIFIED GUEST

No. You will not be ready to change your mind
Until you recover from having made a decision.
10   No. I have come to tell you that you will change your mind,
But that it will not matter. It will be too late.

EDWARD

I have half a mind to change my mind now
To show you that I am free to change it.

UNIDENTIFIED GUEST

You will change your mind, but you are not free.
Your moment of freedom was yesterday.
You made a decision. You set in motion
Forces in your life and in the lives of others
Which cannot be reversed. That is one consideration.
And another is this: it is a serious matter
20   To bring someone back from the dead.*

EDWARD

From the dead?
That figure of speech is somewhat . . . dramatic,
As it was only yesterday that my wife left me.

UNIDENTIFIED GUEST

Ah, but we die to each other daily.*
What we know of other people
Is only our memory of the moments
During which we knew them. And they have changed
        since then.
To pretend that they and we are the same
Is a useful and convenient social convention
Which must sometimes be broken. We must also remember
30   That at every meeting we are meeting a stranger.

EDWARD

So you want me to greet my wife as a stranger?
That will not be easy.

UNIDENTIFIED GUEST
It is very difficult.
But it is perhaps still more difficult
To keep up the pretence that you are not strangers.
The affectionate ghosts: the grandmother,
The lively bachelor uncle at the Christmas party,
The beloved nursemaid — those who enfolded
Your childhood years in comfort, mirth, security —
If they returned, would it not be embarrassing?
What would you say to them, or they to you   40
After the first ten minutes? You would find it difficult
To treat them as strangers, but still more difficult
To pretend that you were not strange to each other.

EDWARD

You can hardly expect me to obliterate 擦掉
The last five years.

UNIDENTIFIED GUEST
I ask you to forget nothing.
To try to forget is to try to conceal.

EDWARD

There are certainly things I should like to forget.

UNIDENTIFIED GUEST

And persons also. But you must not forget them.
You must face them all, but meet them as strangers.

EDWARD

Then I myself must also be a stranger.   50

75

UNIDENTIFIED GUEST

And to yourself as well. But remember,
When you see your wife, you must ask no questions
And give no explanations. I have said the same to her.
Don't strangle each other with knotted memories.
Now I shall go.

EDWARD

Stop! Will you come back with her?

UNIDENTIFIED GUEST

No, I shall not come with her.

EDWARD

I don't know why,
But I think I should like you to bring her yourself.

UNIDENTIFIED GUEST

Yes, I know you would. And for definite reasons*
Which I am not prepared to explain to you
60   I must ask you not to speak of me to her;
And she will not mention me to you.

EDWARD

I promise.

UNIDENTIFIED GUEST

And now you must await your visitors.

EDWARD

Visitors? What visitors?

UNIDENTIFIED GUEST

Whoever comes. The strangers.
As for myself, I shall take the precaution
Of leaving by the service staircase.

76

EDWARD

May I ask one question?

UNIDENTIFIED GUEST
You may ask it.

EDWARD

Who are you?

UNIDENTIFIED GUEST
I also am a stranger.
[*Exit. A pause.* EDWARD *moves about restlessly. The bell
rings, and he goes to the front door.*]

EDWARD

Celia!

CELIA
Has Lavinia arrived?

EDWARD
Celia! Why have you come?
I expect Lavinia at any moment.
You must not be here. Why have you come here?   70

CELIA
Because Lavinia asked me.

EDWARD
Because Lavinia asked you!

CELIA
Well, not directly, Julia had a telegram*
Asking her to come, and to bring me with her.
Julia was delayed, and sent me on ahead.

77

EDWARD

It seems very odd. And not like Lavinia.
I suppose there is nothing to do but wait.
Won't you sit down?

CELIA
Thank you.
[*Pause*]

EDWARD

Oh, my God, what shall we talk about?
We can't sit here in silence.

CELIA
Oh, I could.
80 Just looking at you. Edward, forgive my laughing.
You look like a little boy who's been sent for
To the headmaster's study; and is not quite sure
What he's been found out in. I never saw you so before.
This is really a ludicrous situation.

EDWARD

I'm afraid I can't see the humorous side of it.

CELIA

I'm not really laughing at *you*, Edward.
I couldn't have laughed at anything, yesterday;
But I've learnt a lot in twenty-four hours.
It wasn't a very pleasant experience.
90 Oh, I'm glad I came!
I can see you at last as a human being.
Can't you see me that way too, and laugh about it?*

EDWARD

I wish I could. I wish I understood anything.

78

I'm completely in the dark.

CELIA
But it's all so simple.
Can't you see that . . .
[*The doorbell rings*]

EDWARD
There's Lavinia.
[*Goes to front door*]
Peter!
[*Enter* PETER]

PETER
Where's Lavinia?

EDWARD
Don't tell me that Lavinia
Sent you a telegram . . .

PETER
No, not to me,
But to Alex. She told him to come here
And to bring me with him. He'll be here in a minute.
Celia! Have you heard from Lavinia too?   100
Or am I interrupting?

CELIA
I've just explained to Edward —
I only got here this moment myself —
That she telegraphed to Julia to come and bring me with her.

EDWARD
I wonder whom else Lavinia has invited.

79

PETER

Why, I got the impression that Lavinia intended
To have yesterday's cocktail party to-day
So I don't suppose her aunt can have died.

EDWARD

What aunt?

PETER

The aunt you told us about.
But Edward — you remember our conversation yesterday?

EDWARD

110 Of course.

PETER

I hope you've done nothing about it.

EDWARD

No, I've done nothing.

PETER

I'm so glad.
Because I've changed my mind. I mean, I've decided
That it's all no use. I'm going to California.

CELIA

You're going to California!

PETER

Yes, I have a new job.

EDWARD

And how did that happen, overnight?

80

PETER

Why, it's a man Alex put me in touch with
And we settled everything this morning.
Alex is a wonderful person to know,
Because, you see, he knows everybody, everywhere.
So what I've really come for is to say good-bye.   120

CELIA

Well, Peter, I'm awfully glad, for your sake,
Though of course we . . . I shall miss you;
You know how I depended on you for concerts,
And picture exhibitions — more than you realised.
It *was* fun, wasn't it! But now you'll have a chance,
I hope, to realise your ambitions.
I shall miss you.

PETER
It's nice of you to say so;
But you'll find someone better, to go about with.

CELIA

I don't think that I shall be going to concerts.
I am going away too.   130
        [LAVINIA *lets herself in with a latch-key*]

PETER
You're going abroad?

CELIA

I don't know. Perhaps.

EDWARD
You're both going away!

81

[*Enter* LAVINIA]

LAVINIA
Who's going away? Well, Celia. Well, Peter.
I didn't expect to find either of you here.

PETER *and* CELIA
But the telegram!

LAVINIA
What telegram?

CELIA
The one you sent to Julia.

PETER
And the one you sent to Alex.

LAVINIA
I don't know what you mean.
Edward, have you been sending telegrams?

EDWARD
Of course I haven't sent any telegrams.

LAVINIA
This is some of Julia's mischief. 惡作劇
And is *she* coming?

PETER
Yes, and Alex.

LAVINIA
140 Then I shall ask *them* for an explanation.
Meanwhile, I suppose we might as well sit down.
What shall we talk about?

82

EDWARD
Peter's going to America.

PETER
Yes, and I would have rung you up tomorrow
And come in to say good-bye before I left.

LAVINIA
And Celia's going too? Was that what I heard?
I congratulate you both. To Hollywood, of course?
How exciting for you, Celia! Now you'll have a chance
At last, to realise your ambitions.
You're going together?

PETER
We're not going together.
Celia told us she was going away,
But I don't know where.

150

LAVINIA
You don't know where?
And do you know where you are going, yourself?

PETER
Yes, of course, I'm going to California.

LAVINIA
Well, Celia, why don't you go to California?
Everyone says it's a wonderful climate:
The people who go there never want to leave it.

CELIA
Lavinia, I think I understand about Peter . . .

LAVINIA

I have no doubt you do.

CELIA
And why he is going . . .

LAVINIA

I don't doubt that either.

CELIA
And I believe he is right to go.

LAVINIA

160   Oh, so you advised him?

PETER
She knew nothing about it.

CELIA

But now that I may be going away — somewhere —
I should like to say good-bye — as friends.

LAVINIA

Why, Celia, but haven't we always been friends?
I thought you were one of my dearest friends —
At least, in so far as a girl *can* be a friend
Of a woman so much older than herself.

CELIA
Lavinia,
Don't put me off. I may not see you again.
What I want to say is this: I should like you to remember me
As someone who wants you and Edward to be happy.

84

LAVINIA

You are very kind, but very mysterious.   170
I am sure that we shall manage somehow, thank you,
As we have in the past.

CELIA

Oh, not as in the past!
[*The doorbell rings, and* EDWARD *goes to answer it*]
Oh, I'm afraid that all this sounds rather silly!
But . . .
[EDWARD *re-enters with* JULIA]

JULIA

There you are, Lavinia! I'm sorry to be late.
But your telegram was a bit unexpected.
I dropped everything to come. And how is the dear aunt?

LAVINIA

So far as I know, she is very well, thank you.

JULIA

She must have made a marvellous recovery.
I said so to myself, when I got your telegram.

LAVINIA

But where, may I ask, was this telegram sent from?   180

JULIA

Why, from Essex, of course.

LAVINIA

And why from Essex?

JULIA

Because you've been in Essex.

LAVINIA

> Because I've been in Essex!

JULIA

Lavinia! Don't say you've had a lapse of memory!
Then that accounts for the aunt — and the telegram.

LAVINIA

Well, perhaps I was in Essex. I really don't know.

JULIA

You don't know where you were? Lavinia!
Don't tell me you were abducted! Tell us
I'm thrilled . . .
[*The doorbell rings.* EDWARD *goes to answer it. Enter* ALEX.]

ALEX

Has Lavinia arrived?

EDWARD

> Yes.

ALEX

> Welcome back, Lavinia!

190 When I got your telegram . . .

LAVINIA

> Where from?

ALEX

> *dea*
> *Lavinia*
> Dedham.*
> *metaphorically*
> *return from*
> *the grave.*

LAVINIA

Dedham is in Essex. So it was from Dedham.
Edward, have *you* any friends in Dedham?

86

EDWARD

No, *I* have no connections in Dedham.

JULIA

Well, it's all delightfully mysterious.

ALEX

But what is the mystery?

JULIA

                    Alex, *don't* be inquisitive.
Lavinia has had a lapse of memory,
And so, of course, she sent us telegrams:
And now I don't believe she really wants us.
I can see that she is quite worn out
After her anxiety about her aunt —   200
Who you'll be glad to hear, has quite recovered, Alex —
And after that long journey on the old Great Eastern,
Waiting at junctions. And I suppose she's famished.

ALEX

Ah, in that case I know what I'll do . . .

JULIA

                    No, Alex.
We must leave them alone, and let Lavinia rest.
Now we'll all go back to *my* house. Peter, call a taxi.

                                        [*Exit* PETER]

We'll have a cocktail party at *my* house to-day.

CELIA

Well, I'll go now. Good-bye, Lavinia.
Good-bye, Edward.

EDWARD
Good-bye, Celia.

CELIA
210 Good-bye, Lavinia.

LAVINIA
Good-bye, Celia.

[*Exit* CELIA]

JULIA
And now, Alex, you and I should be going.

EDWARD
Are you sure you haven't left anything, Julia?

JULIA
Left anything? Oh, you mean my spectacles.
No, they're here. Besides, they're no use to me.
I'm not coming back again *this* evening.

LAVINIA
Stop! I want you to explain the telegram.

JULIA
Explain the telegram? What do you think, Alex?

ALEX
No, Julia, *we* can't explain the telegram.

LAVINIA
I am sure that you could explain the telegram.
220 I don't know why. But it seems to me that yesterday
I started some machine,* that goes on working,

And I cannot stop it; no, it's not like a machine —
Or if it's a machine, someone else is running it.
But who? Somebody is always interfering*... Guardian
I don't feel free ... and yet I started it ...

JULIA

Alex, do you think we could explain *anything*?

ALEX

I think not, Julia. She must find out for herself:
That's the only way.

JULIA
How right you are!
Well, my dears, I shall see you very soon.

EDWARD

When shall we see you?   230

JULIA
Did I say you'd see me?
Good-bye. I believe ... I haven't left anything.
[*Enter* PETER]

PETER

I've got a taxi, Julia.

JULIA
Splendid! Good-bye!
                    [*Exeunt* JULIA, ALEX *and* PETER]

LAVINIA

I must say, you don't seem very pleased to see me.

EDWARD

I can't say that I've had much opportunity
To seem anything. But of course I'm glad to see you.

LAVINIA

Yes, that was a silly thing to say.
Like a schoolgirl. Like Celia. I don't know why I said it.
Well, here I am.

EDWARD

I am to ask no questions.

LAVINIA

And I know I am to give no explanations.

EDWARD

240 And I am to give no explanations.

LAVINIA

And I am to ask no questions. And yet . . . why not?

EDWARD

I don't know why not. So what are we to talk about?

LAVINIA

There is one thing I ought to know, because of other people
And what to do about them. It's about that party.
I suppose you won't believe I forgot all about it!
I let you down badly. What did you do about it?
I only remembered after I had left.

EDWARD

I telephoned to everyone I knew was coming
But I couldn't get everyone. And so a few came.

90

LAVINIA
Who came?   250

EDWARD
Just those who were here this evening . . .

LAVINIA
That's odd.

EDWARD
. . . and one other. I don't know who he was,
But *you* ought to know.*

LAVINIA
Yes, I think I know.
But I'm puzzled by Julia. That woman is the devil.
She knows by instinct when something's going to happen.
Trust her not to miss any awkward situation!
And what did you tell them?

EDWARD
I invented an aunt
Who was ill in the country, and had sent for you.

LAVINIA
Really, Edward! You had better have told the truth:
Nothing less that the truth could deceive Julia.
But how did the aunt come to live in Essex?   260

EDWARD
Julia compelled me to make her live somewhere.

LAVINIA
I see. So Julia made her live in Essex;
And made the telegrams come from Essex.

Well, I shall have to tell Julia the truth.
I shall always tell the truth now.
We have wasted such a lot of time in lying.

EDWARD

I don't quite know what you mean.

LAVINIA

Oh, Edward!
The point is, that since I've been away
I see that I've taken you much too seriously.
270   And now I can see how absurd you are.*
                unreasonable

EDWARD

That is a very serious conclusion
To have arrived at in . . . how many? . . . thirty-two hours.

LAVINIA

Yes, a very important discovery,
Finding that you've spent five years of your life
With a man who has no sense of humour;
And that the effect upon me was
That I lost all sense of humour myself.
That's what came of always giving in to you.

EDWARD

I was unaware that you'd always given in to me.
280   It struck me very differently. As we're on the subject,
I thought that it was I who had given in to *you*.

LAVINIA

I know what you mean by giving in to *me*:
You mean, leaving all the practical decisions
That you should have made yourself. I remember —

Oh, I ought to have realised what was coming —
When we were planning our honeymoon,
I couldn't make you say where you wanted to go . . .

EDWARD

But I wanted *you* to make that decision.

LAVINIA

But how could I tell where I wanted to go
Unless you suggested some other place first?   290
And I remember that finally in desperation
I said: 'I suppose you'd as soon go to Peacehaven' —
And you said 'I don't mind'.

EDWARD

                Of course I didn't mind.
I meant it as a compliment.

LAVINIA

                You meant it as a compliment!
And you were so considerate, people said;
And you thought you were unselfish. It was only passivity;
You only wanted to be bolstered, encouraged. . . .

EDWARD

Encouraged? To what?

LAVINIA

                To think well of yourself.
You know it was I who made you work at the Bar . . .

EDWARD

You nagged me because I didn't get enough work   300
And said that I ought to meet more people:

93

But when the briefs began to come in —
And they didn't come through any of *your* friends —
You suddenly found it inconvenient
That I should be always too busy or too tired
To be of use to you socially . . .

LAVINIA
                    I *never* complained.

EDWARD
No; and it was perfectly infuriating,
The way you *didn't* complain . . .

LAVINIA
                              It was you who complained
Of seeing nobody but solicitors and clients . . .

EDWARD
310 And you were never very sympathetic.

LAVINIA
Well, I tried to do something about it.
That was why I took so much trouble
To have those Thursdays, to give you the chance
Of talking to intellectual people . . .

EDWARD
You would have given me about as much opportunity
If you had hired me as your butler:
Some of your guests may have thought I *was* the butler.

LAVINIA
And on several occasions, when somebody was coming
Whom I particularly wanted you to meet,
320 You didn't arrive until just as they were leaving.

94

EDWARD

Well, at least, they can't have thought I was the butler.

LAVINIA

Everything I tried only made matters worse,
And the moment you were offered something that you
    wanted
You wanted something else. I shall treat you very differently
In future.

EDWARD

Thank you for the warning. But tell me,
Since this is how you see me, why did you come back?

LAVINIA

Frankly, I don't know. I was warned of the danger,*
Yet something, or somebody, compelled me to come.
And why did you want me?

EDWARD

I don't know either.
You say you were trying to 'encourage' me: 330
Then why did you always make me feel insignificant?
I may not have known what life I wanted,
But it wasn't the life you chose for me.
You wanted your husband to be *successful*,
You wanted me to supply a public background
For your kind of public life. You wished to be a hostess
For whom my career would be a support.
Well, I tried to be accommodating. But, in future,
I shall behave, I assure you, very differently.

LAVINIA

Bravo! Edward. This is surprising.   340
Now who could have taught you to answer back like that?

95

EDWARD

I have had quite enough humiliation
Lately, to bring me to the point
At which humiliation ceases to humiliate.
You get to the point at which you cease to feel
And then you speak your mind.

LAVINIA
                    That will be a novelty *newness strangeness*
To find that you have a mind to speak.
Anyway, I'm prepared to take you as you are.

EDWARD

You mean you are prepared to take me
350   As I was, or as you think I am.
But what do you think I am?

LAVINIA
                    Oh, what you always were.
As for me, I'm rather a different person
Whom you must get to know.

EDWARD
                    This is very interesting:
But you seem to assume that you've done all the changing —
Though I haven't yet found it a change for the better.
But doesn't it occur to you that possibly
I may have changed too?

LAVINIA
                    Oh, Edward, when you were a little boy,*
I'm sure you were always getting yourself measured
To prove how you had grown since the last holidays.
360   You were always intensely concerned with yourself;

96

And if other people grow, well, you want to grow too.
In what way have you changed?

EDWARD

The change that comes
From seeing oneself through the eyes of other people.

LAVINIA

That must have been very shattering for you.
But never mind, you'll soon get over it
And find yourself another little part to play,
With another face, to take people in.

EDWARD

One of the most infuriating things about you
Has always been your perfect assurance
That you understood me better than I understood myself.   370

LAVINIA

And the most infuriating thing about you
Has always been your placid assumption
That I wasn't worth the trouble of understanding.

EDWARD

So here we are again. Back in the trap,
With only one difference, perhaps — we can fight each
    other,
Instead of each taking his corner of the cage.
Well, it's a better way of passing the evening
Than listening to the gramophone.

LAVINIA

We have very good records;
But I always suspected that you really hated music

380 And that the gramophone was only your escape
From talking to me when we had to be alone.

EDWARD
I've often wondered why you married me.

LAVINIA
Well, you really were rather attractive, you know;
And you kept on *saying* that you were in love with me —
I believe you were trying to persuade yourself you were.
I seemed always on the verge of some wonderful experience
And then it never happened. I wonder now
How you could have thought you were in love with me.

EDWARD
Everybody told me that I was;
390 And they told me how well suited we were.

LAVINIA
It's a pity that you had no opinion of your own.
Oh, Edward, I should like to be good to you —
Or if that's impossible, at least be horrid to you —
Anything but nothing, which is all you seem to want of me.
But I'm sorry for you . . .

EDWARD
Don't say you are sorry for me!
I have had enough of people being sorry for me.

LAVINIA
Yes, because they can never be so sorry for you
As you are for yourself. And that's hard to bear.
I thought that there might be some way out for you
400 If I went away. I thought that if I died

98

To you, I who had been only a ghost to you,
You might be able to find the road back
To a time when you were real — for you must have been
    real
At some time or other, before you ever knew me:
Perhaps only when you were a child.

EDWARD

I don't want you to make yourself responsible for me:
It's only another kind of contempt.
And I do not want you to explain me to myself.
You're still trying to invent a personality for me
Which will only keep me away from myself.   410

LAVINIA

You're complicating what is in fact very simple.
But there is one point which I see clearly:
We are not to relapse into the kind of life we led
Until yesterday morning.

EDWARD
                There was a door
And I could not open it. I could not touch the handle.
Why could I not walk out of my prison?
What is hell? Hell is oneself,
Hell is alone, the other figures in it
Merely projections.* There is nothing to escape from
And nothing to escape to. One is always alone.   420

LAVINIA

Edward, what *are* you talking about?
Talking to yourself. Could you bear, for a moment,
To think about *me*?

99

EDWARD

It was only yesterday*
That damnation took place. And now I must live with it
Day by day, hour by hour, for ever and ever.

LAVINIA

I think you're on the edge of a nervous breakdown!

EDWARD

Don't say that!

LAVINIA

I must say it.
I know . . . of a doctor who I think could help you.

EDWARD

If I go to a doctor, I shall make my own choice;
430 Not take one whom you choose. How do I know
That you wouldn't see him first, and tell him all about me
From *your* point of view? But I don't need a doctor.
I am simply in hell. Where there are no doctors —
At least, not in a professional capacity.

LAVINIA

One can be practical, even in hell:
And you know I am much more practical than you are.

EDWARD

I ought to know by now what you consider practical.
Practical! I remember, on our honeymoon,
You were always wrapping things up in tissue paper
440 And then had to unwrap everything again
To find what you wanted. And I could never teach you
How to put the cap on a tube of tooth-paste.

100

LAVINIA

Very well then, I shall not try to press you.
You're much too divided to know what you want.
But, being divided, you will tend to compromise,
And your sort of compromise will be the old one.

EDWARD

You don't understand me. Have I not made it clear
That in future you will find me a different person?

LAVINIA

Indeed. And has the difference nothing to do
With Celia going to California?   450

EDWARD

Celia? Going to California?

LAVINIA

            Yes, with Peter.*
Really, Edward, if you were human
You would burst out laughing. But you won't.

EDWARD

O God, O God, if I could return to yesterday
Before I thought that I had made a decision.
What devil left the door on the latch
For these doubts to enter? And then you came back, you
The angel of destruction — just as I felt sure.
In a moment, at your touch, there is nothing but ruin.
O God, what have I done? The python. The octopus.   460
Must I become after all what you would make me?

101

LAVINIA

Well, Edward, as I am unable to make you laugh,
And as I can't persuade you to see a doctor,
There's nothing else at present that I can do about it.
I ought to go and have a look in the kitchen.
I know there are some eggs. But we must go out for dinner.
Meanwhile, my luggage is in the hall downstairs:
Will you get the porter to fetch it up for me?

CURTAIN

Act Two

Sir Henry Harcourt-Reilly's *consulting room in London. Morning: several weeks later.* Sir Henry *alone at his desk. He presses an electric button. The* Nurse-Secretary *enters, with Appointment Book.*

REILLY

About those three appointments this morning, Miss
Barraway:
I should like to run over my instructions again.
You understand, of course, that it is important
To avoid any meeting?

NURSE-SECRETARY
You made that clear, Sir Henry:
The first appointment at eleven o'clock.
He is to be shown into the small waiting-room;
And you will see him almost at once.

REILLY

I shall see him at once. And the second?

NURSE-SECRETARY

The second to be shown into the other room
Just as usual. She arrives at a quarter past;   10
But you may keep her waiting.

103

REILLY

Or she may keep me waiting;
But I think she will be punctual.

NURSE-SECRETARY

I telephone through
The moment she arrives. I leave her there
Until you ring three times.

REILLY

And the third patient?

NURSE-SECRETARY

The third one to be shown into the small room;
And I need not let you know that she has arrived.
Then, when you ring, I show the others out;
And only after they have left the house. . . .

REILLY

Quite right, Miss Barraway. That's all for the moment.

NURSE-SECRETARY

20 Mr. Gibbs is here, Sir Henry.

REILLY

Ask him to come straight in.
                    [*Exit* NURSE-SECRETARY]
[ALEX *enters almost immediately*]

ALEX

When is Chamberlayne's appointment?

REILLY

At eleven o'clock,
The conventional hour. We have not much time.

Tell me now, did you have any difficulty
In convincing him I was the man for his case?

ALEX

Difficulty? No! He was only impatient
At having to wait four days for the appointment.

REILLY

It was necessary to delay his appointment
To lower his resistance. But what I mean is,
Does he trust your judgement?

ALEX

                    Yes, implicitly.
It's not that he regards me as very intelligent,   30
But he thinks I'm well informed: the sort of person
Who would know the right doctor, as well as the right shops
Besides, he was ready to consult any doctor
Recommended by anyone except his wife.

REILLY

I had already impressed upon her
That she was not to mention my name to him.

ALEX

With your usual foresight. Now, he's quite triumphant
Because he thinks he's stolen a march on her.
And when you've sent him to a sanatorium*   療養院
Where she can't get at him — then, he believes,   40
She will be very penitent. He's enjoying his illness.
              feeling
              regret

REILLY

Illness offers him a double advantage:
To escape from himself — and get the better of his wife.

105

ALEX

Not to escape from her?

REILLY

He doesn't want to escape from her.

ALEX

He is staying at his club.

REILLY

Yes, that is where he wrote from.
                    [*The house-telephone rings*]
Hello! Yes, show him up.

ALEX

You will have a busy morning!
I will go out by the service staircase
And come back when they've gone.

REILLY

Yes, when they've gone.

                    [*Exit* ALEX *by side door*]
[EDWARD *is shown in by* NURSE-SECRETARY]

EDWARD

50 Sir Henry Harcourt-Reilly —
                    [*Stops and stares at* REILLY]

REILLY

[*Without looking up from his papers*]
                    Good morning, Mr. Chamberlayne.
Please sit down. I won't keep you a moment.
— Now, Mr. Chamberlayne?

EDWARD
It came into my mind
Before I entered the door, that you might be the same
person:
But I dismissed that as just another symptom.
Well, I should have known better than to come here
On the recommendation of a man who did not know you.*
Yet Alex is so plausible. And his recommendations
Of shops, have always been satisfactory.
I beg your pardon. But he *is* a blunderer.
I should like to know . . . but what is the use!   60
I suppose I might as well go away at once.

REILLY
No. If you please, sit down, Mr. Chamberlayne.
You are not going away, so you might as well sit down.
You were going to ask a question.

EDWARD
When you came to my flat
Had you been invited by my wife as a guest
As I supposed? . . . Or did she *send* you?

REILLY
I cannot say that I had been invited;
And Mrs. Chamberlayne did not know that I was coming.
But I knew you would be there, and whom I should find
with you.

EDWARD
But you had seen my wife?   70

REILLY
Oh yes, I had seen her.

EDWARD

So this *is* a trap!

REILLY

Let's not call it a trap.
But if it is a trap, then you cannot escape from it:
And so . . . you might as well sit down.
I think you will find that chair comfortable.

EDWARD

You knew,
Before I began to tell you, what had happened?

REILLY

That is so, that is so. But all in good time.
Let us dismiss that question for the moment.
Tell me first, about the difficulties
On which you want my professional opinion.

EDWARD

80 It's not for me to blame you for bringing my wife back,
I suppose. You seemed to be trying to persuade me
That I was better off without her. But didn't you realise
That I was in no state to make a decision?

REILLY

If I had not brought your wife back, Mr. Chamberlayne,
Do you suppose that things would be any better — now?

EDWARD

I don't know, I'm sure. They could hardly be worse.

REILLY

They might be much worse. You might have ruined three
        lives

108

By your indecision. Now there are only two —
Which you still have the chance of redeeming from ruin.

EDWARD

You talk as if I was capable of action: 90
If I were, I should not need to consult you
Or anyone else. I came here as a patient.
If you take no interest in my case, I can go elsewhere.

REILLY

You have reason to believe that you are very ill?

EDWARD

I should have thought a doctor could see that for himself.
Or at least that he would enquire about the symptoms.
Two people advised me recently,*
Almost in the same words, that I ought to see a doctor.
They said — again, in almost the same words —
That I was on the edge of a nervous breakdown.   100
I didn't know it then myself — but if they saw it
I should have thought that a doctor could see it.

REILLY

'Nervous breakdown' is a term I never use:
It can mean almost anything.

EDWARD

                    And since then, I have realised
That mine is a very unusual case.

REILLY

All cases are unique, and very similar to others.

EDWARD

Is there a sanatorium to which you send such patients

As myself, under your personal observation?

REILLY

You are very impetuous, Mr. Chamberlayne.
110   There are several kinds of sanatoria
For several kinds of patient. And there are also patients
For whom a sanatorium is the worst place possible.
We must first find out what is wrong with you
Before we decide what to do with you.

EDWARD

I doubt if you have ever had a case like mine:
I have ceased to believe in my own personality.

REILLY

Oh, dear yes; this is serious. A very common malady.
Very prevalent indeed.

EDWARD

I remember, in my childhood . . .

REILLY

I always begin from the immediate situation
120   And then go back as far as I find necessary.
You see, your memories of childhood —
I mean, in your present state of mind —
Would be largely fictitious; and as for your dreams,
You would produce amazing dreams, to oblige me.
I could make you dream any kind of dream I suggested,
And it would only go to flatter your vanity
With the temporary stimulus of feeling interesting.

EDWARD

But I am obsessed by the thought of my own insignificance.

REILLY

Precisely. And I could make you feel important,
And you would imagine it a marvellous cure; 130
And you would go on, doing such amount of mischief
As lay within your power — until you came to grief.
Half of the harm that is done in this world
Is due to people who want to feel important.
They don't mean to do harm — but the harm does not
    interest them.
Or they do not see it, or they justify it
Because they are absorbed in the endless struggle
To think well of themselves.

EDWARD
           If I am like that
I must have done a great deal of harm.

REILLY

Oh, not so much as you would like to think: 140
Only, shall we say, within your modest capacity.
Try to explain what has happened since I left you.

EDWARD

I see now why I wanted my wife to come back.
It was because of what she had made me into.
We had not been alone again for fifteen minutes
Before I felt, and still more acutely —
Indeed, acutely, perhaps, for the first time,
The whole oppression, the unreality
Of the role she had always imposed upon me
With the obstinate, unconscious, sub-human strength 150

That some women have. Without her, it was vacancy.
When I thought she had left me, I began to dissolve,
To cease to exist. That was what she had done to me!
I cannot live with her — that is now intolerable;
I cannot live without her, for she has made me incapable
Of having any existence of my own.
That is what she has done to me in five years together!
She has made the world a place I cannot live in
Except on her terms. I must be alone,
160   But not in the same world. So I want you to put me
Into your sanatorium. I could be alone there?
                    [*House-telephone rings*]

REILLY

[*Into telephone*]   Yes.
[*To* EDWARD]   Yes, you could be alone there.

EDWARD

                                          I wonder
If you have understood a word of what I have been saying.

REILLY

You must have patience with me, Mr. Chamberlayne:
I learn a good deal by merely observing you,
And letting you talk as long as you please,
And taking note of what you do not say.

EDWARD

I once experienced the extreme of physical pain,
And now I know there is suffering worse than that.
It is surprising, if one had time to be surprised:
170   I am not afraid of the death of the body,
But this death is terrifying. The death of the spirit —
Can you understand what I suffer?

112

REILLY

I understand what you mean.

EDWARD

I can no longer act for myself.
Coming to see you — that's the last decision
I was capable of making. I am in your hands.
I cannot take any further responsibility.

REILLY

Many patients come in that belief.

EDWARD

And now will you send me to the sanatorium?

REILLY

You have nothing else to tell me?*

tell the full truth about the protraction.

EDWARD

What else can I tell you?
You didn't want to hear about my early history.   180

REILLY

No, I did not want to hear about your *early* history.

EDWARD

And so will you send me to the sanatorium?
I can't go home again. And at my club
They won't let you keep a room for more than seven days;
I haven't the courage to go to a hotel,
And besides, I need more shirts — you can get my wife
To have my things sent on: whatever I shall need.
But of course you mustn't tell her where I am.
Is it far to go?

REILLY

You might say, a long journey.
190   But before I treat a patient like yourself
I need to know a great deal more about him,
Than the patient himself can always tell me.
Indeed, it is often the case that my patients
Are only pieces of a total situation
Which I have to explore. The single patient
Who is ill by himself, is rather the exception.
I have recently had another patient
Whose situation is much the same as your own.
            [*Presses the bell on his desk three times*]
You must accept a rather unusual procedure:
200   I propose to introduce you to the other patient.

EDWARD

What do you mean? Who is this other patient?
I consider this very unprofessional conduct —
I will not discuss my case before another patient.

REILLY

On the contrary. That is the only way
In which it can be discussed. You have told me nothing.
You have had the opportunity, and you have said enough
To convince me that you have been making up your case
So to speak, as you went along. A barrister
Ought to know his brief before he enters the court.

EDWARD

210   I am at least free to leave. And I propose to do so.
My mind is made up. I shall go to a hotel.

REILLY

It is just because you are not free, Mr. Chamberlayne,

That you have come to me. It is for me to give you that —
Your freedom. That is my affair.

    [LAVINIA *is shown in by the* NURSE-SECRETARY]
But here is the other patient.

EDWARD

    Lavinia!

LAVINIA

                    Well, Sir Henry!
I said I would come to talk about my husband:
I didn't say I was prepared to meet him.

EDWARD

And I did not expect to meet *you*, Lavinia.
I call this a very dishonourable trick.

REILLY

Honesty before honour,* Mr. Chamberlayne.   220
Sit down, please, both of you. Mrs. Chamberlayne,
Your husband wishes to enter a sanatorium,
And that is a question which naturally concerns you.

EDWARD

I am not going to any sanatorium.
I am going to a hotel. And I shall ask you, Lavinia,
To be so good as to send me on some clothes.

LAVINIA

Oh, to what hotel?

EDWARD

            I don't know — I mean to say,
That doesn't concern you.

LAVINIA

In that case, Edward,
I don't think your clothes concern me either.

[*To* REILLY]

230 I presume you will send him to the same sanatorium
To which you sent me? Well, he needs it more than I did.

REILLY

I am glad that you have come to see it in that light —
At least, for the moment. But, Mrs. Chamberlayne,
You have never visited my sanatorium.*

LAVINIA

What do you mean? I asked to be sent
And you took me there. If that was not a sanatorium
What was it?

REILLY

A kind of hotel. A retreat
For people who imagine that they need a respite
From everyday life. They return refreshed;
240 And if they believe it to be a sanatorium
That is good reason for not sending them to one.
The people who need my sort of sanatorium
Are not easily deceived.

LAVINIA

Are you a devil
Or merely a lunatic practical joker?

EDWARD

I incline to the second explanation
Without the qualification 'lunatic'.
Why should *you* go to a sanatorium?

I have never known anyone in my life
With fewer mental complications than you;
You're stronger than a . . . battleship. That's what drove me   250
    mad.
I am the one who needs a sanatorium —
But I'm not going there.

REILLY
        You are right, Mr. Chamberlayne.
You are no case for my sanatorium:
You are much too ill.*— *morally ill and self-centred and dishonest.*

EDWARD
        Much too ill?
Then I'll go and be ill in a suburban boarding-house.

LAVINIA
That would never suit you, Edward. Now I know of a hotel
In the New Forest . . .

EDWARD
        How like you, Lavinia.
You always know of something better.

LAVINIA
It's only that I have a more practical mind
Than you have, Edward. You do know that.   260

EDWARD
Only because you've told me so often.
I'd like to see *you* filling up an income-tax form.

LAVINIA
Don't be silly, Edward. When I say practical,
I mean practical in the things that really matter.

REILLY

May I interrupt this interesting discussion?
I say you are both too ill. There several symptoms
Which must occur together, and to a marked degree,
To qualify a patient for *my* sanatorium:
And one of them is an honest mind.
270 That is one of the causes of their suffering.

LAVINIA

No one can say my husband has an honest mind.

EDWARD

And I could not honestly say that of *you*, Lavinia.

REILLY

I congratulate you both on your perspicacity.
Your sympathetic understanding of each other
Will prepare you to appreciate what I have to say to you.
I do not trouble myself with the common cheat,
Or with the insuperably, innocently dull:
My patients such as you are the self-deceivers
Taking infinite pains, exhausting their energy,
280 Yet never quite successful. You have both of you pretended
To be consulting me; both, tried to impose upon me
Your own diagnosis, and prescribe your own cure.
But when you put yourselves into hands like mine
You surrender a great deal more than you meant to.
This is the consequence of trying to lie to me.

LAVINIA

I did not come here to be insulted.

REILLY

You have come where the word 'insult' has no meaning;*

118

And you must put up with that. All that you have told me —
Both of you — was true enough: you described your
     feelings —
Or some of them — omitting the important facts.   290
Let me take your husband first.
            [*To* EDWARD]
                   You were lying to me
By concealing your relations with Miss Coplestone.

EDWARD

This is monstrous! My wife knew nothing about it.

LAVINIA

Really, Edward! Even if I'd been blind
There were plenty of people to let me know about it.
I wonder if there was anyone who didn't know.

REILLY

There was one, in fact.* But you, Mrs. Chamberlayne,
Tried to make me believe that it was this discovery
Precipitated what you called your nervous breakdown.

LAVINIA

But it's true! I was completely prostrated;   300
Even if I have made a partial recovery.

REILLY

Certainly, you were completely prostrated,
And certainly, you have somewhat recovered.
But you failed to mention that the cause of your distress
Was the defection of your lover — who suddenly
For the first time in his life, fell in love with someone,
And with someone of whom you had reason to be jealous.

EDWARD

Really, Lavinia! This is very interesting.
You seem to have been much more successful at concealment
310   Than I was. Now I wonder who it could have been.

LAVINIA

Well, tell him if you like.

REILLY

          A young man named Peter.

EDWARD

Peter? Peter who?

REILLY

          Mr. Peter Quilpe
Was a frequent guest.

EDWARD

          Peter Quilpe.
Peter Quilpe! Really Lavinia!
I congratulate you. You could not have chosen
Anyone I was less likely to suspect.
And then he came to *me* to confide about Celia!
I have never heard anything so utterly ludicrous:
This is the best joke that ever happened.

LAVINIA

320   I never knew you had such a sense of humour.

REILLY

It is the first more hopeful symptom.

LAVINIA

How did you know all this?

REILLY
                That I cannot disclose.
I have my own method of collecting information
About my patients. You must not ask me to reveal it —
That is a matter of professional etiquette.

LAVINIA
I have not noticed much professional etiquette
About your behaviour to-day.

REILLY
                A point well taken.
But permit me to remark that my revelations
About each of you, to one another,
Have not been of anything that you confided to me.   330
The information I have exchanged between you
Was all obtained from outside sources.
Mrs. Chamberlayne, when you came to me two months ago
I was dissatisfied with your explanation
Of your obvious symptoms of emotional strain
And so I made enquiries.

EDWARD
                It was two months ago
That your breakdown began! And I never noticed it.

LAVINIA
You wouldn't notice anything. You never noticed *me*.

REILLY
Now, I want to point out to both of you
How much you have in common. Indeed, I consider   340
That you are exceptionally well-suited to each other.

121

Mr. Chamberlayne, when you thought your wife had left
　　you,
You discovered, to your surprise and consternation,
That you were not really in love with Miss Coplestone . . .

LAVINIA

My husband has never been in love with anybody.

REILLY

And were not prepared to make the least sacrifice
On her account. This injured your vanity.
You liked to think of yourself as a passionate lover.
Then you realised, what your wife has justly remarked,
350　That you had never been in love with anybody;
Which made you suspect that you were incapable
Of loving. To men of a certain type
The suspicion that they are incapable of loving
Is as disturbing to their self-esteem
As, in cruder men, the fear of impotence.

LAVINIA

You *are* cold-hearted, Edward.

REILLY

　　　　　　So you say, Mrs. Chamberlayne.
And now, let us turn to your side of the problem.
When you discovered that your young friend
(Though you knew, in your heart, that he was not in love
　　with you,
360　And were always humiliated by the awareness
That you had forced him into this position) —
When, I say, you discovered that your young friend
Had actually fallen in love with Miss Coplestone,
It took you some time, I have no doubt,

Before you would admit it. Though perhaps you knew it
Before he did. You pretended to yourself,
I suspect, and for as long as you could,
That he was aiming at a higher social distinction
Than the honour conferred by being *your* lover.
When you had to face the fact that his feelings towards her   370
Were different from any you had aroused in him —
It was a shock. You had wanted to be loved;
You had come to see that no one had ever loved you.
Then you began to fear that no one *could* love you.

EDWARD

I'm beginning to feel very sorry for you, Lavinia.
You know, you really are exceptionally unlovable,
And I never quite knew why. I thought it was *my* fault.

REILLY

And now you begin to see, I hope,
How much you have in common. The same isolation.
A man who finds himself incapable of loving   380
And a woman who finds that no man can love her.

LAVINIA

It seems to me that what we have in common
Might be just enough to make us loathe one another.*

REILLY

See it rather as the bond which holds you together.
While still in a state of unenlightenment,
You could always say: 'he could not love any woman;'
You could always say: 'no man could love her.'
You could accuse each other of your own faults,
And so could avoid understanding each other.
Now, you have only to reverse the propositions   390
And put them together.

123

LAVINIA
Is that possible?

REILLY
If I had sent either of you to the sanatorium
In the state in which you came to me — I tell you this:
It would have been a horror beyond your imagining,
For you would have been left with what you brought with
        you:
The shadow of desires of desires.* A prey
To the devils who arrive at their plenitude of power*
When they have you to themselves.

LAVINIA
                    Then what can we do
When we can go neither back nor forward? Edward!*
400 What can we do?

REILLY
                You have answered your own question,
Though you do not know the meaning of what you have
            said.*

EDWARD
Lavinia, we must make the best of a bad job.
That is what he means.

REILLY
                When you find, Mr. Chamberlayne,
The best of a bad job is all any of us make of it —
Except of course, the saints — such as those who go
To the sanatorium — you will forget this phrase,
And in forgetting it will alter the condition.

124

LAVINIA

Edward, there *is* that hotel in the New Forest
If you want to go there. The proprietor
Who has just taken over, is a friend of Alex's.　　　　410
I could go down with you, and then leave you there
If you want to be alone . . .

EDWARD

But I can't go away!
I have a case coming on next Monday.

LAVINIA

Then will you stop at your club?

EDWARD

No, they won't let me.
I must leave tomorrow — but how did you know
I was staying at the club?

LAVINIA

Really, Edward!
I have *some* sense of responsibility.*
I was going to leave some shirts there for you.

EDWARD

It seems to me that I might as well go home.

LAVINIA

Then we can share a taxi, and be economical.　　　　420
Edward, have you anything else to ask him
Before we go?

EDWARD

Yes, I have.
But it's difficult to say.

125

LAVINIA

But I wish you would say it.
At least, there is something I would like you to ask.

EDWARD

It's about the future of . . . the others.
I don't want to build on other people's ruins.

LAVINIA

Exactly. And I have a question too.
Sir Henry, was it you who sent those telegrams?

REILLY

I think I will dispose of your husband's problem.
[*To* EDWARD]
430 Your business is not to clear your conscience
But to learn how to bear the burdens on your conscience.
With the future of the others you are not concerned.

LAVINIA

I think you have answered my question too.*
They had to tell us, themselves, that they had made their
    decision.

EDWARD

Have you anything else to say to us, Sir Henry?

REILLY

No. Not in this capacity.
[EDWARD *takes out his cheque-book.* REILLY *raises his hand.*]
My secretary will send you my account.
Go in peace. And work out your salvation with diligence.*
[*Exeunt* EDWARD *and* LAVINIA]
[REILLY *goes to the couch and lies down. The house-telephone
    rings. He gets up and answers it.*]

126

REILLY

Yes? . . . Yes. Come in.
[*Enter* JULIA *by side door*]
                              She's waiting downstairs.

JULIA

I know that, Henry. I brought her here myself.   440

REILLY

Oh? You didn't let her know you were seeing me first?

JULIA

Of course not. I dropped her at the door
And went on in the taxi, round the corner;
Waited a moment, and slipped in by the back way.
I only came to tell you, I am sure she is ready
To make a decision.

REILLY
                Was she reluctant?
Was that why you brought her?

JULIA
                        Oh no, not reluctant:
Only diffident. She cannot believe
That you will take her seriously.

REILLY
                        That is not uncommon.

JULIA

Or that she deserves to be taken seriously.   450

REILLY

That is most uncommon.

127

JULIA

Henry, get up.

You can't be as tired as that. I shall wait in the next room,
And come back when she's gone.

REILLY

Yes, when she's gone.

JULIA

Will Alex be here?

REILLY

Yes, he'll be here.

[*Exit* JULIA *by side door*]
[REILLY *presses button.*
NURSE-SECRETARY *shows in* CELIA.]

REILLY

Miss Celia Coplestone? . . . Won't you sit down?
I believe you are a friend of Mrs. Shuttlethwaite.

CELIA

Yes, it was Julia . . . Mrs. Shuttlethwaite
Who advised me to come to you. — But I've met you before,
Haven't I, somewhere? . . . Oh, of course.
460   But I didn't know . . .

REILLY

There is nothing you need to know.
I was there at the instance of Mrs. Shuttlethwaite.

CELIA

That makes it even more perplexing. However,
I don't want to waste your time. And I'm awfully afraid
That you'll think that I am wasting it anyway.

128

I suppose most people, when they come to see you,
Are obviously ill, or can give good reasons
For wanting to see you. Well, I can't.
I just came in desperation. And I shan't be offended
If you simply tell me to go away again.

REILLY

Most of my patients begin, Miss Coplestone,   470
By telling me exactly what is the matter with them,
And what I am to do about it. They are quite sure
They have had a nervous breakdown — that is what they
        call it —
And usually they think that someone else is to blame.

CELIA

I at least have no one to blame but myself.

REILLY

And after that, the prologue to my treatment
Is to try to show them that they are mistaken
About the nature of their illness, and lead them to see
That it's not so interesting as they had imagined.
When I get as far as that, there is something to be done.   480

CELIA

Well, I can't pretend that my trouble is interesting;
But I shan't begin that way. I feel perfectly well.
I could lead an active life — if there's anything to work for;
I don't imagine that I am being persecuted;
I don't hear any voices, I have no delusions —
Except that the world I live in seems all a delusion!* *Unreal London city*
But oughtn't I first to tell you the circumstances?
I'd forgotten that you know nothing about me;
And with what I've been going through, these last weeks,
I somehow took it for granted that I needn't explain myself.   490

E   129

REILLY

I know quite enough about you for the moment:
Try first to describe your present state of mind.

[handwritten: general isolation among human beings — surprises of failing]
[handwritten: 1) sense of solitude 2) sense of sin — towards someone or something.]

CELIA

Well, there are two things I can't understand,*
Which you might consider symptoms. But first I must tell you
That I should really *like* to think there's something wrong with me —
Because, if there isn't, then there's something wrong,
Or at least, very different from what it seemed to be,
With the world itself — and that's much more frightening!
That would be terrible. So I'd rather believe
500 There is something wrong with me, that could be put right.
I'd do anything you told me, to get back to normality.

[handwritten: What is a saint. What normal]

REILLY

We must find out about you, before we decide
What *is* normality.* You say there are two things:
What is the first?

CELIA

An awareness of solitude.
But that sounds so flat. I don't mean simply
That there's been a crash: though indeed there has been.
It isn't simply the end of an illusion
In the ordinary way, or being ditched.
Of course that's something that's always happening
510 To all sorts of people, and they get over it
More or less, or at least they carry on.
No. I mean that what has happened has made me aware
That I've always been alone. That one always is alone.
Not simply the ending of one relationship,

130

Not even simply finding that it never existed —
But a revelation about my relationship
With *everybody*. Do you know —
It no longer seems worth while to *speak* to anyone!*

REILLY
And what about your parents?

CELIA
               Oh, they live in the country,
Now they can't afford to have a place in town.   520
It's all they can do to keep the country house going;
But it's been in the family so long, they won't leave it.

REILLY
And you live in London?

CELIA
         I share a flat
With a cousin: but she's abroad at the moment,
And my family want me to come down and stay with them.
But I just can't face it.

REILLY
So you want to see no one?

CELIA
No . . . it isn't that I *want* to be alone,
But that everyone's alone — or so it seems to me.
They make noises, and think they are talking to each other;
They make faces, and think they understand each other.   530
And I'm sure that they don't. Is that a delusion?

REILLY

A delusion is something we must return from.
There are other states of mind,* which we take to be
        delusion,
But which we have to accept and go on from.
And the second symptom?

CELIA

                    That's stranger still.
It sounds ridiculous — but the only word for it
That I can find, is a sense of sin.

REILLY

You suffer from a sense of sin, Miss Coplestone?
This is most unusual.

CELIA

                    It seemed to *me* abnormal.

REILLY

540   We have yet to find what would be normal
For *you*, before we use the term 'abnormal'.
Tell me what you mean by a sense of sin.

CELIA

It's much easier to tell you what I don't mean:
I don't mean sin in the ordinary sense.

REILLY

And what, in your opinion, is the ordinary sense?

CELIA

Well . . . I suppose it's being immoral* —
And I don't feel as if I was immoral:

132

In fact, aren't the people one thinks of as immoral
Just the people who we say have no moral sense?
I've never noticed that immorality   550
Was accompanied by a sense of sin:
At least, I have never come across it.
I suppose it is wicked to hurt other people.
If you know that you're hurting them. I haven't hurt *her*.
I wasn't taking anything away from her —
Anything she wanted. I may have been a fool:
But I don't mind at all having been a fool.

REILLY

And what is the point of view of your family?

CELIA

Well, my bringing up was pretty conventional —
I had always been taught to disbelieve in sin.   560
Oh, I don't mean that it was ever mentioned!*
But anything wrong, from our point of view,
Was either bad form, or was psychological.
And bad form always led to disaster
Because the people one knew disapproved of it.
I don't worry much about form, myself —
But when everything's bad form, or mental kinks,
You either become bad form, and cease to care,
Or else, if you care, you must be kinky.

REILLY

And so you suppose you have what you call a 'kink'?   570

CELIA

But everything seemed so right, at the time!
I've been thinking about it, over and over;
I can see now, it was all a mistake.

But I don't see why mistakes should make one feel sinful!
And yet I can't find any other word for it.
It must be some kind of hallucination;
Yet, at the same time, I'm frightened by the fear
That it is more real than anything I believed in.

REILLY

What is more real than anything you believed in?

CELIA

580 It's not the feeling of anything I've ever *done*,
Which I might get away from, or of anything in me
I could get rid of — but of emptiness, of failure
Towards someone, or something, outside of myself;
And I feel I must . . . *atone* — is that the word?
Can you treat a patient for such a state of mind?

REILLY

What had you believed were your relations with this man?

CELIA

Oh, you'd guessed that, had you? That's clever of you.
No, perhaps I made it obvious. You don't need to know
About him, do you?

REILLY

          No.

CELIA

Perhaps I'm only typical.

REILLY

590 There are different types. Some are rarer than others.

CELIA

Oh, I thought that I was giving him so much!
And he to me — and the giving and the taking
Seemed so right: not in terms of calculation
Of what was good for the persons we had been
But for the new person, *us*. If I could feel
As I did then, even now it would seem right.
And then I found we were only strangers
And that there had been neither giving nor taking
But that we had merely made use of each other
Each for his purpose. That's horrible. Can we only love   600
Something created by our own imagination?
Are we all in fact unloving and unlovable?
Then one *is* alone, and if one is alone
Then lover and belovèd are equally unreal
And the dreamer is no more real than his dreams.

REILLY

And this man. What does he now seem like, to you?

CELIA

Like a child who has wandered into a forest
Playing with an imaginary playmate
And suddenly discovers he is only a child
Lost in a forest, wanting to go home.   610

REILLY

Compassion may be already a clue
Towards finding your own way out of the forest.

CELIA

But even if I find my way out of the forest
I shall be left with the inconsolable memory
Of the treasure I went into the forest to find

135

And never found, and which was not there
And perhaps is not anywhere? But if not anywhere,
Why do I feel guilty at not having found it?

醒覚

REILLY

Disillusion can become itself an illusion
620　If we rest in it.

CELIA

　　　I cannot argue.*
It's not that I'm afraid of being hurt again:
Nothing again can either hurt or heal.
I have thought at moments that the ecstasy is real
Although those who experience it may have no reality.
For what happened is remembered like a dream
In which one is exalted by intensity of loving
In the spirit, a vibration of delight
Without desire, for desire is fulfilled
In the delight of loving. A state one does not know
630　When awake. But what, or whom I loved,
Or what in me was loving, I do not know.
And if that is all meaningless, I want to be cured
Of a craving for something I cannot find
And of the shame of never finding it.
Can you cure me?

REILLY

　　　The condition is curable.
But the form of treatment must be your own choice:
I cannot choose for you. If that is what you wish,
I can reconcile you to the human condition,
The condition to which some who have gone as far as you
640　Have succeeded in returning.* They may remember
The vision they have had, but they cease to regret it,

136

wishing for a visionary love

Maintain themselves by the common routine,
Learn to avoid excessive expectation,
Become tolerant of themselves and others,
Giving and taking, in the usual actions
What there is to give and take. They do not repine;
Are contented with the morning that separates
And with the evening that brings together
For casual talk before the fire
Two people who know they do not understand each other,   650
Breeding children whom they do not understand
And who will never understand them.

CELIA

Is that the best life?

REILLY

It is a good life. Though you will not know how good
Till you come to the end. But you will want nothing else,
And the other life will be only like a book
You have read once, and lost. In a world of lunacy,
Violence, stupidity, greed . . . it is a good life.

CELIA

I know I ought to be able to accept that
If I might still have it. Yet it leaves me cold.
Perhaps that's just a part of my illness,   660
But I feel it would be a kind of surrender —
No, not a surrender — more like a betrayal.
You see, I think I really had a vision of something
Though I don't know what it is. I don't want to forget it.
I want to live with it. I could do without everything,
Put up with anything, if I might cherish it.
In fact, I think it would really be dishonest
For me, now, to try to make a life with *any*body!

137

I couldn't give anyone the kind of love —
670 I wish I could — which belongs to that life.
Oh, I'm afraid this sounds like raving!
Or just cantankerousness . . . still,
If there's no other way . . . then I feel just hopeless.

REILLY

There *is* another way, if you have the courage.
The first I could describe in familiar terms
Because you have seen it, as we all have seen it,
Illustrated, more or less, in lives of those about us.
The second is unknown, and so requires faith —
The kind of faith that issues from despair.*
680 The destination cannot be described;
You will know very little until you get there;
You will journey blind. But the way leads towards possession
Of what you have sought for in the wrong place.

CELIA

That sounds like what I want. But what is my duty?

REILLY

Whichever way you choose will prescribe its own duty.

CELIA

Which way is better?

REILLY
Neither way is better.
Both ways are necessary. It is also necessary
To make a choice between them.

CELIA
Then I choose the second.

138

REILLY

It is a terrifying journey.

CELIA

           I am not frightened
But glad. I suppose it is a lonely way? 690

REILLY

No lonelier than the other. But those who take the other
Can forget their loneliness. You will not forget yours.
Each way means loneliness — and communion.
Both ways avoid the final desolation
Of solitude in the phantasmal world
Of imagination, shuffling memories and desires.

CELIA

That is the hell I have been in.

REILLY

              It isn't hell
Till you become incapable of anything else.
Now — do you feel quite sure?

CELIA

           I want your second way.
So what am I to do? 700

REILLY

        You will go to the sanatorium.

CELIA

Oh, what an anti-climax! I have known people
Who have been to your sanatorium, and come back again —
I don't mean to say they weren't much better for it —
That's why I came to you. But they returned . . .
Well . . . I mean . . . to everyday life.

139

REILLY

True. But the friends you have in mind
Cannot have been to this sanatorium.*
I am very careful whom I send there:
Those who go do not come back as these did.

CELIA

710 It sounds like a prison. But they can't *all* stay there!
I mean, it would make the place so over-crowded.

REILLY

Not very many go. But I said they did not come back
In the sense in which your friends came back.
I did not say they stayed there.

CELIA

What becomes of them?

REILLY

They choose, Miss Coplestone. Nothing is forced on them.
Some of them return, in a physical sense;
No one disappears. They lead very active lives
Very often, in the world.

CELIA

How soon will you send me there?

REILLY

How soon will you be ready?

CELIA

Tonight, by nine o'clock.

REILLY

720 Go home then, and make your preparations.

Here is the address for you to give your friends;
       [*Writes on a slip of paper*]
You had better let your family know at once.
I will send a car for you at nine o'clock.

CELIA

What do I need to take with me?

REILLY
           Nothing.
Everything you need will be provided for you,
And you will have no expenses at the sanatorium.

CELIA

I don't in the least know what I am doing
Or why I am doing it. There is nothing else to do:
That is the only reason.

REILLY
       It is the best reason.

CELIA

But I know it is I who have made the decision: 730
I must tell you that. Oh, I almost forgot —
May I ask what your fee is?

REILLY
          I have told my secretary
That there is no fee.

CELIA
       But . . .

141

REILLY
For a case like yours
There is no fee.
[*Presses button*]

CELIA
You have been very kind.

REILLY
Go in peace, my daughter.
Work out your salvation with diligence.
[NURSE-SECRETARY *appears at door. Exit* CELIA
REILLY *dials on house-telephone.*]

REILLY
[*Into telephone*]
It is finished.* You can come in now.
[*Enter* JULIA *by side door*]
She will go far, that one.

JULIA
Very far, I think.
You do not need to tell me. I knew from the beginning.

REILLY
740 It's the other ones I am worried about.

JULIA
Nonsense, Henry. *I* shall keep an eye on them.

REILLY
To send them back: what have they to go back to?
To the stale food mouldering in the larder,
The stale thoughts mouldering in their minds.

Each unable to disguise his own meanness
From himself, because it is known to the other.
It's not the knowledge of the mutual treachery
But the knowledge that the other understands the motive —
Mirror to mirror, reflecting vanity.
I have taken a great risk.   750

JULIA
                    We must always take risks.
That is our destiny. Since you question the decision
What possible alternative can you imagine?

REILLY
None.

JULIA
                    Very well then. We must take the risk.
All we could do was to give them the chance.
And now, when they are stripped naked to their souls
And can choose, whether to put on proper costumes
Or huddle quickly into new disguises,
They have, for the first time, somewhere to start from.
Oh, of course, they might just murder each other!
But I don't think they will do that. We shall see.   760
It's the thought of Celia that weighs upon my mind.

REILLY
Of Celia?

JULIA
        Of Celia.

REILLY
                    But when I said just now
That she would go far, you agreed with me.

JULIA

Oh yes, she will go far. And we know where she is going.
But what do we know of the terrors of the journey?
You and I don't know the process by which the human is
Transhumanised:* what do we know
Of the kind of suffering they must undergo
On the way of illumination?*

REILLY

Will she be frightened
770 By the first appearance of projected spirits?*

JULIA

Henry, you simply do not understand innocence.
She will be afraid of nothing; she will not even know
That there is anything there to be afraid of.
She is too humble. She will pass between the scolding hills,
Through the valley of derision,* like a child sent on an errand
In eagerness and patience. Yet she must suffer.

REILLY

When I express confidence in anything
You always raise doubts; when I am apprehensive
Then you see no reason for anything but confidence.

JULIA

780 That's one way in which I am so useful to you.
You ought to be grateful.

REILLY

And when I say to one like her
'Work out your salvation with diligence', I do not
    understand
What I myself am saying.

144

JULIA

You must accept your limitations.
— But how much longer will Alex keep us waiting?

REILLY

He should be here by now. I'll speak to Miss Barraway.
[*Takes up house-telephone*]
Miss Barraway, when Mr. Gibbs arrives . . .
Oh, very good.
[*To* JULIA]
He's on his way up.
[*Into telephone*]
You may bring the tray in now, Miss Barraway.
[*Enter* ALEX]

ALEX

Well! Well! and how have we got on?

JULIA

Everything is in order.

ALEX

The Chamberlaynes have chosen?

REILLY

They accept their destiny.

ALEX

And *she* has made the choice?   790

REILLY

She will be fetched this evening.
[NURSE-SECRETARY *enters with a tray, a decanter and three
glasses, and exit.* REILLY *pours drinks.*]
And now we are ready to proceed to the libation.*

145

ALEX

The words for the building of the hearth.
[*They raise their glasses*]

REILLY

Let them build the hearth
Under the protection of the stars.

ALEX

Let them place a chair each side of it.

JULIA

May the holy ones watch over the roof,
May the Moon herself influence the bed.
[*They drink*]

ALEX

The words for those who go upon a journey.

REILLY

Protector of travellers
800   Bless the road.

ALEX

Watch over her in the desert.
Watch over her in the mountain.
Watch over her in the labyrinth.
Watch over her by the quicksand.

JULIA

Protect her from the Voices
Protect her from the Visions
Protect her in the tumult
Protect her in the silence.
[*They drink*]

146

REILLY
There is one for whom the words cannot be spoken.

ALEX
They can not be spoken yet.   810

JULIA
You mean Peter Quilpe.

REILLY
He has not yet come to where the words are valid.*

JULIA
Shall we ever speak them?

ALEX
Others, perhaps, will speak them.
You know, I have connections — even in California.*

CURTAIN

Act Three

The drawing-room of the Chamberlaynes' London flat. Two years later. A late afternoon in July. A CATERER'S MAN *is arranging a buffet table.* LAVINIA *enters from side door.*

CATERER'S MAN

Have you any further orders for us, Madam?

LAVINIA

You could bring in the trolley with the glasses
And leave them ready.

CATERER'S MAN
                Very good, Madam.
[*Exit.* LAVINIA *looks about the room critically and moves bowl of flowers.*]
[*Re-enter* CATERER'S MAN *with trolley*]

LAVINIA

There, in that corner. That's the most convenient;
You can get in and out. Is there anything you need
That you can't find in the kitchen?

CATERER'S MAN
                      Nothing, Madam.
Will there be anything more you require?

LAVINIA

Nothing more, I think, till half past six.

[*Exit* CATERER'S MAN]

[EDWARD *lets himself in at the front door*]

EDWARD

I'm in good time, I think. I hope you've not been worrying.

LAVINIA

Oh no. I did in fact ring up your chambers,   10
And your clerk told me you had already left.
But all I rang up for was to reassure you . . .

EDWARD

[*Smiling*]

That you hadn't run away?

LAVINIA

                    Now Edward, that's unfair!
You know that we've given *several* parties
In the last two years. And I've attended *all* of them.
I hope you're not too tired?

EDWARD

                    Oh no, a quiet day.
Two consultations with solicitors
On quite straightforward cases. It's you who should be tired.*

LAVINIA

I'm not tired yet. But I know that I'll be glad
When it's all over.   20

EDWARD

                    I like the dress you're wearing:
I'm glad you put on that one.

LAVINIA
Well, Edward!
Do you know it's the first time you've paid me a compliment
Before a party? And that's when one needs them.

EDWARD
Well, you deserve it. — We asked too many people.

LAVINIA
It's true, a great many more accepted
Than we thought would want to come. But what can you do?
There's usually a lot who don't want to come
But all the same would be bitterly offended
To hear we'd given a party without asking them.

EDWARD
30 Perhaps we ought to have arranged to have two parties
Instead of one.

LAVINIA
That's never satisfactory.
Everyone who's asked to either party
Suspects that the other one was more important.

EDWARD
That's true. You have a very practical mind.

LAVINIA
But you know, I don't think that you need worry:
They won't all come, out of those who accepted.
You know we said, 'we can ask twenty more
Because they will be going to the Gunnings instead'.

EDWARD

I know, that's what we said at the time;
But I'd forgotten what the Gunnings' parties were like.
Their guests will get just enough to make them thirsty;   40
They'll come on to us later, roaring for drink.
Well, let's hope that those who come to us early
Will be going on to the Gunnings afterwards,
To make room for those who come from the Gunnings.

LAVINIA

And if it's very crowded, they can't get at the cocktails,
And the man won't be able to take the tray about,
So they'll go away again. Anyway, at that stage
There's nothing whatever you can do about it:
And everyone likes to be seen at a party
Where everybody else is, to show they've been invited.   50
That's what makes it a success. Is that picture straight?

EDWARD

Yes, it is.

LAVINIA

No, it isn't. Do please straighten it.

EDWARD

Is it straight now?

LAVINIA

Too much to the left.

EDWARD

How's that now?

151

LAVINIA

No, I meant the right.
That will do. I'm too tired to bother.

EDWARD

After they're all gone, we will have some champagne.
Just ourselves. You lie down now, Lavinia.
No one will be coming for at least half an hour;
So just stretch out.

LAVINIA

You must sit beside me,
60   Then I can relax.

EDWARD

This is the best moment
Of the whole party.

LAVINIA

Oh no, Edward.
The best moment is the moment it's over;
And then to remember, it's the end of the season
And no more parties.

EDWARD

And no more committees.

LAVINIA

Can we get away soon?

EDWARD

By the end of next week
I shall be quite free.

LAVINIA
And we can be alone.
I love that house being so remote.

EDWARD
That's why we took it. And I'm really thankful
To have that excuse for not seeing people;
And you do need to rest now.　　　　　　　　70
[*The doorbell rings*]

LAVINIA
Oh, bother!
Now who would come so early? I simply *can't* get up.

CATERER'S MAN
Mrs. Shuttlethwaite!

LAVINIA
Oh, it's Julia!
[*Enter* JULIA]

JULIA
Well, my dears, and here I am!
I seem *literally* to have caught you napping!
I know I'm much too early; but the fact is, my dears,
That I have to go on to the Gunnings' party —
And you know what *they* offer in the way of food and drink!
And I've had to miss my tea, and I'm simply ravenous
And dying of thirst. What can Parkinson's do for me?
Oh yes, I know this is a Parkinson party;　　　　80
I recognised one of their men at the door —
An old friend of mine, in fact. But I'm forgetting!
I've got a surprise: I've brought Alex with me!
He only got back this morning from somewhere —

153

One of his mysterious expeditions,
And we're going to get him to tell us all about it.
But what's become of him?
[*Enter* ALEX]

EDWARD
Well, Alex!
Where on earth do you turn up from?

ALEX

Where on earth? From the east. From Kinkanja —
90   An island that you won't have heard of
Yet. Got back this morning. I heard about your party
And, as I thought you might be leaving for the country,
I said, I must not miss the opportunity
To see Edward and Lavinia.

LAVINIA
How are you, Alex?

ALEX

I did try to get you on the telephone
After lunch, but my secretary couldn't get through to you.
Never mind, I said — to myself, not to her —
Never mind: the unexpected guest
Is the one to whom they give the warmest welcome.
100   I know them well enough for that.

JULIA
But tell us, Alex.
What were you doing in this strange place —
What's it called?

ALEX
Kinkanja.

JULIA

What were you doing
In Kinkanja? Visiting some Sultan?
You were shooting tigers?

ALEX

There are no tigers, Julia,
In Kinkanja. And there are no sultans.
I have been staying with the Governor.
Three of us have been out on a tour of inspection
Of local conditions.

JULIA

What about? Monkey nuts?

ALEX

That was a nearer guess than you think.*
No, not monkey nuts. But it had to do with monkeys —   110
Though whether the monkeys are the core of the problem
Or merely a symptom, I am not so sure.
At least, the monkeys have become the pretext
For general unrest amongst the natives.

EDWARD

But how do the monkeys create unrest?

ALEX

To begin with, the monkeys are very destructive . . .

JULIA

You don't need to tell me that monkeys are destructive.
I shall never forget Mary Mallington's monkey,
The horrid little beast — stole my ticket to Mentone
And I had to travel in a very slow train   120

And in a *couchette*. She was very angry
When I told her the creature ought to be destroyed.

LAVINIA

But can't they exterminate these monkeys
If they are a pest?

ALEX

Unfortunately,
The majority of the natives are heathen:
They hold these monkeys in peculiar veneration
And do not want them killed. So they blame the
    Government
For the damage that the monkeys do.

EDWARD

That seems unreasonable.

ALEX

It is unreasonable,
130   But characteristic. And that's not the worst of it.
Some of the tribes are Christian converts,
And, naturally, take a different view.
They trap the monkeys. And they eat them.
The young monkeys are extremely palatable:
I've cooked them myself . . .

EDWARD

And did anybody eat them
When you cooked them?

ALEX

Oh yes, indeed.
I invented for the natives several new recipes.

But you see, what with eating the monkeys
And what with protecting their crops from the monkeys
The Christian natives prosper exceedingly: 140
And that creates friction between them and the others.
And that's the real problem. I hope I'm not boring you?

EDWARD
No indeed: we are anxious to learn the solution.

ALEX
I'm not sure that there *is* any solution.
But even this does not bring us to the heart of the matter.
There are also foreign agitators,
Stirring up trouble . . .

LAVINIA
Why don't you expel them?

ALEX
They are citizens of a friendly neighbouring state
Which we have just recognised. You see, Lavinia,
There are very deep waters.   150

EDWARD
And the agitators;
How do they agitate?

ALEX
By convincing the heathen
That the slaughter of monkeys has put a curse on them
Which can only be removed by slaughtering the Christians.
They have even been persuading some of the converts —
Who, after all, prefer not to be slaughtered —

To relapse into heathendom. So, instead of eating monkeys
They are eating Christians.

ALEX

JULIA
Who have eaten monkeys.

ALEX
The native is not, I fear, very logical.

JULIA
I wondered where you were taking us, with your monkeys.
160 I thought I was going to dine out on those monkeys:
But one can't dine out on eating Christians —
Even among pagans!*

ALEX
Not on the *whole* story.

EDWARD
And have any of the English residents been murdered?

ALEX
Yes, but they are not usually eaten.
When these people have done with a European
He is, as a rule, no longer fit to eat.

EDWARD
And what has your commission accomplished?

ALEX
We have just drawn up an interim report.

EDWARD
Will it be made public?

158

ALEX
It cannot be, at present:
There are too many international complications.   170
Eventually, there may be an official publication.

EDWARD
But when?

ALEX
In a year or two.

EDWARD
                                And meanwhile?

ALEX
Meanwhile the monkeys multiply.

LAVINIA
                                And the Christians?

ALEX
Ah, the Christians! Now, I think I ought to tell you
About someone you know — or knew . . .

JULIA
                                                Edward!
Somebody must have walked over my grave:
I'm feeling so chilly. Give me some gin.
Not a cocktail. I'm freezing — in July!

CATERER'S MAN
Mr. Quilpe!

EDWARD
>   Now who . . .
> [*Enter* PETER]
>   Why, it's Peter!

LAVINIA
180 Peter!

PETER
>   Hullo, everybody!

LAVINIA
>   When did you arrive?

PETER
> I flew over from New York last night —
> I left Los Angeles three days ago.
> I saw Sheila Paisley at lunch to-day
> And she told me you were giving a party —
> She's coming on later, after the Gunnings —
> So I said, I really must crash in:
> It's my only chance to see Edward and Lavinia.
> I'm only over for a week, you see,
> And I'm driving down to the country this evening,
190 So I knew you wouldn't mind my looking in so early.
> It does seem ages since I last saw any of you!
> And how are you, Alex? And dear old Julia!

LAVINIA
So you've just come from New York.

PETER
>   Yes, from New York.
> The Bologolomskys saw me off.

You remember Princess Bologolomsky
In the old days? We dined the other night
At the Saffron Monkey. Thàt's the place to go now.

ALEX

How very odd. *My* monkeys are saffron.

PETER

Your monkeys, Alex? I always said
That Alex knew everybody. But I didn't know   200
That he knew any monkeys.

JULIA

But give us your news;
Give us your news of the world, Peter.
We lead such a quiet life, here in London.

PETER

You always did enjoy a leg-pull, Julia:
But you all know I'm working for Pan-Am-Eagle?

EDWARD

No. Tell us, what is Pan-Am-Eagle?

PETER

You must have been living a quiet life!
Don't you go to the movies?

LAVINIA

Occasionally.

PETER

Alex knows.
Did you see my last picture, Alex?

ALEX

210 I knew about it, but I didn't see it.
There is no cinema in Kinkanja.

PETER

Kinkanja? Where's that? They don't have pictures?
Pan-Am-Eagle must look into this.
Perhaps it would be a good place to make one.
— Alex knows all about Pan-Am-Eagle:
It was he who introduced me to the great Bela.

JULIA

And who is the great Bela?

PETER

Why, Bela Szogody —
He's my boss. I thought everyone knew *his* name.

JULIA

Is he your connection in California, Alex?

ALEX

220 Yes, we have sometimes obliged each other.

PETER

Well, it was Bela sent me over
Just for a week. And I have my hands full
I'm going down tonight, to Boltwell.

JULIA

To stay with the Duke?

PETER

And do him a good turn.
We're making a film of English life
And we want to use Boltwell.

JULIA

But I understood that Boltwell
Is in a very decayed condition.

PETER

Exactly. It is. And that's why we're interested.
The most decayed noble mansion in England!
At least, of any that are still inhabited.   230
We've got a team of experts over
To study the decay, so as to reproduce it.
Then we build another Boltwell in California.

JULIA

But what is your position, Peter?
Have you become an expert on decaying houses?

PETER

Oh dear no! I've written the script of this film,
And Bela is very pleased with it.
He thought I should see the original Boltwell;
And besides, he thought that as I'm English
I ought to know the best way to handle a duke.   240
Besides that, we've got the casting director:
He's looking for some typical English faces —
Of course, only for minor parts —
And I'll help him decide what faces are typical.

JULIA

Peter, I've thought of a wonderful idea!
I've always wanted to go to California:
Couldn't you persuade your casting director
To take us all over? We're all very typical.

PETER

No, I'm afraid . . .

163

CATERER'S MAN
Sir Henry Harcourt-Reilly!

JULIA

250 Oh, I forgot! I'd another surprise for you.
[*Enter* REILLY]
I want you to meet Sir Henry Harcourt-Reilly —

EDWARD
We're delighted to see him. But we *have* met before.

JULIA
Then if you know him already, you won't be afraid of him.
You know, I was afraid of him at first:
He looks so forbidding . . .

REILLY
My dear Julia,
You are giving me a very bad introduction —
Supposing that an introduction was necessary.

JULIA
My dear Henry, you are interrupting me.

LAVINIA
If you can interrupt Julia, Sir Henry,
260 You are the perfect guest we've been looking for.

REILLY
I should not dream of trying to interrupt Julia . . .

JULIA
But you're both interrupting!

164

REILLY
                    Who is interrupting now?

JULIA
Well, you shouldn't interrupt my interruptions:
That's really worse than interrupting.
Now my head's fairly spinning. I must have a cocktail.

EDWARD
                    [*To* REILLY]
And will you have a cocktail?

REILLY
                    Might I have a glass of water?

EDWARD
Anything with it?

REILLY
                    Nothing, thank you.

LAVINIA
May I introduce Mr. Peter Quilpe?
Sir Henry Harcourt-Reilly. Peter's an old friend
Of my husband and myself. Oh, I forgot —   270
                    [*Turning to* ALEX]
I rather assumed that you knew each other —
I don't know why I should. Mr. MacColgie Gibbs.

ALEX
Indeed, yes, we have met.

REILLY
                    On several commissions.

JULIA

We've been having such an interesting conversation.
Peter's just over from California
Where he's something very important in films.
He's making a film of English life
And he's going to find parts for all of us. Think of it!

PETER

But, Julia, I was just about to explain —
280   I'm afraid I can't find parts for anybody
In *this* film — it's not my business;
And that's not the way we do it.

JULIA

                              But, Peter;
If you're taking Boltwell to California
Why can't you take me?

PETER

                              We're not taking Boltwell.
We reconstruct a Boltwell.

JULIA

                              Very well, then:
Why not reconstruct *me*? It's very much cheaper.
Oh, dear, I can see you're determined not to have me:
So good-bye to my hopes of seeing California.

PETER

You know you'd never come if we invited you.
290   But there's someone I wanted to ask about,
Who did really want to get into films,
And I always thought she could make a success of it
If she only got the chance. It's Celia Coplestone.

166

She always wanted to. And now I could help her.
I've already spoken to Bela about her,
And I want to introduce her to our casting director.
I've got an idea for another film.
Can you tell me where she is? I couldn't find her
In the telephone directory.

JULIA
                    Not in the directory,
Or in any directory. You can tell them now, Alex.   300

LAVINIA
What does Julia mean?

ALEX
                    I was about to speak of her
When you came in, Peter. I'm afraid you can't have Celia.

PETER
Oh . . . Is she married?

ALEX
Not married, but dead.*

LAVINIA
Celia?

ALEX
    Dead.

PETER
Dead. That knocks the bottom out of it.

EDWARD
Celia dead.

JULIA

You had better tell them, Alex,
The news that you bring back from Kinkanja.

LAVINIA

Kinkanja? What was Celia doing in Kinkanja?
We heard that she had joined some nursing order . . .

ALEX

She had joined an order. A very austere one.
310 And as she already had experience of nursing . . .

LAVINIA

Yes, she had been a V.A.D. I remember.*

ALEX

She was directed to Kinkanja,
Where there are various endemic diseases
Besides, of course, those brought by Europeans,
And where the conditions are favourable to plague.

EDWARD

Go on.

ALEX

It seems that there were three of them —
Three sisters at this station, in a Christian village;
And half the natives were dying of pestilence.
They must have been overworked for weeks.

EDWARD

320 And then?

ALEX

And then, the insurrection broke out
Among the heathen, of which I was telling you.

168

They knew of it, but would not leave the dying natives.
Eventually, two of them escaped:
One died in the jungle, and the other
Will never be fit for normal life again.
But Celia Coplestone, she was taken.
When our people got there, they questioned the villagers —
Those who survived. And then they found her body,
Or at least, they found the traces of it.

                    EDWARD
But before that . . .   330

                    ALEX
          It was difficult to tell.
But from what we know of local practices
It would seem that she must have been crucified
Very near an ant-hill.

                    LAVINIA
          But Celia! . . . Of all people . . .

                    EDWARD
And just for a handful of plague-stricken natives
Who would have died anyway.

                    ALEX
                    Yes, the patients died anyway;
Being tainted with the plague, they were not eaten.

                    LAVINIA
Oh, Edward, I'm so sorry — what a feeble thing to say!
But you know what I mean.

                    EDWARD
                    And you know what I'm thinking.

PETER

I don't understand at all.* But then I've been away
340 For two years, and don't know what happened
To Celia, during those two years.
Two years! Thinking about Celia.

EDWARD

It's the waste that I resent.

PETER

You know more than I do:
For *me*, it's everything else that's a waste.
Two years! And it was all a mistake.
Julia! Why don't *you* say anything?

JULIA

You gave her those two years, as best you could.

PETER

When did she . . . take up this career?

JULIA

Two years ago.

PETER

Two years ago! I tried to forget about her,
350 Until I began to think myself a success
And got a little more self-confidence;
And then I thought about her again. More and more.
At first I did not want to know about Celia
And so I never asked. Then I wanted to know
And did not dare to ask. It took all my courage
To ask you about her just now; but I never thought
Of anything like this. I suppose I didn't know her,
I didn't understand her. I understand nothing.

170

REILLY

You understand your *métier*, Mr. Quilpe —
Which is the most that any of us can ask for.   360

PETER

And what a *métier*! I've tried to believe in it
So that I might believe in myself.
I thought I had ideas to make a revolution
In the cinema, that no one could ignore —
And here I am, making a second-rate film!
But I thought it was going to lead to something better,
And that seemed possible, while Celia was alive.
I wanted it, believed in it, for Celia.
And, of course, I wanted to do something for Celia —
But what mattered was, that Celia was alive.   370
And now it's all worthless. Celia's not alive.

LAVINIA

No, it's not all worthless, Peter. You've only just begun.
I mean, this only brings you to the point
At which you *must* begin. You were saying just now
That you never knew Celia. We none of us did.
What you've been living on is an image of Celia
Which you made for yourself, to meet your own needs.
Peter, please don't think I'm being unkind . . .

PETER

No, I don't think you're being unkind, Lavinia;
And I know that you're right.   380

LAVINIA

                    And perhaps what I've been saying
Will seem less unkind if I can make you understand
That in fact I've been talking about myself.

EDWARD

Lavinia is right. This is where you start from.
If you find out now, Peter, things about yourself
That you don't like to face: well, just remember
That some men have to learn much worse things
About themselves, and learn them later
When it's harder to recover, and make a new beginning.
It's not so hard for you. You're naturally good.

PETER

390   I'm sorry. I don't believe I've taken in
All that you've been saying. But I'm grateful all the same.
You know, all the time that you've been talking,
One thought has been going round and round in my head —
That I've only been interested in myself:
And that isn't good enough for Celia.

JULIA

You must have learned how to look at people, Peter,
When you look at them with an eye for the films:
That is, when you're not concerned with yourself
But just being an eye. You will come to think of Celia
400   Like that, one day. And then you'll understand her
And be reconciled, and be happy in the thought of her.

LAVINIA

Sir Henry, there is something I want to say to you.
While Alex was telling us what had happened to Celia
I was looking at your face. And it seemed from your
         expression
That the way in which she died did not disturb you
Or the fact that she died because she would not leave
A few dying natives.

172

REILLY

Who knows, Mrs. Chamberlayne,
The difference that made to the natives who were dying
Or the state of mind in which they died?

LAVINIA

I'm willing to grant that. What struck me, though,   410
Was that your face showed no surprise or horror
At the way in which she died. I don't know if you knew her.
I suspect that you did. In any case you knew *about* her.
Yet I thought your expression was one of . . . satisfaction!

REILLY

Mrs. Chamberlayne, I must be very transparent
Or else you are very perceptive.

JULIA

Oh, Henry!
Lavinia is much more observant than you think.
I believe that she has forced you to a show-down.

REILLY

You state the position correctly, Julia.
Do you mind if I quote poetry, Mrs. Chamberlayne?   420

LAVINIA

Oh no, I should love to hear you speaking poetry . . .

JULIA

She has made a point, Henry.

LAVINIA

. . . if it answers my question.

REILLY
*Ere Babylon was dust**
The magus Zoroaster, my dead child,
Met his own image walking in the garden.
That apparition, sole of men, he saw.
For know there are two worlds of life and death:
One that which thou beholdest; but the other
Is underneath the grave, where do inhabit
430 *The shadows of all forms that think and live*
Till death unite them and they part no more!

When I first met Miss Coplestone, in this room,
I saw the image, standing behind her chair,
Of a Celia Coplestone whose face showed the astonishment
Of the first five minutes after a violent death.
If this strains your credulity, Mrs. Chamberlayne,
I ask you only to entertain the suggestion
That a sudden intuition, in certain minds,
May tend to express itself at once in a picture.
440 That happens to me, sometimes. So it was obvious
That here was a woman under sentence of death.
That was her destiny. The only question
Then was, what sort of death?* I could not know;
Because it was for her to choose the way of life
To lead to death, and, without knowing the end
Yet choose the form of death. We know the death she chose.
I did not know that she would die in this way;
She did not know. So all that I could do
Was to direct her in the way of preparation.
450 That way, which she accepted, led to this death.
And if that is not a happy death, what death is happy?

EDWARD
Do you mean that having chosen this form of death

She did not suffer as ordinary people suffer?

REILLY

Not at all what I mean. Rather the contrary.
I'd say that she suffered all that we should suffer
In fear and pain and loathing — all these together —
And reluctance of the body to become a *thing*.
I'd say she suffered more, because more conscious
Than the rest of us. She paid the highest price
In suffering. That is part of the design.*   460

LAVINIA

Perhaps she had been through greater agony beforehand.
I mean — I know nothing of her last two years.

REILLY

That shows some insight on your part, Mrs. Chamberlayne;
But such experience can only be hinted at
In myths and images.* To speak about it
We talk of darkness, labyrinths, Minotaur terrors.
But that world does not take the place of this one.
Do you imagine that the Saint in the desert
With spiritual evil always at his shoulder
Suffered any less from hunger, damp, exposure,   470
Bowel trouble, and the fear of lions,
Cold of the night and heat of the day, than we should?

EDWARD

But if this was right — if this was right for Celia —
There must be something else that is terribly wrong,*
And the rest of us are somehow involved in the wrong.
I should only speak for myself. I'm sure that *I* am.

REILLY

Let me free your mind from one impediment:

175

You must try to detach yourself from what you still feel
As your responsibility.

EDWARD
I cannot help the feeling*
480 That, in some way, my responsibility
Is greater than that of a band of half-crazed savages.

LAVINIA
Oh, Edward, I knew! I knew what you were thinking!
Doesn't it help you, that I feel guilty too?

REILLY
If we were all judged according to the consequences
Of all our words and deeds, beyond the intention
And beyond our limited understanding
Of ourselves and others, we should all be condemned.
Mrs. Chamberlayne, I often have to make a decision
Which may mean restoration or ruin to a patient —
490 And sometimes I have made the wrong decision.
As for Miss Coplestone, because you think her death was waste
You blame yourselves, and because you blame yourselves
You think her life was wasted. It was triumphant.
But I am no more responsible for the triumph —
And just as responsible for her death as you are.

LAVINIA
Yet I know I shall go on blaming myself
For being so unkind to her . . . so spiteful.
I shall go on seeing her at the moment
When she said good-bye to us, two years ago.

EDWARD
500 Your responsibility is nothing to mine, Lavinia.

LAVINIA

I'm not sure about that. If I had understood you
Then I might not have misunderstood Celia.

REILLY

You will have to live with these memories and make them
Into something new. Only by acceptance*
Of the past will you alter its meaning.

JULIA

Henry, I think it is time that *I* said something:
Everyone makes a choice, of one kind or another,
And then must take the consequences. Celia chose
A way of which the consequence was Kinkanja.
Peter chose a way that leads him to Boltwell: 510
And he's got to go there . . .

PETER

         I see what you mean.
I wish I didn't have to. But the car will be waiting,
And the experts — I'd almost forgotten them.
I realise that I can't get out of it —
And what else can I do?

ALEX

         It is your film.
And I know that Bela expects great things of it.

PETER

So now I'll be going.

EDWARD

         Shall we see you again, Peter,
Before you leave England?

LAVINIA
Do try to come to see us.
You know, I think it would do us all good —
520   You and me and Edward . . . to talk about Celia

PETER
Thanks very much. But not this time —
I simply shan't be able to.

EDWARD
But on your next visit?

PETER
The next time I come to England, I promise you.
I really do want to see you both, very much.
Good-bye, Julia. Good-bye, Alex. Good-bye, Sir Henry.
[*Exit*]

JULIA
. . . And now the consequences of the Chamberlaynes' choice
Is a cocktail party. They must be ready for it.
Their guests may be arriving at any moment.

REILLY
Julia, you are right. It is also right
530   That the Chamberlaynes should now be giving a party.

LAVINIA
And I have been thinking, for these last five minutes,
How I could face my guests. I wish it was over.
I mean . . . I am glad you came . . . I am glad Alex told us . . .
And Peter had to know . . .

EDWARD
Now I think I understand . . .

178

LAVINIA

Then I hope you will explain it to me!

EDWARD

Oh, it isn't much
That I understand yet! But Sir Henry has been saying,
I think, that every moment is a fresh beginning;
And Julia, that life is only keeping on;
And somehow, the two ideas seem to fit together.

LAVINIA

But all the same . . . I don't want to see these people.   540

REILLY

It is your appointed burden. And as for the party,
I am sure it will be a success.

JULIA

And I think, Henry,
That we should leave before the party begins.
They will get on better without us. You too, Alex.

LAVINIA

We don't *want* you to go!

ALEX

We have another engagement.

REILLY

And on this occasion I shall not be unexpected.

JULIA

Now, Henry. Now, Alex. We're going to the Gunnings.
                    [*Exeunt* JULIA, REILLY *and* ALEX]

179

LAVINIA

Edward, how am I looking?

EDWARD
Very well.
I might almost say, your best. But you always look your best.

LAVINIA

550 Oh, Edward, that spoils it. No woman can believe
That she always looks her best. You're rather transparent,
You know, when you're trying to cheer me up.
To say I always look my best can only mean the worst.

EDWARD

I never shall learn how to pay a compliment.

LAVINIA

What you should have done was to admire my dress.

EDWARD

But I've already told you how much I like it.

LAVINIA

But so much has happened since then. And besides,
One sometimes likes to hear the same compliment twice.

EDWARD

And now for the party.

LAVINIA
Now for the party.

EDWARD

560 It will soon be over.

LAVINIA
I wish it would begin.

EDWARD
There's the doorbell.

LAVINIA
Oh, I'm glad. It's begun.

CURTAIN

Appendix

The tune of *One-Eyed Riley* (page 38), as scored from the author's dictation by Miss Mary Trevelyan.

As I was walk-ing round and round and round in ev'-ry quar-ter I walk'd in to a

REFRAIN

pub-lic house and or-der'd up my gin and wa-ter

Too - ri - oo-ley, Too - ri - i - ley, What's the mat-ter with

One-Eyed Ri-ley

As I was drink-in' gin and wa-ter

(And me be-in' the One-Eyed Ri-ley) Who came in but the

REFRAIN

land-lord's daugh-ter And she took my heart en-tire-ly

Too - ri - oo-ley, Too-ri - i - ley, What's the mat-ter with

One-Eyed Ri-ley

The Cast of the First Production
at the
Edinburgh Festival,
August 22-27, 1949

Edward Chamberlayne	ROBERT FLEMYNG
Julia (Mrs. Shuttlethwaite)	CATHLEEN NESBITT
Celia Coplestone	IRENE WORTH
Alexander McColgie Gibbs	ERNEST CLARK
Peter Quilpe	DONALD HOUSTON
An Unidentified Guest, *later identified* as Sir Henry Harcourt-Reilly	ALEC GUINNESS
Lavinia Chamberlayne	URSULA JEANS
A Nurse-Secretary	CHRISTINA HORNIMAN
Two Caterer's Men	DONALD BAIN MARTIN BECKWITH

Directed by E. MARTIN BROWNE

Settings designed by ANTHONY HOLLAND

Produced by SHEREK PLAYERS LTD.

in association with THE ARTS COUNCIL

2   Some Comments on the Play, taken from the author's private correspondence

2 Some Comments on the Play, taken from the author's private correspondence

I would like once again to thank Mrs. Eliot for allowing me the privilege of selecting and publishing the following extracts from her husband's correspondence, for the most part hitherto unpublished, and also for her help and criticism in the work of preparing this edition.

1. From a letter from T. S. Eliot to Mr. Martin Browne, dated 25 January 1948:

> My dear Martin,
>
> I am sorry for the delay in answering your letter of the 19th. I certainly expect the play to be born this year. I do not know how long it will be before it learns to walk, to say nothing of an acrobatic turn worthy of the theatre. Knowing how slowly I work and the amount of time it is likely to take up to get up a head of steam with an engine which has been out of action for so long, I know that the thought of working to a date for this summer would throw me into a panic. I should be quite happy with the prospect of spring 1949, and if, as I hope, I can break the back of the new-born infant during the summer, I should be able to do polishing work even while at Princeton. I hope to be able to start work — or more exactly perhaps I should say sit down morning after morning with nothing else to do — in two or three weeks.

2. The longest and most revealing letter on the play is one written by Eliot in answer to one from his friend and

partner, Sir Geoffrey Faber, whose acutely critical mind touches on many essential points in the play. Extracts from Sir Geoffrey's letter are printed in italics:

(a) *Aug. 25 '49*

I do, quite simply, think the play a masterpiece, and as a sexagenarian, I am now qualified to express my admiration — not to say sheer envy — of your power of making new growth. Invention, simplicity of dialogue and versification — these are what make the play so exceptionally impressive. Given, of course, the underlying gravity which is the necessary core of your Ribston Pippin of a Play: but that, as the Daily Graphic *surprisingly perceives, is already known to readers of the* Four Quartets.

(b) From Eliot's reply, dated 'Trinity XI': 1949 (Postmark = 29 August):

I am specially gratified by what you say of 'power of making new growth'. This meant a lot to me, because I had always believed a Nobel Prize to be a sort of advance death certificate, and I was putting everything I had into this play in the effort to keep alive.

(Eliot had been awarded the Nobel Prize in 1948)

(c) *Heretic as I am — and fear am doomed to remain — in the sense that I am unable to find or to use the prescribed Exit from Hell, I accept your definition of Hell, and on the whole I agree with Reilly's diagnosis. Not entirely by any means . . .*

Sir Geoffrey seems to be referring to the conversation between Reilly and Celia (II. 690–9), where he distinguishes the loneliness felt by the saints (who also have their communion) and the 'solitude in the phantasmal world of imagination, shuffling memories and desires', a kind of lonely Hell within oneself, from which some can find their way out in marriage, in which some communion can be found and the loneliness be forgotten. But even that kind of companionship falls short of perfection, for, as Sir Henry suggests elsewhere (II. 650–2), a kind of contentment is as much as can be hoped for between

> Two people who know they do not understand each other,
> Breeding children whom they do not understand
> And who will never understand them.

This is the passage that Sir Geoffrey Faber considers '*an over-simplification*'. There is another passage in the play that seems relevant to the idea of Hell as loneliness, which appears in an earlier draft as follows:

> *Edward* What is hell? hell is oneself,
> Hell is alone, the other figures in it
> One's own projections.

In rewriting the speech in which these lines occur, Eliot salvaged them and they stand virtually unaltered in his final text at I. 3. 417–19. Eliot intended this view of Hell (that Hell is oneself) as a counterblast to the view of Hell (that Hell is other people) presented by Jean-Paul Sartre in *Huis-Clos* (1944), as Martin Browne interestingly records (*The Making of T. S. Eliot's Plays*, p. 233).

Continuing the passage from Sir Geoffrey's letter, at the point at which I interrupted it to explain the references to Hell:

(d)   . . . *The two possible lives, as Reilly states them to Celia, are (I think) a very much too narrow an account of the matter. The lines where Reilly speaks of parents who don't understand each other, and neither understand or are under-*

stood by their children, are not true of marriage and parenthood as I have been fortunate enough to experience these states — far as I fall short of deserving them (and that is not mere conventional modesty). That was the one point in the play where I felt you had perhaps been led by dramatic necessity into an over-simplification which came near to being a falsification. Of course, I know it was Reilly who said it, and not you; and Reilly is not at all to be taken as infallible! All the same . . . there is no correction anywhere else in the play. And perhaps that is because it is concentrated — so far as E. and L. are concerned — upon a marital relationship which doesn't seem even to contain the idea of children.

(e) Eliot's reply, taken from the same letter of 29 August, runs:

About the Choice — ah, yes, of course I must agree, as you put it. But, whatever the point of view, it is obvious that Reilly must make the contrast as sharp as possible; and as for the problem of communication, it is a question of the universe of discourse in which one is moving. There are undoubtedly degrees of understanding — but in the universe of discourse in which Reilly is moving during that speech, there are two primary propositions: (1) nobody understands you but God; (2) all real love is ultimately the love of God.

(f) Oh, and as for Lavinia, I thought it was obvious, from one line at the end of Act III and one line in the opening dialogue of Act IV, that Lavinia was going to have a baby. At her age, I fear it will be an only child . . .

(g) From Mr. Martin Browne, dated 31 March 1949:

. . . I am very glad to hear that the early part of Act IV has gone well in revision. . . . Don't forget Edward and

> *Lavinia in that latter part: we are very much attached to*
> *them by now, and pleased at their achievement of a* modus
> vivendi, *so we should like to hear how they managed it —*
> *this might well be useful material in the Peter section. I*
> *think you will find that in playing they will assume great*
> *importance — the play will seem to be largely* about *them:*
> *and on that importance you can build.*

It will be seen from the passage I have numbered 2(f) how
Eliot responded to this suggestion. I cannot positively
identify the 'line at the end of Act III' and the 'line in the
opening dialogue of Act IV', because, as will be seen from
the next extract, there were changes made in the number-
ing of the Acts.

3.(a)   Eliot to Mr Martin Browne, 18 July 1948:

Dear Martin,
    Having finished the first draft of three acts, I think that
I might as well let you have a copy now. The original
scheme was for three acts and an 'epilogue'. I have not
changed this scheme, but I propose to call the Epilogue
'Act IV'. I think the term 'epilogue', read in the programme, is discouraging for the audience: it suggests that
everything will be finished by then, and the epilogue
might be omitted.
    Act IV, as I now propose it, will repeat the scene, and
most of the personages of Act I. The only person absent
will of course be Celia. It should be a year, or perhaps two
years later than the rest of the play. Some indication of the
fate of Celia will be given in the conversation: this is tricky,
but I don't want to leave her in the air like Harry. The
interesting problem, however, is that of the behaviour of
the several persons while Celia is being discussed.

Note: the 'Harry' mentioned here is the protagonist of *The
Family Reunion*, who also receives a call to a religious life,

> To the worship in the desert, the thirst and deprivation,
> A stony sanctuary and a primitive altar,
> The heat of the sun and the icy vigil,
> A care over lives of humble people,
> The lesson of ignorance, of incurable diseases.
>
> (*The Family Reunion*, II. 2. 331–5)

We are never told in the play what became of him, in obedience to this call, which nevertheless, like Celia, he obeys, bidding farewell to his family.

(b) Continuing from Eliot's letter to Mr. Martin Browne of 18 July 1948, we find an early reference to the Libation scene:

> In order to use the same set for Act IV as for Act I, I have put in a final scene at the end of Act III, which was not contemplated in this form when I last saw you, so as to get Julia, Reilly and Gibbs together with all the others out of the way. This is a kind of scene which I, naturally, rather fancy; and which, equally naturally, I fear you will disallow.

(c) I should think we might allow another 20 pages for the last act. One question will be whether this will work out at anything near the right length. On the one hand, there are probably passages where there are more words than necessary to carry forward the situation, and others where there are gaps. I don't feel that I can myself judge whether I have plotted the emotional curve of the important scenes successfully. One sees the situation at the beginning of the scene, and the situation one wants to arrive at, at the end; but it is, I feel sure, only too easy to leave out indications of sufficient changes, in the course of the dialogue, which the audience must have. I suspect, for instance, that the transformation of Edward and Lavinia, and the development of Celia in the hands of Reilly occurs too abruptly

194

to be convincing. At the same time, I believe that there is always a way of solving the problem *within the time limits of the form*, if one selects the essential words which will do the work within that time. I suppose it is the business of the dramatist to be able to give, in ten minutes on the stage, the illusion of an operation which in life would take at least half an hour.

Yours ever

P.S. I am inclined to think that a better title would be THE COCKTAIL PARTY. A cocktail party of guests whom the host didn't want, corresponds very well to a family reunion from which part of the family was absent.

(It may be noted here that Eliot had at first chosen *One-Eyed Riley* for the title of his comedy, in order strongly to stress the name he had decided to give his principal character; though his identity is not at first disclosed, his raucous music-hall song implants the name which, in its grander form — Sir Henry Harcourt-Reilly — that character will bear. However, as he wrote he changed his mind apparently for the reason here given.)

4.   Eliot to Mr. Martin Browne, dated 15 March 1949:

Dear Martin,

I think it might be possible for me to devise a better opening for Act IV, rewriting the first few pages, and especially if you could allow me a couple of caterer's men to be present at the very beginning. It seems to me that a little business would enliven the opening and stimulate the interest of the audience instead of the mere dialogue. Besides I am not sure that that light comedy dialogue doesn't go on too long and perhaps give the impression of being rather forced.

On the other hand having now worked the thing out to an end I incline to revert to the view that this act works out

195

best timed in this way — *before* the cocktail party — rather than if I tried to reset it to take place just *after* all the other guests had left. I don't mind in the least writing quite a different opening to indicate that the party is over, but if I made that change I wonder whether the conclusion might not be less effective. It seems to me to add to the point of the scene for the audience to have in mind that my people have got to go on with their party in spite of everything; and this ending also seems to provide an effective exit for the other three. I shall be glad if you will think about this carefully. Of course I appear to be assuming that the centre of the scene is all right, and I am certainly not confident about anything.

Yours ever

5. To which Eliot added a postscript on the following day (16 March 1949):

Dear Martin,

A point I forgot. I should like Peter's talk checked to make sure that it does not betray too much ignorance of the film industry. I don't know whether, if he was a script writer, he could be given anything so important to do as engaging minor characters in England. And it is important that his chief interest lay in getting a good part designed for Celia, and persuading her to take it.

Yours ever

6. How willing to change and polish his text, how flexible as a craftsman, how sensitive to the criterion of what will best make its point in a theatre (*'within the time limits of the form'*, to use his own phrase), not only when first putting pen to paper, but also after the play had been successfully performed, may be seen from the following excerpts from two letters to Mr. Martin Browne:

196

(a)   1st June 1948

Dear Martin,

Here is the first draft of three scenes which I promised you to examine at your convenience. When you are ready for a preliminary talk about it please let me know and we will arrange a meeting.

You will understand of course that this is only a first rough draft and that everything, including a good deal of the actual dialogue, is subject to revision. The verse is still in a very rough state and will in any case need a good deal of polishing. On the other hand I understand how little you can say about what is little more than a third of a play. Possibly no more than whether you think it is worth pursuing or not . . .

The first performance of *The Cocktail Party* was given at the Royal Lyceum Theatre, Edinburgh, as part of the Edinburgh International Festival, on 22 August 1949 and was a nationally acclaimed success. This made a London run during the winter a seeming certainty; but in the event no theatre there was available and the play went to New York instead, where it became the 'talking-point of the season', as Martin Browne records in *The Making of T. S. Eliot's Plays*, p. 241. It opened in London on 3 May 1950 and became, once again, a centre of excited controversy. Eliot was still concerned with perfecting the text, in spite of the praise it had received after the Edinburgh opening, as the following extract from a further letter of his to Martin Browne, dated 7 September 1949 testifies:

(b)   . . . I return from a long week-end in the country, somewhat refreshed but still very tired. I am worried by the fact that I have now to prepare three lectures before I go to Germany on October 26th. If the play is to come to London in November, when I shall be away, I shall be hard put to it to effect any actual re-writing . . .

. . . if the play is to be resumed this autumn, or before Christmas, then I must rely upon you pretty heavily for the shortening of it.

I certainly look to Act I (as now constituted) to provide opportunities. I should be sorry to cut the opening, as it seems to me that the light note is very important to the total effect of the play . . .

. . . Well, will you take the initiative about the cutting? I can do a little patchwork in writing in new lines, but I feel quite incapable of thinking the whole play out again for myself.

3   Notes to *The Cocktail Party*

3   Notes to *The Cocktail Party*

ACT I   Scene 1

Lines 14–18
The conversational repetitions in these lines recall the
rhythms and repetitions of the first fragment of *Sweeney
Agonistes*, which are further marked by thudding rhymes.
Here the rhymes have been dropped and the rhythms broken
a little, to approximate more closely to normal interchanges
of speech, and yet retain the ghost of a feeling of comic verse-
energy.

Line 120
Go away yourself! Celia is amazed at the possibility of
Edward's vague plan to go away, when the situation as she
sees it, specially needs his presence, now that Lavinia has
left him and so given him the chance to declare and pursue
his relationship with Celia, his mistress; she is confused by
his spineless attitude as her next speech shows.

Line 133
Are there any prospects? Julia means will Lavinia's aunt
leave her any money? (She is keeping up her pose as a
worldly-minded 'tough old woman', as she describes herself
in her next speech.)

Line 213
Your wife has left you? The Unidentified Guest asks this
question to keep up the pretence of being a stranger to the
whole situation, that Edward may converse all the more
freely. Actually he knows the whole story as is clear from his
confession in Act II, line 70. It is part of the trap in which
Edward finds himself at that point.

Line 217

This is an occasion. 'The Unknown Guest warms to his work' Professor John Lawlor, 'The Formal Achievement of *The Cocktail Party*', *Virginia Quarterly Review*, 30, 1954, p. 446.

Line 286

I never thought I should be any happier

With another person. Edward is keeping up the lie he has told in saying that his wife had nothing to complain of in his behaviour (line 231); he is shielding himself and his relationship with Celia. *protecting.*

Lines 328–9

You are nothing but a set

Of obsolete responses. He is a person who has lost the sense of his identity which he had derived from the habits of five years as Lavinia's husband; now that Lavinia has left him, his habits are out of date and he does not know how to respond to events, since the accustomed way has been taken from him. Presently, Edward, unconsciously taking his cue from this speech of the Unidentified Guest, declares '*I must find out who she is, to find out who I am*' (line 356); his Guest is already establishing an authority over him. This is what makes it possible for him to make promises, defy questions and issue orders to Edward, as he does in lines 364, 366 and 374.

Line 384

because one lens is missing. Symbol hunters have linked Julia's one-eyed spectacles with the Unidentified Guest's music-hall ballad of the One-Eyed Riley, and so with the Unidentified Guest himself (Sir Henry Harcourt-Reilly) who in some productions wears a monocle, though this does not appear to be mandatory from the text. D. W. Harding in an essay called 'Progression of Theme in Eliot's Modern Plays' (*Kenyon Review*, Vol. XIII, No. 3, 1956) suggests that

Julia and Sir Henry 'both are metaphorically one-eyed and need each other to give a whole vision'. It is certain that these two need each other; they share the risks they take in pursuing their destiny as Guardians:

> *Reilly* I have taken a great risk.
> *Julia*   We must always take risks.
>   That is our destiny.
>
>   (II. 750–1)

Moreover their method of working together is later defined by Sir Henry with some clarity:

> When I express confidence in anything
> You always raise doubts; when I am apprehensive
> Then you see no reason for anything but confidence.
>
>   (II. 777–9)

But I see no reason to think they are 'metaphorically one-eyed' and need each other to give a whole vision. Spiritual insight is abnormally acute in each of them; there is no point at which Julia's insight corrects Sir Henry's, or his hers. They have different functions of course — she the sheep-dog, he the shepherd — but they have the same visions. The passage about the lost lens can be taken quite simply as a joke — the scatter-brained chatterbox that Julia makes herself out to be in the pretended quest for her spectacles, which are in her pocket all the time, and the joke of a burst of music-hall balladry about the One-Eyed Riley suggested by the one-eyed spectacles and the fact (which we don't yet know) that the Unidentified Guest happens to be called Reilly too.

Line 421

St. Anthony. St. Anthony of Padua (1195–1231), Portu-guese by birth, famous preacher in Italy and France, called 'hammer of heretics', and a notable wonder-worker, especially in the matter of finding lost belongings for you. See Donald Attwater, *A Dictionary of Saints* (1958). This is a Christian reference that has slipped out, as it were without Eliot noticing, in Julia's irrepressible rotations of tongue.

Line 507

starting a salon. A way of acquiring social distinction — even fame — by inducing literary lions and lion-cubs to come and prowl round your drawing-room consuming light refreshment and making memorable remarks, on certain regular days; Lavinia's days were Thursdays (line 527); in addition to the lions would be the lionisers, especially women of fashion, such as Celia Coplestone. It is said she was also a poetess, and a good one in line 469; Peter Quilpe was a lion-cub, having published a novel (line 457), and aspiring to direct films. To start a salon, as the word 'salon' suggests (salon = drawing-room) was an idea popular among society hostesses in nineteenth-century Paris.

Line 568

With some secret excitement which I cannot share. Perhaps the excitement of her love for Edward, of which Peter is ignorant. Perhaps an excitement created in her by a more 'indefinable experience' (line 573) than her love for Edward, namely an experience for which her love for Edward turns out to be a substitute, and which ultimately leads to her martyrdom.

Line 601

Excuse me a moment. Edward is being rung by Celia, at an awkward moment. See I. 2. 3.

Line 612

the fool you are. Edward is unconsciously continuing to show how great an influence the Unidentified Guest has already acquired over him, first noted at line 356 (see note to I. 1. 328–9); he is snubbing Peter in much the same way as the Unidentified Guest has snubbed him. He adopts his way of thinking, when Peter says he must see Celia, by remarking 'Will it be the same Celia?', which recalls the idea of the Unidentified Guest that our identities change very easily and swiftly (I. 1. 322–30) and now, in using this phrase to Peter, he is simply passing on the scornful advice given to him at line 334, to 'Resign yourself to be the fool you are'.

Line 641

I'd rather you didn't tell her. Peter seems to know that Lavinia takes a proprietary, almost an amatory interest in him, and would prefer her not to know of his attachment to Celia, to avoid a scene with Lavinia.

ACT I   Scene 2

Line 44

Slipper what? One may conjecture that Alex said 'Slivovica', a Jugoslav brandy made from plums, their national drink; Edward must have misheard him over the telephone; or Alex may have got the name a little wrong, since he speaks of prunes, not plums.

Line 76

He was left at an inn. See Luke 10. 34.

Line 91

He has some sort of power. A spiritual nature like Celia's might well have unprompted intuitions of this kind; but perhaps she noticed him at the moment when he had the strange vision of her he had had standing behind her chair, which he describes in Act III, lines 425–33, which gave him the idea that she was 'under sentence of death'.

Line 95

Unless he is the Devil! There is, of course nothing diabolical about the Unidentified Guest, as some critics have supposed. He seems diabolical at the moment to Celia because he has

惡魔

promised to restore Lavinia to Edward's arms, where Celia intends, or thinks she intends to be herself.

Line 150

— *and his name* is *Reilly!* Celia has heard of Sir Henry Harcourt-Reilly from Julia (II. 457–8), but does not yet know he is the Unidentified Guest of Act I scene 1. This is not revealed to her till they meet again in II. 460.

Line 172

I have heard of that experience. Edward, totally immersed in the problems of his own egotism and unable to commit himself or give himself unconditionally to another person, sacrificing all else in his life to it, has never known the kind of ecstasy that his filled Celia, has never been 'in love'. He hotly denies that he has taken Celia '*as a passing diversion*' (I. 2. 191) but the best he seems able to say of her by way of concluding his affair with her is the feeble comment '*And I think you are a very rare person*' (I. 2. 161). We have already heard his advice, or pretended advice, to Peter Quilpe (who believes himself in love with Celia) that it is a mere fever that will cool (I. 1. 579) and that he is to be congratulated on a timely escape (I. 1. 581); this is not the language of a man deeply affected by love or friendship. It may be true that he is trying to protect his relationship with Celia from discovery, and so adopts a cynical tone, but there would be other ways of doing this without such sneers, which either belittle the worth of loving Celia or the worth of his own sincerity towards Peter. He still has much to learn about himself and others.

Line 177

the dream was not enough. Celia hungers for reality thinking to have found it in her love of Edward, which, by the departure of Lavinia, she now feels able to proclaim to the world, and, by a divorce and remarriage, to make real, in the public world, as well as in '*a private world of* ours' (line

170). But now that Edward has repudiated their relation-ship and says he wishes to have Lavinia back '*the dream was better. It seemed the real reality,*' (I. 2. 179).

Line 181

Perhaps it was I. Unlike most people in such circumstances, Celia blames nobody but herself, and feels humiliated at her own self-betrayal; she makes no reproaches to Edward for letting her down with such a seeming crash; but we are shown at once that this is not due to mere poor-spiritedness in her, but to a real inner magnanimity and sense of truth, for she delivers an annihilating attack on him in her next speech ('Oh, don't think that you can humiliate me!') accusing him of being a self-deceiving sham. This is a true insight into Edward's nature, though during the course of the play, he becomes modestly capable of better things. She does not hit back at him in revenge for having hurt her, but accuses herself of having humiliated herself and her in-ward vision of love by supposing it could be realised (made real) in Edward. The difference between Edward and Celia can be instantly seen when he feels himself attacked for taking her as a '*passing diversion*' (I. 2. 191); he hits back defensively, but to hurt her, with '*How did you take Peter?*' (line 196). Nevertheless she leads the dialogue back (after this oblique attack has been fended off by her obvious innocence in the matter of Peter) to the central issue, namely that Edward wants Lavinia back, and if that is what suits him, he had better have her back (lines 212–13), and the sooner the better.

Line 220

You should have a man . . . nearer your own age. Perhaps because he is kindled by Celia's intentness on reaching the truth, Edward shows the first signs of a capacity for self-criticism, which increases in strength as the scene pro-gresses. It is as if her sincerity were infectious.

Line 238

But I want to understand you. Here again Celia shows she is not just striving for victory over Edward in an argument, but is full of sorrow and compassion for him, for the kind of life he seems to be choosing; she wants him to be happy, but how can he be so with Lavinia? (line 243).

Line 244

No — not happy. Edward sunk in the self-absorbed conventional routine of his uninspired character, resigns himself to it once more, to a meaningless, humdrum existence, after his recognition of failure to escape into a make-believe love-affair with Celia. He has met himself as a middle-aged man (line 229) who feels he has lost the desire for all that was most desirable, that is (in his idea) for a perfect relationship in human love and union, having no longer the energy for it. He sees that he must take what happiness he can from not having forced himself to continue feeding on an exhausted passion, which I think may be the sense of his phrase:

> *of knowing*
> *That the misery does not feed on the ruin of loveliness.*

(I. 2. 246)

Line 247

That the tedium is not the residue of ecstasy. The sense of ecstasy in a love-relationship is an important criterion to Eliot. In *The Family Reunion*, Harry says of the relationship between his father and mother 'There was no ecstasy' (II. 2. 72); for a fuller understanding of the underlying idea, there could be no better commentary than John Donne's poem *The Extasie*:

> This Extasie doth unperplex
> (We said) and tell us what we love,
> Wee see by this, it was not sexe,
> Wee see, we saw not what did move . . .

> When love, with one another so
>   Interinanimates two soules,
> That abler soule, which thence doth flow,
>   Defects of loneliness controules.

It is a moment of spiritual wonder in a union possible to such as are capable of it; the 'tedium' of which Edward speaks would be the fruit of an attempt to force a continuance of this ineffable experience after it had ceased to 'interinanimate' the lovers.

Line 257

And who in some men may be the guardian. Edward is thinking and talking at a far more perceptive level than one would expect from a man of his conventionality, and there was, in the earlier version of this scene, a passage in which he shows himself aware of this:

> I have had a vision of my own mediocrity;
> But I shall return shortly, I suppose,
> To my proper dimness. Now while I am awake,
> For the first, and for the last time,
> Good-bye.

> (Martin Browne, op. cit., p. 199)

It is to Edward's credit that he has the insight to find the word 'Guardian'. It replaces the word '*daemon*' which is to be found in an earlier draft of the speech we are discussing (lines 244–62). There the lines run:

> I see that my life was determined long ago
> And that the struggle to escape from it
> Is only a make-believe, a pretence
> That what is, is not, or could be changed.
> The self that can say 'I want this — or want that' —
> The self that *wills* — he is a feeble creature;
> He has come to terms in the end
> With the real, tougher self, who does not speak,

Who never talks, who does not argue;
And who in some men may be the daemon, the genius,
And in others, like myself, the dull, implacable,
The indomitable spirit of mediocrity.

(Ibid., pp. 183–4)

Socrates was said to have a *daemon*, or indwelling spirit, to which he gave obedience, a kind of oracle or conscience that seemed to prompt him with a power not his own, not to be disobeyed. It is to some such power Edward is referring, a power that may inspire other men, but not himself; what keeps and prompts Edward is a deadweight of commonplace conventionality. To have realised this is something of an advance in Edward's self-knowledge; perhaps it is Celia's presence that has inspired him to this flight of thought; and a sign of her magnanimity towards him, after he has let her down so unexpectedly, is seen in her willingness to drink a toast with him to 'the Guardians', a word she has done him the honour of borrowing from him. In the earlier version, already quoted from, the toast she proposes is '*To the daemons*' (ibid., p. 200).

Line 267

Twice you have changed. At her first entry in this scene, Edward had appeared to her as the man she loved and was prepared to acknowledge to the world; but his refusal to take the course of claiming his freedom from Lavinia (after her seeming desertion) in order to marry Celia, revealed his mean-hearted, poor-spirited, conventional, mummy-like, dried-up, bloodless nature. That was the first change Celia saw. It was all that was left of what she had thought he was. But now she sees him freshly, as he really is

> I see another person,
I see you as a person whom I never saw before.

(I. 2. 283–4)

This is a second change.

Line 285
a projection. That is, an embodiment, in Edward, of a certain vision she had had of the nature of love; it existed in her imagination and she had 'projected' it on him, as one may project a film on a screen; the picture seems to be on the screen, but it 'really' is in the projector.

ACT I   Scene 3

Line 20
To bring someone back from the dead. This is the first fairly explicit reference to the Alcestis theme, from which Eliot tells us the play took its origin. (See Section (h) on Influences and Sources.)

Line 23
Ah, but we die to each other daily. This is a stroke of serious wit by the Unidentified Guest. He is half-quoting from St. Paul's famous phrase in the first Epistle to the Corinthians (Ch. 15. 30–1)

> And why stand we in jeopardy every hour?
> I protest by your rejoicing which I have in Jesus Christ our Lord, I die daily.

St. Paul under constant threat feels his life as a daily death. Sir Henry takes his phrase and plays with it to suggest that human beings are continually ceasing to be what they had seemed to be and becoming something else, as if they had suffered a little death and rebirth. This is illustrated by Celia's remark already noted, that Edward had twice changed while she watched him (I. 2. 267). He had 'died' to her as a lover. The phrase is taken up again later by Lavinia when alone with Edward:

211

I thought that there might be some way out for you
If I went away. *I thought that if I died*
To you, I who had only been a ghost to you,
You might be able to find the road back
To a time when you were real — for you must have
  been real
At some time or other, before you ever knew me.

(I. 3. 399–404. My italics)

This willingness to sacrifice herself for Edward reflects the willingness of Alcestis to sacrifice herself for Admetus. The parallel is somewhat faint, but see the note on the word *Dedham* (I. 3. 190).

Line 58

for definite reasons. The Unidentified Guest is allowed to remain unidentified for many reasons; one is Eliot's wish to sustain the mystery and so increase the suspense of the situation for the audience; another reason is that Sir Henry does not wish Edward and Lavinia to realise the trap he has devised for them, from which they could still escape if they knew of it; secondly he wishes them to find themselves bickering just as before, as soon as they are alone together. This will make them both·more than ever convinced that they need his promised help; their waspish incompatibility will also be demonstrated to the audience the first time they are seen left to themselves. For all these reasons, and others, perhaps, Eliot has made Sir Henry keep his secret for a little longer.

Line 72

Julia had a telegram. Here begins the comedy of the telegrams. Julia claims to have had a telegram from Lavinia with a message for Celia. Alex claims to have had a telegram from Lavinia with a message for Peter (line 98). Lavinia knows nothing about the telegrams (line 134) but instantly, and perhaps rightly, judges them to be 'some of

Julia's mischief' (line 138); Alex may have had a hand in it too (line 227). But the simplest explanation is that they were all sent by the Unidentified Guest, with the other Guardians in collusion; the scene makes for lively comedy before the play plunges into the more serious business of the Consulting Room of Sir Henry Harcourt-Reilly.

Line 92

Can't you see me that way too, and laugh about it? Reilly regards the return of a sense of humour as a hopeful symptom (II. 321). Celia has been able to see Edward, first, as the embodiment of the spiritual things she was blindly seeking, then, as a mummy or insect, and, at last, with more truth, as an ordinary human being with absurd foibles and faults, and puffed up with a laughable conceit, blinkered by egotism. To be able to accept all this with a warm laugh is a sign of sanity and friendliness. Celia seems willing to admit she has her own laughable aspects; she says later in Sir Henry's Consulting Room

> I may have been a fool:
> But I don't mind at all having been a fool.
>
> (II. 556)

Line 190

Dedham. Note that this name is rammed into the reader and into the audience — *five times in four lines.* Can it be that the name was chosen by Eliot half as a pun, half as a symbol, to remind us of Alcestis-Lavinia's return from the Home of the Dead (Dead-home)? Of course this would be etymological nonsense, for the name has originally nothing to do with the idea of death, and means 'Dydda's Home' (Eilert Ekwall, *The Concise Oxford Dictionary of English Place-names*, Clarendon Press, 1960); but the sound, so insistently repeated, might recall, to alert eyes and ears, the notion of Lavinia's metaphorical return from the grave.

I can think of no other reason to explain the reiteration; with a writer like Eliot it cannot be an accident.

Lines 220–1

yesterday I started some machine. She started a train of events by leaving Edward which because her action involved the taking of decisions by other people, seems now beyond her control, and indeed is.

Line 224

Somebody is always interfering. She is conscious of the work the Guardians are doing without knowing of their existence.

Line 252

But you *ought to know.* She ought to know because the Unidentified Guest has brought her back, as he promised, and she therefore must know him.

Line 270

And now I can see how absurd you are. Compare Lavinia's manner of announcing this tart discovery with Celia's more affectionate, indulgent way in I. 3. 80–4. So too later in the scene, Lavinia also makes fun of Edward by her school-boy imagery (lines 357–62), but more cuttingly.

Line 327

I was warned of the danger. The danger of returning to the prison-house of matrimonial squabbles with a man who showed no spirit, instead of staying safely in the secluded, restful Hotel-Nursing-Home, which she thinks of as one of Sir Henry's 'sanatoria' (see II. 230–4), and enjoying her 'nervous breakdown'. It must have been Sir Henry who issued the 'warning' she speaks of, using his usual technique with self-obsessed patients like Edward and Lavinia, of advising them to do the opposite of what he intends they shall do, and this drives them into a wilful contradiction of his 'advice' which is just what he has aimed at. In the same way he had seemed to advise Edward that he ought to be thankful for Lavinia's 'desertion',

> And yet, the effect of all his argument
> Was to make me see that I wanted her back.
>
> (I. 2. 128–9)

Line 357

Oh, Edward, when you were a little boy. See note on line 270 above.

Line 419

Merely projections. See note on I. 2. 285, where Celia's 'projection' was one of love, a heaven of her imagination that she was mistakenly seeing in Edward; here (I. 3. 419) we are told of Edward's projections; locked inside his own self-obsession, he has Hell within him, which he projects upon others, but he is always *alone* in the Hell-prison-cell of Self; contrast Celia, who thinks of this alone-ness of the individual as a 'solitude' of which she has become aware (II. 505), but without fear or regret, and suggests that she is gradually becoming free of worldly attachment (now that Edward has broken her illusion about him) and is approaching a knowledge of the love of God. These two kinds of alone-ness, that at first seem similar, are really opposites. Her whole character and situation reflect the maxim taken by Eliot from St. John of the Cross for the epigraph on *Sweeney Agonistes: 'Hence the soul cannot be possessed of the divine union, until it has divested itself of the love of created beings.'*

Line 423

It was only yesterday. It was only yesterday that Edward had made the decision that he wanted Lavinia back, and that decision has damned him (condemned him) to the old Hell of solitude and total immersion in himself.

Line 451

Celia? Going to California? Yes, with Peter. Lavinia knows perfectly well that this is a false suggestion. She has already been told it is not the case (lines 149–50). Edward cannot have been attending when Peter told Lavinia that he and Celia were not going away together, for now the anguish of having lost Celia strikes him freshly and fiercely, though conventionally too, to make him exclaim:

> O God, O God, if I could return to yesterday
> Before I thought that I had made a decision.
>
> (I. 3. 454–5)

Edward's exclamation had its model in Thomas Heywood's play *A Woman Killed with Kindness* (1603), in Act IV, scene 6:

> O God! O God! that it were possible
> To undo things done; to call back yesterday!

These lines are quoted in Eliot's essay on Thomas Heywood (*Selected Essays*, p. 181), with the comment:

His nearest approach to those deeper emotions which shake the veil of Time is in that fine speech of Frankford which surely no men or women past their youth can read without a twinge of personal feeling.

The most poignant of all phrases expressing this idea, however, is to be heard in Lady Macbeth's 'What's done cannot be undone.'

ACT II

Line 39
a sanatorium. Sir Henry's connections with sanatoria are never quite clearly defined, nor is it clear what kind of sanatoria they are. We learn from him that '*There are several kinds of sanatoria*' (line 110) for several kinds of

patient. Sir Henry evades questions on the subject, but admits in answer to Edward's question whether it was far to go '*You might say, a long journey*' (II. 189). Lavinia believes she has spent some time in one of Sir Henry's sanatoria (II. 230) but he assures her '*You have never visited my sanatorium*' (line 234), as if he only had one after all; he adds that he had sent her to '*a kind if hotel*' (II. 237). People, he says, who need his sanatorium 'are not easily deceived' (line 243) and they must have honest minds (line 269); whereas Edward and Lavinia are self-deceivers (lines 278–80). Those who go to the Sanatorium are the *saints* (line 405). Yet some people have been to Sir Henry's sanatorium, and have come back, 'to everyday life' (II. 705), or so Celia thinks; but Sir Henry mysteriously contradicts her; they cannot have been to the sanatorium, to which he proposes to send Celia (line 707); nevertheless some of those who have been to it have returned 'to lead very active lives, very often, in the world'. (II. 717–18).

To make a guess at the situation behind these hints, Sir Henry has official connections with various kinds of medical, quasi-medical and religious institutions, to which he can send such patients as he judges to be in need of one or other of them; loosely they may all be classed among his 'sana-toria', though they vary from something resembling a private hotel or a nursing-home to the most austere re-ligious, missionary and nursing Orders. This last is a special kind of sanatorium referred to by Sir Henry in II. 234, where those who are not easily deceived are sent (lines 242–3), where also the saints go (line 405). It is to this kind of 'sanatorium' that Celia will be sent; when fully trained there, she will return to lead a very active life in the world, yet no longer in London Society, but among plague-stricken natives in the Christianised parts of Kinkanja, as we learn from Alex in III. 310, and the lines that follow.

Line 56

a man who did not know you. Edward is of course mistaken in thinking Alex does not know Sir Henry; the Guardians keep their association secret to the end.

Line 87

They might be much worse. If he had not decided that he wanted Lavinia back he might have lived with Celia and allowed Lavinia to divorce him. This would have ruined all three of them, in Sir Henry's opinion; and we are meant to agree with him.

Line 97

Two people advised me recently. Celia in Act I scene 2 line 150, and Lavinia in Act I scene 3 line 428.

Line 179

You have nothing else to tell me? Sir Henry is giving Edward a chance to tell the full truth about his situation in regard to Celia as well as to Lavinia, but Edward dodges the question.

Line 220

Honesty before honour, Mr. Chamberlayne. Edward has accused Sir Henry of behaving dishonourably by his breach of confidence in exposing him to his wife, and by disregarding the medical convention by which the secrets of a patient are never divulged to an outsider. Sir Henry raps out this epigram rather slickly; what he means is that Edward has been suppressing the truth about himself and Celia, and this is more important than a fine point in medical etiquette.

Line 234

You have never visited my sanatorium. See note on Act II, line 39.

Line 254

You are much too ill. He is morally ill, self-centred and dishonest; he is in no condition for undertaking the kind of life to which a saint is called; truthfulness and humility such as we shall presently see in Celia are the first requisites, the signs of the spiritual health and strength that she has and he has not. Therefore Sir Henry's special kind of 'sanatorium' is not for him. He presently tells Edward and Lavinia that *you are both too ill* (line 266); and this is apparent from their embittered interchanges.

Line 287

where the word 'insult' has no meaning. In a Consulting Room a truthful diagnosis is what you go for; it is not a personal but a scientific matter to be told the nature of your complaint, whether the knowledge be painful or not.

Line 297

There was one, in fact. Peter Quilpe, of course.

Line 383

just enough to make us loathe one another; another 'point well taken'. Sir Henry is taking a great risk as he very fully understands and later acknowledges; see lines 343–51 in this scene.

Line 396

The shadow of desires of desires. Edward would be haunted by the desire to desire Celia; Lavinia would be haunted by a desire to desire Peter; these would be barren desires for a past now impossible or for an impossible future. These barren desires would be all that they had to think about if they had been sent to sanatoria, whether together or separately. It is not absolutely explicit which of Sir Henry's kinds of sanatoria he has in mind, but (since honesty is the criterion for entry into the kind to which Celia will be sent) one may suppose he is thinking of a sanatorium like 'a kind of hotel' mentioned in II. 237.

Line 397

the devils who arrive at their plentitude of power. This is an allusion to Christ's parable of the unclean spirit that returns to a soul it has quitted and finds it clean and garnished and empty; and it goes out again to collect seven other spirits more wicked than itself; and the last state of that soul is worse than the first (Matthew 12. 43–5).

Line 399

Edward! In the earlier version of this passage, Lavinia does not use his name, as Mr. Martin Browne points out (op. cit., p. 212), but simply says:

> Then what can we do
> When we can go neither back nor forward?

By adding '*Edward!*' she intensifies her anguish of mind by making a personal appeal for his help, as any affectionate wife might make to a trusted husband in a moment of crisis. It is the first time she has used his Christian name without her habitual cold sneer. It gives hope that their marriage may, after all, succeed.

Line 401

Though you do not know the meaning of what you have said. The meaning of what Lavinia has just said (though in saying it she acted impulsively and did not realise that meaning) is that she and Edward must learn how to make a habit of turning towards each other, rather than against each other, in any personal problem, and to respond as allies, rather than by scoring petty points against each other. The result may not be perfect, for this is an imperfect world, but it will help to '*make the best of a bad job*' as Edward says (line 402). This pessimistic view of normal human relationships, which I suppose Edward utters with a rueful look and a half-laugh at his conventional gibe, seems to be echoed and endorsed more seriously by Sir Henry Harcourt-Reilly, in commenting:

> The best of a bad job is all any of us make of it
> Except, of course, the saints . . .

(lines 404–5)

220

Sir Henry however means more than Edward in using this phrase. He is making reference to the philosophical and theological view that ours is a 'fallen' world, in which, at some point in Time, things went wrong, and a rebellion, in which the human race joined and to which it became permanently committed, broke out against the will of the Creator. In such a world the only way to do better than 'make the best of a bad job' of the world and its ways, is to 'divest itself of the love of created beings' and seek the love and will of God.

Eliot has also expressed this vision of pervading sin in a fallen world and the effort to escape it in a life of sanctity and expiation, in the person of Harry in *The Family Reunion*; there the theme is more powerfully, more poetically, treated, and at greater length. Sir Geoffrey Faber's letter about *The Cocktail Party* and Eliot's reply, is worth study in this context of the discussion of sacred and profane love (see pages 189–92 and 241).

Line 417

Really, Edward! I have some *sense of responsibility*. Deftly Eliot begins to turn our sympathies towards Lavinia; she reveals some thought for others and some practical ability — she has always boasted herself Edward's superior in practical matters (except in things which in her opinion don't really matter, like Income Tax forms) and now, while Edward's mind is still grappling with his moral problem of not wanting 'to build on other people's ruins', she is already able to think in terms of shirts, taxis and telegrams; after all Edward's hesitations, her mind is made up with a snap.

Line 433

I think you have answered my question too. By evading an answer Sir Henry has virtually admitted that the answer should be 'Yes'.

Line 438

work out your salvation with diligence. The last words of the dying Buddha to his disciples.

'But the Buddha laid stress on the final perseverance of the saints, saying that even the least among the disciples who had entered the first path only, still had his heart fixed on the way to perfection, and constantly strove after the three higher paths. "No doubt," he said, "can be found in the mind of a true disciple." After another pause he said, "Behold, now, brethren, this is my exhortation to you. Decay is inherent in all component things. *Work out, therefore, your emancipation with diligence!*" These were the last words the Buddha spoke. . . .'

(From the translation in Rhys David's *Buddhist Suttas*, quoted in the *Encyclopaedia Britannica*, 11th Edition, p. 742, under the article on Buddha.)

Line 486

Except that the world I live in seems all a delusion! The world of London, especially of fashionable London, 'Unreal City' as Eliot calls it in *The Waste Land*, l. 60.

Line 493

Well, there are two things I can't understand. For some discussion of these, see the Introduction, p. 267.

Line 503

What is normality. What is normal for a saint? The question is insisted on again in lines 541–2.

Line 518

It no longer seems worth while to speak to anyone! Yet she is speaking to Sir Henry and establishes a genuine communication with him; this must heighten our opinion of him.

Line 533

There are other states of mind. Sir Henry is speaking from experience, as we learn later (III. 434) when he seemed to see the image of Celia standing behind her chair. This he 'accepted and went on from', to use his own phrase.

Line 546

I suppose it's being immoral. Celia seems to say that she has a moral sense, but does not feel as if she had offended against it; immorality, she thinks, is generally held to be the mark of people who are deficient in moral sense; they feel no guilt, though being 'sinful in the ordinary sense'. It must be admitted her thought in this argument is not quite clear; for by being Edward's mistress she has been 'immoral'; in that case she resembles those whose immorality is not accompanied by a sense of sin. The contrast between them and herself is unclear. Her criterion of wickedness is whether your action hurts someone else, and she claims not to have hurt Lavinia by taking Edward from her (lines 555–556). It would be interesting to know what Lavinia would have retorted.

Line 561

Oh, I don't mean that it was ever mentioned! The question of sin is one of those 'overwhelming questions' which J. Alfred Prufrock, in Eliot's poem, may have wanted to ask, but for the fact that it would have been very bad form to do so in polite society. Misbehaviour, by Celia's account, was regarded (in the circles among which they moved, namely the circles of a West End theatre audience) as either something 'not done', or as something for which one could not be held responsible, a kink in one's nature which one had been born with or which one had acquired in infancy. Celia tells us she is indifferent to the disapproval earned by 'bad form' (567) yet she has not ceased to care about her deviation from conventional morality, so she must be 'kinky' (569–70). But now her deviation seems to her just a mistake (573); but why should one feel '*sinful*' for a *mistake*? Yet she can find no other word for her feelings.

However she does find a word — the word '*emptiness*', and a failure towards something outside herself (582); it is as if she had belittled herself, not lived to her full stature, had let herself down in relation to this 'something', and that she now *ought to make up for it* — to atone. To *atone* is the word she was looking for, and which she finds presently (line 584).

Line 620

I cannot argue. Celia is making a blind attempt to express the newly felt promptings of the mystical side of her nature; for the moment she has passed beyond the grief and shock of the 'crash' (line 506) and being 'ditched' (508) by Edward, to the realisation that she is alone and aware of guilt, or sin, or failure, because of mistaking the love between her and Edward for the real thing; whereas the treasure she was seeking, the love she is looking for, may be an illusion: lover and beloved, dream and dreamer, all equally unreal (605–6); unless the ecstasy of love is real, though those experiencing it have no reality (624), if that is possible. She attempts to describe this ecstasy as 'an intensity of loving in the spirit, a vibration of delight without desire, for desire is fulfilled in the delight of loving' (626–9). But what or whom it is that she loves she does not know, and is ashamed for not being able to find out (634).

Lines 639–40

The condition to which some who have gone as far as you have succeeded in returning. Celia is asking whether she can be cured of a longing for a visionary love she has not found and cannot find, and which may be an illusion. Reilly offers her a choice of alternatives: the first is the possibility of having a glimpse of some spiritual vocation, and of answering it fully enough to reach Celia's condition, without, after all, pursuing it further; it remains with them as a memory and a regret, but the regret diminishes in time. This may be a reflection of the idea summed up in the words of Jesus 'for many be called but few chosen' (Matthew 20. 16). These who are not 'transhumanised' (line 767) come to accept the 'human condition' that finds its way of love in marriage and a family.

Line 679

The kind of faith that issues from despair. A faith in the truth of her vision, though she may despair of finding it. Perhaps Sir Henry is also warning her of what St. John of the Cross calls 'the dark night of the soul', when your vision fails you and nothing is left you but faith. See *The Ascent of Mount Carmel* by St. John of the Cross, mystical Spanish writer (1549–91).

Line 707

Cannot have been to this sanatorium. See note to II. 39.

Line 737

It is finished. The last words spoken by Jesus from the Cross, according to the *Gospel of St. John* (XIX. 30). Sir Henry certainly knows he is quoting these words from the Gospel and applying them to his own work in bringing Celia to a clear decision and the choice of a 'transhumanised' way of life. He does not, however, know that he is speaking prophetically and that Celia too will be crucified; but these three words should alert an audience to an awareness, however dim, of this significance.

Line 767

Transhumanised. This word may be translated as 'brought to a condition of more than human virtue or power; a nature supernaturally lifted above its natural capacity'. Eliot takes it from Dante's *Paradiso*, I. 70–1:

> Transumanar significar per verba
> non si poria.

('Words may not tell of that transhuman change')

Line 769

the way of illumination. 'A phrase reminiscent of the Buddhist way of life which 'conduces to enlightenment by the noble eight-fold path: right views; right intentions; right actions; right livelihood; right effort; right speech; right mindfulness; right concentration'. (*Encyclopaedia Britannica*, 14th Edn., article on *Buddhism*.)

Line 770

projected spirits. Something has been said of 'projections' in the note on I. 3. 419 and I. 2. 285. It is hard to be quite certain what kind of experience Julia is referring to; there are many possibilities. There is, for instance the long tradition of demonic apparition to Christian Saints, such as St. Anthony of St. Dunstan, to tempt or terrify them, and I think we may best imagine what Julia means by imagining ourselves beset by some nightmare of haunting, or of the sense of some supernatural power of pure evil being present, especially in one's moments of solitude or defencelessness and darkness, or of isolation; some such experience as Coleridge paints in *The Ancient Mariner:*

> Like one, that on a lonesome road
> Doth walk in fear and dread,
> And having once turned round walks on,
> And turns no more his head;
> Because he knows, a frightful fiend
> Doth close behind him tread.

Lines 774–5

She will pass between the scolding hills,

Through the valley of derision. I have been unable to recall or trace the source of these allegorical phrases; they are very unlike the language and way of thinking we associate with Julia's rattling tongue; they sound rather as if they had escaped from John Bunyan; Pofessor Grover Smith suggests it is reminiscent of *The Ascent of Mt. Carmel* (*T. S. Eliot's Poetry and Plays*, University of Chicago Press, 1966, p. 226), but I have not found these exact expressions there.

Line 791
And now we are ready to proceed to the libation. See Section (f), pages 270–4.

Line 811
He has not yet come to where the words are valid. Peter is young; a kind of calf-love and an inner conviction that he will become famous as a revolutionary film-director seem to be his highest experiences in the world of the spirit so far; he is in no urgent psychological danger which would give validity to the kind of prayer which the Guardians feel are needed by Celia and the Chamberlaynes.

Line 813
You know, I have connections — even in California. Another example of the irrepressible comedy by which the Guardians send the play spanking along at its most serious moments; the curtain falls on a solemnity of blessing lightened by a laugh.

ACT III

Line 18
It's you who should be tired. Edward thinks Lavinia may be tired after the work of getting things ready for a party, seeing that she is expecting a baby. (See page 192.)

Line 109
That was a nearer guess than you think. Of course Julia is not guessing, as Alex knows perfectly well, but they are playing their habitual game of concealing their secret association as 'Guardians'. Julia knows the whole Kinkanja story, as later

appears (III. 300), and she has brought Alex with her to the Chamberlaynes to tell them. It is she who starts the subject (lines 101–3) and, with her usual verve, elicits enough about Kinkanja to amuse and whet our curiosity; but she doesn't allow the whole story to come out until Peter Quilpe and Sir Henry have arrived to complete Alex's audience. Does she know that Peter is on his way? We are not told so in so many words, but Peter informs us that he has had lunch with Sheila Paisley (line 183) and had told her he intended to 'crash in' on the Chamberlaynes' party; so we may well imagine that Sheila told Julia.

Lines 161–2

But one can't dine out on eating Christians —

Even among pagans! Julia (and Eliot) are here referring to their religion-less London Society audiences, who were pagan without being heathen, like the Greeks and Romans; whereas the Kinkanjans were heathen but not pagan.

Line 303

Not married, but dead. Notice the rhythms, and the repetitions of the word *dead* in these lines:

> *Alex*   Not married, but *dead*.
> *Lavinia* Celia?
> *Alex*   *Dead*.
> *Peter*   *Dead*. That knocks the bottom out of it.
> *Edward* Celia *dead*.

I think it likely that Eliot found these irresistibly impressive cadences in Shakespeare's *Antony and Cleopatra*, Act I, scene 2, lines 151 onwards:

> *Antony*   Fulvia is *dead*.
> *Enobarbus* Sir?
> *Antony*   Fulvia is *dead*.
> *Enobarbus* Fulvia?
> *Antony*   *Dead*.

Line 311
Yes, she had been a V.A.D. I remember. The Voluntary Aid
Detachment to which nurses belonged in the 1914–18
War.

Line 339
I don't understand at all. The reactions of Lavinia, Edward
and Peter to the news of Celia's crucifixion are of some
interest, and Martin Browne's notes on the effect of this
scene upon audiences are specially helpful; they are given
in his *The Making of T. S. Eliot's Plays*, pp. 229–30, from
which I make the following quotation:

(a) The reaction of the three non-guardians to the story
didn't seem violent enough.

(b) *Peter* in particular worried everybody. Why didn't he
rebel actively against the Hollywood he only worked
in for Celia's sake? How could he, after helpless
protests, just go gaily back there?

Lavinia's reaction, though tame in its expression, is
generous both to Edward and to Celia; at least she is no
longer thinking only about herself. Edward is thinking of
Celia and the waste of Celia's life — for that is how it seems
to him, not yet having Sir Henry's viewpoint to guide him.
Peter is only thinking of himself, and the waste of two years
in Hollywood, spent in thinking about Celia and whether he
could find a part for her in a film. One can easily see that he
'has not yet come to where the words are valid' (II. 811).
He has hardly begun, and that is what Lavinia tries to tell
him (III. 374). But it is too late in the play to attempt a
rescue for Peter's character; the audience has heard the
fate of Celia, with stupefaction for those who do not know
the story, and all that it is now waiting for is Sir Henry
Harcourt-Reilly to rise to the occasion: and this he does with
sudden impressiveness.

Lines 423–31

Ere Babylon was dust . . . part no more! These lines come
from Shelley's lyrical drama *Prometheus Unbound* (published in 1820), among the most splendid masterpieces of
the Romantic Movement. They are lines 191–9 of Act I, and
are spoken to Prometheus by his mother, Earth. The Act
opens in a ravine among the icy rocks of the Indian Caucasus,
where Prometheus is chained to a precipice. There the
Tyrant Jove has decreed he shall stay for ever in unceasing
torment. 'Three thousand years of sleep-unsheltered hours'
Prometheus has hung there, defiant, but no longer hating
his Supreme Adversary; he has even forgotten the words
of the earth-shaking curse he had uttered against Jove, and
he now addresses the Mountains, Springs, Air and Whirl-
winds, asking them what were the words he had spoken.
Their voices reply describing their terrible effect, and the
voice of Earth joins with theirs; she had heard the curse
which he remembers no longer and would now retract, but
not before he has been reminded what the actual words of
the curse were. Earth replies that they shall be told him.
Then comes the passage quoted by Sir Henry, from Earth's
speech. Earth is saying that underneath the grave there is
another world, a kind of duplicate of the world we know,
where the shadows of all that has ever existed, of all that has
ever been thought of or imagined, have their being:

> Dreams and the light imaginings of men,
> And all that faith creates or love desires,
> Terrible, strange, sublime and beauteous shapes.

Prometheus (Earth tells him) could call upon his own
shadow to tell him what his words had been; for his 'double'
is in that shadowy region too: 'Ask and they must reply' she
says. She tells him also that death will unite reality and
shadow, and then they will part no more.

Sir Henry quotes this mysterious passage to explain a strange experience of his own that he has hitherto kept to himself, namely that at the original cocktail party with which the play opens, he had seen a vision of Celia, close to Celia herself, her double (as it were) from the region described by Shelley, and that her face 'showed the astonishment of the first five minutes after a violent death' (lines 434–5). He had concluded from this vision, insight, or intuition, that she was about to be united with her shadow and was under sentence of death (line 441). For this reason Sir Henry's face had shown no 'surprise or horror' (line 411) at the news from Kinkanja.

Line 443

what sort of death? He could not know whether it was a natural death or a death by martyrdom, 'because it was for her to choose the way of life to lead to death, and without knowing the end, yet choose the form of death.' She had not then made her choice of death by martyrdom.

Line 460

That is part of the design. See pages 273–80.

Lines 465–6

In myths and images. To speak about it

We talk of darkness, labyrinths, Minotaur terrors. Sir Henry is saying that there are spiritual terrors to face in the spiritual world in which Celia had found her vocation, of which we can only speak in imaginative or poetic terms, but they are not the less real for that. The Minotaur was a mythical monster, half-bull, half-man, that was housed in the labyrinth built by Daedalus in Crete. It was fed on human flesh — seven boys and seven girls, sent every year as tribute from Athens. Sir Henry is saying that the horror of 'spiritual evil always at his shoulder' (line 469) felt by the saints can only be described in terms of nightmare and other monstrous imaginations. The Minotaur image has already

231

been suggested in the litany of the Libation scene, in the line:

Watch over her in the labyrinth

(II. 803)

Lines 473–4

But if this was right — if this was right for Celia —
There must be something else that is terribly wrong. Edward is unconsciously repeating an idea already expressed by Celia (II. 495–9) when she says she would rather believe there was something wrong with *her* than that there was something so massively wrong in the whole world; she never precisely defines what she is thinking of, but it has to do with her discovery of a sense of sin (II. 535–7) and of emptiness and failure in herself, for which she must *atone* (II. 584). Edward puts the thought differently; if Celia was right in making atonement by her crucifixion, then there *is* something massively wrong with a world that calls for such a sacrifice. The idea behind both these passages is the traditional Christian view, to be found in the Thirty-nine Articles (Articles IX and XV particularly), that man's nature is 'inclined to evil', bent, twisted or fallen from its primal innocence, and is born guilty in a guilty world; this is usually called the doctrine of the Fall, or of Original Sin. Our human wills are corrupt from the start; we can only make atonement by surrendering our wills into the will of God. The call to do so is heard and answered by the saints. The way of redemption from the sins of the world was made open to it by the Incarnation and Crucifixion of Christ, in whose footsteps Celia has found her way of love. A sense of sin, or evil, was the first premonition of her conversion as it was also of Harry's conversion in *The Family Reunion*. Harry also chooses a life of expiation. Considered as the hero of a play, however, he is unhappily dislikeable, violent, inconsiderate, contemptuous and abrupt; there is no feeling

that he has won to grace. But with Celia it is different; she is humble; she is capable of love. *The Cocktail Party* marks a great advance in Eliot's power to express the idea of holiness.

Line 479

I cannot help the feeling. Edward, who had self-deceivingly thought himself in love with Celia and had made her his mistress and, after that, had 'ditched her' (to use her own word in II. 508) feels that his behaviour has contributed to her choice of a way of life which resulted in a terrible death for her. Lavinia tries to help Edward to bear this guilt by sharing it, in that she was unkind and spiteful to her (III. 497); as she was in Act I scene 3, 158–60.

Lines 504–5

Only by acceptance of the past will you alter its meaning. To have that knowledge of yourself that the past reveals gives a new perspective, and so a new meaning and purpose in what lies ahead. 'Every moment is a fresh beginning' says Edward, in a sudden understanding (line 537), to which one may add from Eliot's *East Coker*: 'In my beginning is my end.'

4 An Essay on the Structure and Meaning of the Play

4 An Essay on the Structure and Meaning of the Play

(a) *Two modes of comedy and two of love*

Although in some monumental yet admirable way *Murder in the Cathedral* must be rated as Eliot's greatest dramatic masterpiece, I prefer the spanking *allegro* of *The Cocktail Party*, which takes his problems in holiness out of Church in order to show them to us in our comparatively godless daily lives, where we need not keep straight faces for more than a brief moment. As a play it is the easiest, most cursive and actable, intelligently naturalistic yet poetical comedy he has given us, and the readiest of all his comedies to rouse argument and speculation. It gives an amusingly satirical picture of the fashionable West End world of London between the two wars, and yet is charged with a sense of the mystical destiny of a soul chosen for something greater — the soul of a society girl unforeseeably called upon to lay down her life for others in a far-off, primitive and heathen place, and die unknown, the death of martyrdom. This is the greatness of the play, that it not only convincingly presents a spiritual calling of this kind, but also the antics of our secular, modern world of troubled sexual relationships, in what seems a maladjusted marriage, for the cure of which a brilliant psychoanalysis is amusingly presented. All this is done with great vitality, in a continuous blend of laughter and gravity. No other English comedy has linked these two kinds of spiritual quest — the quest for love in marriage and the quest for the love of God. All I have to say of it is an elaboration of this proposition.

237

In an undated letter about *The Cocktail Party* to its first director, Mr. Martin Browne, Eliot wrote:

> I am not anxious that people should have the play explained to them before they have seen it.

If he had thought of it, he might have added 'or read it'. By placing this essay after the play, as an appendage, rather than before it, as an introduction, I have sought to fall in with Eliot's wishes and to encourage readers to begin with the play itself.

Best of all is to see it in a theatre, without knowing anything about it in advance, but with an eye and an ear open to all impressions; for that is the experience for which it was designed. Next best is to read it; this will give a ghost of the experience at least (for by being printed, a play dies a little death). After that may come a time for discussion and argument, for this play abounds in combative ideas and, if we judge by the critics, may be taken in different ways. But first things should come first; it is a lucid play (in spite of many twists of surprise and paradox) and can easily be taken at sight; but after it has been so taken, questions begin to arise.

The Cocktail Party has the sparkle and dash of a comedy of manners; a brilliant surface, with underlying depths. More and more seriously the strange, spiritual criss-cross of affections, passions and desires that it pictures unfolds itself as the play proceeds; yet it does so with continuous comedy, almost, indeed, with farce — at the least with hilarious touches. Steadily, however, the story intensifies to reach a moment of great gravity and shock, and this (as it were) brings a silence in heaven.

With this silence comes a richer and happier understanding of love, seen in its two-fold aspects — the human or natural (such as is seen in marriage) and the mystical or divine (such as is seen in Christian sanctity and martyrdom) which reconciles grief with joy and makes disaster seem triumphant. It becomes clearer what Eliot meant when he wrote to Sir Geoffrey Faber that there were two primary propositions in the play: (1) nobody understands you but God; (2) all real love is ultimately the love of God.

These propositions are nowhere explicitly stated in the play, but they undergird it, as they assert the supremacy of love, whether on the mystical or on the natural plane. So, after the grave climax to which I have referred, the story can return to laughter, to another cocktail party, and to a new hope.

Two modes of comedy as well as two of love are merged and blended in this unique play — for I know of no other which combines them all. These modes are the *satiric*, which laughs at folly and affectation out of countenance and punishes vanity with ridicule, and the *romantic*, which is centred in the happy fulfilment of love and has a humane sympathy for all its characters, even in their failings, and is touched throughout with poetry. These are the familiar modes of Congreve and Shakespeare* respectively. Even when we laugh at them we are not to stand aloof from them, but rather realise how we fall under the same condemnation; no concept of 'alienation' should separate the characters in the play from the audience and deny them the empathy they invite. (We may recall Eliot's quotation, at the end of 'The Burial of the Dead' that opens *The Waste Land*, taken from the Preface of Baudelaire's *Les Fleurs du Mal*: 'You! hypocrite lecteur! — mon semblable, — mon frère!', which is a repudiation of the idea that we are in a position to withdraw our charity from those a poet has imagined in order that they may seek it.) Tiresome at moments, ridiculous at others, all the characters are basically likable and intelligent, and even if Peter Quilpe is no great genius, he is companionable enough, and was more so in an earlier draft, as we can see from Martin Browne's *The Making of T. S. Eliot's Plays* (pp. 220–5).

As for Edward and Lavinia, with all their faults and follies, we meet with what seems to be the way in which we are intended to regard them in a passage already quoted from Mr. Martin Browne to Eliot:

> *Don't forget Edward and Lavinia in that latter part: we are very much attached to them by now, and pleased at their achievement of a* modus vivendi, *so we should like to hear how they managed it . . . I think you will find that in playing they will assume great importance — the play will seem to be largely* about *them: and on that importance you can build.*

In *The Cocktail Party*, what is satirical and punitive is funny enough; the pompous Edward and the frigid Lavinia are properly exposed to each other and to us, but they accept their humiliation, they take their medicine, and in the end they are cured. What is satirical and Congrevian, then, is overarched by what is romantic and Shakespearian; consequently the dialogue is a blend of wit and poetry; consequently, too (for it is found, notwithstanding his punitive satire, in Congreve as in Shakespeare), love not ridicule, is the heart's core of the comedy. It ends happily for all.

Yet the shadow of death falls darkly over this happy ending. This too is found in Shakespeare, early and late; early in *Love's Labour's Lost* and late in *The Winter's Tale*. The ridicule in *The Cocktail Party* is light, if sharp, not inflicted as a punishment (as in Ben Jonson) but in the form of therapy; the victims recover from their treatment, and because of it, though they are laughable they are likable, and the more so for the amusement given by them in their moments of absurdity, and for their manner of taking their medicine.

Love, as I have said, is also presented under two traditional modes, and we are meant, at the end, to feel that each has been finely fulfilled; one of them heroically. These modes derive their being from the deepest and most ancient roots of religious thought, coming from far beyond Christianity, yet modified through many Christian centuries, in our parts of the world, into distinctively Christian shapes. One of them is that mode which withdraws from the humdrum world of daily secular life under vows of chastity, poverty and obedience, into monasteries and convents, or in missionary and healing work under a religious discipline. The other is that of a life lived in the normal, natural bustle of the world, and which, if moved by love, takes other vows — the vows of marriage, which it calls a sacrament. In both ways of life, love is seen religiously, as a calling, a vocation, either to the love of God, or to the love that makes a human family.

These two loves were so well recognised as normal alternatives that Chaucer, writing in about 1385, assumed them as a matter of course, trotting them out on the tongue of Pandarus, during a conversation with Troilus about his niece Criseyde who, he thinks, might well be capable of a response to love:

> 'Was nevere man or woman yet bigete
> That was unapt to suffren love's hete,
> Celestial, or elles love of kynde.'
>
> (*Troilus and Criseyde*, I. 977–9)

'Never', he says 'was man or woman yet begotten who was not liable to suffer the pangs of love, natural or celestial.' It was a platitude, almost a proverb. One of Titian's most famous paintings, entitled *Sacred and Profane Love*, is an

241

allegorical presentation of the same basic idea. In *The Cock-tail Party* it lies at the heart of the matter; the love of God awakens in Celia Coplestone and a love for each other awakens in Edward Chamberlayne and his wife Lavinia; each love discovers its right fulfilment, one in the making of a saint, and the other in the remaking of a broken marriage. It is asked in the course of the play which way of love is the better, and the answer given is:

> Neither way is better.
> Both ways are necessary.

(II. 686–7)

This is the fourth and culminating study of Christian sainthood to which Eliot has given dramatic form; he had previously shown a great part of his thought on the subject in *The Rock* (1934), *Murder in the Cathedral* (1935), and *The Family Reunion* (1939).* *The Cocktail Party* was written between May 1948 and August 1949, and grows out of all that he had written on it before.

(b) *One group of characters (Julia, Alex, The Unidentified Guest)*

The characters in *The Cocktail Party* resolve themselves into two groups of which we only gradually become aware, as the painful complexities of the outwardly carefree company of the opening scene unfold themselves. They seem at first as casual a collection of friends as might have been met in any fashionable London flat, in the middle of our century, a little after sundown. They exhibit that somewhat forced yet corporate liveliness that is partly due to a loyal wish to keep the party going, and partly to the power of the abundant cocktails that have been, and are being, served to them. The scene has the cut-glass sparkle of bright epigram and anecdote, rewarded with laughter.

The talk is in the hands of two conspicuous guests when the play opens, whose vivacity singles them out as the self-appointed entertainers of the gathering. These, as the programme will tell us, are Mrs. Julia Shuttlethwaite and Mr. Alexander MacColgie Gibbs. Mrs. Shuttlethwaite is of the kind that would obviously be the life (and death) of any party she attended; Mr. Gibbs aids and abets her.

When the curtain rises — for it is a play written for a 'picture-frame stage' that aims at creating an exact illusion of actuality, in the tradition of drawing-room comedy — Alex and Julia have an audience of two, Celia Coplestone, a young and beautiful society girl, and Peter Quilpe, a rather ordinary young man. A little aloof from these, Edward Chamberlayne, their harassed host, is busy with serving and replenishing drinks, and near him is a strange and striking figure whom nobody seems to know; he wears an eye-glass, says little and drinks gin and water; in marked contrast to the volubility of Alexander and Julia, he is monosyllabic.

These three — Julia, Alexander and the as yet Unidentified Guest — dominate the first scene and although we do not yet know that they are working in collusion with each other and are, secretly, a group of benevolent conspirators, they focus our attention as a kind of Clown-Trio at Edward Chamberlayne's rather sparsely attended cocktail party.

But there is a sense of malaise underlying the party spirit, presently voiced by the delightful but intolerable Julia. She turns on the harassed Edward and probes him for information about Lavinia. Where is Lavinia? Why is she not at her party? This is hideously embarrassing for Edward; Lavinia is Edward's wife, and the horrid truth is that he has no idea where she is, for she has left him, that very afternoon, left him with her cocktail party on his hands. Yet to confess such a thing to this talkative old woman would make him look a fool. To avoid looking like a fool is a powerful motive with Edward, who is soon involved in a number of palpable fibs, having been cornered, 'driven into a toil' as Hamlet would say, by the searching questions put to him by Julia. He has been obliged to invent a sick Aunt for Lavinia to be visiting. Nobody believes in the aunt, but everyone pretends to. Meanwhile it is established that Lavinia is not at home, for reasons undisclosed, and that fact is what starts the action of the play, under the cover of the chit-chat and persiflage, the probings and evasions. When Julia feels herself to have sufficiently bared Edward's secret, she sweeps out, taking with her the main body of the party, like an outgoing tide with its foam, to reveal the rock on which Edward's family craft has split — his wife's disappearance; he finds himself alone with that somewhat grotesque yet impressive stranger, the Unidentified Guest.

We can sometimes find relief in confessing to a stranger what we cannot admit to a friend, and Edward falls into this trap — for trap it is, as we begin later to understand, laid by Julia in collaboration with Alex and the Unidentified Guest himself. When left alone with this unknown person, Edward at once announces to him, not without that faint touch of the self-importance we feel when delivering bad news, that his wife has left him. As he does this, the pattern of relationships begins to shift. Edward has abdicated his position as Host in exchange for that of Client; whereas the Unidentified Guest rises in status from that of an oddity to that of an expert; he at once reveals his acute psychological powers, and before he has finished he is ordering Edward about, in the manner of a psychoanalyst with a patient who needs a dose of humiliation. After telling him that his wife's desertion is all for the best, he delivers the brutal but no doubt necessary advice in a sharp line of (seemingly un-intentional) blank verse:

> Resign yourself to be the fool you are.
>
> (I. 1. 334)

Humbled, almost mesmerised as Edward seems to be by this unexpectedly remarkable stranger, he still has some-thing within himself that refuses to admit that Lavinia's desertion may be all for the best. He finds himself domi-nated by an inexplicable need to get her back, if only to find out who and what he is, and who is she? What can have happened to them during their five years of loveless, childless marriage? He had always taken her for granted and now he cannot even recall exactly what she looks like; he is lost in a painful mystery:

> I am not quite sure that I could describe her
> If I had to ask the police to search for her.
> I'm sure I don't know what she was wearing
> When I saw her last. And yet I want her back.
> And I *must* get her back, to find out what has happened
> During the five years that we've been married.
> I must find out who she is, to find out who I am.
>
> (I. 1. 350–6)

Edward's amazing guest seems to understand this too and undertakes, with absolute confidence, to bring Lavinia back to him within twenty-four hours. Astounded that this stranger should seem to know everything about him and to be able to control the movements of his vanished wife, Edward exclaims:

> Do you mean to say that you know where she is?
>
> (I. 1. 365)

and receives the mysterious, yet still authoritative answer:

245

That question is not worth the trouble of an answer.
But if I bring her back it must be on one condition:
That you promise to ask her no questions
Of where she has been.

(I. 1. 366–9)

Edward meekly gives his promise, and the Unidentified Guest continues:

In twenty-four hours
She will come to you here. You will be here to meet her.

(I. 1. 373–4)

This appointment seems to be the climax of the scene, but it is only the first crest in a range of further climaxes. The inescapable Julia (who has already returned to interrupt them to retrieve her umbrella) now bursts in once more to look for her spectacles (which turn out to be in her pocket all the time). Her reappearance has an astonishing effect upon the Unidentified Guest; he turns instantly into a kind of clown, rising tipsily to his feet, and he sings a stanza of a well-known popular ballad, peculiarly appropriate to himself on account of his eye-glass, and his favourite tipple, and to Julia because of her having so suddenly come in:

> *As I was drinkin' gin and water,*
> *And me bein' the One-Eyed Riley,*
> *Who came in but the landlord's daughter*
> *And she took my heart entirely.*

Then, after a swift and sober aside to Edward 'You will keep our appointment?' to which Edward replies 'I shall keep it', he totters out singing the chorus:

> *Tooryooly toory-iley*
> *What's the matter with One-Eyed Riley?*

He has evidently had too much gin, too little water. Julia seems not to know who he is:

> Edward who *is* that dreadful man? . . .
> . . . Tell me about him. You've been *drinking* together!
> (I. 1. 392–6)

But drunk as the Unidentified Guest may seem, he has got his message through to her, namely that he has succeeded in securing Edward's co-operation with him in what the audience knows to be the return of Lavinia. This was what Julia had come back to discover; the tale of her lost spectacles was another of her fibs, and when Edward tells her to look in her bag for them, she finds them.

But Julia has another motive in coming back: she has brought Peter back too. He is the sort of young man whom elderly ladies of her social position like to have about, to catch them taxis (I. 1. 177), but she now decants him on the long-suffering Edward, whose one wish is to be alone. We begin, more and more strongly, to suspect that a kind of strategy is being woven around Edward by these three serio-comic figures, Julia, Alex and the One-Eyed Riley, for presently Alex also returns to look in on Edward, ostensibly to cook some supper for him — Alex takes great pride in his gifts as a chef — but actually to get rid of Peter, who by now has had time for the important talk with Edward which he needed and which Julia had dexterously arranged for him — a talk about Celia.

(c) *A second group of characters (Edward, Peter, Celia, Lavinia)*

It must be confessed that there is a regrettable insipidity about Peter Quilpe, so unceremoniously landed, as it were, by Julia on Edward's lap. Peter is in a kind of quandary; he needs to talk about himself to Edward, as Edward had needed to talk about himself to the Unidentified Guest.

Peter's quandary is not a mature matrimonial one, like Edward's; it is a quandary of calf love; he is wondering whether he has been in love, whether he is still in love, whether he is, or has been loved in return, and if so, what has happened to that return of love? Why does Celia — for it is, of course, she of whom he is speaking — no longer seem to wish for his company that had once seemed agreeable to her, as if she were 'preoccupied with some secret excitement' which he cannot share (I. 1. 566–7). Perhaps Edward, as a disinterested friend, could find out from Celia what has happened to produce this estrangement, this fading-out of Celia from Peter's quasi-amorous life?

Eliot seems unconsciously to have written Peter down; he is commonplace and self-absorbed; nothing he says bears the sharp interest of a creative observation, nothing sparks unexpectedly out of him, he carries no feeling of power or imagination — he is supposed to be a young and rising film-director and he believes himself to be revolutionary in that capacity — but one cannot even imagine him handling a prickly film-star let alone a revolution; during the course of the play, he loses his belief, both in films and in himself, but fades out in the direction of Hollywood with a kindly pat on the back from the One-Eyed Riley, Sir Henry Harcourt-Reilly, as we by then will have learnt to call him.

Yet Peter is in some sort useful, since he helps to communicate to us a certain serenity of character in Celia — her power of contemplation, of absorbed attention — he tells us she went alone to concerts and to picture galleries (I. 1. 540) and that when she allowed him to accompany her:

> And I was so happy when we were together —
> So . . . contented, so . . . at peace: I can't express it;
> I had never imagined such quiet happiness.

> (I. 1. 550–2)

She stirred in him no desire for possession, but simply for her company, her presence — 'There was such . . . tranquility' (I. 1. 555).

Peter's visit to Edward corrects and gives depth to the first impressions we had of her in the opening scene. Then we were only aware of her young beauty, her height of fashion, her laughter; now we are won over to her by a sense of enrichment in her, of a nature touched, perhaps, by some mystical inwardness.

All this is in preparation for our first full realisation of her nature and circumstances; these are kept back from us until, in the second scene, we at last see her alone with her lover, Edward Chamberlayne; for Celia is Edward's mistress.

This is the first great surprise of the play; only the most percipient member of an audience could guess the relationship in advance. Yet the hints are there in the text, ready to be conveyed by infinitesimal suggestions in timing and tones of an actor's voice, by glances very reserved and yet indicative, by some abruptness, it may be, in their shaking hands at the end of the party; it is a subtlety for the actors to convey:

Celia	Good-bye, Edward
	Shall I see you soon?
Edward	Perhaps. I don't know.
Celia	Perhaps you don't know? Very well, good-bye.
Edward	Good-bye, Celia.

(I. 1. 181–4)

Later on she rings him up, but we can only guess it is she, for we do not hear her name (I. 1. 600). But we hear it in the last lines of the scene in a climax whose significance is not always instantly perceived; we see its importance in retrospect, a quiet climax, pointer towards the main business of the play, the two ways of love that are to branch out of this relationship.

This climax is handled thus:

Edward *picks up the telephone, and dials a number.*
Edward Is Miss Celia Coplestone in? . . . How long ago? . . .
    No, it doesn't matter.

(I. 1. 647–8)

So slight are these indications that we cannot fairly blame Peter Quilpe for his maladroit choice of Edward as his confidant. But Peter is too self-absorbed to be aware of what is going on in Edward, that dull grown-up, as he must seem to him, kind but dull; elderly. Yet there is another use in Peter's choice of Edward, a satirical use; for we hear Edward echoing the Unidentified Guest in the advice he gives to Peter; he tells him he is lucky to have escaped from Celia, as he had himself been told he was lucky to have escaped from Lavinia; it was all for the best. And he tells him, rather contemptuously, that he doesn't know why he is taking so much trouble to protect him from the fool he is (I. 1. 611). The influence of the Unidentified Guest is palpable enough: he had used almost the same words to Edward a few moments before (I. 1. 334).

As the curtain falls at the end of Scene 1, Edward, disappointed in his attempt to ring Celia, sits down to play a game of Patience. He is still playing when the curtain rises again; the door-bell rings and he rises to answer. It is Celia. We soon feel her clear and fearless strength. Having given herself wholly to Edward, she is ready, now that Lavinia has left him, for the world to know it; ready to live with him openly through the scandal and difficulties of divorce, ready to take the social blame herself, rather than force him to go through the miserable pretences of adultery; she rejoices at their being at last free to face the world of London society, in which she is so admired a figure, and challenge it with the integrity of her love for Edward. This

250

love, no doubt, was the 'secret excitement' which Peter had said was preoccupying her and which he could not share (I. 1. 561–2).

But Edward has changed. Unaccountably he wants Lavinia back. At first Celia cannot believe it, and puts it down to a temporary weakness, overwork, mental illness; she tries to lend him her strength:

> Will you assure me that everything is right,
> That you do not mean to have Lavinia back
> And that you do mean to gain your freedom,
> And that everything is all right between us?
> That's all that matters. Truly, Edward,
> If that is right, everything else will be,
> I promise you.
>
> (I. 2. 153–9)

But Edward remains firm in his weakness. It is too late. He is too old. He has lost the desire for all that is most desirable (I. 2. 231–2). There is a kind of climax in self-realisation for each of them as the scene draws to its strange close. Edward sees that the effort to escape from his own mediocrity through his love-affair with Celia, was only a make-believe, a furtive attempt to find a way out of the joyless realities of his marriage:

> a pretence
> That what is, is not, or could be changed.
>
> (I. 2. 250)

His life had been determined long ago in the conventional ways of the world; his mere emotional wants were not strong enough to compete with the massive, protective inertia of his own commonplaceness. The pretence, he says, could no longer be kept up; and for once Edward, in elaborating this assertion, makes a striking remark, unexpected in so uninspired a man. He says he must submit to the dull, dominating apathy of his nature, which keeps him safe, guards him from adventure, and rules him as much as some other men are ruled by an inner genius:

> . . . the obstinate, the tougher self; who does not speak,
> Who never talks, who cannot argue;
> And who in some men may be the *guardian* —
> But in men like me, the dull, the implacable,
> The indomitable spirit of mediocrity.

(I. 2. 255–9)

As he makes this confession, it seems to Celia that she is witnessing a total change in Edward's nature; it is as if scales had dropped from her eyes and she was seeing him as he really was, and not (as she had imagined him before) a lover matching her in love; this new vision of him she clothes in a poetry of candour well-suited to her, though (since imagery can exaggerate) a little hard on him; she sees him as a mummy being unwrapped, whose voice was the voice of an insect:

> Dry, endless, meaningless, inhuman —

(I. 2. 274)

and whose true likeness appeared to her as 'only a beetle the size of a man', as if he had undergone some hideous metamorphosis, like the unhappy wretch in Kafka's story, *The Metamorphosis*, changed during the night into a beetle:

> With nothing more inside it than what comes out
> When you tread on a beetle

(I. 2. 279–80)

Edward rises to a little moment of greatness by accepting this wounding description as the truth:

> Perhaps that is what I am.
> Tread on me, if you like.

(I. 2. 281–2)

But Celia spares him; she does not reproach him for what he cannot help being, still less does she tread on him; for she now realises her own mistaking. It had been her fault to idealise him, to think he embodied a reality that existed elsewhere, that she was desparately seeking. There is something in her thought that resembles a thought of Madame Odintsov in Turgenev's *Fathers and Sons*:*

> Why is it that when one is enjoying, say, a piece of music or a beautiful summer evening, or a conversation with a sympathetic companion, the occasion seems rather a hint at an infinite felicity existent elsewhere, than a real felicity actually being experienced?

Celia puts it this way, as she meditates her feelings for Edward:

> The man I saw before, he was only a projection —
> I see that now — of something that I wanted —
> No, not *wanted* — something I aspired to —
> Something that I desperately wanted to exist.
> It must happen somewhere — but what, and where is it?
>
> (I. 2. 285–9)

Though she does not yet realise it, it had been a vision of divine love, which she had 'projected' on Edward and of which she only knows, or desparately wishes, that 'it must happen somewhere'. She had thought to find it in a human relationship, but she had been deluded, self-deluded, as she now sees; she must look elsewhere. The last thing she takes from her former lover is his striking phrase, the Guardian; together they drink, at her suggestion, 'to the Guardians.' By the kind of swift, decisive intuition we have come to expect of her, and shall meet in her again, she has seen her need for guidance, and is willing to recognise a Guardian, even in Julia:

> It may be that even Julia is a guardian.
> Perhaps she is *my* guardian.
>
> (I. 2. 311–12)

and this is the truth.

The last member of the second group of characters to appear and be recognised is Lavinia. True to his word the Unidentified Guest produces her in Edward's flat within twenty-four hours. She walks in, unannounced, using her own key, as if she had never been away, as cool as if she were the mistress of the situation. It is the last scene of Act I, the first purpose of which is a long farewell; it is the last that the other characters will see of Peter for a long time; he is off to California. It is the last, though they do not know it, that they will ever see of Celia Coplestone.

But the scene has another purpose; when Celia has gone, followed, after a moment by Julia, Alex and Peter, we are left with Edward and Lavinia, alone together once again, coldly man and wife.

'I must say, you don't seem very pleased to see me', she cannot help remarking (I. 3. 233). Their incompatible cat-and-dog lives recommence. Lavinia cannot resist humiliating her husband; Edward shields himself behind his seemingly invulnerable conventionality. She can now see (she tells him) how absurd he is; he has no sense of humour; he can never make a practical decision. And so the dialogue of polite fury begins again; every repartee hits a tender spot. Yet there are signs of love under the ice:

> O, Edward, I should like to be good to you —
> Or if that's impossible, at least be horrid to you —
> Anything but nothing, which is all you seem to want of me.
>
> (I. 3. 392–4)

and again, when she says:

> I thought that there might be some way out for you
> If I went away. I thought that if I died

> To you, I who had been only a ghost to you,
> You might be able to find the road back
> To a time when you were real —
>
> (I. 3. 399–403)

Edward is no match for her; he is cowed by the knowledge that he might have been free of her, if only he had not insisted on having her brought back to him! She is the angel of destruction. Desperately he is driven to rhetorical questions:

> O God, what have I done? The python. The octopus.
> Must I become after all what you would make me?
>
> (I. 3. 460–1)

She remains the cool mistress of the situation:

> Meanwhile my luggage is in the hall downstairs:
> Will you get the porter to fetch it up for me?
>
> (I. 3. 467–8)

(d) *Guardians and guardianship* 68 & 71

By the end of Act I the exposition is complete. The two groups of characters and their spiritual relationships have been indicated, and all is poised to go forward. Eliot's love of mystification, his talent for creating suspense out of almost nothing, still teases us in the matter of the Unidentified Guest, and though the existence of Guardians has been half-laughingly suggested by Celia, we have as yet no certainty of it. The certainty, however, is not long delayed after we are shown the Consulting Room of Sir Henry Harcourt-Reilly, and recognise him as the One-Eyed Riley of the first Act. That Alexander MacColgie Gibbs and Julia Shuttlethwaite are his secret-service agents is soon obvious enough. They do not think of themselves, never speak of themselves, as Guardians; they give their association no name, but they work together, like a harmonious committee in which each from time to time may take the Chair, though Sir Henry is felt to be their leader, since he has overriding authority as a psychotherapist. This, however, does not prevent Julia from saying what she thinks, with a 'Nonsense, Henry!' when she feels inclined.

Though their association is never revealed by them, or discovered by the others, and the word Guardians is never specifically applied to them in the play, we may take it and use it for the convenience of discussing the work of Sir Henry and his associates, which starts many hares. The first is the symbolic overtone we cannot but hear in the word *Guardian*; it inevitably suggests *Guardian Angel*, and consequently a kind of hint that the Guardians have some supernatural element or authority, a mysterious touch of priesthood, or even of something indefinably more than human, though appearing to be human flesh and blood; or, if that is too extreme a suggestion, they are corporately to be considered as *symbolising* the Church in its care of souls. From this thought it is easy to go further and see in Sir Henry's Consulting Room something analogous to a Confessional, and in the 'Libation scene' (to be discussed later), something suggestive of a sacrament, if not (for Celia, at least) a last sacament, a *viaticum*.

Another significant overtone may be heard from a non-Christian context, the thought of which cannot but have been present to Eliot when he settled on the word *Guardian* to put in Edward's mouth — a context unknown, doubtless to Edward, but very familiar to Eliot, namely that of *The Republic* of Plato. Here, in Plato's blueprint for a perfect State, is a long account of the education proper to its 'Guardians', or philosopher-kings, and their place in the establishment of justice, the essential both for the State and for every individual within it.

Too much weight should not be given to these overtones or correspondences; it is true that symbolism had always appealed to Eliot, and this permits the slightly luminous haze into which such interpretations tempt us to wander and wonder, without being absolutely misled; but the play makes very good sense without them, and there are other aspects of the Guardians that are more fruitful to think about.

The Family Reunion opens with a situation in the life of a family cursed with loveless marriage in two consecutive generations, and we learn, as the play unfolds, a great deal about its earlier history, which Eliot had imagined and conveyed in careful detail. But *The Cocktail Party* has no such long pre-history; at most we can say that if it began with the marriage of Edward and Lavinia, it began five years before the opening scene, for Edward tells us so (I. 1. 225). But how or when the Guardians began to form themselves into an active, secret group, we are not told. Clearly, however, they are by no means beginners. Any account of them must start with *One-Eyed Riley*, and that was the title originally proposed by Eliot for the comedy.* This striking figure with his tipsy snatch of music-hall song is revealed at the opening of the second Act as Sir Henry Harcourt-Reilly, a leading psychoanalyst, who pursues methods of his own in the conduct of his profession, often of a somewhat unorthodox kind; they include prescribing rest-cures in secluded '*sanatoria*' that resemble private hotels rather than clinics, and to these he sends wealthy patients who are, or believe themselves to be, suffering from 'a nervous breakdown' — a phrase Sir Henry never uses. But he is also in touch with certain religious, medical and missionary Orders, whose religious houses he also calls '*sanatoria*', and to these he entrusts those patients whose malaise is a sense of the sins of the world and a spiritual craving to expiate or atone for them by a life of dedication, a self-surrender to a power whose beauty and attraction they have felt or glimpsed and which may be called the will or love of God. To enter such a 'sanatorium' is to abandon all earthly ties, other than those to which their Order directs them, such as the care of the sick and destitute, and the extension of their message of love in far countries and among heathen peoples.

Sir Henry's methods of recruiting his patients are also startling, for they include the services of his two socialite assistants (Julia and Alex), who have a gift for sensing where spiritual crises are building up in the circles of their acquaintance. Julia seems to have the keener nose in this respect, and has discerned that all is not well between Edward and Lavinia. She has persuaded Lavinia to become Sir Henry's patient, without her husband's knowledge, a little time before the play begins (II. 230–1). We do not know the nature of Lavinia's malady, but it may be imagined as the effect of five years of a barren and meaningless marriage on a quick-witted and sensitive woman.

Sir Henry decides to send her to one of his secular sanatoria (of the luxury-hotel kind) whither she departs, completely forgetting, if we may believe her assurance (I. 3. 245), that she had invited friends round for cocktails that very afternoon. Sir Henry, however, had not forgotten, and so he arrives as 'an Unidentified Guest', assumed, no doubt, by Edward, Celia and Peter to be a friend of the absent Lavinia. He has thus put himself in a position to observe the immediate effect on Edward of Lavinia's disappearance — (into Sir Henry's 'sanatorium'). His allies, Julia and Alex, take on the task of diverting the company while he observes it. That he is also, and most deeply, observing Celia we learn much later in the play, when he tells of the strange vision he had had of her at the opening cocktail party (III. 434–8). Julia had perhaps suggested he should observe Celia as well as Edward, for Celia too had been advised by Julia to consult Sir Henry (II. 457). Celia, like Lavinia, accepts the advice, after the breakdown of her relationship with Edward. Peter Quilpe, on the periphery of these crises, is doubly, if dimly, involved; for he imagines himself to be in love with Celia, while Lavinia imagines herself to be in love with him (II. 308–15). But the Guardians realise that Peter is in no need of them; he is not faced by a momentous spiritual choice, as the others are: 'He has not yet come to where the words are valid', as Sir Henry puts it, when considering whether the Guardians should speak a prayer for him (II. 811). For the present all Peter need do is to pursue his job as a film-director to the best of his ability; he has no need of either kind of sanatorium.

But Edward, Celia and Lavinia are in deeper waters, and Act I pilots them into port, that is, into the Consulting Room of Sir Henry Harcourt-Reilly, that their hearts may be laid bare to him, and to us.

Before we watch them enter the sanctum of the One-Eyed Riley, there is a question to be faced which presses more and more upon us as we realise how Edward, Celia, Lavinia and possibly Peter, have been netted by this secret conspiracy of self-appointed moral straighteners. We feel it an unwarrantable presumption for the Guardians to interfere, unasked, in the spiritual destinies of three, perhaps four, souls, who have been manoeuvred into seeking Sir Henry's advice. This charge against the Guardians is never levelled in the play, but it is one which audiences are likely to formulate and hold against them. The charge has some justice in it, and must be faced later; but first their function in the play may be considered on a lighter level.

The Guardians are a two-way force or impetus that drives the play along on each of its different planes; the first plane is one of frivolous comedy, rising to farce. They give the play all its comic energy. The play opens with a burst of their laughter and their clowning continues in scene after scene, right up to that moment of supreme gravity and shock when Alex tells us that Celia has been crucified by monkey-worshipping savages near an ant-hill.

In contrary motion, on another plane, not divulged to us until the second Act, the Guardians reveal themselves as people who have secretly, but religiously, banded themselves together, to keep watch over their friends and others whom they know to be reaching a spiritual crisis in their lives. Their business is to shepherd them into the Consulting-Room of their leader, in whose humane wisdom they have put their trust.

As this underlying seriousness unfolds itself and we learn the complexities of the situation, their comic power harnesses itself to their graver purposes, their jokes sparkle through the crises, and there are more music-hall tricks — the greater the gravity, the finer the fun. The tale of Lady Klootz and her false teeth (which never gets told), the tipsy ballad of the One-Eyed Riley, Julia's maddening intrusions in search, first of her umbrella, next of her spectacles, Alex's kindly but infuriating return when he is not wanted, and his insisting on cooking Edward 'a toothsome meal' which uses all tomorrow's breakfast eggs and is burnt to a cinder, the continual ringing of telephone and doorbell, the comedy of the mysterious telegrams — all these things springing from Eliot's comic invention and given to the Guardians, supply the comic energy of the play. It maintains its momentum 'to move wild laughter in the throat of death' right up to the account of the saffron monkeys of Kinkanja, though these preposterous creatures are an indirect cause of Celia's martyrdom; and so we reach the sublime by the ridiculous.

Structurally considered, then, the Guardians correspond in one sense to the Eumenides in *The Family Reunion*; they supply what Dryden or Byron and the older kind of criticism, based on the epic and drama of ancient Greece, might have called 'the supernatural machinery' for they lead in the direction of a supernatural love to which it was Eliot's main hope to awaken his audiences. Yet, as I have claimed, they are not to be thought of as supernatural themselves, but as two men and a woman seeking to do good by stealth through a conspiracy of enlightened benevolence. It is a dangerous trade to play Providence, as the case of the hapless Friar Laurence in *Romeo and Juliet* shows; yet we are moved to accept and delight in the Guardians, as we do in Friar Laurence, though for not the same reasons. We like and forgive them their interference first because they make us laugh; they are the *primum mobile* of the play, the laughter that moves it; secondly they acknowledge that they are working and moving among mysteries beyond their understanding, at least in the case of Celia; even in the cases of Edward and Lavinia Sir Henry admits doubtingly and humbly, that he has 'taken a great risk' (II. 351); as for Celia, he admits:

> And when I say to one like her
> 'Work out your salvation with diligence', I do not understand
> What I myself am saying.

> (II. 781–3)

So these seemingly over-reaching clowns, that have taken so much upon themselves, are 'holy and humble men of heart' and earn our affection and respect as healers, as richly as they do as jesters.

It is in embodying the notion of the Guardians, however,

that this play diverges from what it pretends to be — a slice
of life cut from the cake-stand of drawing-room comedy;
for through the Guardians it enters the world of serious
moral questioning. It does so to put forward an answer to
one of those 'overwhelming questions' that are not much
asked in drawing-rooms; Eliot had remarked on this some
seven-and-thirty years before in that brief masterpiece *The
Love Song of J. Alfred Prufrock*. Prufrock, the diffident
lover, dare not approach the drawing-room of his beloved
and formulate any of the disturbing questions that perhaps
can only be answered by a Lazarus, that is, by one returned
from the dead; for such questions in a drawing-room would
seem superfluous, impertinent, irrelevant, unsophisticated.
Here, in the Chamberlayne drawing-room, however, the
Prufrock in Eliot has plucked up courage, and poses Cain's
momentous question:

Am I my brother's keeper?

and to this, the answer given by the play, and by Christianity, is '*Yes, you are.*'

St. Paul said we are all members one of another (*Ephesi-
ans* 4. 25). And we may say that if Julia is Celia's Guardian
— as Celia thought she might be — then, by a like reason-
ing, Celia is also Julia's Guardian; it is always the duty of
each to care for all and all to care for each, a counsel of
perfection, like other unattainable Christian imperatives,
and one well known by Eliot. But to ask him to make this
larger assertion his theme would be to ask for a different
play, or perhaps for any essay; and indeed Eliot *had* written
such an essay ten years before, in a series of lectures
entitled *The Idea of a Christian Society* (1939).* Mr.
David E. Jones and Mr. Martin Browne concur in thinking
these lectures are significant in a discussion of the nature of
the Guardians; how relevant they are may be seen from the

following passages which I have taken from the third lecture; they describe a society in which groups like the Guardians might well exist and operate:

> It would be a society in which the natural end of man — virtue and well-being in community — is acknowledged for all, and the supernatural end — beatitude — for those who have the eye to see it.

> We need therefore what I have called 'The Community of Christians', by which I mean not local groups, and not the Church in any one of its senses, unless we call it 'the Church within the Church'. These will be the consciously and thoughtfully practising Christians, especially those of intellectual and spiritual superiority.

> The Community of Christians is not an organisation, but a body of indefinite outline; composed both of clergy and of laity, of the more conscious, more spiritually developed of both.

and again, in an Appendix, the Church is said to:

> maintain the paradox that while we are responsible for our own souls, we are all responsible for all other souls.

There is something chilling in these concepts; if the Guardians had been so conscious of their intellectual and spiritual superiority, who would ever have invited them to a cocktail party? But the 'Church within the Church' proclaims two important principles that are reflected in the Guardians also — the acceptance of responsibility for the welfare of the souls of others as well as of their own, and the affirmation of a choice that may have to be made in harmony with an inward vocation; one will lead to 'virtue and well-being in community', as in the case of the Chamberlaynes, and the other to 'beatitude', that is, to sainthood, as in the case of Celia Coplestone; they are the two ways of Christian love, neither better than the other, but both necessary, which are the subject of the play,

Seen in this light the question by what right the Guardians take it upon themselves to intervene in the inmost lives of others falls to the ground; they do so not as a *right* but as a *duty*, and try to live the life of a Good Samaritan according to the parable, and not 'pass by on the other side'. In other respects the Guardians do not much resemble 'the Church within the Church', for they are full of fun; but after all, Eliot was ten years wiser when he created them than when he first tried to formulate the nature of a Christian community.

(e) *In the consulting room*

Julia and Alex, Sir Henry's sheep-dogs, have succeeded in driving Edward and Lavinia, the black sheep, and Celia the white, into their several pens in his Consulting Rooms at their prearranged times, and the excitements of psycho-analytical treatment begin with the startling deflation of the Chamberlaynes; it is Edward's turn first to be submitted to the necessary humiliations to puncture his ingrown self-deception; when this process seems complete and he declares he has had enough of it and tries to break off the interview, Sir Henry rings the bell for his Nurse-Secretary who brings in Lavinia, whose turn has come; husband and wife are stunned by this highly unprofessional confrontation — for Group Therapy was not in vogue in 1940. Edward's relationship with Celia is laid bare in front of his wife (who claims to have known it all before) and Lavinia's unrequited attachment to Peter Quilpe is also revealed, to the delight of Edward, who, vain and obtuse, had never imagined such

a thing. It is a scene of highest satirical pleasure to listen to
Sir Henry's remorseless analysis, which reaches its climax in
its demonstration that their situations are so similar as to
create a bond between them:

> Reilly   And now you begin to see, I hope,
> How much you have in common. The same isolation.
> A man who finds himself incapable of loving
> And a woman who finds that no man can love her.
>
> Lavinia It seems to me that what we have in common
> Might be just enough to make us loathe one another.
>
> Reilly   See it rather as the bond which holds you together.
> While still in a state of unenlightenment,
> *You* could always say: 'he could not love any woman;'
> *You* could always say: 'no man could love her.'
> You could accuse each other of your own faults,
> And so could avoid understanding each other.
> Now, you have only to reverse the propositions
> And put them together.
>
>   (II. 378–91)

You could accuse each other of your own faults — and
therefore they could punish each other for their own guilts;
but now that they have been enlightened, she should see
that he might love her if only she were more lovable, and
he that she was lovable, if only he could learn to love. It
may be that in writing this, Eliot was remembering the
ultimate advice given by Nature to the Dreamer, at the
end of the B Text of *Piers Plowman*:

> 'Conseille me, Kynde,' quod I 'what crafte is best to lerne?'
> 'Lerne to love,' quod Kynde, 'and leve of alle othre.'
>   (B. XX. 206–7)

> ('Counsel me, Nature,' said I, 'what knowledge is the best to
>   learn?'
> 'Learn to love', said Nature, 'and leave all other learning.')

Sharp-eyed and practical, Lavinia sees the truth of what Sir Henry has said to them, and she sees the risk in following his advice; to be fair to Sir Henry, he foresees it too:

> what have they to go back to?
> To the stale food mouldering in the larder,
> The stale thoughts mouldering in their minds.
> Each unable to disguise his own meanness
> From himself, because it is known to the other . . .
> I have taken a great risk.

(II. 742–50)

But if it is the way of danger, it is also the way of hope, and Lavinia presses forward to it, not by asserting her will or laying down a course of action, but more subtly, more generously, appealing to Edward, to take command and solve their problem, as if she trusted in him for guidance and strength; she launches her appeal to him over Sir Henry's head, as to a final authority:

> Then what can we do
> When we can go neither back nor forward? Edward!
> What can we do?

(II. 399–401)

and Edward is touched and rises to the occasion, humbly, and yet with a certain grandeur, in another little moment of greatness, notwithstanding the utter mediocrity of his turn of phrase:

> Lavinia, we must make the best of a bad job.
> That is what he means.

(II. 403–4)

It is the first time she has used his Christian name without a sneer, the first time he has used hers with kindly affection. In the first draft this subtle touch was not present; it is one of 'the felicities' of which Martin Browne speaks, in describing Eliot's craftsmanship,* added in production. This tense appeal has brought them to the threshold of a reconciliation and so it is the moment for a return from drama to comedy; Edward, a little ruefully, decides that he had better go home. The ever-practical Lavinia pounces on his decision and clinches it:

> Then we can share a taxi, and be economical.
>
> (II. 420)

It is a touch that would have delighted Congreve.

It is now Celia's turn, and, when the Chamberlaynes have left, she is admitted to the Consulting Room. Her approach to her problems is markedly different from theirs; it is almost as if she belonged to another order of human beings. This beautiful society girl comes in humble and bewildered, 'in desperation' she says (II. 468); she has no one to blame but herself (475) and cannot think her trouble is of any interest to others. When pressed to explain her perplexity, she diffidently speaks of two unusual symptoms that she has experienced. The first is a sense of her *solitude*, not only hers, but the general isolation of all human beings from each other; everyone is profoundly alone. 'They make noises', she says, 'and think they are talking to each other; they make faces and think they understand each other' (II. 529-30).

Yet she is speaking to Sir Henry, and it seems that he understands her well. Her second symptom is more remarkable still; she has a sense of *sin*. By that she does not mean that she feels 'immoral' (in her relations with Edward); she means far more:

> It's not the feeling of anything I've ever *done*,
> Which I might get away from, or of anything in me
> I could get rid of — but of emptiness, of failure
> Towards someone, or something, outside of myself;

> And I feel I must . . . *atone* — is that the word?
> Can you treat a patient for such a state of mind?
>
> (II. 580–5)

Celia has other phrases that hint at her condition; the world she lives in 'seems all a delusion' (486), whereas her sense of sin might prove more real than anything she had believed in (578). And again she says she is like a child who has wandered into a forest playing with an imaginary playmate, who suddenly discovers he is only a child lost in a forest, wanting to go home (607–10).

> But even if I find my way out of the forest
> I shall be left with the inconsolable memory
> Of the treasure I went into the forest to find
> And never found, and which is not there
> And perhaps is not anywhere? But if not anywhere,
> Why do I feel guilty at not having found it?
>
> (II. 613–18)

What are we to make of these hints and imageries? She says also that she thinks she has had a vision, but of what she cannot say; but it is a vision which above all things she would wish to cherish and live with, that demands a kind of love that she could give to no one else:

> I couldn't give anyone the kind of love —
> I wish I could — which belongs to that life.
>
> (II. 669–70)

These are among the stirrings of her conversion, whose compelling purposes are as yet unclear to her, yet she feels her way towards them poetically, as we might expect of her, since we have been told she is a poet (I. 1. 465). Her intuition tells her of a treasure in a forest sought for in vain, yet so precious as to leave her inconsolable in its loss; yet it must happen somewhere, this 'infinite felicity', if we may borrow Madame Odintsov's phrase.

268

These insights have much in common with those of
Harry in *The Family Reunion*, though his sense of sin is
more violent than hers and his search for expiation cruder;
love is what marks the great advance which *The Cocktail
Party* makes over *The Family Reunion*, in its account of a
religious conversion. Harry, of course, is a wilder, un-
happier figure than Celia; he believes himself to have
murdered his wife. Celia is gentler and wiser, and she is
capable of a life:

> In which one is exalted by intensity of loving
> In the spirit, a vibration of delight
> Without desire, for desire is fulfilled
> In the delight of loving . . .
> > . . . But what, or whom I loved,
> Or what in me was loving, I do not know.
>
> (II. 626–31)

Yet Celia is unsure whether this vision of hers is false or
meaningless, and if so, whether she can be cured of 'the
shame of never finding it' (II. 634).

Sir Henry confirms her intuitions; there is another kind
of life, based upon faith, he says:

> The kind of faith that issues from despair.
> The destination cannot be described;
> You will know very little until you get there;
> You will journey blind. But the way leads towards possession
> Of what you have sought for in the wrong place.
>
> (II. 679–83)

He shows her that she must choose between this dangerous
way and the way of common humanity, 'the human
condition' of ordinary love in marriage:

> with the morning that separates
> And with the evening that brings together
> For casual talk before the fire

269

Two people who know they do not understand each other,
Breeding children whom they do not understand
And who will never understand them.

(II. 647–52)

Celia chooses the unknown and more dangerous way and, in
doing so, passes beyond the point at which Sir Henry can
help her, except by sending her to his special sanatorium,
that is, to a religious Order, where she will be trained to
fulfil her austere vocation. After her departure, Julia enters
by a side door, and presently she and Sir Henry are joined by
Alex. For the first time we see the three Guardians alone
together.

(f) *The Libation*

They have met to pray for those they have guarded and
guided: for the Chamberlaynes in their homely but home-
creating task of making a real marriage out of their empty
union, and for Celia on her austere journey into the unknown dangers of a mystical vocation. It was to be a little
ceremony of prayer which they called '*a Libation*', because
it included a pouring out of wine in a kind of drink-offering.
It could suggest a classic ritual for those to whom a Christian
prayer might cause offence or embarrassment, and at the
same time symbolise a sacramental act for those whose
imaginations were of a Christian cast. The form the
Libation takes more nearly resembles a toast over a glass of
sherry and this ingeniously keeps in sight the cocktail party
element in the play, while turning it to a more serious,
ritual use.

In making so daring an experiment in drawing-room
comedy, Eliot faced a major self-contradiction in the
strategy he had chosen for offering Christian plays to

agnostic audiences; he had denied himself the open preaching of a Christian sermon, for he had already said his say by way of sermons in the choruses of *The Rock* and in *Murder in the Cathedral* — Christian sermons addressed to Christian audiences. But now he had adopted a technique of symbolism, a form of poetic imagination that he had learnt from France in earlier years. So in *The Family Reunion* he had used the imagery of the Eumenides to suggest how a soul, convinced of sin, could be first hounded, but at last guided, by the angels of conscience, towards expiation, through a better understanding of love and sacrifice; he had achieved this, however, at the cost of deep obscurity. Yet it had permitted him to indulge his feeling for liturgy or ceremonial of a quasi-religious kind, by concluding the play with a magical incantation and a processional blowing-out of candles.

The Libation scene in *The Cocktail Party* attempts a comparable effect. It was essential to bring the second Act to a climax which should declare the religious character of the Guardians in a corporate action, that would gather the purposes of the play together and speed it along towards its spiritual goal. It should be a climax that would crown all that has gone before, and, at the same time, engender feelings of surprise and suspense, on which to launch the last Act.

Up till this point in the play, Eliot had succeeded in avoiding all mention of Christianity; it is true that 'the saints' had been spoken of (II. 406), but there are saints in other religions; there are even agnostic saints. Now, however, intent upon the religious ritual which his love of classical Greek had taught him to think of as an essential of drama, he was faced with the task of writing a prayer for one about to become a Christian martyr, to be spoken by those who, though not apparently Christian themselves, had helped to send her to her martyrdom. Were they in fact Christians? Should their prayers be Christian prayers, or conceived in some elevated pagan style suited to their 'intellectual superiority'? Or should they be neutral, non-committal?

Had it been Eliot's intention to write an openly Christian play, or a play to illustrate his *Idea of a Christian Society*, the natural thing would have been for the Guardians, at least when alone with each other, to confess their Christianity and kneel down to offer up a Christian prayer; but naturalism is not everything, even in a drawing-room comedy; what was needed at the end of a long and serious Act was a sudden bright surprise, in keeping with the Guardian character of unpredictable levity blended with high seriousness — the gesture of a toast, the language of a prayer.

Eliot found a model for such a language in a work by Dr. Alexander Carmichael called *Carmina Gadelica*, that began to be published in a series of volumes in 1900. They consisted of 'hymns and incantations . . . orally collected in the Highlands and Islands of Scotland'. A more recent volume, comprising the first four volumes of Carmichael's collection, with additions, was published under the title *Poems from the Western Highlanders* (1961), from the Gaelic, by G. R. D. McLean. Examples taken from this work show how it kindled Eliot's imagination:

> I have over thee the power of the silver moon,
> I have over thee the power of the fierce sun,
> I have over thee the power of the rain's wet shoon,
> I have over thee the power of the dew spun . . .
>
> Be with us through the time of each day,
> Be with us through the time of each night . . .
>
> White-beamed Father, Son, Holy Spirit bright,
> Be the Three-in-One with us day and night,

> On the sandy plain, on the hill-ridge led,
> Three-in-One with us, guide-hand in our head,
> Three-in-One our helmet-hand round the head.

In his original draft Eliot indulged his fantasy; indeed, he *over*-indulged it with a mixture of symbols which he later repented and ruled out; they read more like mystification than mysticism (see Martin Browne, op. cit., p. 187):

Alex   The prayer for the building of the hearth:
            Let them build the hearth
            Under the protection of the Moon,
            And place a chair on each side of it.
            Who shall surround the house?
J and R The four higher protectors.
Alex   Who shall watch over the roof?
J and R The two winged ones shall watch over the roof.
Alex   Under what sign shall it be erected?
J and R Under the sign of the seven stars.
Alex   Who shall cast influence upon the bed?
J and R The Moon shall influence the bed.
Alex   In what name shall she act?
J and R In the name of the fructifying Sun.

Rational thought, rejecting the intrusion of things symbolic, might pause here prosily to ask whether so eminent a scientist as Sir Henry Harcourt-Reilly really believed that the sun, moon and stars could hear and grant his prayers, or whether it was a piece of mumbo-jumbo for theatrical effect; and there might be further questions: Who were 'the four higher protectors'? Could they be Matthew, Mark, Luke and John? Were the 'two winged ones' over the roof (changed later to 'two holy ones') a cherub and a seraph? Or a reminiscence of a famous Botticelli Nativity in the National Gallery, in which angels dance on the roof of the Bethlehem manger?

Eliot has removed the necessity of answering these questions by removing 'the higher protectors' and 'the winged ones' from his final text, leaving us with the simpler symbolism of Nature-Worship (sun, moon and stars) to do duty for a Christian acknowledgement of:

the Name which is not spoken,

to use the phrase which concluded the prayer in its earlier draft, but which was later cancelled, perhaps for consistency. These cancellations are more than made up for in the final version by a last twist of wit; the draft had ended thus:

R　　But there is one for whom we do nothing.
J　　It is Peter whom he means.
A　　Peter? What Peter?
R　　The young man Peter Quilpe.
A　　There are things beyond our powers
　　　Which must be left to the mystery and the mercy.

Fortunately these lines were dropped; in their stead Eliot wrote:

R　　There is one for whom the words cannot be spoken.
A　　They cannot be spoken yet.
J　　You mean Peter Quilpe.
R　　He has not yet come to where the words are valid.
J　　Shall we ever speak them?
A　　Others, perhaps, will speak them.
　　　You know, I have connections — even in California.
　　　　　　　　　　　　　　　　　　　　　(II. 809–13)

The idea that by the time Peter Quilpe needs spiritual guidance there may be a Christian society, even in California, brings down the curtain with a run.

It is hard to assess what Eliot has achieved in this astonishing second Act. It creates and sustains an absorbed attention or empathy; every word of the pyschoanalysis sharpens excitement: the Libation is a startling, last-moment surprise: it is serious and it is comic: Eliot has kept to his strategy: he has kept to his love of ritual and symbolism: he has kept the excitement alive to the last instant: he has created a kind of cliff-hanger suspense, to lead us to the heart of the last Act: above all he has kept his secret — the Christian cat is still safely in the seemingly pagan bag, ready for the stunning effect when it is to spring out with the news of Celia's crucifixion, brought by Alex from far Kinkanja.

(g) *The fulfilments of love*

Two years have passed and the intensity of the Consulting Room now gives way to the frivolity of the Chamberlayne flat. The Chamberlaynes are about to give another cocktail party. Lavinia gives her final orders to the caterer's man as her husband returns from a day's work in his chambers. The audience settles itself pleasurably for the business of the last Act, which can be no other than to satisfy its curiosity about the success or failure of Sir Henry's psychotherapy.

The Chamberlaynes are certainly on friendly terms, for they chaff each other on the very subject that might be expected to produce explosions; Lavinia says:

> . . . all I rang up for was to reassure you . . .
> *Edward* (smiling) That you hadn't run away?
> *Lavinia* Now Edward, that's unfair!
> You know that we've given *several* parties
> In the last two years. And I've attended *all* of them.
>
> (III. 12–15)

A gay but humdrum conversation flows along, suggesting their unity, even their amity — a little too strongly, perhaps; the embarrassing suspicion arises in our minds that they are being *too* kind to each other, or, worse still, *'polite'*, in their mutual solicitude: we hear phrases liike 'I hope you're not too tired' . . . 'It's you who should be tired' . . . 'I like the dress you're wearing' which set a satirical mind wondering how long a marriage could last on mere good manners and soft sugar. However the question is swiftly swept aside by the imperious doorbell rung (of course) by Julia, who has brought Alex with her.

Where has he come from? From Kinkanja! And with a globe-trotter's enthusiasm he launches into a ludicrous account of the monkey-problem in that remote and little-known region. We are back in the mood of high comedy that started the play off so amusingly with talk of tigers and Maharajahs, and which is now extended to Sultans and monkeys, heathens and Christians. The heathens revere the monkeys, the Christian converts eat them; Alex has not only cooked and eaten them himself, but has invented several new recipes for the natives.

As the talk butterflies its way along among these topics, the mood is suddenly, for an instant, changed by Alex, taking up his cue from Lavinia:

> Ah, the Christians! Now I think I ought to tell you
> About someone you know — or knew . . .
>
> (III. 174–5)

Julia knows the news he is about to deliver; it is about Celia, and she breaks in to delay it until those who should hear it have all gathered in the Chamberlaynes' flat. 'Edward' she says, 'Somebody must have walked over my grave . . . Give me some gin.' It is a subtle warning, the creation of a *frisson* of suspense tinged with anxiety, and produces a presentiment, vague as yet, but chilling. The effect, however, is almost instantly dispelled by the arrival of .Peter Quilpe. We are not told whether Julia or Alex knew he would be joining the party once more, but it may be guessed that she did, since Peter had told Sheila Paisley that he was going to call on the Chamberlaynes (III. 186) and she may well have passed the news on to Julia, ever in the thick of things social.

Peter has just flown in from New York, full of his own doings, and by one of those coincidences that so often happen in life — far more often than they are allowed to happen in literature — he tells them of a newly fashionable restaurant where he had dined a few nights before:

> We dined the other night
> At the Saffron Monkey. That's the place to go now.
>
> (III. 196–7)

'How very odd!' comments Alex, '*My* monkeys are saffron.' The subject of the Kinkanja monkeys is once again about to be developed, but once again Julia fends it off; we may assume she is secretly waiting for the arrival of Sir Henry Harcourt-Reilly before allowing Alex to give his news. Is it because she knows he is the only one among them who is of sufficient stature in understanding to expound the inward truth of Celia's martyrdom, and what we should think of it?

At last Sir Henry enters; the whole company has thus assembled once more in the Chamberlaynes' flat, all except one. Where is Celia?

The question is put by Peter Quilpe; he wants to cast her for his next film, but he cannot find her name in the telephone directory. Julia says:

> Not in the directory,
> Or in any directory. You can tell them now, Alex.
>
> (III. 299–300)

Alex tells them that Celia is dead. In telling them that she died in Kinkanja, and how she died, we see the sudden relevance of the monkeys, worshipped by the heathen there. An insurrection had broken out among the heathen against the Christians. Celia, nursing the natives in a Christian village, where they were dying of war and pestilence, had been taken prisoner:

> When our people got there, they questioned the villagers —
> Those who survived. And then they found her body,
> Or at least, they found the traces of it.
>
> (III. 327–9)

> . . . from what we know of local practices
> It would seem that she must have been crucified
> Very near an ant-hill.
>
> (III. 331–3)

Those who reject this climax as too horrible for comedy have missed the point of the play, one of the purposes of which, as we have seen, is to show a saint and martyr in the making and the kind of love demanded of a saint. This is a perspective that is not commonly shown in comedies, or in drawing-rooms either, and it falls to Sir Henry to tell his hearers how they should think of the news that has so briefly and so brutally been delivered.

It is a perspective long since explained by Eliot through the mouth of St. Thomas of Canterbury in *Murder in the Cathedral*, a play which is the tragic Christian pillar that supports so much of what is in this secular comedy. In the sermon at the centre of this play, St. Thomas tells us how to think of martyrdom:

> Beloved, we do not think of a martyr simply as a good Christian who has been killed because he is a Christian: for that would be solely to mourn. We do not think of him simply as a good Christian who has been elevated to the company of the Saints: for that would be simply to rejoice: and neither our mourning nor our rejoicing is as the

world's is. A Christian martyrdom is never an accident, for Saints are not made by accident . . . A martyrdom is always the design of God . . . for the true martyr is he who has become the instrument of God . . . and who no longer desires anything for himself, not even the glory of being a martyr. So thus as on earth the Church mourns and rejoices at once, in a fashion that the world cannot understand.

This vision of heroic sanctity, seen by Eliot in the martyrdom of St. Thomas of Canterbury in the twelfth century, was equally seen by him in that of Celia Coplestone in the twentieth. How was he to expound it, in its inevitability, its terror and its glory, above all, perhaps, in its mystery, in a London drawing-room?

There was only one among his characters of a sufficient spiritual stature to speak of such things — Sir Henry Harcourt-Reilly; yet even he and his finely phrased, conversational habit of speech, would not sound very plausible if he were suddenly to rise, on his own, to great intensities of poetic language. Yet great intensities were needed of him. Eliot hit on an expedient of the greatest ingenuity. He would make Sir Henry quote Shelley. Sir Henry would know his Shelley, Shelley would supply the intensity.

He found the passage he needed already quoted in a novel called *Descent into Hell* by Charles Williams, a close friend of his. It had recently been published in 1937. The passage came from the first Act of *Prometheus Unbound* and described the eerie experience of meeting with one's double:

> Ere Babylon was dust
> The magus Zoroaster, my dead child,
> Met his own image walking in the garden.
> That apparition, sole of men, he saw.

(III. 423–6)

There was no reason to suppose that Sir Henry would be

incapable of quoting Shelley; there was equally no reason why sir Henry might not be endowed with the strange gift of Second Sight, upon occasion. It is a well-attested phenomenon ever among the hardest-headed. Eliot settled for this way of solving his problem. Sir Henry (after asking permission from Lavinia, the least poetical person present) preludes his story with ten of Shelley's eeriest lines, to prepare them for his strange experience:

> When I first met Miss Coplestone, in this room,
> I saw the image, standing behind her chair,
> Of a Celia Coplestone whose face showed the astonishment
> Of the first five minutes after a violent death.
> If this strains your credulity, Mrs. Chamberlayne,
> I ask you only to entertain the suggestion
> That a sudden intuition, in certain minds,
> May tend to express itself at once in a picture.
> That happens to me, sometimes. So it was obvious
> That here was a woman under sentence of death.

> (III. 432–41)

That Celia's death could be thus 'foreseen' suggests the presence of the 'design' that St. Thomas speaks of, a design to which Celia, by the surrender of her will and power of loving into the will and love of God, has freely consented. Reilly also refers to this 'design'; in speaking of what Celia suffered in the way of pain, compared with what ordinary people, not martyrs or ecstatics, might suffer, he says:

> She paid the highest price
> In suffering. That is part of the design.

> (III. 460)

For some approach to a definition of this mystical 'design' as Eliot saw it, we may again turn to *Murder in the Cathedral*:

> . . . action is suffering
> And suffering is action. Neither does the agent suffer

> Nor the patient act. Both are fixed
> In an eternal action, an eternal patience
> To which all must consent that it may be willed
> And which all must suffer that they may will it,
> That the pattern may subsist, for the pattern is the action
> And the suffering, that the wheel may turn and still
> Be forever still.
>
> (Part I, 209–17)

It is the pattern set by the Incarnation and Crucifixion of Christ. Celia has willingly filled in her part in the pattern; so Reilly can declare her death to have been triumphant.

Celia has found, in her way of life and death, the fulfilment of her power to love, 'to suffren love's hete celestial'. As Sir Henry says:

> That way, which she accepted, led to this death.
> And if that is not a happy death, what death is happy?
>
> (III. 450–1)

The little party breaks up; Peter leaves for California; Julia collects her fellow Guardians and sweeps them imperiously off to another party and the Chamberlaynes are left alone, awaiting the guests they have invited; they are still in the same idyllic mood in which the scene started; Lavinia fishes, Edward dotes:

Lavinia Edward, how am I looking?
Edward   Very well.
         I might almost say, your best. But you always look your
         best.

> (III. 548–9)

The explanation of Edward's extreme solicitude, his flattering tenderness, is given in Eliot's letter to Sir Geoffrey Faber (see p. 192 f.). Lavinia is going to have a baby. This is the fulfilment of the love of kynde.

281

(h) *Influences and sources*

We should distinguish between influences and sources in considering the conceptions on which *The Cocktail Party* is based. Its sources are those works from which specific passages are directly and identifiably taken and used, or imitated, in Eliot's play; there are four of these. There is first the ballad of *One-Eyed Riley*, the work of the anonymous popular Muse, from which Eliot took a verse and chorus to supply Sir Henry with a necessary music-hall song. It is necessary because of what happens in the second source, to which Eliot confessed with glee in his well-known Harvard lecture on 'Poetry and Drama', given in 1950. His debt in *The Cocktail Party*, he told his astonished hearers, was to the *Alcestis* of Euripides:

> I was still inclined to go to a Greek dramatist for my theme, but I was determined to do so merely as a point of departure, and to conceal the origins so well that nobody would identify them until I pointed them out myself. In this last I have been successful; for no one of my acquaintance (and no dramatic critics) recognised the source of my story in the *Alcestis* of Euripides. In fact I have had to go into detailed explanation to convince them — I mean, of course, those who were familiar with the plot of that play — of the genuineness of the inspiration. But those who were at first disturbed by the eccentric behaviour of my unknown guest, and his apparently intemperate habits and tendency to burst into song, have found some consolation after I have called their attention to the behaviour of Heracles in Euripides' play.

Alcestis was the wife of Admetus, who had put the god Apollo under an obligation. To discharge his obligation, Apollo cheated the Fates into allowing Admetus to escape death, if he could find anyone willing to take his place and die instead of him. Admetus tried to persuade his father and mother to do him this service, but he had no success with them. His wife, Alcestis, however freely offered to take his place and die that he might live, and the play opens with the news that she is at the point of death already, and the whole house is in mourning for her impending doom.

At this moment Heracles, an old friend of Admetus, unexpectedly arrives, on the way to perform his Eighth Labour (the capture of the man-eating horses of Diomedes) and is hospitably received by Admetus, who conceals from him the cause of the general grief, inviting him in and offering him a feast, so as not to seem inhospitable. Heracles enters, is lavishly provided for, and takes full advantage of what is set before him and more. By the time Alcestis is borne off lifeless to her tomb, Heracles is so drunk as to scandalise the servants, one of whom enters to tell the audience all about it:

> 'He refused to understand the situation and be content with anything we could provide, but when we failed to bring him something, demanded it, and took a cup with ivy on it in both hands and drank the wine of our dark mother, straight until the flame of the wine went all through him, and heated him, and then he wreathed branches of myrtle on his head and howled off key. There were two kinds of music now to hear, for while he sang and never gave a thought to the sorrows of Admetus, we servants were mourning for our mistress . . .'*

Heracles then returns to the scene, drunk but not incapable, and by cross-examining the servant learns the truth about Alcestis. He determines at once to save her by watching for 'Death of the Black Robes', whom he means to hold in the circle of his huge arms until he gives the woman up to him. It need hardly be said that in the Euripedean version of this myth, the drunken demi-god is successful and brings Alcestis safely back to the arms of her husband. In like manner the One-Eyed Riley arrives on the very afternoon of Lavinia's desertion of Edward, drinks a lot of gin and water, at Edward's expense, promises to bring her back within twenty-four hours, and makes his exit singing a lewd song, 'howled off-key'.

Verbal touches of poetic reminder give things, slender enough to elude the source-seeker, but strong enough to be triumphantly pointed out by the author, when all the critics had failed; for instance, Sir Henry says:

> it is a serious matter
> *To bring someone back from the dead*.
> Edward   *From the dead?*
> That figure of speech is somewhat . . . dramatic,
> As it was only yesterday my wife left me.
> *Unidentified Guest*   Ah, but we die to each other daily.
> (I. 3. 20–23 My italics)

Another hint to tease non-Euripideans with comes later in the play, when Lavinia has been brought back from her 'sanatorium', and is talking, for once with some tenderness, to her husband of their broken marriage:

> I thought there might be some way out for you
> If I went away. *I thought that if I died*
> *To you*, I who had only been a ghost to you,
> You might be able to find the road back
> To a time when you were real. . . .
> (I. 3. 399–403 My italics)

Sources can be demonstrated; they leave their finger-prints. Influences permeate but are less specific. I have already mentioned the pervading influences of Shakespeare and of the Comedy of Manners; but there are others also, at a greater depth, traceable to the excitement of those early discoveries in anthropology made famous by Sir James

Fraser's *Golden Bough* (1890–1915), which started many trains of thought at the time; one of them was embodied in a work by F. M. Cornford, called *The Origin of Attic Comedy* (1914, republished in 1934) to which Eliot confessed he was deeply indebted for its insistence on ritual significance in drama.* In this book Cornford contended that the comedies of Aristophanes contained a ritual of a Dionysiac or phallic kind; they invariably included a Sacrifice, a Feast, a Marriage and a Phallic Procession. We are shown Sacrifice in Celia, Marriage in Edward and Lavinia, whose pregnancy represents the phallic element; the Feast is treated as a joke; it is the 'toothsome morsel' concocted by Alexander MacColgie Gibbs for the distracted Edward, and which is burnt to a cinder.

This is an Aristophanic joke that Eliot has used once before, in the second fragment of *Sweeney Agonistes*; we have Eliot's authority for saying that when the fragment is performed, Sweeney should be cooking a dish of eggs;* an egg is of course a symbol of life at its most elementary and primitive; as Sweeney says:

> You see this egg
> You see this egg
> Well that's life on a crocodile isle.

MacColgie Gibbs is the comic cook, preparing the ritual meal.

These are the esoteric significances or creative allusions that are semi-secretly mixed in with other elements that go to make *The Cocktail Party*, for the pleasure of those who can detect and appreciate them, and perhaps for the even greater pleasure of the author when they are *not* detected.

(i) *'Poetry' and verse*

The dialogue of *The Cocktail Party*, as of all Eliot's plays, is printed in lines of verse, to help the reader or actor to speak them properly by indicating their intended rhythms; they suggest pauses and stresses and breath lengths, singling out words of special importance; for instance, a reader confronted by the following sentence:

> You and I don't know the process by which the human is transhumanised: what do we know of the kind of suffering they must undergo on the way of illumination?

might well miss the infinitesimal pauses and stresses of:

> You and I don't know the process by which the human is/
> *Transhumanised*: what do *we* know
> Of the kind of suffering *they* must undergo/
> On the way to illumination?

(II. 766–9)

The unusual word *transhumanised* is picked out by a kind of hesitation at the end of the line, before the speaker 'finds' it, and a similar pause is placed after *undergo*, to make the contrast between *suffering* and *illumination*: this draws our attention to the further contrast between *we* and *they*. I have supplied clumsy italics and bar-lines to emphasise the nuances of the text that Eliot has indicated by writing the speech in verses. This method of helping an actor is more necessary in *The Family Reunion*, where there are far greater obscurities of thought than in *The Cocktail Party*. Indeed, the latter is a play as lucid as any play of Shaw, the great master of lucidity in prose dialogue.

That the lines are written in verses does not mean that they are staking a claim to be considered as 'poetry'. Nor is it useful to describe them as 'prose cut up into lengths'. They are cut up into *rhythms* that have meaning; each line asks for the kind of attention which it specially deserves as a component in the general meaning of the passage in which it comes, and in the general effect of human talk, with its irregular stresses and pauses. Yet human talk has its moments of poetry, which Eliot has ever been careful to capture; he shows a rare ear for natural idiom and how to make it tell in a poem; one has only to read *The Love Song of J. Alfred Prufrock*, *The Waste Land* (especially the rejected passages now made available to us by Mrs. Eliot's splendid edition) and *Sweeney Agonistes*, to perceive his extraordinary gift in this art of talk, that so deftly intensifies his effects. That intensity rather than metre is the true source of poetry is claimed by him in a lecture on 'The Three Voices of Poetry', given in 1953 to the National Book League:

> In a verse play, you will probably have to find words for several characters differing widely from each other in background, temperament, education and intelligence. You cannot afford to identify one of these characters with yourself, and give him or her all the 'poetry' to speak. The poetry (*I mean the language at those dramatic moments when it reaches intensity*) must be as widely distributed as characterisation permits; and each of your characters, when he has words to speak which are poetry and not merely verse, must be given lines appropriate to himself.

I have italicised the essential idea, that poetry is language used with intensity, and I would like to contrast this account of its nature with a famous definition offered by S. T. Coleridge in his *Table Talk* (12 July 1827):

> I wish our clever young poets would remember my homely definitions of prose and poetry; that is, prose equals words in their best order; — poetry equals the *best* words in the best order.

It is evident that to substitute 'intensity' for 'goodness' is a great step forward from Coleridge; one can think of many sentences superlatively well-expressed that are still not what we mean by 'poetry'; for instance *'Two and two are four.'* These are certainly the best words in the best order for the particular notion they express, but they would be judged by most people to be purest prose, in spite of A. E. Housman's rueful quatrain:

> To think that two and two are four,
>   And neither five nor three,
> The heart of man has long been sore,
>   And long is like to be.

When Eliot began on his great work of restoring poetry to our stage, he tried to find or fashion a language that achieved an intensity of rhythm, as well as of imagery. Of this achievement he wrote later (in his Theodore Spencer Memorial Lecture, 1950):

> As for the versification, I was only aware at this stage that the essential was to avoid any echo of Shakespeare. . . . The rhythm of regular blank verse had become too remote from the movement of modern speech. Therefore what I kept in mind was the versification of *Everyman*.

This revolutionary versification, which was based on 'an avoidance of too much iambic', continued to develop towards an increasingly conversational movement and tone, adhering, but not slavishly, to the rules he tells us he formulated for himself:

> What I worked out is substantially what I have continued to employ: a line of varying length and varying number of syllables, with a caesura and three stresses. The caesura and the stresses may come at different places almost anywhere in the line; the stresses may be close together or well separated by light syllables, the only rule being that there must be one stress on one side of the caesura and two on the other.

He came even to relaxing his avoidance of iambic move-
ment and of admitting brief intrusions of blank verse itself.
Many such intrusions will be found in *The Cocktail Party*.
For instance:

> There *is* another way, if you have the courage.
> The first I could describe in familiar terms
> * Because you have seen it, as we all have seen it,
> Illustrated, more or less, in lives of those about us.
> The second is unknown, and so requires faith —
> * The kind of faith that issues from despair.
> * The destination cannot be described.
>
> (II. 674–80)

I have marked with an asterisk three normal blank-verse
lines, and might include a fourth by a slight elision, thus:

> There is another way if you've the courage.

The caesuras fall after way/ describe/ seen it/ or less/
unknown/. There is no caesura in either of the last two
lines, no hint of pause; the last but one has four lightish
stresses:

> The *kind* of *faith* that *is*sues from des*pair*

and the last has but three:

> The *dest*ination *can*not be des*cribed*

This is traditional blank verse usage; compare:

> The *qual*ity of *mer*cy is not *strained* (3)
> It *drop*peth as the *gen*tle *rain* from *heaven* (4)
> (*The Merchant of Venice*, IV. 183–4)

or

> But *see* the *ang*ry *Vic*tor hath *recalled* (4)
> His *Min*isters of *ven*geance and pur*suit* (3)
> (*Paradise Lost*, I. 169–70)

Perhaps Eliot's most ingenious use of blank verse in *The Cocktail Party* is in the mouth of Sir Henry Harcourt-Reilly, when he seeks to pierce Lavinia's boasted practicality with a touch of poetry, by quoting the mysterious passage from Shelley's *Prometheus Unbound* (III. 423–31). It creates a sudden escalation of intensity which may be due as much to its majestic regularity of iambic movement as to the strangeness of the experience it describes. It is in a language beyond the reach of conversation.

To sum up: in *The Cocktail Party*, each line, as printed, has its own autonomous length and rhythm as a sentence, or part of a sentence, lightly indicating how it is to be spoken, where the emphasis should fall, and where the pauses (if any) are to come, if the meaning is to be fully expressed, and the quality of conversation is to be preserved. The 'poetry' (that is, the intensity) flows through the lines with varying strength, related to the situation and the character of the speaker.

Lines are sometimes broken up between two speakers. I have no warrant for saying so, but I think that when this happens, the broken pieces are meant to take each other up in brief interchange. For instance:

Celia	That's all that matters. Truly, Edward,
	If that is right, everything else will be,
	I promise you.
Edward	No, Celia.
	It has been very wonderful, and I'm very grateful,
	And I think you are a very rare person.
	But it is too late. And I should have known
	That it wasn't fair to you.
Celia	It wasn't fair to *me*!
	You can stand there and talk about being fair to *me*!
	(I. 2. 157–64)

Here 'No Celia' belongs to the sequence of meaning that

culminates in 'I promise you'; but 'It has been very wonderful' starts a new idea — Edward's gauche effort to pat Celia on the back; if the lines had been printed thus:

> *Celia* If that is right, everything else will be,
>   I promise you.
> *Edward* No, Celia. It has been very wonderful
>   And I'm very grateful, and I think
>   You are a very rare person.

Edward's refusal would seem a more settled, a more deliberate choice. Similarly Celia's repetition of Edward's phrase:

>   it wasn't fair to you.
>   It wasn't fair to *me*!

belongs to her anger at this notion, rather than to her amazement (which is her next emotion) given a line to itself:

> You can stand there and talk about being fair to *me*!

No doubt her amazement has some anger in it still, but it is amazement that predominates in the repetition, to my ear, at least. Typography does not make poetry, but it may help the speaker to recognise and speak it. There is no new doctrine as to the nature of poetry in relation to verse or even to prose, in *The Cocktail Party*. There is simply the culmination of a long search for a way of writing that would admit the intensity of poetry without losing the flavour of conversation. When for a moment Eliot needs something of even greater intensity, he abandons conversation and turns to Shelley.

5   Notes to the Essay

5 Notes to the Essay

Page 239
Congreve and Shakespeare. Compare John Lawlor, 'The Formal Achievement of *The Cocktail Party*', *Virginia Quarterly Review*, Vol. 30, 1954, pp. 431–51.

Page 242
The Rock, Murder in the Cathedral and *The Family Reunion*. For an elaboration of this statement, see my Introduction to the Educational Edition of *The Family Reunion*, Faber, 1969, pp. 11–64.

Page 253
Fathers and Sons by Ivan Turgenev, translated by C. J. Hogarth, Everyman Edition, 1921, Chapter 18.

Page 257
See Martin Browne, *The Making of T. S. Eliot's Plays*, Cambridge University Press, 1969, p. 173. An indispensable book for students of Eliot's drama.

Page 262
The Idea of a Christian Society. This was first noted as a parallel reflection of Eliot's opinion by David E. Jones, in *The Plays of T. S. Eliot*, Routledge & Kegan Paul, 1960, p. 123. The observation is confirmed by Martin Browne, op. cit., p. 185.

Page 267
One of the felicities. Martin Browne, op. cit., p. 212.

Page 283
This quotation is taken from the translation by Richmond Lattimore in *The Complete Greek Tragedies*, edited by

David Grene and Richmond Lattimore, University of Chicago Press, 1955.

Page 285

See Eliot's letter to Hallie Flanagan, printed in her book, *Dynamo*, New York, 1943. She had directed his *Sweeney Agonistes* at Vassar in 1933, and had written to Eliot for elucidation of certain points; he replied explaining the importance, in the second fragment of the play, of the ritual cooking of eggs in accordance with Aristophanic precedence.

Page 285

A dish of eggs. See previous note.

6 List of Dates

6 List of Dates

Thomas Stearns Eliot born in St. Louis, U.S.A.

1910 A.B. and A.M. at Harvard University; and studied later at the University of Paris and Merton College, Oxford.

1911 *The Love Song of J. Alfred Prufrock* written.

1915 *The Love Song of J. Alfred Prufrock* published in *Poetry*, 1915.
Married Vivienne Haigh Haigh-Wood.
Taught at High Wycombe Grammar School and Highgate School.

1917 Entered the foreign department of Lloyds Bank in the City of London.

1922 Founded and edited *The Criterion* until 1939, in which he published *The Waste Land* in October 1922.

1925 Published *The Hollow Men*.
Joined Messrs Faber & Gwyer, reconstituted as Faber & Faber in 1929.

1926–7 Published *Sweeney Agonistes* in *The Criterion*.

1927 Became a naturalised British subject; was confirmed into the Church of England.

1934 Wrote *The Rock* from a scenario suggested by the Rev. Webb-Odell and composed by E. Martin Browne, a pageant-play, performed at Sadler's Wells Theatre in May–June.

1935	*Murder in the Cathedral* written for the Canterbury Festival and produced there in June.
1939	Published *The Idea of a Christian Society*.
	Published *The Family Reunion*, which opened at the Westminster Theatre in March.
1944	Published the *Four Quartets*.
1948	Published *Notes Towards the Definition of Culture*.
	Awarded the Nobel Prize for Literature.
	Awarded the Order of Merit.
1949	*The Cocktail Party* produced at the Royal Lyceum Theatre during the Edinburgh International Festival.
1953	*The Confidential Clerk* produced at the Royal Lyceum Theatre during the Edinburgh International Festival; published the following year.
1957	Married Esmé Valerie Fletcher.
1958	*The Elder Statesman* produced during the Edinburgh International Festival; published the following year.
1965	Eliot died on 4 January.

7 Selected Reading List

7   Selected Reading List

T. S. Eliot

POETRY

The Waste Land (1923) (See also a facsimile and transcript
of the original drafts including the annotations of
Ezra Pound, edited by Valerie Eliot, 1971)

Old Possum's Book of Practical Cats (1939)

Four Quartets (1944)

Collected Poems 1909–1962 (1963)

Poems Written in Early Youth (1967)

DRAMA

The Rock (1934)

Murder in the Cathedral (1935) (Educational edition
with an introduction and notes by Nevill Coghill, 1965)

The Family Reunion (1939) (Educational edition with an
introduction and notes by Nevill Coghill, 1965)

The Elder Statesman (1959)

CRITICISM

The Sacred Wood (1920)

The Idea of a Christian Society (1939)

Selected Essays (1951)

Poetry and Drama (1951)

The Three Voices of Poetry (1953)

Browne, E. Martin *The Making of T. S. Eliot's Plays* (1969)
(This work is indispensable to a study of Eliot's development as a practical poet and dramatist.)

Gallup, Donald *T. S. Eliot: A Bibliography* (1969)

SELECTED READING LIST

Gardner, Dame Helen *The Art of T. S. Eliot* (1949)
  'The Comedies of T. S. Eliot' (in *Essays by Diverse Hands*,
  New Series, Royal Society of Literature, Vol. 34, 1964)

Howarth, Herbert *Notes on Some Figures behind T. S. Eliot*
  (1965)

Jones, David E. *The Plays of T. S. Eliot* (1960)

Kojecky, Roger *T. S. Eliot's Social Criticism* (1971)

Lawlor, John 'The Formal Achievement of *The Cocktail
  Party*' (in *Virginia Quarterly Review*, Vol. 30, 1954)

March, Richard and Tambimuttu (eds.) *T. S. Eliot: A Sym-
  posium* (1948)

Matthiessen, F. O. *The Achievement of T. S. Eliot* (3rd
  edition 1958)

Smith, Carol H. *T. S. Eliot's Dramatic Theory and Practice*
  (1963)

Smith, Grover *T. S. Eliot's Poetry and Plays* (1956)

Unger, L. *T. S. Eliot: A Selected Critique* (1948)
  The Man in the Name (1956)

Williamson, G. A. *A Reader's Guide to T. S. Eliot* (1953)